6/96

CIVIC CENTER

SKINNER'S TRAIL

SKINNER'S TRAIL

Also by Quintin Jardine

Skinner's Rules
Skinner's Festival

SKINNER'S TRAIL

Quintin Jardine

St. Martin's Press ☀ New York

A THOMAS DUNNE BOOK.
An imprint of St. Martin's Press.

SKINNER'S TRAIL. Copyright © 1994 by Quintin Jardine.
All rights reserved. Printed in the United States of
America. No part of this book may be used or reproduced
in any manner whatsoever without written permission
except in the case of brief quotations embodied in critical
articles or reviews. For information, address St. Martin's
Press, 175 Fifth Avenue, New York, N.Y. 10010.

ISBN 0-312-14417-2

First published in Great Britain by Headline Book
Publishing

First U.S. Edition: May 1996

10 9 8 7 6 5 4 3 2 1

This is for Allan and Susie, chips off the old blocks

ACKNOWLEDGEMENTS

The author's grateful thanks go to

Carlos and Kathleen Pallares, of Trattoria La Clota, L'Escala, Spain, for being real and thus saving him the impossible task of inventing them

Mary Clark, of Villa Service, L'Escala

Mr V

Paul Grace

1

It was only a small scream.

Not much of a scream at all, really. Yet it had a profound effect on Bob Skinner.

His broad shoulders and his ramrod straight spine, which had been rigid with tension, relaxed and sagged. In the same instant his eyes overflowed with hot, sudden, unexpected tears. They ran down his face, mingling with the sweat of the two-hour drama in which, although only a bit player, he had been involved as intensely as the two principals.

The scream, spontaneous from the shock of the first inflation of the lungs, faltered quickly, became for a second or two a hiccuping splutter, then settled into a long-drawn-out wailing cry.

Bob Skinner stared in awe at the miracle of new life, at the infant fresh from the womb, held upside-down before him by the young doctor whose white cap and mask seemed to add lustre to the shining blackness of his face. Then, through his trance, Bob felt the pressure of his wife's strong grip and turned towards her. His mouth shaped words, but no sound came. He was for that time, indeed for the first time in his forty-five years, struck quite dumb.

Sarah said it for him, 'We have a son.' She looked back towards the baby, as his crying took on added volume with the cutting of the umbilical. A few seconds later, he was swaddled and placed in her arms. She kissed the tiny forehead above the slitted eyes, oblivious of the smears of blood and mucus.

'Welcome to the world, James Andrew Skinner,' she whispered.

Bob's left arm slipped round her shoulders as she lay propped up on the delivery table, legs still spread in the position of birth. He leaned down and peered at the white bundle of soft blankets, looking into his son's face for the first time. The power of speech returned. 'Yes, wee fella. Hello, there. You'll like it out here, I think, Master JAS. Hope you'll like us.'

'No doubt about that, copper,' said his wife. 'Hey! JAS – I like the sound of that. James Andrew Skinner, aka Jazz. Spelled J-A-Z-Z. That's what we'll call him. Yes, Bob?'

The new father threw back his head and laughed. The movement loosened his surgical cap, and he shook it off completely, freeing his thick, steel-grey hair. 'Yes! That's great. Our boy Jazz. It sort of suits him doesn't it. He looks pretty cool already.'

The baby's crying had stopped. The crumpled face had begun to relax, a wrinkle line across the forehead disappearing as it did. A small right hand forced its way from within the bundle. Very gently, Bob touched the tiny palm with his index finger. The fingers closed in a reflex action on its tip. He was amazed by the strength of the grip. 'My God! Feel that.'

Sarah nodded. 'I know. I am a doctor, remember. The human animal is proportionately stronger, in relation to body weight, at the moment of birth, than it will ever be again, even suppose it grows up to be an Olympic weight-lifter.' She offered the middle joint of her little finger to the bud-like mouth. It clamped on tight, and began to suck voraciously. 'Ow! Jazz, baby, what have I let myself in for?'

The young nurse who had handed Sarah her baby for the first time returned and took him back, to have all his regulation parts checked and counted, to be weighed, to be washed and to be spruced up generally for his debut. Bob glanced at the big wall-clock, to mark the time in his memory. It was two minutes before midday on Sunday the twelfth of May.

He helped a second member of the delivery team restore Sarah to a more conventional and comfortable position, with her back propped up on the birth table high enough for her to be able to watch the first nurse at work.

The new-born Jazz Skinner was stretched out on the blanket which had served as his first robe, while the girl washed him gently, from top to toe. 'Look at him, Bob,' said Sarah. Fit as she was, her breathing was still slightly heavy from the exertion of the birth, and its irregularity gave an added edge to the wonderment in her voice. 'Look at him. He's just like you.'

Bob beamed, then chuckled. 'Hair's a bit darker, though!'

'Yes but it looks as if it'll lie the same way once it's dried off. And look at the shape of his body; how long and lean he is. Just like you. And his little face: that frown line above the bridge of his nose. That's yours, too.'

He squeezed her shoulder. 'Sarah, love. He's like all new-born babies. He's got a face like a well-skelped arse, and he will have until he opens his eyes properly. Talking of arses, when the doc held him up there, something looked familiar. That's one thing of yours he's got, at least.'

'Bob!'

'Come on, girl. That's a compliment. You've got the nicest arse in Edinburgh!'

'Hmm. Wonder if you'll still say that when you see the effect carrying young Jazz has on it?'

''Course I will. Anything on you is the best by me. You're a wonder, Doctor – sorry, Professor – and you've just proved it again.'

From the breathless moment when they had confirmed it, using an over-the-counter test kit, through to the uncomplicated delivery, two days early, in the grandly-named Simpson Memorial Maternity Pavilion within the crowded precincts of Edinburgh Royal Infirmary, Sarah's pregnancy had been a model – without major upsets for either mother or father. Bob had been outraged on one occasion by a junior doctor's description of his thirty-year-old wife as an 'elderly prim', but had been mollified by Sarah's explanation that the term was medical jargon for first-time mothers over twenty-five.

Alex, Bob's daughter by his all-too-brief first marriage, had been born over twenty years before, in an age and under a regime in which fathers were excluded as a matter of policy once their biological task had been completed. So the growth of Sarah's bump, and the gestation process of the individual who had just emerged from the dark chrysalis of the womb as his son Jazz, had been in effect as new an experience for him as for his wife. He had shared in the preparation every step of the way, attending all of Sarah's training classes, and the consultant's sincere enquiry as to whether he wished to attend the birth had been greeted with a sternly raised eyebrow and a curt, 'Of course.'

Even Bob's work had seemed to co-operate in allowing him to spend as much time as possible at his wife's side. After a terrible twelve months, with drama following drama, life had become, since the previous September, even quieter than was normal in Edinburgh. It was as if the city's criminal underclass had been awed by the grand scale of the crises of the previous year, and cowed also by the force with which Assistant Chief Constable Robert Skinner had dealt with each one. As a result, Skinner had been able to establish a normal working routine for the first time since his promotion to Executive Officer rank. Even the demands of his 'second job', as security adviser to Andrew Hardie, the recently appointed Secretary of State for Scotland, had slackened off, through a general lessening in the terrorist threat.

So marked had been the change that, in addition to sharing the routine tasks of Sarah's pregnancy, Bob had been able to resume his stewardship of his police force's karate club and rejoin the squash ladder. He had even entered, for the first time in five years, the spring knock-out golf tournament, where his path to the final had been blocked by a suspiciously good fourteen-handicapper who would now find it difficult as a result, or so it was hinted by colleagues, ever to escape from the humdrum of the traffic department. The new routine had been badly needed therapy for Bob Skinner, after a year during which he had faced the greatest challenges of his life, shocking himself at times by the things of which, in hours of need, he had proved capable, encountering an inner self whose existence he had never suspected, and whose ruthlessness he feared.

But now, as the young nurse put his son into his arms for the first time, the questioning voices within him were stilled. Perched carefully on the table, he looked down at tiny Jazz, looking for his own likeness, and finding it, as Sarah had said he would, in the quiff of hair which fell over the child's forehead, and in the strange deep vertical line between his eyebrows. The baby blinked, and Bob was sure that he was peering at him, trying to focus on his face, adjusting his eyes to these strange new phenomena of light and movement that had come into his world.

For months, Bob had anticipated this moment when first he would cradle his son in his arms. He had thought of many profound, wise, and probably pompous things that he would say to him. But, now that the time had come, there were no words. Only the widest smile of his life, only the happiness of journey's end, only the private thought: *'If you can do this, Skinner, you're okay. You're okay.'*

He kissed the tiny forehead. 'And you're okay, too, Jazz my boy . . . and how!' he said softly.

He held the baby proudly, as the nurses eased Sarah into a wheel chair, and he followed as they pushed her back along the corridor to the private room in which she had been installed on their arrival at the hospital three hours earlier. She climbed into bed gingerly, but still smiling. Without waiting to be asked, Bob bent and passed their child, from the cradle of his arms, to his mother. He stripped off his green robe and tore open the Velcro fastening of the face mask which hung around his neck, forgotten until that moment. Throwing both on to a chair beside the window, he walked over and retrieved his leather jacket from the small wardrobe facing the bed. 'Let's tell some people,' he said, and took his mobile telephone from the right-hand pocket. He switched it on and punched in an American number, handing the small instrument to Sarah as he pushed the SEND button. 'Your father.'

The call was picked up on the fourth ring.

'Dad? Sorry, that's Grandad!' She cried a few happy tears with her

4

father in New York State, then, promising to write, said her goodbyes.

Bob took back the phone, and called his daughter. As he had anticipated, Alex was at home in her Glasgow flat studying for the last of her university Law exams, in hot pursuit of a first-class honours degree.

'I am sorry, Pops,' she said, after he had broken his news. 'I am twenty-one years old, and I just cannot get my head round the idea of having a baby brother. He's going to have to call me Auntie – that's all there is to it.' She laughed at the other end of the line. 'Seriously, I am so pleased for you both. And so proud. He's a new chapter in all our lives, and you know what? We deserve him.' Her voice sounded suddenly wistful, almost vulnerable.

Bob's third call was to another mobile. It rang out several times; then, just as a puzzled look began to creep across his face, the ringing stopped.

'Martin.' The man on the other end sounded testy, annoyed at the interruption.

'Skinner.'

Detective Superintendent Andy Martin's tone changed in an instant. 'Bob! News?'

'Aye, news indeed, uncle. James Andrew Skinner checked in around half an hour ago. He and his mother are both A1 – repeat A1, my boy.'

'Bob, that's wonderful. No problems?'

'None at all.'

'Smashin'. Hey, did you say Andrew?'

'Yes . . . Sarah's idea, of course. I don't know which is more dodgy: naming him after two coppers or after two saints Anyway, we're not going to call him either one. His using name's going to be Jazz – that's spelt as in Acker Bilk. It sort of suits his American half. He's a well-behaved wee chap too; hardly a murmur since he was tidied up.'

'Terrific. When can I come to see him?'

'You can come today, if you like.' He glanced at Sarah for confirmation, and saw her nod vigorously. 'They're in the posh parent ward, so visiting hours aren't a problem. Come this evening if you like.'

'Fine. I should be clear by then.'

'Okay. Where are you just now? You sounded a bit grumpy when you answered.'

'Looking at stiffs still gets me that way. I'm at a murder scene.'

Skinner frowned. Since his promotion at the beginning of April, following a three-month secondment to the Los Angeles Police

5

Department, Andy Martin had been in command of the force's Drugs and Vice Squad, two formerly separate units combined by Skinner into a single department because of the strong link between narcotics and prostitution, and the AIDS-related dangers which this trend had created.

'What are you doing at a murder?'

'Ah, boss, this isn't any old murder. The stiff here's a celebrity.' Martin paused, and Skinner's eyebrows rose. 'But you don't want to know about this just now, do you?'

'Come on, boy. Who've you got there?'

'Well, if you insist. Tell Sarah you forced it out of me, though. The guest of honour here is only Mr Tony Manson, that's all.'

Skinner's surprise expressed itself in a low, drawn-out whistle. 'Terrible Tony! Murdered? There's no doubt it was murder?'

'If it wasn't, he's made a bloody good job of hiding the suicide weapon.'

'Where are you?'

'At his place, out in Barnton. I'll show you the pictures tomorrow.'

'Trinity? Oh yes, I remember. I knocked that house over a few years back, when I was doing your job. Found bugger all, of course.' Skinner paused. He glanced over at the bed. 'Listen, Andy. Stuff the pictures! Keep him on ice. This one I've got to see for myself.Sarah and wee Jazz will probably go for a sleep soon. I'll be down then.'

2

The dead ones bothered him so much more now.

Before ... well, before it had been part of the job. He had been called in and there they were: carcasses, no more than that. It didn't matter whether they had been men, women or children. At the moment of his first contact, they were all just victims, and Skinner had been able to deal with them on that basis, however bloody the remains, however cruel the killing.

Oh, he had been righteously angered on many occasions. There had been a child killer a decade ago; Bob had seen to it, with a word to an assistant governor, that the man's first night as a convicted prisoner had been spent in open association with the rest. His next three weeks had been spent in hospital, and all the years since then in segregation. Yet, on the whole, Skinner had coped dispassionately with the nasty side of the job. It was, after all, an essential part of leadership. It had helped him take the fast track to his present exalted position as Assistant Chief Constable and head of criminal investigation in Scotland's capital, a city whose cruel streak is never shown to the tourists but which lurks there, nonetheless.

Yet Bob Skinner, like the great majority, had reached his forties without ever having seen another human being actually die, without looking into a person's face as the last breath was drawn. Now he had been there, done that. In fact, he had done more – much more. Now, every time he was called to a murder scene, the centre of attraction was more than just a victim. Skinner found himself stepping into that person's mind, thinking their thoughts, forming a picture of that last moment, not as an observer but as a participant experiencing the rage and terror of the life as it was stolen.

'*Theft. That's what murder is.*' As he opened the heavy brass-bound front-door, flanked on either side by a row of four granite curling stones, Skinner recalled a sombre speech made to a police-force dinner party by a senior judge. '*The most serious theft of all: the theft of life, of time, of years unfulfilled. And for what? Once it's stolen, it can't be used. It has no resale value, no value to anyone other than its owner, to whom of course it is beyond price. Mostly, the theft takes place without thought, in a moment of anger, and is regretted the instant it is done. But life isn't a magazine filched from a rack, or a can of beans from a supermarket shelf. You can't sneak a stolen life back to the shop and pretend that nothing happened.'*

The eyes stared at Skinner, upside-down, as he climbed the staircase. The head lolled backwards over the landing; the dark hair looked as if it was standing on end, the mouth hung open, grotesque and oddly obscene, the tip of the tongue licking out over the top lip. The banisters hung by shreds of wood. They were solid mahogany, yet they had been smashed by the bulk of the body and the force with which it had crashed backwards through them.

The tableau of death offered a surreal and stark contrast to the scene in which Bob had been involved only four hours before, and the private room in the Simpson where he had left mother and son asleep. From birth to death in twenty minutes, he thought. His mind swam for a second, and a violent shudder ran through him.

Andy Martin was waiting for him in the upper hallway at the top of the staircase, with Alan Royston the force press officer.

If Martin had noticed Skinner's reaction, he gave no sign. 'Stone cold, boss. There's hardly any blood. Single puncture wound straight into the heart. Whoever did this either knew exactly where to hit, or they were dead lucky.'

'Whoever did this didn't rely on luck. How long has he been dead?'

'The doctor's first guess was that he was done between one and two a.m. The cleaning lady found him. She lets herself in around nine every morning.'

'He lived alone, still, did he?'

'Always has done. He's never been married. The odd girlfriend, but mostly he used the tarts from his saunas.'

Skinner grunted. 'Hmm. A man of simple tastes, then. Who's the senior bod here from Division?'

The answer came from a room off the landing. 'So far, it's me, sir. DI Donaldson's on leave, and Miss Higgins is over in the west, crewing her brother's yacht on the Clyde.' The husky shape of Detective Sergeant Mario McGuire appeared, framed in the doorway.

'Where's Roy Old?'

'Away in Hawick with the Chief and Brian Mackie, looking after the Princess Royal,' said Martin.

Skinner nodded. 'Of course. Right, Mario, what have we got, then?'

'Here, sir?' said McGuire. 'Not a lot, you might say. Only a very dead Anthony Manson. Owner and operator of a dozen housing-scheme laundrettes, eight takeaways, six dodgy lock-up public houses, four saunas of ill repute, and one curling club complete with blue-chip membership to make Tony there look halfway respectable. The ideal set-up for the biggest drug baron in Scotland.'

Skinner laughed ironically. 'Come on now, sergeant. The late Mr Manson has never been charged with a single crime or mis-demeanour. Okay, so half a dozen of his former employees are doing time for dealing, but that's still no reason to speak ill of the dead.'

McGuire snorted. 'The only thing I've got to say to the dead, sir, is, "Cheerio, Tony, you won't be missed." We all know what he was.'

Skinner nodded. 'So the place is clean, then. He hasn't left anything we can stick on him beyond the grave?'

'Clean as a whistle, boss,' said Martin. 'Not as much as a Beechams powder.'

'What about motive? Any chance it was a house-breaking interrupted?'

Martin grinned, raising his blond eyebrows. 'Who'd be daft enough to burgle Tony Manson, boss? No sign of theft. His jewellery's untouched, the video's still there, and there's a few thousand in cash in a drawer in his desk downstairs.'

'So what *do* we know?'

'Not a lot, so far. He took a taxi home from the casino in Kent Street a bit after midnight. We traced the driver. Tony bunged him a tenner tip apparently. He'd had a good night. There was a glass with the end of a whisky in it, in the study downstairs. It looks as if he came in, had himself a nightcap, and wandered up the stairs. Your man – and it has to be a man, from the way the body was rammed through that balustrade – seems to have been waiting just inside the bedroom. Tony's prints are fresh on the door handle. He opens the door, and . . .' The sentence tailed off, unfinished.

Skinner leaned over the body. 'With a knife, too, lads. Now that's unusual, if this was a contract job. I have only once, that I can recall, seen a hit where a knife was used. And we cleared that one up. You know the usual story: the pros nearly always use big-calibre pistols, or sawn-offs '

'Mm.' Martin nodded his agreement. 'That's right: weapons that don't leave any room for doubt. And it wasn't as if there was any need to be quiet about this one. You could fire a cannon in here and the folk next-door wouldn't hear, the houses are so far apart.'

'Another thing,' said Skinner. 'If this was done by a specialist act, he's from out of town. From out of Scotland, I'll bet. If this guy had worked up here before, I'd have heard of it. And that could paint a

9

very scary picture. Tony never allowed any organised opposition to develop in Edinburgh. A hard guy in a horrible trade, but at least with him around we've known the extent of the problem, and we've been able to keep it in check. I think he even had the sense a few years back to realise that he was going over the score, and to rein himself in. So if someone's had him bumped, that could mean a takeover bid. That's the devil we knew lying there, that heap of dead meat. If we're going to face a new team, Andy, it looks as if I've put you in charge of the squad in the nick of time.'

'Thanks, boss. Thanks a million. You're always doing things like this to me. Mind you, I've had no sniff of any rival bidders for Tony's franchise. I'll put out feelers when we get back to base.'

'Yes, and *I'll* put Maggie Rose to work, trying to trace similar killings through the PNC. I'll have Brian Mackie check his network, too. You never know, this could even have been overseas talent.' He turned. 'Mario, you've searched the place once. Now do it again, looking for anything funny – anything that doesn't seem natural.'

Skinner called to the press officer. 'Alan, you're free to make a statement to the media outside. You can't confirm without formal identification that this is Tony Manson, but tell them that no one will sue them if they say it is. Beyond that, just say that a full-scale murder inquiry is being set up. Then we can sit back and wait for the GANG WARS headlines that we will surely see tomorrow.'

Skinner paused and smiled. 'And while we're waiting, you, Andy, can come back to the Simpson and meet your new godson.'

3

'No danger of him growing up to be a ballet dancer. Look at the size of those feet!'

'Just a minute, Martin! That's my wee brother you're talking about.' Alex Skinner laughed and threw her arms in delight around Andy's broad shoulders, as they perched on the edge of the bed.

His vivid green eyes sparkled as he glanced sideways at her. '*And* your father!' he said. 'Where d'you think he got those plates from? Tell you what, Sarah, it'll be special-order trainers for him by the time he's fourteen.'

Bob looked across at Alex and Andy, thoughtfully. They had each come through terrible times, only a few months before. In the aftermath they had seemed to come closer together in their friendship, each helping the other to heal. The medicine seemed to have worked. Sitting side by side, they looked for all the world like two happy people without a care. But, still, Bob fancied that he saw the occasional shadow pass across his daughter's face, and noted a sombre side to his friend's sunny nature that had not been there a year before.

Sarah was seated at the window, in a high-backed armchair, cradling Jazz in her right arm. His shawl – a Skinner family heirloom in which Alex herself had once been wrapped – was loosened, and one corner hung towards the floor. Golden evening sun flooded in, washing over mother and son, and glinting in the grey of Bob's hair as he leaned over the chair back. He whistled softly, and Jazz looked upwards toward the sound, curiosity stilling the kicking of his feet . . . which were, Bob had to admit, generously sized.

'Do you hear what that policeman's saying about us, wee man. Good honest working feet those are. Just made for pounding a beat. Which is what that cheeky bugger'll be doin' before too long, if he doesn't watch it! He'll make a good godfather though, Jazz. Biggest gangster in the force, so the boys say. Your godmother will see you okay, too. You Baptists don't have some rule against sisters being godmothers, do you, love?'

Sarah smiled across at Alex. 'If we did, I'd look for another church

11

that didn't.' She switched her glance, and her grin, to Andy Martin. 'So, Superintendent, where did you drag my old man off to this afternoon, the moment our eyes closed? Didn't you think he might be feeling as tired as we did?'

Andy shook his blond head, throwing up his hands in a fending-off gesture. 'I didn't drag him anywhere, honest. He dragged himself. It wasn't any old crime scene either, mother. Talk of godfathers: that's who this was – Edinburgh's own. One Tony Manson.'

Sarah's eyes widened. 'Even *I've* heard of him! What happened? Wish I'd been there.'

'Steady on, Sarah,' said Alex. 'You're out of that line now. You're a professor, remember.'

'Ah, but I can still be called in to crime scenes!'

Five months before, when word of her impending withdrawal from general practice had reached the Principal of Edinburgh University, Sarah had been made a surprising and totally unexpected offer. The Faculty of Advocates, the Scottish Bar, had just agreed to sponsor a new chair of Criminal Forensics and Pathology within the University's Medical School, and was pressing for a high-profile appointment. Without Bob's knowledge, Archie Nelson, the recently elected Dean of Faculty, had proposed Dr Sarah Grace Skinner, already recognised, after less than two years in post, as Scotland's leading police surgeon. Recognising both the power of the paymaster and the merit of the appointment, the Principal had approached Sarah, and offered her the chair on a three-year tenure. When she had recovered from her surprise, Sarah, with Bob's agreement, had accepted, and had been installed as Scotland's youngest professor. She had spent the latter part of her pregnancy planning her course, and working on her lectures, which were scheduled to begin with the new term, in the autumn.

'So, come on, boys,' she said. 'Tell me about it. My professional curiosity's well wound up now.'

Bob sighed and shrugged his shoulders. 'Well, if you insist. But there was nothing spectacular about it. Single blow with a long-bladed knife, Dr Banks said. Victim taken by surprise by an intruder, late at night. It's likely he was half asleep, and so an easy target. Banks is doing the PM himself.'

'Banks!' Sarah snorted. 'Couldn't you have got Burke and Hare? They'd have done a better job. What else did that horse-doctor have to tell you?'

'What more should there be?' asked Bob, but even as he spoke he recognised that the doctor's scene-of-crime examination *had* been perfunctory. And he knew that his wife had a special talent. She could

12

look at a murder scene and put together a description of the crime which would later prove unerringly accurate.

'What more?' said Sarah. 'Plenty! How tall was the attacker? Was it a man or woman? Was he or she left-handed or orthodox? Did Manson do any damage himself? All *that* stuff.'

Bob smiled. 'Come on, love. Don't be so hard on the man. I'm sure all that'll be in his PM report.'

'Yes, and he'll give you the Derby winner, too! Listen, your people are going to be under pressure on this one. You can guess what the media coverage will be like tomorrow. Let me help. I'm going to cool my heels in here until Wednesday at least, practising the nuts and bolt of this motherhood thing. Why don't you bring me in the PM report and the photographs tomorrow, and I'll try to fill in some of the gaps that Banks will have left?'

Bob opened his mouth to protest, but his wife fixed him with a look which told him that refusal was not an option, so he closed it again. Andy and Alex, looking on from their bedside perch, smiled at this silent exchange.

'Okay, Prof, if it'll make you happy, I'll do that. You're in a strong negotiating position today, I suppose. See what you're up against in life's battles of wills, wee Jazz?'

As if in response, Jazz wriggled in Sarah's arms, released a mewling cat-like cry, and turned his face towards his mother's breast in a gesture which was pure reflex, but which could have only one meaning.

Sarah laughed. 'I think you'll find that this one won't take no for an answer either! Go on you lot. Go and wet his head, or whatever. I've got some mothering to do here.'

4

'It'll be the standard routine, sheer back-breaking drudgery, this investigation, but it's the only way.'

Two men and a woman faced Skinner across his rosewood desk in the big office located in the command suite of the ugly, hybrid building in Fettes Avenue which was Edinburgh's police headquarters. Detective Inspector Maggie Rose, the ACC's recently promoted personal assistant, sat to his left, a notebook on her lap, ready to record decisions taken and orders issued. Ranged beside her were Detective Chief Superintendent Roy Old who was Skinner's immediate deputy, Andy Martin, and Detective Superintendent Alison Higgins who had day-to-day responsibility for criminal investigation in Edinburgh's Eastern Division.

'Neither our own criminal intelligence sources nor the PNC has thrown up any hint that Manson had been a target, or has given us any warning that a rival outfit might have fancied his territory. Yet all the evidence points to this having been a premeditated murder. The attending officers went over the place twice yesterday, the first time with the cleaning woman, and the second time with Manson's lawyer. They both said that everything looked normal and that no valuables seemed to be missing.'

He glanced around at them, then continued. 'That means we have to look into every area of Manson's life, both the legitimate side and the things we've never been able to nail down before. I want every one of his managers brought in for interview. Put them under a bit of pressure, especially those we've got under the closest observation already. We know that Tony was too cute to push stuff through all his places at once. He only ever ran his candy stall in *one* place at any given time, always moving it around to cut down our chances of nailing the operation.'

'How did the buyers know where to go then, sir?' asked Superintendent Higgins.

Skinner raised an eyebrow in surprise at the question. 'Come on, Alison, these are addicts we're talking about. They've got a bush telegraph that's like no other. Word gets round like lightning. But it's

14

a very tight-knit club, and difficult for us to penetrate. We had an informant for a while, who gave us three or four tips that led to dealer arrests, but she died of an overdose. We suspected at the time – in fact I'm still bloody certain – that her death wasn't an accident. Since then, all we've been able to do is try to read Tony's mind, and keep an eye on some of the places that haven't been used in a while, hoping to catch one of them dirty. That's worked precisely once over the years. My darkest suspicion is that Manson had one of our own people on his payroll. Maybe now he's dead, we'll have a chance of finding out whether I'm right – or, I pray, proving that I'm wrong.'

He paused, to look out of the picture window, contemplatively, for a second or two.

'That's another thing I want done. Interview Manson's lawyer, accountant, bank manager, everyone who was ever involved with him in business. See if any of them know of any argument he had in the pubs, the laundrettes, the curling club, anywhere. Interview every bugger you can find who ever knew Manson. His hairdresser, the taxi driver who brought him home, the cellar men in his pubs, the whores in his saunas, everyone. Andy, you and your Vice people interview the women. They'll be on first-name terms with most of them. Divisional CID does the rest. Roy, if you need an overtime tab for all this, just let me know what it's likely to run to, and I'll ask the Management Services Director to adjust the budget. It's boring old stuff, as I say, but it's all we have.'

He turned to DS Higgins. 'Alison, you scrutinise all the interview transcripts, and report to Roy daily, in summary. You, Roy, keep me in touch. Anything that you think I should see, get it to me right away. I'll be around until Wednesday, then I'm taking a few days off. I'll still be close by, though.'

He sat forward in his chair and put his hands palm-down on the desk. 'Right, that's almost everything. Maggie, Andy, could you leave us now. Mags, check if the PM report is in yet. If it is, make me an extra copy and get me a full set of photos, scene-of-crime and postmortem.'

Maggie Rose nodded and left the room with Martin. As the door closed behind them, Skinner turned back to Old and Higgins. He looked the woman straight in the eye, suddenly serious. 'I've got a bone to pick with you Alison. I don't think it's too clever to leave a detective sergeant as acting divisional head of CID. Presumably you knew that Donaldson was on leave, and that Roy was away with a Royal.'

The detective superintendent, reddening, nodded her close-cropped blonde head.

'In that case, you should have known better than to put yourself out of reach at the same time. It's as well that big McGuire is a good operator, and that Andy Martin was available, otherwise you'd have been in the shit. Look, you know me. I try to be even-handed. That means, whether you're a detective constable or detective superintendent, if you screw up, I'll tell you. Now, you're fairly new in rank and in post, and I've got faith in you. I won't chop you for one error of judgement. But for two of the same kind, I will. Make sure that this is part of the learning experience. Okay?'

'Yes, sir.'

Skinner looked across at Old. 'You can consider your arse kicked, too, Roy. As Alison's line commander, when she drops one, it's down to you as well, Make sure that none of your divisional supers make the same mistake.'

He paused, easing the atmosphere with a smile. 'And don't go taking it out on Alison.'

Old, looking relieved, smiled in his turn, and shook his head vigorously.

Skinner stood up, and his two colleagues followed. He led them out into the corridor of the command suite. 'Okay, into battle. Remember, every detail might fit together with another detail, and amount to something. So note every tiny piece of information. Good luck.'

As Old and Higgins disappeared through the swing doors at the end of the corridor, Skinner turned to look for Maggie Rose – to find her standing behind him, comb-bound reports and photographs held in both hands.

'That's Banks's report, is it?'

The red-haired Inspector nodded.

'Did the big man tell you all about his moment of glory last night, then?'

'Oh yes, sir. Every detail, every fingerprint. I'm surprised he hasn't got *himself* into the photos.'

Skinner smiled. Maggie Rose and Mario McGuire's eighteen-month relationship had just been formalised by an engagement, and by their acquisition of a new flat in Liberton, in the south of the city.

'What he has got himself into is a stretch of overtime. He could be in for a few late nights.'

Maggie's smile brightened. 'Good, that'll take care of the curtains.'

As Skinner turned to go back into his office, she called after him. 'Oh, boss, Sir James's secretary called. He just got in. Can you look in on him.'

16

5

The big silver-haired man rushed across the room, hands out-stretched when Skinner entered. 'Congratulations, Bob! I couldn't be more pleased for you and Sarah. Both doing very well, I hear. What did he weigh?' He paused. 'Now why do people of my age always ask that?'

Sir James Proud, the Chief Constable, was Skinner's mentor. Their relationship had become even closer over the past eighteen months, until Skinner had come to see Proud Jimmy – as he was popularly known – almost as a father figure.

Skinner laughed. 'Thanks, Jimmy. Eight pounds and twelve ounces, they said. That's one thing that hasn't gone metric yet. Not in the Simpson, at least.'

'So what the Hell are you still doing here? Why aren't you on paternity leave?'

'Things to do, Chief. Getting the Tony Manson show on the road, for one.'

'Yes. That fairly knocked our Royal Visit off the front page. What d'you think, Bob – is it a "gang war"?'

'Buggered if I know. Tony Manson must have had a thousand small-time enemies, but obviously one was serious enough to put a contract out on him. At least that's how it looks. A thoroughly professional job.'

As they sat at his low coffee table, Proud Jimmy pointed to the comb-bound documents which Skinner carried. 'Are those part of it?'

'Mmm. Autopsy report and the picture gallery.'

'Why the extra set?'

'I'm taking them in to let Sarah have a look.'

The Chief Constable's jaw dropped in a sudden comic gesture. 'You're joking!' He paused for a second, and a smile spread across his face. 'But of course you're not. That's typical Sarah. Off you go to see her, then. Her and wee James Andrew.'

'That's Jazz, Chief.'

'Eh!'

17

Skinner smiled and nodded. 'His name. It suits him down to the ground. You'll get used to it.'

'I'm sure I will,' said the conservative Proud Jimmy. 'Hope *he* does.'

6

If Sarah felt any reaction to her physical exertion of the previous day, none was on show to the world.

She sat at the window, fully dressed and lightly made up, ready to receive callers. When Bob arrived just after eleven a.m. he found her reading a magazine. Jazz was sleeping by her side, in his crib.

'Mornin', Mom,' he said. He bent into the crib and kissed the baby gently on the cheek. As he did, he caught the sweet milky scent of his breath, and felt a totally unexpected thrill. For a second, Bob's eyes moistened once more. When he turned towards Sarah, she was standing facing him. He took her in his arms and kissed her long and lingering.

'Sarah my love, you are an incredibly clever woman, to create someone like that.'

She smiled. 'At another time I'd call you a patronising so-and-so. But right now, as it happens, I agree with you.'

Her foot bumped against his briefcase, and she looked down. 'Have you got them? Good. Now let me try to show you what else I'm good at. Gimme.'

She sat down again while he unlocked his case, and took out the reports and photographs. 'There, get stuck into that lot. You can keep the report, but I'll take the pics back with me. We can't have them lying around here.' Behind him, Jazz made a small sound in his sleep. 'I'll tell you what. You get started, and I'll show my son off to the world, and the world off to my son.'

Terribly carefully, as if he were handling explosives, he lifted the baby from the crib and, holding him in the crook of his left arm, stepped across to the window. 'Good morning, Edinburgh,' he said, softly. 'May I present James Andrew Skinner, your newest citizen and potential man-about-town. Now there, Jazz, is a phrase that should be brought back into the language. That'll be you: Jazz Skinner, a man about town of your time.'

The baby's eyes blinked open and looked up at him. Bob grinned broadly. The corners of the baby's mouth twitched upwards. 'Hey, Sarah,' he whispered. 'He's smiling at me!'

Behind him she laughed. 'Wind, darling. It's wind.'

He looked back down at Jazz, whose eyes were wider open now, peering, as if focusing on Bob's grin and mimicking it. Turning the baby to face the window, Bob tilted him up slightly. 'There you are, my son, let me present to you your city, Edinburgh as ever is. That nice tree-lined bit out there is called the Meadows. Looks nice, doesn't it. They play cricket there at weekends in the summer. Maybe you will too. And they have Festival shows there, in tents. I'll take you to one, soon. There are swings, too. We'll like swings, you and I. It's a real utility place the Meadows.'

Jazz looked towards the window, as if weighing his father's words, and contemplating treats to come.

'That's enough excitement for now, though,' said Bob. As gingerly as he had picked him up, he laid the child, still less than a day old, back down in the crib. 'We'll take another walk later.'

He turned towards Sarah, and found her still scanning the autopsy report, turning pages quickly, pausing every so often at something which she found of special interest. The bound sheaf of photographs lay at her feet, open at a close-up shot of the fatal wound.

Bob sat on the edge of the bed and waited silently for several minutes, watching her as she studied, admiring the depth of her concentration, amused by the occasional furrowing of her brow as she considered the implications of different parts of the report, frequently snorting and shaking her head as she found something with which to take issue. Eventually, she laid the book in her lap and leaned back in her chair, looking over at Bob.

'For a professional report, this shows some of, but not all, the imagination of a particularly dense rock. It tells you that Manson was killed by a knife-wound to the heart – and that's it. Mary the tea-lady in my old surgery could have told you the same! No suggestions, no conclusions, nothing that will take your inquiry one step further. I suggest that in future you use this man for looking after the police horses . . . no, maybe not.'

'What do you draw from it, then?' said Bob. 'Can you make suggestions?'

She shot him a look which was almost withering. He smiled at her professional pride.

'Yes. The first is a heavy probability; the second is a God-damned certainty! I'll excuse Banks the first one, but the other . . . My God! A horse-doctor, I tell you.'

She leaned over and picked up the book of photographs. 'How big was Manson?'

'Tony? About five-eleven, I'd say. Weight? Let's see, he was a light-heavyweight boxer when he was young. That would make him twelve-and-a-half stone in his prime. He hadn't run much to fat, as you can see from the photos. Let's say fourteen stone, tops.'

'Age? Oh, yes, the report said forty-eight. Reasonably fit?'

'For sure. He could still have done his own bouncing in the pubs if necessary . . . not that any of his regulars would have been so daft. What does all that tell you?'

Sarah paused.

'What I think it tells me is that whoever killed Manson was someone he knew, and he was either expecting or wasn't surprised to see.'

'How do you work that out?'

She paused again, considering her answer, examining her logic once more before committing herself. Eventually she leaned forward in her chair and looked him earnestly in the eye.

'This is a tough guy, right. A no-nonsense guy. A hard man, as you would say.'

Skinner nodded.

She lifted up the book of photographs from her lap, and turned to a wide-angle shot of the death scene that she had marked with her thumb. 'This is exactly as your people found it, yes? I assume all of them knew to touch nothing.' Again, Skinner nodded. 'Right, look at the door. Fresh prints on the handle, and it's all the way open. That means that Manson was all the way into his bedroom when he was attacked. And a fresh thumb-print on the switch means that the light was on.'

She turned back to the close-up shot of the wound. 'Look here. The angle of entry, as Banks describes it, and the force of the wound can mean only that he was attacked from the front by a strong right-handed person, let's assume a man. He was stabbed, and then he was run backwards, all two-hundred pounds of him, fast enough to smash that damned heavy balustrade when he was forced into it. For that to have happened, there must have been no defensive reflex at all from Manson as he was being attacked with the knife. If there had been, then not even Arnold Schwarzenegger would have been able to generate the sort of force and speed with which he was moved backwards. And he must have been travelling that fast for the body to have such an effect on that solid wood.'

She paused, considering her words. 'Now you're Tony Manson, major operator, experienced villain of repute, afraid of nothing and very hard man. You walk into your bedroom, switch on the light and there's a stranger facing you with a knife. Even if he's coming at you fast, you react. It's your instinct. So even as he's sticking the knife into you, you're moving against him, resisting, your last active thought being to take a pop at this intruder. You're heavy, so even a strong man will have trouble holding you up, let alone moving you backwards.'

She shook her head. 'No, Bob, I believe that Manson came into the room, switched on the light, saw someone that he knew, and was so surprised that he was frozen, his muscles completely relaxed as he was killed. Look at his face, even. He died with his jaw dropped and his eyes wide open ... in surprise. The man just slammed right into him with the knife and kept moving, making sure to get him down, to be able to finish him if he had to. Only he didn't. He'd done the job first time of asking. That's how I see it. Questions?'

Skinner looked at his wife, considering everything she had said. He stood up from the bed and walked across to the window. He gazed out at the Meadows for a few seconds, still thinking, then glanced back over his shoulder towards Sarah. 'Could he have in fact resisted, and could they have struggled together *back* through the doorway on to the landing?'

She shook her head with conviction. 'No way. The wound is too clean and too deep; and that way the body wouldn't have developed pace enough to smash the balustrade. Look at the photos – see how solid it is.'

He cast his mind back to the day before, and nodded his agreement. 'Yes, you're right. They were built to stop people falling, those things, not to simply give way. 'Could he have been attacked from behind by a stranger, and stumbled backwards?'

'Again, no way. The angle of the wound is wrong. No, either Tony was a closet wimp and froze with fright—'

'You can rule that one out!'

'—or he was *surprised* to death.'

Skinner looked at her for a few seconds more, then smiled. 'Okay, Prof. If that's your heavy probability, I'll buy it. Now what's your certainty.'

She smiled back, pleased, and picked up the photographs once more. As she flicked through them she asked, 'Was Manson left-handed?'

'Eh? Buggered if I know.' Bob's forehead wrinkled as he searched his memory. 'Hey no! Wait a minute! I remember seeing him box once; must be twenty-five years ago. He was a southpaw. Yes, that would mean that he was left-handed. Why d'you need to know?'

She found the photograph for which she had been looking. 'See here.' She held it up to Skinner. Taken at the postmortem, the shot

22

was a close-up view of the ends of the fingers of Manson's left hand, facing palm upwards.

'Yes?'

'Standard practice at an autopsy: look under the fingernails.' She turned to the next photograph. 'This is what they found under the nails of Manson's left hand.' Skinner looked again. The ragged bits were magnified so that, in the colour exposure, Skinner recognised them easily as scraps of skin all flecked with blood, and one clearly with tissue attached.

He stared back at Sarah, his question clear in his eyes, and she answered at once.

'The knife's gone in. Manson's dead but he doesn't quite know it yet. Even as he's hurtling backwards, with the blade in his heart, his left hand clamps on to the wrist holding the knife. Like this.'

She reached up and grabbed his arm, her palm underneath, her fingers touching the base of his hand.

'The nails dig in, deep. It's a death grip. When he goes down, the man rips his hand free, and Manson's nails tear a great chunk out of his wrist. Just about there.' As she released him, she stroked the area which she had held. 'When you find the man who killed Tony Manson, you may take it from me, he will have either deep, ragged scratches or – if you don't catch him that quick – small scars on the inside of his right wrist.'

23

7

'What are you implying, Mr Skinner?'

Richard Cocozza, Tony Manson's lawyer, and now executor, leaned forward aggressively. Skinner disliked the man intensely. He had always believed that he must be completely aware of all the details of Manson's business activities, legitimate and covert. Though he was not by nature vindictive, he had long harboured a secret dream of catching Cocozza in some situation that was either criminally or professionally compromising. With Manson dead, that dream had dwindled to the faintest of hopes. Now the little man's reaction fanned that antipathy once more.

'Implying, Richard? What should I be implying? In the two days since your client was murdered, we have learned nothing from our inquiries that suggests any motive. Now, I am asking you and Mr John to allow my officers access to his personal and business bank accounts to see if they throw up any line of inquiry.'

The two men, lawyer and detective, sat facing each other on either side of a grey-surfaced designer desk in the office of the senior manager of the Greenside branch of Bank of Scotland. The banker, Andrew John, a burly, bearded figure, leaned back in his swivel chair, sensing the animosity, but remaining silent as the exchange developed.

'You expect me to believe that's all you're after?'

Skinner shook his head. 'I don't give a toss what you believe. I've explained to you what we want. Tell you what, though, the way you're going on, I'm beginning to think there might be something in there that you don't want me to find. We've always taken the view that Tony Manson was far too careful ever to have tried laundering any drug money through the legitimate businesses. Don't tell me we were wrong about that. Because if it turns out that we were, if we can trace large unaccounted movements of cash in and out of any of those accounts, we'd have to take a very close look at *you* and at what you might have known. Is that what your problem is, Richard? Is that why you're being obstructive?'

The fat little lawyer sat bolt upright, trembling with indignation.

Whether this was real or pretence, Skinner did not know, but he was pleased that the man's customary arrogance had been rattled.

'I'm *not* being obstructive!'

'Then why the questions? Why aren't you falling over yourself to help us find out who killed Manson? You can't want me to go to Court. We both know what the Law Society would think of that.'

He stood up and walked over to the first-floor bay window, his back turned to Cocozza as he looked across Picardy Place, past the life-size bronze statue of Sherlock Holmes – his fictional colleague – and beyond to the Paolozzi sculptures, vastly different in concept and execution, which dominated the pedestrian way in front of the Roman Catholic Cathedral. Skinner watched the traffic, as it circled the Picardy Place roundabout and exited in three directions: towards Princes Street, towards Leith, towards the west. In mid-morning May the traffic was relatively light in comparison with the peak summer months, when tourist cars and camper vans would abound.

For almost a minute only the traffic noise could be heard in the panelled office. Finally, Andrew John broke the silence. 'Look, Mr Cocozza, we're all busy people. You've no good reason not to agree to this, and you know it. So can you stop wasting our time!'

Skinner turned around. 'It's all right, Richard. There'll be no comeback. Tony's dead, remember.' He paused. 'Or is it the guy who killed him that you're scared of?'

Cocozza flushed, and suddenly Skinner knew that he had hit the mark.

'Very well. If it's in the interests of justice, I'll agree. With the proviso that the files do not leave this office, and that I am present whenever your people have access to them.'

Skinner nodded. 'Suits me. I'm sure points will come up that we'll have to ask you about.' He looked towards the manager. 'Do you have a spare office for my people?'

'Sure. When?'

'Now. They're waiting outside.'

8

'At times like this, sir, d'you never wish you were back in the clean air of Special Branch?'

Detective Sergeant Neil McIlhenney leaned his broad back against the drab grey wall of the windowless room. It still smelled of its last occupant, and perhaps, of two or three earlier ones.

Andy Martin smiled. 'Come on, Neil. We're doing a worthwhile job here too.'

'Maybe so, sir, but these low-lifers ... It's the constant procession of the miserable bastards that wears me down. Shifty-eyed, lying so-and-sos, and every one o' them in need of a good scrub. At least the agitators and general nutters we used to keep tabs on in the SB had nothing against underarm deodorant.

'Christ, that last tart we had in here – she was fuckin' honkin'.'

Martin laughed out loud. 'Aye, it must be working in a sauna that does it! All that sweat! Still, I wasn't kidding when I asked you to come to Drugs and Vice with me. I said it'd be a challenge.'

'Fine, but what you didn't say was that the challenge would be in keepin' down your lunch!'

Martin and McIlhenney had been interviewing non-stop for six hours in the Torphichen Place office, near Haymarket Station. Since nine a.m. they had seen and questioned a constant stream of managers and staff from Tony Manson's four saunas. The managers had all been picked up early that morning and ordered to provide complete lists of their staff – present and recent past. The responses of the four managers to Martin's questions about Tony Manson were so similar that it was clear the men had been well schooled.

'Mr Manson? A gent.'

'Mr Manson? Used to drop by every now and again to check on the takings. No, no, he never handled cash himself.'

'What d'ye mean, did he use any particular girls? Ah don't run that sort of place.'

The women had been a different story. Although none would say, it was clear that they regarded Manson's death as liberation from a

26

form of bondage. Most were ready to talk . . . within reason. But one went way beyond that.

Martin had recognised Big Joanne at once. When he had first encountered her on a street corner off Leith Walk – he in his uniform, she in hers – she had been more than something of a looker. Ten years on, he had been impressed to note that, even with her thirtieth milestone a year or two behind her, and hauled out of bed early after a hard night's work, she was still holding it together.

'Ah remember you! PC Martin it wis then. My, youse has fairly come up in the world.' Her transplanted Glaswegian tones were a contrast to the clipped Edinburgh accents with which Martin and McIlhenney were used to dealing.

'Tony Manson? Good riddance. Every workin' girl in Edinburgh should chip in a pony for the guy that did it. A fuckin' brute, he was. Once a lassie went tae work in one of his places, she wis dogmeat. There were only three ways out: get knocked up, get the clap, or get marked by a punter. Tony, he wid use the places like a harem, any time he felt like gettin' his end away . . .

'Away games? Sometimes. Every now and again, he'd pick up a lassie and take her out tae his place. A Tony takeaway, he used tae call it. Ah've been there a couple of times myself . . .

'Did he have any specials? If you got out tae Barnton more than once, ah suppose ye might have thought ye were special . . . until the next time he came in and took someone else! There was supposed tae be one lassie, though, that he did fancy. She didnae work in the same place as me. She was in that one down near Powderhall. Her name wis Linda somethin' or other. Apparently she was out at Tony's place a lot. Eventually she only did turns at the sauna fur Tony's pals. Too good fur the ordinary punters, so they said. Ah did hear that Tony kent her frae somewhere else. She's no there ony mair though. She must have got knocked up, or got the clap, or got cut, 'cos she stopped workin' awfy quick . . .

'Drugs? Know nothin' about that, Mr Martin. Nothin' . . .

'How much did he pay us? Where did ye get this guy, Mr Martin? *We* paid Tony, son. The workin' girls paid him!'

And that had been that. The sum total of six hours' work. They had checked the staff lists of the Powderhall sauna, but there was no mention of any girl named Linda. They had brought the manager back in, but he had been as tight-lipped as before. 'Linda? Linda who? Linda bloody Ronstadt for all I know. Never had anyone by that name working at my place.'

McIlhenney pushed himself off the wall against which he had been leaning. The heat of his body left a sheen on the dirty paint. 'That's us finished wi' the low-life, sir. What do we do next?'

'Just keep on looking for Linda, Neil,' said Martin. 'That's all we've got.'

9

'You didn't expect it to be easy, did you?' sneered Richard Cocozza.

Alison Higgins' jaw dropped when she saw the folders stacked on the table in the small office.

'There are thirty-two files in total, Superintendent,' said Andrew John. 'Each separate business has its own account. Take each laundrette, takeaway, pub, sauna, and the curling club, and you have a total of thirty-one accounts. Then there's a central Premier deposit account into which cash surpluses from each are transferred annually. That's kept at around a hundred thousand pounds. Cash surpluses beyond that go to longer-term investments. Any questions?'

'Who did the banking?'

'Managers in each business.'

'How were payments made?'

'The total payroll was processed by a firm of accountants, and debits were made from each account. Each business rendered its own tax and NI and its VAT. The same accountants handled all that. Very expensive in accounting terms, but it kept each of the businesses free-standing. That's the way Mr Manson wanted it. All other payments were made on his signature. He controlled every penny going out.'

'Good luck, then. I imagine that you could be here for some time.' John closed the door softly behind him.

Higgins and her assistant, Inspector David Ogilvie, a young officer with an accountancy degree, pulled chairs up to the table and sat down. Cocozza took his place alongside Higgins, watching her every move.

They began with the Premier deposit account file. Soon they saw that it offered no help at all. As the manager had described, they showed a series of inward transfers from named accounts, and occasional withdrawals by transfer of funds to an Edinburgh stockbroker.

'Okay, David,' said Higgins, closing the folder. 'Let's get into this lot. You take the laundrettes. I'll take the pubs and the takeaways.

Shout if you find anything that looks odd.' They selected the files according to the superintendent's allocation, and set to work.

Two hours later they broke for coffee. Cocozza, who had sat silent through all that time, could contain his mounting impatience no longer. 'Are you going any further with this farce, Superintendent?' he demanded.

Alison Higgins smiled across the table. 'Just as far as I have to, Mr Cocozza.'

It was Ogilvie who spotted the only anomaly in the meticulous records. 'Look here, ma'am.'

Higgins leaned across to follow his pointing finger. The file which was open before him was that of the Powderhall sauna.

'So far, the payment pattern in these statements is just the same as the rest,' Payroll out. Tax and NI out. Supplier bills out. In these sauna accounts, the main suppliers are the Council, for business rates, the Evening News for small ads, one of Manson's own laundrettes, and Scottish Power. They're all paid by direct debit. The odd petty cash cheque, thirty quid or so, and that's it. An established pattern. Then all of a sudden, look at this.' He pointed out an entry on the page, showing a debit of four thousand pounds through a cheque drawn on the account. 'Drawn six days ago, last Wednesday. I wonder who copped for that one.'

Higgins looked at the fat little lawyer. 'Well?' Cocozza said nothing. He sat there, grim-faced, and shook his head. She could not tell whether the gesture was one of refusal or ignorance.

'Let's find out, then.'

She left the room and returned just over a minute later, followed by Andrew John. The manager looked at the entry, then switched on a computer terminal which sat at a side table. He keyed in several numbers before he found the detail he sought. 'Cheque number 001237, drawn on the Powderhall sauna account. Presented to the Clydesdale Bank in Comiston on Monday last week, and cleared by us two days later. Payee is one L. Plenderleith. There's no other information I can tap into through this.'

'Can you call the manager of the Clydesdale and get more from him?'

'I can try. Let me go back to my office. I can check from there who he is. I suppose there's a chance I might know him personally.'

Higgins nodded, and the burly banker bustled from the room. As the door closed, the detective looked across once more at Cocozza. 'Well? L. Plenderleith. Does that name mean anything to you?'

Again the lawyer shook his head.

'You sure?'

'Quite sure.' His voice was quiet, his head still down.

'And you know nothing at all about any exceptional payment that your client might have made?'

'No.'

'I'll have to ask you to make a formal statement to that effect. You may wish to have another lawyer present when you do.'

Cocozza flashed her a sudden glance with suspicion bordering on alarm showing in his eyes. 'What do you mean by that?'

Alison Higgins smiled coolly back. 'Mr Cocozza, this is a murder inquiry, and we are under no illusions about your late client. I am suggesting that you might wish to take objective advice about everything you say to us. If you find that threatening, we have to ask ourselves why.'

Silence fell across the room, and hung there heavily until Andrew John returned two or three minutes later. He wore a satisfied smile.

'That was a stroke of luck. The manager wasn't a he but a she, Wendy Black, and she and I sat our bank exams at the same time. She'd have been within her rights to tell me to get stuffed, and to make you go through all the hoops to get what you're after. But the old pals act worked its charm.'

He sat down and continued. 'L stands for Linda. Mrs Linda Plenderleith, no kids, lives alone in a flat at 492 Morningside Road. She lives alone because Mr Plenderleith is doing time for something or other. Wendy didn't know anything else about her. She did say that this was the first cheque the woman had ever paid into her account, other than giros. All the previous deposits were cash. She was well in credit, though, even without the four-grand cheque from Manson. No mortgage or rent payments for her flat.'

Higgins' surprise showed on her face. 'How long has she lived there?'

'She was already at that address when she opened the account in 1990, and deposited ten thousand pounds cash.'

The detective whistled softly. 'Wonder where that came from. Did you ask whether there's been any further action since the cheque was cashed?'

For a second, John's enthusiasm was tempered by an offended look. 'Of course. And there has been. She drew out five hundred cash on Thursday, and asked for four grand in traveller's cheques. She had them picked up by courier on Friday. Banks don't like that, normally, but she made a special arrangement and the courier carried her letter of authority.'

Higgins' teeth sparkled as she smiled. 'Good work, Mr John! You can join my team any time.' She looked round at Ogilvie. 'David, you stay here and finish going through these files. Just in case there are any more Linda Plenderleiths. I'm going back to Torphichen Place to report this. Manson seems to have been keen to help this woman leave the country. Let's see if we can find out why.'

10

Andy Martin sat bolt upright in his chair.

'Did you say Linda?'

Skinner, in the process of pouring himself a cup of tea from the pot which the divisional commander's secretary had just brought in, put it down quickly on the conference table and straightened up, his eyes alert and questioning.

'Did you say Plenderleith?'

Detective Superintendent Higgins was taken aback by the speed and vehemence of her two colleagues' simultaneous reactions. She looked at each in turn, puzzlement wrinkling her eyes.

'Yes. Linda Plenderleith, 492 Morningside Road. Tony Manson paid her four grand last Wednesday, through the Powderhall sauna account. Why the interest?'

Once more, Skinner and Martin opened their mouths in tandem, to reply. They paused and looked at each other, smiling. 'Okay, Andy,' said the ACC. 'You first.'

'A girl called Linda something-or-other seems to have been Tony Manson's personal tart. Tony's and his friends, that is. Off limits to anyone else. We were told that she worked out of Powderhall, but the manager there denied it. We were also told that she'd dropped out of sight. So what does she mean to you, boss?'

Skinner looked at him. 'The girl? She means nothing to me . . . but her surname does. D'you remember big Lennie Plenderleith?'

For a few seconds, Martin searched his mental filing system, then he nodded vigorously. 'Yes! You put him away, must be about six or seven years ago now, for serious assault. Didn't he work for Manson?'

'Uh-huh.' Skinner nodded in his turn. 'He was head barman in that pub of Manson's in Leith Walk. You know the rough-looking one, the Milton Vaults. The one they call the War Office. While big Lennie worked there, it was as peaceful as a Sunday school. The trouble was bar-tending wasn't all that he did for Manson. He did heavy stuff as well . . . and I don't mean cellar work! Even as a lad, big

Lennie was a real gorilla. Tough, tough boy. He was in the Newhaven gang, and that got him into all sorts of trouble. He was never dishonest, or did drugs, and as far as I know he didn't go looking for trouble. But whenever any of the other gangs came on to the Newhaven patch, they had to deal with him; only none of them could. Through the gang he built up quite a record of assault convictions in his teens and early twenties; one of them was for using a blade – although he didn't need it. But then he went to work for Tony Manson, and all of sudden the arrests stopped. There were none for, oh, maybe for ten years.'

Skinner stopped to reflect, then continued. 'One or two people upset Manson over the years. They usually wound up in the Royal – "Don't know what happened, doctor. Ah just felt dizzy and fell down the stairs" – you know the story. We had a fair idea that big Lennie was Manson's "staircase", but none of the accident victims would talk, so we never nabbed him – until finally we got lucky. Dalkeith CID were keeping loose tabs on a suspected housebreaker What they didn't know – none of us knew – was that the guy had burgled Tony's sister's house a couple of weeks earlier. So anyway, they're watching the guy one night as he's walking home from the pub, as per usual, when big Lennie steps out of a close and breaks his kneecaps, one, two, nice as you like, with a baseball bat. The CID officers saw the whole thing. Plenderleith didn't try to run for it, or resist, or anything else. He just shrugged his shoulders, gave the guy one last whack in the head, then dropped the bat and held out his wrists for the cuffs.

'If he hadn't given the guy that last whack he'd probably have got no more than two or three years. As it was, he fractured the victim's skull and left him brain-damaged, so the Fiscal charged him with attempt to murder. Eventually his counsel did a deal and Lennie pleaded to serious assault, but he still got ten. He wouldn't say a dicky-bird about why he did it or who had paid him, and the judge took a dim view of that.'

Skinner paused, scratching his chin. 'You know, I always liked big Lennie, in a funny sort of way. When he wasn't smashing kneecaps, he was just a plain, polite, ordinary bloke who seemed to do more thinking than talking. Ran a good bar, collected tons of money for charity, was good to his granny. He just had a talent for violence, like *you* have a talent for detecting, Andy, and like you, he put it to work. Someone would have done it for Manson. It was probably just as well that it was Lennie than some mindless hooligan. As far as I know, Lennie never broke any bones that he wasn't paid to break. I've never doubted that when he fractured that guy's skull, that was what Manson had told him to do. Let's think, when did he go down –

1988,1989? No, 1990, that was it. And I remember hearing he'd married a young thing a year or two before that.'

Alison Higgins cut in. 'Excuse me boss, but Linda Plenderleith's bank account was opened in 1990 . . . with ten grand in cash.'

'Hah! Wonder whose cash it was. Big Lennie's bonus for keeping his mouth shut, or a down-payment to Linda for future services. Who was paying her mortgage?'

'No one, sir. According to her bank she didn't have one.'

'Find out, then, who owns the flat. It'll be one of the Plenderleiths, or both of them, or one of Tony Manson's companies. The last of these, I'd guess. I remember another thing about Big Lennie. When he was done, his address was given as Leith Walk, the flat above the pub.'

'If he got ten in 1990, he should still be inside,' said Martin.

'Aye, in theory, but you know our fine, politically correct Parole Board. That four grand might tell a different story. We should have been told if he was getting out but, again, nobody's perfect. Alison, will you get one of your people on to Scottish Prisons and check on the scheduled release date of one Leonard Plenderleith, last known address Care of Her Majesty, Shotts.'

He turned back to Martin. 'Makes for. some interesting possibilities, doesn't it. Big Lennie does a job for Manson, keeps his mouth shut, thinking no doubt that Tony'll look after his wife while he's away. Tony looks after her all right. Puts her on the game, and eventually turns her into a group concubine for himself and his pals. Tell you what, Andy. I don't get out of the office nearly enough these days. Let's you and I take a run up to 492 Morningside Road. There's no way she'll be there, but there's just the odd chance that Mrs Plenderleith might have given the neighbours a clue to where she was headed.'

11

Even in the cheek-by-jowl world of the tenement dweller, where other people's supposed secrets make commonplace conversation, Linda Plenderleith was a figure of rumour and mystery to her neighbours.

'A naice enough lassie, but she keeps to herself. None of us know what she does for a living. Maind you, I've always thought it's bar work, or hotel reception. She always gets home late, by taxi.' Mrs Angus occupied the ground-floor flat to the right of the mouth of the tiled close, directly below that of Linda Plenderleith. Her distinctive, flattened Morningside tones suggested disappointment over the gap in her knowledge, rather than disapproval of Linda Plenderleith's unsocial working hours.

Skinner imagined that, through the eyes of Mrs Angus, commuting by taxi was a mark of respectability.

The neighbour stood in her doorway, wearing the uniform of the Morningside matron, tweed skirt, twin-set and imitation pearls. Her arms were folded across her ample bosom as she eyed the two policemen, weighing in her mind the significance of their visit.

'When did you last see Mrs Plenderleith?' asked Martin.

'Let me think. It must have been last Friday. Yes, last Friday afternoon.'

'And was she going out or coming home?'

'Coming home.'

'And you didn't see her leave after that?'

'No. I don't think she's been to her work for a couple of weeks. At least I haven't heard any taxis after midnight.'

'Has there been any sound from upstairs since last Friday?'

'Not at all. But I never hear anything from above. This is a good building. There's a layer of ash between the floors. That's what they did in those days. No noise gets through that. Are you sure her doorbell was working?'

Skinner nodded. 'Yes, quite sure. Has Mrs Plenderleith had any visitors lately?'

Mrs Angus thought for a moment or two. 'She hardly ever had visitors. But I did see her leaving with a man last Wednesday. It would have been early afternoon. Then she came back alone, an hour later.'

'What did he look like?' asked Martin.

'Well he'd be about your size, I'd have said. Very well dressed: one of those expensive shiny suits. Beautifully groomed. Looked like a very nice man. Maybe a friend of Mr Plenderleith?'

Neither detective responded to the heavily loaded question in her tone. Skinner simply smiled. The quality of Tony Manson's tailoring had been a legend in his lifetime. 'Thank you, Mrs Angus.'

'Andy, let's try again upstairs. Maybe Mrs Plenderleith was asleep last time.'

The sentinel of 492 Morningside Road peered after them as they disappeared once more into the tiled close.

They trotted up the stone stairway. Linda Plenderleith's green front door was on the first landing. Skinner pressed the brass button of the doorbell once more, leaning on it for several seconds. He and Martin stood in silence for almost a minute, listening for any sound within the flat, but hearing none. Skinner frowned at Martin. He tried the door handle, but the Yale lock was dropped. Suddenly he crouched down and, flipping up the letter-box, peered into the narrow hall. He shoved his nose into the rectangular opening, and sniffed deeply. Then, without a word, he stood upright once more, took a pace backwards, sprang up, and slammed the heel of his right shoe powerfully against the shiny brass circle of the door's Yale lock.

With a sound of ripping wood, the door burst open.

As soon as he stepped into the hall, Martin realised that it was the unmistakable smell of death which had alerted Skinner. They followed it into a bedroom, facing out on to Morningside Road, and found her there.

Where Tony Manson's ending had been clean, almost bloodless, Linda Plenderleith had been butchered.

She was sprawled on her back, naked, on the bed. The duvet had been thrown across the room, and lay against the wall on the right. The pillows were crimson. The sheets were crumpled, saturated with blood, and in one place stained with faeces.

Martin took a deep breath and stepped towards the body. Skinner followed slowly suppressing his revulsion and looking round the room. He saw, on the tiny dressing table unit, a small framed photograph of a red-haired woman and a tall man. He noticed that one of the three doors of the white wardrobe unit lay open and saw, discarded on the floor before it, a bloody sweatshirt and a pair of black jeans. A pink dressing-gown had been thrown across a canvas director chair which faced the dressing mirror. Finally he steeled himself and stepped up beside Martin to look closely at what had been Linda Plenderleith.

The bloodless, pale-blue lips were beginning to shrink back from the teeth, giving them a look of protuberance. Already, with its sunken cheeks, the woman's face had taken on a skull-like appearance. The eyes were half open, but only the whites showed. The red hair was swept back, or had been pulled back, from the high forehead. The skin, where it was not smeared with blood, was exceptionally pale, almost translucent.

Skinner leaned over the carcass. As he studied it, he spoke to Martin, to maintain his detachment more than anything else. 'I think I can count six wounds to the throat. A big, crescent-shaped slash from ear to ear, probably not deep enough to do the job. Then three shorter deep cuts on the right side, and two on the left. It looks as if he straddled her, jerked her head back by the hair, and just hacked away until the blood was pumping. Look at that streak up the headboard and on to the wall. That must have happened when he hit the main artery.'

He looked more closely at the wall, his eyes widening. 'Jesus Christ, Andy. Look at that. The daft bastard must have pushed against the wall when he was getting off her. That looks like a perfect left-hand print.'

Martin followed his pointing finger, and nodded agreement. 'Incredible. Whoever it was must have been in a complete frenzy. He certainly wasn't thinking about making things hard for us. Who's your money on? Was this the same bloke who did Manson? Or could this have been Tony getting even with the woman for blackmailing him?'

Skinner stood up from the woman's body and walked away. 'Andy, son, you know how much I detest jumping to conclusions, but big Lennie is a stick-on fucking certainty for this one. And I say that without even having confirmed that he's out of jail. Take a gander in here.' Martin looked around. Skinner was standing by the wardrobe units.

'There's man's stuff in here, and it's not Tony Manson's. Cheap suits, jeans, bomber jackets, all XL size. This is Lennie's kit. And look at these things on the floor. He's dumped his bloodstained stuff and changed clothes. Look at this, too.'

Beckoning Martin to follow, Skinner stepped slowly alongside a trail of brownish smudges on the smoke-grey carpet, taking care not to tread on any of them. They led out of the bedroom into the hall, and from there into a long narrow bathroom. On the white PVC flooring, the brown stains were quite clearly dried blood. An electric shower was plumbed into the wall above the bath taps, and a white plastic curtain hung from a rectangular rail. A big pale-blue towel lay discarded across the toilet seat. Skinner moved carefully into the room, and looked into the bath. The safety mat had trapped some of the water from the shower. It was pink, matching that trapped in the channel between the white tiling and the edge of the tub. On the soap, in its dish, Skinner could see clearly a large, rusty-brown thumb-print.

He shook his head. 'God, he must have been covered in it! You're right, Andy. He must have been out of his tree. Wonder how long he knew. I wonder who told him about Manson and what he'd done to her. Get on the phone, Andy, and call the scene-of-crime people down here right away.'

As Martin took out his mobile phone, so Skinner pulled his own from his pocket. He searched his memory for a number, recalled it without reference to his diary, and dialled it in. 'Room 35, please.'

There was a pause, then, 'Sarah Skinner.'

'Hello, my love. How are you and Jazz?'

'We're great. Jazz is out like a light. I've just fed him. God, what an appetite. I don't know how I'm going to keep up with him.'

Even in his grim surroundings, Skinner laughed. 'Listen, let me take your mind off your mammaries for a bit. I'm at another murder scene. There's a connection with Tony Manson. After your critique of Banks's performance on Sunday, I don't want to call him in on this one. I need to know with authority when the victim here died. Looking at her, I'd say she's been dead for two days at the very least, but I need to know for certain whether she could have been killed by the same person who did Tony Manson. If the answer is yes, then it looks as if all the pieces fit. Who else would you recommend?'

There was a drawn-out silence on the other end. 'No one. Send a car for me.'

'Sarah, you're kidding!'

'The hell I am. Look, I'm fit as a flea. Jazz is going to sleep for three or four hours. Where are you?'

'Morningside Road.'

'Even better. That's only a mile or so from here. Now, come on, get that car down here, or you'll just have to call in old horse-doctor Banks!'

12

By the time that she arrived at 492 Morningside Road, Sarah's outright enthusiasm had been watered down into a strange mix of pleasure and agitation; pleasure at being back in action after her pregnancy-enforced lay-off, but a brand-new and totally unexpected restlessness over her first separation from her first-born.

A grim-faced constable stood at the entrance to the close. Another, even more solemn, guarded the door to Linda Plenderleith's flat. Sarah identified herself to each, and was admitted to the little apartment. Skinner, meeting her in the hall, caught her mood at once.

'Are you feeling guilty about rushing down here?'

She smiled ruefully. 'It's nature, I suppose. I mean, I know he couldn't be in better hands. It's just . . . I don't know, didn't expect it, that's all. I mean, he's sleeping, and I'll only be a couple of hours.'

Bob smiled. 'Make that ten minutes, if you like. Come through and have a look.' He was reaching out to open the bathroom door for Sarah, when his mobile phone sounded.

The caller was Alison Higgins. 'I've run both those checks you ordered, sir. Linda Plenderleith's flat was owned by a company called Samson Properties, registered number SC 122783, directors Anthony Manson and Richard Cocozza. And Leonard Plenderleith was released from Shotts Prison, on parole, on Saturday morning. Get this: they were expecting to be short-staffed at the prison over the weekend, so they let him out a day early. The officer on gate duty remembers that he was picked up by a small, fat, dark-haired man driving a white Astra GSi.'

'Thanks, Superintendent. Small, fat and dark, eh. Can we find out—?'

'I have done, sir. Richard Cocozza drives a white Astra GSi.'

'Nice one. Perhaps you could arrange for Mr Cocozza to join us at Torphichen Place. I'm looking forward to watching that slimy wee bastard sweat. Let me know when you pick him up. You and I will interview him together. Ask Roy Old to sit in too, and I'll arrange for

41

Andy Martin and Maggie Rose to be there as well. We'll terrify him by weight of numbers if nothing else!'

Skinner ended the call, and put the miniature phone back in its customary place in the pocket of his shirt. Sarah was still standing beside him at the door to Linda Plenderleith's bloody bedroom.

'Come on, then,' he said. 'Have a look at the mess, and tell me what you think. The technicians have barely started yet, so mind what you touch.'

She gave him her best withering look as he opened the door. A photographer was at work beside the bed, taking close-up shots of the wounds to the neck. Sarah knew him well from other crime scenes. 'Excuse me please, Dave,' she said as she approached.

The man looked up, surprised by the sound of her voice. 'Doc! What're you doing here? Haven't you just had a—?'

She stopped him with a smile and a nod, and stepped up to the bed. She leaned close to the body and looked at the face and at the cuts on the neck. She touched the flesh of the abdomen to test the temperature, and lifted one of the hands to judge the rigidity of the joints. Then she leaned over the groin, probing, testing, exploring gently. The woman's legs were spread apart in a V shape. Sarah looked closely at the inside of her thighs, then quickly at each of the upper arms.

She stood up and walked over to the discarded clothing on the floor. 'Can I touch these?' she asked Skinner.

'Sure, but put them back more or less where they were.'

She picked up the underpants, and looked at them inside and out. She lifted them to her nose and sniffed. Next she examined the shirt, and finally, the jeans.

Replacing the last garment as close as possible to its original position, she stood up and turned back to face Skinner.

'Three days, at least. She was killed not less than three days ago. That would make it Saturday.'

'Afternoon?'

'Just about spot on, I'd say. But no later.'

'No possibility of early Sunday morning?'

'No way. It'll take the autopsy to confirm it, but I know I'm right.'

'So I can go on believing that the man who did this could have gone on to kill Manson?'

'Sure. Who do you think it was?'

'The husband. Just released from jail. While he was inside, Manson gave his wife gainful employment as a prostitute.'

Sarah nodded. 'Is that so? Well, I'd say he spent his time in the pen thinking about all this, and planning it. Know what he did? He made

42

love to her, then he did that. It wasn't forcible sex – not rape. Look where her dressing-gown is. I'd say *she* put it there, rather than him. He's horny . . . he's just out of jail after how long?'

'Five years,' Skinner responded.

'Jesus, yes, he's horny. He throws the duvet across the room, he lays her on the bed. He doesn't bother to undress. He's in too much of a hurry, although there's another reason. He just undoes his belt and unzips his jeans – or she does – frees his penis, and enters her straight away. Her pubic hair is matted. There's semen dried in it. There are other semen stains on his underpants, and on his shirt. This is when it gets really calculated. They've just made love. She's lying back, maybe saying how good it was, how much she's missed him. But she hasn't seen the knife. This wasn't a spur-of-the moment thing. All along, he meant to kill her. He took the knife into the bedroom with him.'

'Why didn't she see it?'

'Because it was in the back pocket of his jeans. It could have been something small: a Stanley knife, say. It could have been any size, but one thing I do know: it was pointed. Look at the jeans. They're new. Well, on the back, right-hand pocket, near the bottom, you'll find a tear. I think that he slipped the knife into that pocket, and its point went through the cloth. It was there all the time he was humping her. When he's finished, when he's got his rocks off, the bastard . . .'

For a second her professional mask slipped and a woman's outrage at sexual violence showed through.

'Just when she's telling him he's Superman, he grabs her hair, forces her head back, pulls the knife, and does that. He's never cut anyone's throat before, so the first cut is the big one. The song's wrong, you know. The first cut is rarely the deepest. Maybe she gets off a scream, but she doesn't have time to struggle. The fingers aren't clenched. When the first cut doesn't kill her, when he finds that it isn't as easy as that, he just starts hacking away, to finish her off as quickly as he can. He isn't thinking any more. He cuts deep, on either side of the throat, to make sure. Eventually he hits the big one, and the blood spurts. It goes everywhere. Up the wall, all over the bed, all over him. She blacks out as soon as the blood supply to her brain stops, and she's dead in seconds after that. He's got blood all over his clothes. So he strips them off, washes . . . ?'

She glanced at Skinner for confirmation.

'Yes, he took a shower.'

'Mmm. Then he changes into clean stuff and off, presumably, he goes on his merry way. And *you* think his merry way took him to kill Manson?'

Skinner nodded.

'It fits, I suppose. Have you found the murder weapon?'

'No, but come here and look at this.' Skinner led her into the flat's spacious dining-kitchen. There was a work surface next to the sink, and on it stood a set of kitchen knives, housed in a wooden block. One of the six slots in the block was empty. 'We've got a set much like this one at home,' said Skinner. 'From what I can remember the knife that fills that slot should be a big, broad-bladed job.'

'That's right. The blade is about eight inches long, and comes to a point. In our set the blade's like a razor and the point's like a needle.'

'From what you saw, could a knife like that one have killed Manson?'

Sarah nodded firmly. 'Absolutely. It had to be a blade that long. It travelled upward and ripped the heart open.'

'That looks like the answer, then. Big Lennie kills his wife then shows up at Manson's. He does the alarm. That's no problem; he's been in the nick for five years; he'll have learned how in there. Tony comes in, flushed with success at the tables. It's Big Lennie he sees in the bedroom. His jaw drops as he figures out why Big Lennie's there, and in that short time he's a dead man.'

'Where do you think he is now?'

'I *know* where he is now. Last week Tony Manson gave Linda four grand. She turned it into traveller's cheques. We've found out that there was a seat booked on a flight from Glasgow to Alicante on Sunday in the name of L. Plenderleith. It looks as if Manson was trying to whisk her out of town before Lennie got out. Seems like he didn't quite make it. Nice windfall for Lennie, though. The traveller's cheques – unsigned we believe – and the plane ticket are gone. Britannia tell us that the ticket was used. They said that there was some confusion when a man turned up, but the surname checked and they assumed it had been a booking error. So there you have it. The whole story. Lennie gets home early, exacts a terrible and bloody revenge on Linda and Manson, and buggers off to Spain with Manson's cash and her ticket.'

'Okay, husband, if that is the obvious pattern of events – and it is glaringly obvious – then tell me why you don't believe it.'

Skinner looked at her, a smile twitching the corner of his mouth. 'Who says I don't.'

'*I* do. I see the telltale signs of a Skinner niggle. There's something there that doesn't fit.'

The twitch turned into a grin. 'Well, just a couple of wee things. First, why did Manson leave her in the flat for big Lennie to find; and, second, why did Richard Cocozza, his lawyer, pick him up from

Shotts prison on Saturday morning? Tony can't give us the answers, but Cocozza can, and he sure as hell better. Otherwise I'm going to charge him with being a party to *two* murders! But before I see him again, my love, let's you and I go back to the Simpson, to say hello to our son.'

13

Cocozza crouched forward in his seat so suddenly that Skinner thought for an instant that the little fat man's bladder had betrayed him.

'What!' It was more squawk than speech.

'You heard me, Cocozza. You dropped Plenderleith, a violent man, at his wife's door. Why should I, or a jury for that matter, not assume that you knew he was likely to kill her, and Tony Manson, after what they had done to him while he was inside. Why shouldn't I believe that you set them up? Why shouldn't I believe that you were a party to their murders? You're the lawyer here. You know what that means. You're as guilty as big Lennie is, and I'm going to charge you with the girl's murder, at the very least!'

'No, you can't!'

'Like fuck I can't! You're a dead certainty to go down for the girl's murder. Jesus Christ, Manson puts her on the game, then plans to get her out of town – out of Lennie's way. You show up at the prison and pick the big bugger up – a day early. Then you drop him at her front door.'

Cocozza summoned the last of his defiance. 'Who says I did?'

'A very reliable witness. A neighbour. You know the type, Cocozza. Logs every movement in and out of the building. A flash white car was seen dropping a big man in jeans and a cowboy shirt at Linda Plenderleith's close. The witness has picked Lennie out already from mug shots. And the driver was seen clearly too. All we need is to stick you in front of an identity parade. The bit I can't understand is why? Why did you shop the girl? And Manson? He was your meal ticket. You don't have another significant client. Why set him up for the chop?' Skinner's voice was soft, but his eyes were hard as they stared across the old, scratched table-top at Richard Cocozza.

The lawyer sat with bowed head, still crouched forward on his chair, gripping it on either side, with his knees pressed together and his fingers under his thighs. When he looked up, there were tears in his eyes.

'Plenderleith didn't know. He didn't know what Linda has been

46

doing while he was inside!' he wailed plaintively. 'It wasn't like you said. Tony didn't force her into anything. When Lennie went inside, he offered her a job in my office, but she said she'd rather make real money. So he controlled her. He vetted all her punters. No one in the place knew her surname, not even the manager. She wasn't on the payroll, like the other girls are. They're employed, you see, so that no one can be nailed for living on the proceeds or anything like that. The theory is that what they make on their backs is pin-money.'

He looked across at Alison Higgins and nodded his head in a peculiar gesture, as if offering an apology for the crudeness of his phrase.

'Pin-money,' Skinner snorted. 'But they still kick back enough to the house to cover their pay-packets and a bit more too. Your Tony was a fucking pimp on a big scale!'

'I don't know anything about that,' Cocozza pleaded.

'Aye, sure you don't,' said Skinner with a chuckle. 'But we won't pursue that. No you're still in the frame, wee man. If Lennie was a poor, unsuspecting cuckold, what was the four grand for? Why was there a plane ticket for Linda? It still stacks up like they had her getaway arranged. Then you found out that he was getting out a day early, picked him up and dropped him off, primed and ready to do the dirty deeds, then vanish with Linda's hard-earned dough.'

Cocozza shook his head, violently from side to side. 'No! No! No! You've still got it wrong! The plane ticket and the money were for Lennie. Tony told me that, as soon as he was released, he was going to send him on a sort of working holiday to Spain. The idea was that Linda would fly over to join him in a week or two, once he was settled in. There was a place out there that Tony was thinking of buying into: a Country Club and timeshare resort. Lennie was to go out there right away and spend a couple of months looking the place over, without anyone knowing who he was. Then, if it seemed all right to him, Tony was going to put his cash in, and Lennie and Linda were going to stay there as his people on the ground.'

Skinner looked at him, grinning gently. 'You're thinking fast, Cocozza, but I've still got you by the balls. I prefer my version, and so will the Crown Office. You've still got some work to do.'

'Look, Tony visited him at Shotts just last week. He went out to see him, to tell him what he wanted. He came back and he said to me, "That's fine about the Spanish thing. I've talked to the big fella and he's up for it." He said that he would sort out his traveller's cheques through Linda's bank account. There was another ten thousand waiting for him in a bank account out there. It was the second part of his pay-off for . . .'

Skinner's grin widened into a smile as Cocozza realised that he was about to implicate himself in the six-year-old Dalkeith assault, and choked off his sentence.

'You can check on the visit. They keep records in prisons, don't they? It was only the second time that Tony had been to see him in all that time. I'm sure if there had been any argument they'd have noticed.'

'I'll check, Cocozza. Don't you worry. But the prison office will be closed by now, so you'll be our guest at least until it opens in the morning . . . and then you'll be theirs if they don't back up your story! Meantime, keep talking. The Spanish bank account. Which bank?'

'It's a convertible peseta account at Banco Central, in Alicante. Lennie signed an authorisation form when Tony went to see him, so that he could go in when he got there and draw cash whenever he liked, without fuss. The bank-book should have been at Linda's place too.' Cocozza had recovered some of his composure, but none of his insolence. There was still a plea in his eye. 'Is that enough for you, Skinner?'

'Enough for now, Cocozza. Enough for us to check. But if just one wee piece turns out to be crap, you're for the jump. Even if you walk out of here, you're standing on the edge of being struck off by the Law Society. Who knows, maybe you could pick up a job managing a sauna. That's about your strength!'

14

'Lucky lady, Maggie. You're going to get to do something that I've never done: you're going to Spain on the Company. And before you ask, no, you can't take McGuire!'

It was 8:27 a.m. on Wednesday 15 May. Skinner and his personal assistant had been at work for almost an hour. The remains of their breakfast, of bacon rolls from the canteen and coffee from Skinner's filter, lay on the rosewood desk.

'There's no doubt at all that Big Lennie's in Spain. Maybe he thinks we won't come after him; but if he reckons he can knock off two people and simply become just another anonymous hoodlum among the crowds of villains on the Costa Del Crime, well, he's got another think coming. I saw the mess he made of that woman. I can't get too worked up about Tony Manson, but wherever Lennie is, and whatever provocation he thought he had, I've – we've *all* got a duty to make sure that he can't do to another woman what he did to his wife. That's why I want you out there: to make sure that the Guardia Civil don't treat this as just another request for assistance from a foreign police force.'

Maggie Rose looked Skinner in the eye. 'Why me, boss? You could send Brian Mackie. After all, international liaison's part of his Special Branch brief now. You're not just giving me a perk, are you?'

'Hah!' Skinner laughed; a sudden, short, snorting laugh. 'No, I am not! Since when did I hand out sweeties? Anyway, you haven't been in this post long enough to have earned a freebie. There's a good reason for *your* going, rather than Brian. Even though things have changed for the SB, he still has to be kept anonymous. And that's the last thing I want on this investigation. I want to generate as much publicity for this as I can. I've already told Alan Royston to call a press conference as soon as he can, for first thing this morning, and then I'm going to tell all. You'll be with me at the top table. I'm going to announce that we're anxious to interview the victim's husband, and that we know he's in Spain. Then I'm going to introduce you as the detective responsible for liaison with the Spanish bobbies – Skinner's personal emissary and all that stuff. Fancy being a media superstar, Maggie?'

'Not a lot, sir. Much more up Mario's street. Why don't you send him?'

'Apart from the fact that he's not senior enough, he's a bull. You're a diplomat. This isn't just PR for home consumption. I want the story to follow you out there. I want the Spanish to realise that this isn't just another domestic murderer we're after. This is a man who has made a career out of violence. I want the Scottish media pressuring the Spanish for results, so that I know they're giving us their best efforts. Your job out there will be to brief the Guardia Civil, and to join them in pursuing certain lines of inquiry. You'll really be leading them, in that you'll be making sure that those lines of inquiry are followed up.'

He pointed to his desk. 'Take the picture book out with you, and all the reports: scene-of-crime, forensic, postmortem. Contact Edinburgh University this morning and arrange to have them all translated into Spanish. How good is yours, by the way?'

'Quite good. I've been doing it at the Colegio Español for years. How did you know about that?'

'It's on your file.' Maggie raised her eyebrows in surprise. 'You don't think you'd be where you are now without some vetting, do you?' said Skinner. 'That's yet another reason why I'm sending you rather than anyone else. I want you to be involved in this as actively as you can.'

Rose nodded. 'What special lines of enquiry did you mean, sir?'

'Two really. I want you to check out that place Cocozza told us about, the one that Manson was thinking about putting his dough into. Check there for any sightings of the big man, but while you're at it, find out all you can about the place, and about the types who own it. The other thing you should do is check up on the bank account Cocozza told us about, in the Banco Central in Alicante. See whether it's been activated.'

'One thing, boss. You haven't mentioned Manson at all. Do I take the pics and reports of his murder too?'

Skinner shook his head. 'No. Leave that out.'

'Will you be telling the press that we want to talk to Plenderleith about Manson as well?'

'No.'

'Why not?'

'I don't want to do that for now. When someone like Manson gets knocked off – not that gangland killings are ten a penny in Edinburgh, but we've had a few – people get nervous until it's cleared up. The criminal community doesn't like uncertainty. When a power vacuum develops, people react in two ways. Some get scared: often important people in the network who had nothing to do with it, but wonder whether they might be the next target. Others get brave: the wee folk with a grudge, who might have been shat on by the dear departed or his team. Whatever the reason, they begin to tell us things anonymously or right out in the open, things we'd never hear in normal times. Eventually a new top dog emerges and everything goes back to normal, but until that happens we've got the whip hand.

'Since Manson was knocked off, Andy Martin's squad has had tip-offs about three of his dealers from disgruntled punters. They're all locked up now. We might not get convictions against any of them, but at least they're all blown. They're out of business, and the network's damaged.'

'Who'll be top dog after Manson?'

'I don't know, but neither does anyone else yet, and that's to our good. There'll be one eventually, you can be sure, but until he can show himself, the vacuum's still there. If we let it be known that Tony only got killed because he was shagging someone's wife, it'll be filled in a week. The network will close up.'

'But why should it? Without Manson, might it not just fall apart?'

'Not a chance, Maggie. The trade is bigger than Manson. It isn't driven by the dealers alone. It's driven first by the exporters, then the importers, then the dealers. Always three key links in the chain. Whether the supply comes from Sicily, Corsica, Eastern Europe, or wherever, there's a natural market for the product in every developed country. If the chain loses a link somewhere, it always finds another.'

He paused and looked across the desk at his assistant. 'So that's the main reason why I don't want to finger big Lennie for Manson's murder right now. With a break in the chain, there's always a chance that the other two players will show themselves, trying to plug the gap. If we can nail them, then we *can* break the whole thing up.'

'The main reason, boss? What's the other?'

'Och, I don't know. There probably isn't one. It's just that – well, you know me: I like all the bits to fit. And there's still a piece of this jigsaw that doesn't quite mesh.'

'What do you mean?'

Skinner hesitated. As he opened his mouth to reply, there was a heavy knock on the door. 'Come!' he shouted.

A second later, Roy Old's head showed round the door. 'I've just had a call from Alison Higgins, sir. Cocozza's story about Manson's visit checked out all the way. He *did* go to see big Lennie last week. They were watched They were even videoed. It was all quite cordial.

51

The officers on duty that day said that big Lennie seemed like a dog with two cocks – oh, sorry Maggie.'

'Lucky bitch!' interjected Rose, dead-pan.

Old grinned self-consciously, as he advanced into the room, closing the door behind him. 'That is, he seemed pleased as Punch by a visit from the big boss. Began with a hug and ended with a handshake.'

Skinner pushed himself up from his chair. 'Right. Tough that it seems to leave us with nothing to pin on that wee shit Cocozza. We'll have to spring him. Maggie, give Alison Higgins the word, will you, please. While you're doing that, I'll observe the niceties and call José Pompo, the Spanish Consul. It'll give you added clout if I fix up your trip through him. And then get the translation job under way. But make sure you're ready for the press conference at nine-thirty.'

'That's earlier than usual, isn't it?' said Roy Old.

'Maybe so,' said Skinner, beaming. 'But the hacks can dance to *my* tune for a change. I've got a wife and son to collect from the Simpson by ten-thirty, and nothing – not even the assembled Edinburgh media corps in all its glory – will make me late for that!'

15

'You fancy your new room, wee man, don't you?'

The baby's eyes were wide open as Bob cradled him in the crook of his arm. They seemed to follow the movement of the brightly coloured mobile suspended above his cradle, as it swung in a slow circle in response to Sarah's touch. That, and the American-style satin-lined cradle, had been her choice. Bob had picked the nursery-rhyme motif of the wallpaper. A huge stuffed panda, which he had bought in John Lewis that morning, en route for the Simpson, filled a high-backed rocking-chair by the dormer window.

Bob carried his three-day-old son over to the window and showed him the mature back garden, flooded in mid–day sunshine. 'See that tree down there, Jazz? That nice silver birch with the strong branches. That's where we'll hang your swing in a year or so. The climbing frame can go on the grass just over there, and the sandpit can go up against the garage. You'll be a lucky lad, 'cos there's the same again in your other house out at Gullane, the very swing and frame that your big sister Alex had when she was a nipper. She didn't have a sandpit though. There was hardly any point, was there, with a beach out there.'

Sarah reached up and ruffled her husband's hair. 'You're really looking forward to all this, Pops, ain't you?'

'Too right, I am. His first childhood, but my third. What I'm looking forward to is doing all the things right this time that I might have got wrong with Alex. There's not too many guys my age get that chance.'

'From what Alex says, you didn't get too much wrong. Come on, set him down in the cradle. Let him get used to it.'

Gently, Bob laid the bright-eyed child down in his crib. For a second it seemed as if Jazz would cry at the breaking of the contact, but then his eye was caught once more by the blue-painted balsa-wood birds of the mobile, and he stared following their movement. Quietly, mother and father backed away from the cradle, and stood together by the window.

'It's a dream, isn't it, honey?' said Sarah softly.

53

Bob said nothing. He could only grin, happier than he could express in words.

'What's a dream, too,' she went on, 'is the idea that you'll actually be off work for a few days. How long are you taking?'

'Best part of a week. I've cleared my diary until Tuesday morning. Roy Old's looking after things. It's just you and me and Jazz, apart from tomorrow night. Remember, I told you about it – a meeting of Murrayfield and Cramond Rotary Club. Peter asked me to do it a while back. It's in their programme, so I don't like to back out. Is that okay? They start at half-six, so I should be back around eight-thirty.'

Sarah smiled. 'Well, since you're taking us to Spain in a couple of weeks, I don't really think I can bitch about it. Anyway, Alex is coming through for the night, and Andy said he'd look in later. You'll be back for him, won't you?'

'Mm, sure. Listen, about Spain. You sure it's okay, with Jazz being so young?'

Sarah turned to face him. His arms circled her waist as she placed the flat of her hands on his chest.

'Listen, you can be the fussiest Dad of all time, but trust me on the medical side, just like I leave the detecting to you. I told you already, before we set off I'll take him back to the paediatrician for a 500-mile check-up. If there's the slightest flicker of disapproval on her face, we cancel the ferry and stay home. But worry not, my love. That boy of ours is the thrivingest baby you'll find in a day's march.'

'It won't be too hot?'

'Would it be too hot for a Spanish baby? It's early summer, and so it won't be baking. Believe me, he'll be fine. He'll be in shade all the time. That buggy you bought for him has got everything save air-conditioning, and the house does have that. As for his food, I carry my own supply, remember.' She tapped her chest with a long finger. 'D-cup these days, boy. Tits like racing Zeppelins!'

Bob laughed and hugged her, gently. 'Right, I'm convinced. He'll be fine. But how about you? Will you be all right by then?'

She smiled slyly as she looked up at him. 'Three days after the birth *might* be a bit soon, but before long, you'll have found out just how all right I am. And that, my love, is a promise that I will surely enjoy keeping!'

16

'The bar service is better than usual this evening, Bob. They must have noticed that you were coming!'

Peter Payne held a brimming pint of lager in each hand as he approached the alcove in the Barnton Hotel's main bar where Skinner was waiting. He was a tall ruddy-faced man with a shock of black hair which belied his fifty-something years. The two had met some years before, not in Edinburgh but in L'Escala, in Catalonia, where each had a holiday home. The normally reserved Peter, fuelled by alcohol, had introduced himself towards the end of a party. In the years since then they had met more frequently in Spain than in Edinburgh, since their trips there often coincided, although they found time for golf at Skinner's club in Gullane or in Edinburgh at least once a year.

'Anthea and I were delighted to hear about the little chap. You'll give Sarah our congratulations, won't you?'

'That's kind of you. Of course I will.'

'What's his name? What did your *Scotsman* notice say again? James Andrew, that was it. Which will it be?'

'Neither. Jazz is the name, my friend. Mark it well. He's going to be a star!'

Peter's eyes glazed for a second, while he sought an appropriate response. 'Jazz, eh.'

Bob grinned at his friend's reaction, then moved him on to the evening's business. 'I have a fairly bog-standard presentation for evenings like this, Peter. The changing role of the police, then the role of the CID, that sort of thing. Alternatively I can talk about experiences: great moments in a memorable career, that sort of self-effacing stuff. Which would your members prefer, do you think?'

'The latter, I should think. I'm sure they'd love to hear the inside story of that affair last year.'

Skinner smiled. 'Okay, I'll give them the blood and thunder!'

'Great!' Peter took a swig of his beer and glanced at his watch. 'Look, let's go in to supper. Bring your pint with you.'

He stood up to lead the way, then paused. 'Oh, before I forget, there's a chap here you must meet. A new member. Apparently, he has a place in Lar Escala' – Peter's English accent rolled the vowels together as he used the Castillian form of the name – 'but he always goes in June and September. He said he was keen to meet you too. I'll introduce you after your address.'

They moved into the function room which had been set aside for the meeting. Skinner, a regular speaker to Rotarians and Round Tablers, smiled to himself when he saw the two-course menu of minestrone soup and steak, standard fare at such events. The speed with which the meal was consumed was standard practice also, as if it was a chore to be completed, rather than fare to be enjoyed. Forty-three minutes after they had entered the dining room, Peter Payne introduced his guest, succinctly but generously.

Skinner rose to his feet. 'Good evening, gentlemen.' The emancipation of women in the Rotary movement was still not universal in Edinburgh. 'I have a standard opening line for events such as this. Are there any journalists in the house, and if there are, will they please identify themselves?'

The news editor of a right-wing tabloid rose, smiling, to his feet. He took a small tape-recorder from a pocket of his jacket, and ostentatiously removed the micro-cassette.

'That's fine, Gregor,' said Skinner, smiling. 'Now just keep your hands where I can see them, so I can speak as freely as I like.'

As he had promised Peter Payne, his thirty-minute address contained considerable thunder and the odd drop of blood. Skinner recognised the presence of a ghoulish element in every group he addressed, however sophisticated it might be. He never pandered to it, but at the same time he took pains never to glamorise his job. Several fathers in the audience winced at one point as he described the injuries inflicted by a serial killer of children on his young victims, and others nodded as if from experience when he described the ease with which young people could be led along the path of drug-taking, from the first taste of marijuana to mainlining. As always, Skinner took care to sprinkle his speech liberally with examples of the black humour which is commonplace among policemen, from the tale of the masked and armed post-office robber who dropped his credit cards at the scene of his crime, and who had then called his bank to report the loss, to an in-house legend of a middle aged Special Branch constable whose elevated observation post at a Royal visit had given him an entirely

56

unexpected view of the Royal retiring room, the use of which he recorded for posterity with his 300mm telephoto lens.

Finally, he wound up by inviting questions. 'You understand I can't say anything about current investigations, but that should still leave plenty of scope.'

A plump, dark-haired man in a severely cut business suit raised a hand. 'I believe in arming the police. What's *your* view, Mr Skinner?'

Skinner nodded, unconsciously, at this question which he was regularly asked. 'When it's necessary, we do it, and we're pretty good at judging necessity. Like most policemen, I am dead against general arming. Community relations are tricky enough to manage without making life even more difficult for our officers by hanging pistols from their waist. There's the familiarity angle too. If all our coppers had guns, pretty soon all the hoodlums would have them too. Then, night generally following day as it does, we'd have an increase in their use in muggings and in trivial situations; arguments in pubs, that sort of thing. Apart from all that, the use of firearms is a skilled business. If you're an armed and threatening bad guy, and you see me or any other officer showing a gun, you'd better be bloody careful, because we are all qualified marksmen. I've got a man in my team who could singe your eyebrows from one hundred yards.'

He turned to indicate his host. 'Now, look for example, at the place where Peter and I live in Spain. I'm relaxed about the Guardia, but the local police carry guns, and that scares me witless. There's a young fellow patrols the beaches. He has a bike and he wears shorts and trainers as part of his uniform. His job takes him into the midst of crowds of children, yet he carries a gun. They use girls on traffic duty. Their uniforms don't even fit properly, but they carry bloody great .38 magnums. God forbid that any of them should ever think to draw a weapon. I'd bet you that none of them could hit an elephant in the arse if they were holding its tail! Those young traffic girls would dislocate their wrists if they fired those things they carry. That's what general arming of police means, and I hope we never see it here. Right now, I have guns when I need them . . . and in normal times that is a rare occurrence.'

A bald man at a table twenty feet from Skinner raised a hand. 'How does a policeman feel when he kills a man?'

Skinner shrugged. 'I can tell you how he – or she – *should* feel. Concerned, and personally upset. Its a hell of a serious thing. But if the officer has acted properly and professionally, then that concern will be countered by the knowledge that the criminal

57

committed effective suicide by putting himself in that killing situation.'

'Mr Skinner.' A bulky man in a tweed jacket, with heavy eyebrows and a beard, broke in over his answer. 'Wasn't it the case that one of your officers shot and killed a man last year as he was leaving a crime scene, but the unarmed victim was shot in the back? What do you say to that?'

There was a smile on Skinner's lips as he answered, but his eyes were suddenly icy-cold. 'I say that was the finest shot I have ever seen in my life.'

He paused for several seconds to allow his answer to sink in, holding the bearded man in his gaze. Then, 'You seem well read, sir. In which case I'd ask you to recall that the criminal in question had just killed a number of people, including one of my officers. And I expect you realise that in such circumstances it was the duty of the police to ensure that man did not escape us to kill again. I'd have made that shot myself, if I had the skill and the necessary weapon.'

'*Have* you ever shot anyone?' asked the man in the business suit.

Skinner nodded.

'How did you feel?'

'Better than he did.'

Peter Payne sensed that the mood needed lightening. 'Come on, colleagues, let's have another question. Anyone want to ask about traffic wardens?'

'Sorry,' said Skinner. 'You are definitely not allowed to shoot them. Although, on occasion . . .'

Welcome laughter lightened the atmosphere.

Towards the rear of the room, a thin, middle-aged man raised a hand. 'Mr Skinner, could you say something about the level of co-operation these days between European police forces?'

'Yes. I'd say it's getting better – certainly within the EU. We're finding that it's easier for police colleagues in different countries to get together to solve problems. We're all working harder at it, I think. For example, my head of Special Branch now has general responsibility for international relations. And only this week, as you may have read, I was able to send a detective to Spain to advise the Guardia Civil in their search for a man we want to talk to back here about a current murder investigation.'

'When he's caught, will it be easy to get him back?'

'Sure. The Spanish won't want to feed him for any longer than they have to.'

58

The questioner smiled. 'Can you tell me, if a person in this country feels that he may have been the victim of dishonesty in another country, can he make a complaint *here*?'

'Technically, no. As an investigator, I work for the Crown Office and the Procurator Fiscal. If the crime occurs abroad, then the complaint should be raised in that country. In practice, if anyone on my patch feels that they may have been stitched up in a foreign country, then my department will certainly listen to them. If it is warranted, we might even raise the complaint on their behalf ... unofficially of course.'

The bald man raised a hand again. 'Mr Skinner, about the traffic wardens...'

The question session ran on for a little longer, growing more light-hearted by the minute, until Peter Payne drew it to a close, eliciting a final round of applause for Bob's contribution to the evening. As the gathering broke up, Skinner noticed that the thin man who had spoken from the back of the room seemed to be holding back as if waiting. Peter Payne spotted him in the same moment, and beckoned him across.

'Bob, this is the chap I mentioned earlier,' he said as the man approached.

'Greg Pitkeathly,' said the thin man, shaking Skinner's hand.

'Pleased to meet you,' said Skinner.

'Tell me, am I right in thinking that your questions back there had some purpose to them?'

The man smiled, and nodded. 'Afraid so. I rather think I've been defrauded. Probably in Spain, but I'm not certain. Is there someone who'll speak to me?'

'If it's in Spain, and you're a L'Escala dweller, that makes it almost personal. I'll take a look at it myself.'

'That's very good of you. If you're sure of that, I've got a file on it all. When can I let you see it?'

'Well, if it'll keep till Tuesday, I'll be back in my office then. Why don't you call my secretary tomorrow and fix a time. Tell her where we met.'

Pitkeathly's thin face broke into a smile of gratitude. 'That's very good of you. I'll look forward to telling you my story. It seems almost too obvious to be a fraud but, the way the figures add up, I don't see any other answer.'

'Well, let's find out on Tuesday. I must go now, I'm in danger of being absent without leave!'

He shook Peter Payne's hand and hurried off, leaving Pitkeathly staring in some surprise at his disappearing back.

17

When Bob returned to Fairyhouse Avenue, he found the scene already set in the nursery for the ritual of Jazz Skinner's first bath-time before guests in his new home.

Sarah's advance planning had been meticulous. The yellow plastic bath was in place, held in its collapsible frame beside a low changing table, and a simple wooden stool stood between the two. Andy Martin and Alex had arrived ahead of schedule and, to Sarah's surprise, together in Alex's car. They stood in a corner of the bright nursery and looked on as the new mother undressed her infant, dumped his disposable nappy, wrapped around its colourful contents, in a lined bin beneath the table, and gave him a preliminary wipe before lowering him carefully into the warm water.

Jazz chuckled as the water lapped over his skin, and he kicked his long, strong legs in pleasure, splashing his mother's apron, and his father's slacks. When the waves subsided, Sarah washed him gently with Johnson's soap. It was only when she began to shampoo his dark hair that the baby's equanimity was broken, as he screwed up his eyes and whimpered.

When she had rinsed off the last of the suds, she looked up at Bob. 'How'm I doing then, Dad?'

'Well, as the only person here with relevant experience, I'd say you were doing okay. So would Jazz, I think.' With the annoyance of the suds behind him, the baby had resumed his energetic kicking. 'Better get him out of there before he empties the bath!'

'Okay. You can do the next bit.' Sarah lifted him from the bath and laid him on a soft fluffy blue towel which Bob had spread on the table. She stood to the side and watched as her husband dressed his son for the night, greasing his bottom liberally with Vaseline before fitting the bulky disposable nappy, then easing him – arms first, then legs – into the one-piece white sleep-suit. All the time, he spoke to Jazz in a matter-of-fact way. 'It amazes me, you know, wee pal, looking at that last nappy, how the stuff you get out of your mother converts into the stuff that comes out of you. I suppose there are some things in life that it's better not to know. What d'you think?'

Jazz blew a bubble in response. Bob nodded. 'Yes, I suppose that's as good an answer as any!'

Sarah smiled. As he lifted up the baby with both hands, supporting his head as he passed him to Alex, she reflected on the change that fatherhood had wrought in Bob Skinner. The troubled man of the summer before had vanished. Bob seemed to have despatched his private demons. Sarah hoped that they were gone for good.

Alex's laughter broke her mood. 'Hey, brother, wrong chest!' As she cradled the baby in her arms his mouth was searching, puckering, feeling for her breast through her shirt.

Sarah reached out her arms. 'It's that time again, Jazz. Come to Momma.' She took the baby from Alex and walked over to a low seat by the window, flicking open the buttons of her blouse as she went. Seated, and holding Jazz in the crook of her left arm, she tugged at the hooks of her nursing bra. 'Goddam contraption! Necessary though, Alex. One doesn't want them to start the long journey south before their time.' She freed her left breast, and Jazz set to feeding at once, sucking hungrily. As she settled back in her chair, Sarah's eye was caught by Andy Martin, edging self-consciously towards the door. 'What's the matter, Andy? Never seen one of these things before?'

'Sure, but always in pairs, and never in use.'

'Get accustomed to it, then, man. This here is Nineties woman.' She paused, then looked up again, struck by a sudden thought. 'Hey, I'm sorry, you two. Everybody here's been fed but you. Alex, take Andy downstairs and find yourselves some supper.'

'Thanks, Sarah,' said Andy, 'but we've got a table booked at the Loon Fung for nine-thirty. I thought that Alex could use some lemon chicken to give her a break from all that studying.'

Sarah thrust out her bottom lip in a petulant gesture. 'Lucky Alex. That just makes me think of the downside of this here bundle of joy. My social life's his from now on.'

'Hah!' said Alex. 'I weep for you. I'm sitting finals in two weeks, while you're off to Spain.'

'Yeah,' said Bob. 'Life's a bitch, kid.'

'Well, make up for it. Get us a drink. I'll call a taxi for nine-twenty.'

Bob led the way downstairs. He disappeared into the kitchen, and re-emerged with three uncapped bottles of Sol beer.

'The Loon Fung, eh,' he said, grinning, as he handed them round. 'Should I be giving you the heavy father routine, Martin?'

'Don't you dare!' said Alex with a sharp edge to her voice which was not entirely affected – and which took Bob by surprise. 'I'm

Nineties woman, too. Anyway, Andy's ... well, Andy's ... Andy. He's my mate. Isn't that right Superintendent?' Martin smiled and nodded sheepishly, his green eyes shining. He looked suddenly younger than thirty-something, just as Alex could be taken for mid rather than early twenties.

Bob grinned and shrugged his shoulders. 'Sure, what the hell. I keep forgetting that Andy's known you since you were smoking in the bike sheds.'

Alex looked at him, surprised. 'How did you ... ?'

'Don't be daft, kid. Everyone smokes in the bike shed when they're eleven!'

Andy laughed and took a mouthful of beer. 'When are you going to Spain?'

'I'm back in the office on Tuesday. There's a Police Board meeting on Wednesday, and I'm standing in for the Chief, so I'll go in on the day before to brief myself. I'm in for the rest of the week, then we head off on the following Tuesday.'

'How are you travelling?'

'By car, slowly. You know me, normally I just blaze down there. But this time, with the baby, we'll have a couple of overnight stops: on the ferry and then down in France. Sarah's never been to Cherbourg, so we're taking that route. It's a nice drive at this time of year.'

'Will you see Maggie out there?'

'Not unless the Spanish find Big Lennie. If they don't she'll be back by then. I'll be in the shit if they do turn up our man. Sarah'll kill me if I have to go down to Alicante. Apart from it being our first holiday with Jazz, I've promised her I'll do some writing when I'm out there. I'm taking my Powerbook.'

'Have you indeed! Memoirs?'

'Not yet. No, it'll be the theory and practice of police and security work. This is the age of open government and it should be the age of open policing too, as far as we can manage. But the public don't have the faintest idea of what our job's really like. All they know comes from fictional characters, and all of *them* are still at chief inspector rank in their fifties. It hasn't dawned on the public that if these guys were that fucking clever they'd have made chief super at least! Anyway, as for Maggie, she's well south of L'Escala, and she should be back before I leave. I think big Brian Mackie's a bit huffy that she got to go instead of him. But when I said to him *"Que tal, señor?"* and he said "Eh?" in response, he sort of blew his case out of the water!'

'Any feedback yet?'

'Give the woman a chance. She only got there this afternoon.

Anyway, big Lennie's had a three-day start on us. Chances are he's cashed up and he's in South America already.'

The doorbell rang.

'That must be your taxi. Have a nice meal. And don't be late home, girl!'

Alex glared at him over her shoulder as she headed for the door.

18

'When did Maggie's report come in?'

'She faxed yesterday morning from the Guardia Civil office in Alicante. I was going to send it out to you, but Ruth vetoed that idea!'

Skinner laughed. 'She's a good girl, my secretary. She sees herself as my personal Rottweiler. So where is it, then, this report the boss wasn't allowed to see?'

Roy Old passed a yellow folder across the desk.

'Thanks.' Skinner took it from him and flipped it open. The neatness and precision of the typed lay-out were typical of Maggie Rose, and the text itself was, as ever, concise and informative. He scanned down the page.

Fax message
ACC Skinner
from
DI Rose.

Summary:
Plenderleith has been in Alicante, but the likelihood is that he has now left the area, and very probably that he has left Spain. The Banco Central account has been emptied, and the traveller's cheques cashed. Cocozza's story of a potential investment seems to hold up, but there have been no sightings of Plenderleith at that location.

Main points:
1) Guardia co-operation has been excellent. On the day of my arrival, I was asked to brief local media on my visit at a press conference arranged by the GC commander. Press and television have carried details of the story, with photographs of Plenderleith. Significantly there have been no reported sightings.
2) I visited the Banco Central on Friday with the GC commander, who overcame quickly the manager's reluctance to discuss

account details. His senior assistant, on sight of Plenderleith's photograph, confirmed that he visited the bank on Monday morning and withdrew all the funds on deposit. He also cashed all of his traveller's cheques.

The assistant, who speaks good English, asked him why he needed such a large amount of cash. Plenderleith said that he was putting down a deposit on an apartment.

The Guardia are not best pleased with the bank, which is expected to keep it informed of foreign nationals moving large amounts of cash.

3) Since Friday, the Guardia has contacted all banks in the Alicante area, and has confirmed that no other accounts exist, or have been opened, in Plenderleith's name.

4) On Saturday, I visited Rancho del Sol, the club/timeshare complex in which Cocozza claimed that Manson was thinking of making an investment. Advance intelligence gathered by the GC confirmed that the place is for sale. Officially it belongs to a development company, but behind that the real owner is a Barcelona gangster who has just begun a twenty-year jail sentence for drug-dealing.

The manager had never heard of Plenderleith. Nor did he recognise the photograph.

5) There is a report that a man answering Plenderleith's description bought a plane ticket for Morocco on Monday afternoon, paying in cash. The flight, a holiday charter, left on Tuesday morning. The operator keeps no record of whether bookings are taken up, but the supposition must be that Plenderleith has left European Union territory.

Recommendations:

That the Guardia Civil be asked to retain Plenderleith on their wanted list, against the possibility, however unlikely, that he may be in Spain.

That the authorities in Morocco should be asked to confirm, if possible, Plenderleith's arrival in that country, and if so, to institute a search within their territory.

That other forces be alerted through Interpol.

The Guardia Civil are continuing a sweep of the many hostels and campsites in the Alicante area. In line with your orders, I will remain until Friday to assist them in that task.

Skinner put the folder down on his desk, and looked up at Roy Old. 'Doesn't seem much room for doubt in that, does there?'

'Not much, sir. If the big yin's pulled his cash and jumped across to North Africa, he could be anywhere now. Christ, he could have joined the bloody legion!'

Skinner laughed. 'Maybe we should send Maggie to check that out!'

'Okay, Roy, thanks for that. I'll send Maggie a response. On your way past, would you ask Ruth McConnell to look in here.'

Old acknowledged the request – and his own dismissal – with a nod. Less than a minute later, Skinner heard his secretary's soft knock on the door. 'Come in.' he shouted.

'You wanted to see me?'

'Yes, Ruth, thanks. I'd like you to send DI Rose a fax in Alicante. Thank her for her report, confirm that she should remain there on duty until the end of the week. Tell her she can travel back whenever she likes over the weekend, but that I'd like to touch base with her on Monday here, before I head off myself. Will you ask her also to spend some more time at Rancho del Sol, and to find out as much as she can about the place, and its owner. If he's doing time for drug offences, it may be that he connects into Manson's operation. If he does, maybe we can identify some of the other points in the supply chain.'

'Got all that?' Ruth nodded. 'Good. Knock something out along those lines and I'll sign it. Before you do that, ask Alan Royston to step up and see me. Tell him I want to issue a press release on the basis of Maggie's report.'

'Very good. By the way, did you see the note in your diary about Mr Pitkeathly?'

For a second, Skinner looked puzzled; then the conversation in the Barnton Hotel came back to him. 'I missed that. What have you fixed up?'

'Lunchtime. He suggested it, and I decided that would be best for you, too. He's booked a table at Mr V's for one o'clock. He said he thought that would be fairly discreet.'

'That's nice of him. I hope I can help him.'

19

The diminutive Mr V welcomed Skinner like a long-lost brother to the West End courtyard restaurant which bore his name, and showed him to a table in the small downstairs bar, where Greg Pitkeathly was waiting.

The thin man stood up, hand outstretched. 'Good of you to see me, Mr Skinner. I hope this lunchtime arrangement is all right for you.'

'Mmm. Sure. But I'd have been happy to fit you in at Fettes in the course of the day.'

'Not at all. This is the least I can do. I thought I'd be lucky to get to see a constable, and here I am telling my story to Scotland's most famous detective.'

Their opening exchange was interrupted by Mr V, as he handed them leather-bound menus. 'I have given you the table in the far corner, Mr Pitkeathly. You won't be disturbed there. You want to go up now, yes?'

They rose and followed the little restaurateur, carrying their menus as they climbed the narrow staircase in single file. As he surveyed the long dining room lit by the May sunshine flooding through its south-facing windows, Skinner smiled inwardly at Pitkeathly's notion of discretion. He knew that, while Mr V's might not be the largest restaurant in Edinburgh, it was one of the most popular with the city's chattering classes. As he followed his host across to the table in the far left-hand corner, he recognised and nodded to a Sunday newspaper editor, two business journalists and four chartered surveyors, all assiduous grinders of the rumour mill. He wondered what would be made of his lunchtime meeting.

They chose identical items from the *à la carte* menu, stracciatella followed by pan-fried steak, and Pitkeathly ordered a bottle of red Caruso, the meaty house wine. As the proprietor strolled off to the kitchen, the thin man picked up the tan leather briefcase which he had been carrying, rolled the combinations into place and flicked it open. He withdrew a yellow folder and placed it on the table.

'How long have you owned property in L'Escala, Mr Skinner?' he asked.

'Bob, please. It'll be around ten years now. I went there first on holiday with my daughter to a rented apartment up behind Montgo Bay. We both loved the place. I had some spare cash at the time, and so I bought a two-bed in a block which was being finished off in the same development. The peseta was dirt cheap then, and I was able to forward-buy currency, which made it an even better deal.'

Pitkeathly's brow furrowed for a second. 'I thought Peter Payne said you had a villa.'

Skinner nodded. 'That's right. A couple of years after we bought, an old aunt died and left me her house ... I always think of old Auntie Jessie with great affection. I didn't need another house at the time, and certainly not a huge bloody thing in Aberfeldy with two and a half acres attached. So I sold the land to a builder, and the house to a couple who wanted to turn it into a nursing home, put half the proceeds into an investment trust with a Japanese portfolio, and the other half into a really nice three-bedroom villa up on Puig Pedro, overlooking the bay. It has a sort of pool, more of a swimming puddle really, in the garden ... and very heavy shutters for when the Tramuntana blows down over the Pyrenees.'

'Oh yes,' said Pitkeathly. 'The famous L'Escala north wind. Tell me, did you have much trouble selling your apartment?'

'I didn't try. I still own it, but I rent it out. I advertise in police publications, and I let only to coppers, active or retired. Being who I am, I never have any problem tenants. A very nice English lady called Mary manages it for me. It's hardly ever empty, and so the income covers all my overhead expenses out there, and puts fruit in the bowl as well. I'm a lucky guy, in every way. But tell me about you, Greg, and about your problem.'

Pitkeathly paused while Mr V's young waitress served the soup. He tasted the Caruso, which the wine waiter had opened, and nodded his approval. The young man filled the two glasses. As the staff then withdrew, he offered Skinner bread from a small basket.

'I've been in L'Escala for three years,' he began. 'Just to fill you in on my background, I own and run a medium-sized printing business called GFP. I have an office in Stafford Street, but my printing shop is in Slateford. I supply letterheads, computer stationery, labels, and marketing materials, mostly to professionals and service businesses: lawyers, accountants, surveyors, PR consultancies, and so forth. My wife and I started the business fifteen years ago, and we've built the turnover steadily ever since. We don't have children, so we're both fully committed to the job. Even through the worst of the recession, we managed to make modest profits, and in the better years we've done quite well. We reinvest profits in plant and machinery, to ensure that we are always up with the technology. Quick response to customer needs is very important, and we have to maintain that capability.'

He sipped some wine, and continued. 'In the early years we pushed all of our spare money into our pension fund, and through that we bought the property which we occupy, and the factory unit next-door to us – for possible expansion, you understand. About five years ago, with the business stable, the pension fund very healthy, and good back-up staff in place, we began to think that we should enjoy some of the fruits of success. So we started to look around for a holiday home. We decided that it should be reachable by car, since Jean doesn't like flying too much. And since I don't like the French too much, the Costa Brava was the obvious place. We did our research through the *Sunday Times*, approached a few companies with properties advertised, and took a trip out there to look at some of them. We saw Pals, Llafranc, Pallafrugel and L'Estartit, before we came upon L'Escala. But once we did, we were hooked. It was just the right size and had just the right feel to it.'

He glanced at Skinner. 'The L'Escala properties which we had arranged to view were being handled by a company called InterCosta. Does the name mean anything to you?'

Skinner thought for a moment. 'Yes, I think it does. Don't they have an office on the Passeig Maritim?'

'Yes, that's right. InterCosta seems to be some sort of limited partnership, operating in Spain and in the UK. In Scotland in fact. Our first contact, through the *Sunday Times*, was with an office in Stirling, in a business centre there, run by a man named Ainscow, Paul Ainscow. Have you ever heard of him?'

'Yes. I've even met him. A neighbour introduced us a few years back, in the bar of El Golf Isabel. A nice enough bloke, as I remember. Not as flashy as most of the property guys. I knew he was in that line, but I didn't connect him with InterCosta. I've seen him around a couple of times since then, so you could say we're nodding acquaintances.'

Pitkeathly grimaced. 'I hope that doesn't make the rest of my story awkward for you.'

'Let's see. Go on.'

'Well, we didn't meet Ainscow on that first trip. We were

received by his Spanish director, a man named Santiago Alberni. He's a good English speaker, a very outgoing chap, and he couldn't do enough for us. He showed us two apartments in the price range we specified. One was quite noisy, with a lot of people around the pool, but the other was very quiet, and very secluded, away up at the top of the Riells area, almost in the woods, with a small garden and a south-facing terrace. Jean loved it, so we did some ritual haggling and bought it, furniture and fittings included. Santi was a big help to us settling in, and in lots of other ways. He told us where the best shops were, which restaurants to avoid, and so on. He's a great chap, and seems to have lots of friends, especially among the British community.'

He paused in his narrative to attack his stracciatella. Skinner replaced his spoon in his empty bowl.

'Yes, I've heard of Santi Alberni. I have several friends who know him, but I've never met him. Most of what I've heard squares with your experience. I did hear that he's just bought a new villa in Camp dels Pilans, where most of the head boys in the town hall live. So how did your problem arise?'

Pitkeathly took another sip of wine as the soup bowls were removed. 'That happened only recently.'

He paused as the staff returned with the main course. Skinner looked in appreciation at his steak, which had been hammered flat, then delicately fried in a pepper sauce and garnished with a few vegetables. They ate in silence for perhaps thirty seconds before Pitkeathly put down his cutlery. 'You don't mind if I go on while we're eating, do you?'

Skinner shook his head, and Pitkeathly launched into the next chapter in his story.

'Our new apartment was fine for the first couple of years, as we got to know L'Escala. But after a while, the downside began to develop. The bonking Belgians for a start. I don't know if you've noticed, but the common-or-garden domestic Spanish brick has remarkable acoustic properties. It gives you no sound-proofing at all. In fact it does the opposite: it seems to carry sound. Well, a Belgian couple owned the apartment above us, a big beefy pair, and they always seemed to be there at the same time as us. Their bedroom was directly above ours, and they seemed to be at it non-stop. Like it or not – and we didn't – Jean and I heard every grunt, every moan, every groan, every squeaking spring. We used to read until the performance was over, because there was no point in trying to sleep through it. That was a major irritation, but there were others. The roads aren't great up there, and every time it rained, new ruts and valleys appeared. Also, while it was very secluded, conversely we were a long way from the centre, so we tended to drive everywhere. Finally, as time went on, we made more and more friends among the British property owners. It wasn't long before we had quite a social circle out there.'

Skinner nodded. 'I know what you're going to say now. You were invited to lots of drinks parties and, before you knew it, you discovered that your apartment was just too small for you to entertain properly. Am I right?'

Pitkeathly had returned to his steak. He nodded vigorously as he finished the mouthful.

'Spot on! That's just how it was. So the upshot of it all was that last autumn we went to Santi, and told him that we were interested in a move. That very same day, he took us to see a new development up behind Avinguda Girona, near the Guardia Civil barracks. He said that the builder was under pressure from his bank, and that he had cut his prices to achieve quick sales. Even as incomplete shells, they were beautiful apartments. Three bedrooms, two bathrooms, a big terrace looking out on the Pyrenees, all built to a very high standard, and all for eight million pesetas.'

Skinner did a mental calculation. 'That's under forty K at last year's exchange rate. Sounds like a good buy.'

'It was. It is. We did the deal. As a sweetener, Santi said that he would sell the other place for us at zero commission, and that he would get us over five million for it. He was as good as his word. We were due to take possession of the new place at Easter, and, in January, Paul Ainscow called to say that they had sold the old one for five million two. The buyers were a couple from Sussex named Comfort. I've never met them, not to this day. When he called us to give us the good news, Ainscow said that the Comforts had paid a deposit – around twenty per cent or so; those were his exact words – and that InterCosta had credited that amount towards the purchase of the new apartment. A few days later we received a receipt, bearing the company stamp, from Santi Alberni for one million pesetas.'

He frowned for a moment before continuing. 'So far so good. We were due to complete both transactions at Easter, before the notary in L'Escala, only there was a hitch. The Comforts were involved in a bad car accident in March and were both hospitalised. We thought that the whole thing might collapse, but the Comforts gave power of attorney to a local lawyer, and we went to completion of both sale and purchase. Santi, the builder of our new place, the Comforts' lawyer, Jean and I all turned up at the notary's office. We had a certified cheque for two-point-eight million, the balance of our purchase price, on top of what we were due for the old place. We did our sale first. The notary took us through the deed, noted the price and we were all ready to sign on the dotted. But when the Comforts' lawyer presented their cheque, it was only for three-point-seven million, not the four-point-two we were expecting. We looked at Santi, and he looked puzzled. He swore blind that he had only received one million from Ainscow. We showed the lawyer our receipt from Santi, but he showed us a receipt given to the Comforts by Ainscow for one-point-five million pesetas. I have copies of them both in here.' He tapped the yellow file.

Skinner looked across the table. Pitkeathly's brow was knotted with concern. 'So what did you do?'

'We didn't have much choice. We could have scrapped the deal with the Comforts, but frankly, we needed their cheque, even if it was half a million light. So we went through with it, and I wrote a second cheque on our Spanish bank account for the missing half million, assuming, or hoping at least, that it was all a misunderstanding and that Santi would sort it out with Ainscow.'

'And didn't he?'

'No. He told us that Ainscow was on holiday in America. So we said, sod it all; we decided to forget about it until we got home, and to clear things up ourselves with Ainscow. We spent the rest of our trip fitting out our new apartment. Quite frankly, if it did cost us half a million more, we've still got a bargain.'

'And have you seen Ainscow?'

'No, not yet. He wasn't due back from the States until last Friday, according to Santi. I did call his office once, but there was no reply. Eventually, Jean and I decided that it would be better to speak to the police. I hope you agree with us. It's no small sum after all, well over two thousand pounds, and it's more than a bit suspicious. I mean, even if Ainscow says sorry, it's all a mistake, and gives us half a million pesetas, how can we be sure that he isn't covering up? Maybe there are other people in the same boat as us.'

'Or maybe Alberni's the one on the fiddle. Don't you see that as equally likely?'

Pitkeathly shook his head. 'Santi's as honest as the day is long. I'm convinced of that.'

'Hmm,' said Skinner sceptically. 'They have shorter days than us in Spain for a good chunk of the year! Greg, I'm a policeman. I'm never convinced until I see the proof. If you give me that file, I'll look at everything that's in there. From what you've told me, there's been a theft all right, but it's just as likely, maybe even more likely, that it took place in Spain, not in Scotland. Still, you were quite right to bring it to me, rather than deal with it yourself. If Ainscow is a conman, then he'd probably talk his way out of it. If Alberni's bent, you're obviously far too chummy with him to suspect it. If they're both in on it, then all of the company's business will need to be investigated, here and in Spain. And if it is all a mistake, then it's one that should never have happened. A visit from the police will make sure that they're more careful with clients' funds in future.'

He reached across the table. 'Here. Gimme your file, and a business card too, so I can get it back to you. Do you have copies, or would you like me to send you a set?'

Pitkeathly handed over the file. 'Those are my only copies, but I don't need duplicates. What will you do?'

'I'll read this lot, and then I'll probably go out to interview Ainscow myself. That'll get his attention.'

'What if he proves to you that Santi is responsible, and that the theft occurred in Spain?'

'If that happens, I'll take your documents with me when I go to L'Escala next week. I know Arturo Pujol, the local Guardia commander, on a copper-to-copper basis. His boys keep a special eye on my properties. If it looks like Santi's the man, I'll just hand a copy of your file over to Pujol. I might have to ask you to file a complaint at the consulate in due course, but otherwise, it should be painless for you. I should warn you, though, if Alberni is a thief, you won't see your missing half million for a hell of a long time, if ever. The Spanish criminal justice system is slower than God's mills. On top of that, Greg, if he's convicted, you'll have to sue him for recovery, and their civil courts can be even slower.'

'Maybe I should just forget it all, in that case, and swallow my loss.'

'Too late for that now. You've shown me evidence of a possible crime in this country, so now I have a duty to investigate it. Even if it does turn into a Spanish matter, I have a sort of ethical duty to pass it on to them. Now that you've started the ball rolling, it has to go all the way down the hill.'

'Ah, well,' said Pitkeathly. 'So the die is cast for Mr Ainscow and Santi. In that case, there's nothing for it now but to finish Mr V's fine wine!'

20

'Have you had a chance to read those papers I gave you on Wednesday, Brian?' Behind his desk in the inner office of the Special Branch suite at Fettes Avenue, Chief Inspector Brian Mackie nodded his balding head.

'What do you make of it?'

'Nothing really, boss. From what you told me, Pitkeathly thinks the sun shines out of Alberni's arse, but that alone doesn't put him in the clear. I've faxed the Spanish equivalent of the CRO and asked them to run a check on him for any previous. I've had a look through ours already for Mr Paul Ainscow. He's clean as a whistle. Chances are it was all a mistake.'

Skinner pushed himself up from the table on which he had been sitting. 'I'm not so sure. There are some terrible cowboys in the property game out there. They take outrageous commissions. They make false declarations to the notary on price – with the collusion of the banks – so as to beat the taxman. They complete sales of properties when the developer doesn't even own all the land he's building on. All that stuff's happened in the wee town where my own place is, and in hundreds more like it. So, when the odd half-million pesetas goes missing in a property transaction, probability falls on the side of theft, not human error. I called my friend Pujol in L'Escala on Tuesday evening, and asked him about Alberni. He said that he's a nice enough guy, but he's not local, so no one really knows all that much about him. The local gossip has it, though, that he's pretty heavily borrowed. He's just moved into a big new house, yet his wife has two jobs, to help pay for it, they say.'

'A motive for theft, then.'

'Sure, but what thief needs a motive?'

Mackie leaned back in his chair and gazed at the ceiling. 'Aye, right enough.' He paused for a moment, then looked across at Skinner, as he stood by the window.

'What's to be done about Ainscow, then, boss?'

'Fancy a trip to Stirling, Chief Inspector? 'Cos that's where we're going this afternoon.'

'You're going to see him personally, sir? It's a bit low-grade for you, surely. And for me, for that matter. It is only a two-and-a-half-grand fraud, after all, and maybe not even that.'

'It's the international dimension, Brian. That's why I want you there. As for me? Ach well, Pitkeathly bought me a good lunch. He deserves my personal attention.' Skinner grinned. 'A taste of corruption, eh? No, I'm going along because I might have to take the papers across to L'Escala with me, and brief the Guardia. If it comes to that, it'll be as well if I've been involved in this interview with Ainscow.'

'Yes,' said Mackie. 'That makes sense, all right. What time's he expecting us?'

'He isn't. Not as coppers, anyway. Ruth called his secretary and arranged a meeting for three with a Mr Mackie, to discuss a property matter. He thinks you're a punter. I don't want him to know what the hell this is about until the minute we walk through the door. I want to drop the story on him absolutely cold, to see how he reacts. I'll drive us there. Look into my office around two. But, before that, let the boys in the Stirling CID know that we're going fishing in their patch. See you later!'

21

'Must have been some man, that Wallace, for them to have built that erection in his memory.'

The Wallace Monument glowered over Stirling, its phallic presence a permanent reminder of the great Scottish patriot. The morning's breeze had dropped, and the town seemed to shimmer in the early summer heat as the two detectives drew closer, following the line of the M9 motorway into Scotland's rural heart, leaving behind them the ugly skeletal steel sprawl of the Grangemouth Refinery, the flat drabness of Falkirk, and the dirty River Carron.

A succession of five roundabouts led them from the motorway into the centre of the historic old town, a scaled-down Edinburgh with its castle on the hill.

The Stirling Business Centre was as easy to find as the local CID had promised. Following their directions Skinner drove past an imposing bank, and took the first turn on the left. He negotiated a security barrier and parked his white BMW in front of an attractive, wide, two-storey, brick office building. Over twenty tenant companies were listed on a big noticeboard in the Centre's foyer.

'How can I help you, gentlemen?' The receptionist's manner was as pleasant as her gleaming smile.

'Could you tell us where we'll find InterCosta?' asked Mackie.

'Certainly, sir. Through that door to your right, and along the corridor. It's the – let me see, one, two, three – yes, it's the fourth door on the left. The name's on it.'

'Thanks very much.' The normally diffident Brian Mackie smiled at the girl, struck by her resemblance to his wife. He led the way to the door to which she pointed with her right fore-finger, and pushed it open. As he and Skinner proceeded, they read the names on each of the first three doors on the left.

'Accountant, lawyer, design company,' said Skinner. 'All they need's a sandwich shop and you'd never have to leave here!'

'This is us, boss,' said Mackie. He read aloud the name on the door: '"InterCosta Limited. Spanish Property Consultancy. AIPC Registered." What's AIPC?'

'Christ knows. Probably meant to be some sort of governing body. If it is, it's doing a rotten job. Come on. Let's beard friend Ainscow.'

Mackie rapped on the door, and opened it without waiting for an acknowledgement. A plump, middle-aged woman with dyed auburn hair and ornately framed spectacles sat behind a desk-top computer. She looked up at the two newcomers.

'Yes?' she said, slightly querulously, looking from one to the other.

Brian Mackie stepped towards the desk. 'Afternoon. I've an appointment with Mr Ainscow around now. The name's Mackie.'

'And you're dead on time.' The woman's reply was anticipated by the booming voice which said it. In the same second its owner stepped into the main office from behind two screens which partitioned off its left-hand corner. He was a tall, well-built man wearing a salesman's professional smile and with his hand out-stretched in greeting. Gold links shone in the long shirt cuffs. He advanced towards Mackie, moving with an easy grace. Then all of a sudden he caught sight of Skinner standing by the door, as it was swung shut by its auto-closer. The smile faded, and was replaced by a puzzled look.

'Hello, Mr Ainscow. Good to see you in Scotland for a change. I'm sorry to spring this on you, but something's been brought to our attention and we'd like a wee chat with you about it. Nothing serious, now. I'm sure you'll clear it up in a second. That's the reason for the discreet approach.'

Skinner kept his face absolutely impassive as he spoke, belying deliberately with his expression the reassurance in his words. He kept his eyes fixed on Ainscow, reading him – looking for any sign to counter the first impression that his arrival had taken the man completely by surprise. But he found none. Ainscow's smile returned, but this time it was one that Skinner had seen on a thousand faces in similar circumstances: puzzled and uncertain, wondering what would come next.

'Well, Mr Skinner. You'd better come through here and tell me about it. Nessie, could you rustle up some coffee, please. Unless you'd prefer tea, gentlemen?'

Skinner shook his head. As Ainscow disappeared behind the partition, he glanced around the room. Its walls were covered with posters of Spain, many of them showing familiar views of L'Escala and its bay.

Behind the screen, Ainscow took his place behind a table which served as a desk, offering chairs to his visitors. Skinner sat down and placed his briefcase on his knees. He opened it and took out Greg Pitkeathly's file.

'Before we begin,' said Ainscow, 'would you prefer it if Nessie stepped outside?'

Skinner shook his head. 'Not at all. In fact it may be useful for you to have her here.' As he spoke, the woman reappeared, carrying a tray laden with three mugs of coffee and a plate of chocolate sandwich biscuits, which Skinner recognised as his favourites from Spain. He smiled his thanks to the secretary.

'Mr Ainscow, we know each other, but I should introduce DCI Brian Mackie, the head of my international liaison unit.'

Ainscow, serious now, nodded towards Mackie.

'I'm sorry about the surprise, as I said, but we thought it best not to alarm you unnecessarily. Mr Ainscow, I think you know Greg Pitkeathly.'

'Greg and Jean, yes.'

'John and Claire Comfort?'

'Yes.' Ainscow's tone took on a note of anticipation, almost intrigue. He leaned forward in his chair, anxious, Skinner assumed, to hear what was coming next.

'Have you had any recent contact with Santi Alberni, your partner?'

Ainscow shook his head. 'No. I've been away for a while. I had a couple of weeks in the States, then spent another fortnight just farting about in Scotland. This is my first day back in this office. So why do you ask about Santi? What's he been up to?'

'Why do you ask that?'

'No reason. A joke really.'

'Mr Ainscow, where do you bank your UK clients' funds?'

'Here initially, then we transfer the money to a convertible peseta account in Spain.'

'How. Banker's transfer?'

'No. That costs an arm and a leg. We just write sterling cheques on the Scottish account, and pay them into Banca Catalana.'

'Who are the signatories on the Scottish account?'

'Just me. Santi and I have a very simple system. I leave him a supply of blank, signed cheques. When we need to transfer dough across, I just give him a call and he completes a cheque and pays it in. It's a bit unorthodox, but it's practical. It keeps costs down and it's perfectly legal ... isn't it?'

'Let's give you the benefit of the doubt on that last point ... for now. Don't you think it's a kind of slapdash way to treat clients' money? D'you never worry about security?'

'Mr Skinner, I trust Santi Alberni like a brother.'

Skinner snorted. 'A bloke called Abel said something similar. Mr Ainscow, take a look at this.' He took a document from the folder and passed it across the table. 'Can you confirm that it's a copy of your receipt to Mr and Mrs Comfort for their deposit on the Pitkeathly apartment?' Ainscow accepted the paper, looked at it for a few seconds, and nodded. 'Yes, it is.'

'And all that money was transferred to Spain?'

'Yes. So?'

'Okay, look at this one. It's Santi Alberni's receipt to the Pitkeathlys. And remember, this was a no-commission deal. He took a second page from the file, and handed it across the table.

Ainscow studied it, his brow furrowing as he did. He looked up. 'Jesus.'

'That's what Pitkeathly said, too. Alberni said that one million pesetas was all he got. What's your version? Was all the Comfort money sent to Spain?'

'For sure! Look, I have to give detailed monthly management accounts to my bank. The guy along the corridor does them for me, and he's shit hot. If there was an anomaly of that size, he'd have picked it up.'

A nervous twitch fluttered in the corner of Ainscow's right eye. He opened his mouth to speak, hesitated, then sighed. 'Oh, look. I have to tell you this. I said I trusted Santi like a brother. That's always been true, but just recently – since he bought that new house, in fact – I've been getting a bit worried about him. He's borrowed up to here.' Ainscow drew a finger across his throat. 'I just hope he hasn't been a silly bugger.'

'You maintain that you're certain that the Comfort money all went to Spain? There's no possibility of error?'

'I wish there were. Then I could just say "Sorry, it's all a mistake!", pay Pitkeathly, and clean the mess up. But my accountant hasn't given me that option. It's all gone, and I can prove it.' He paused. 'There'd be two cheques. Five grand is the maximum we put on a single cheque, so it'd be one for that value, in pesetas, and another for the balance. Just over seven grand in total at current rates. Hold on a sec.'

Ainscow jumped up and stepped across to a filing cabinet against the back wall. He pulled open a drawer, and took out a sheaf of bank statements.

'Look, there you are. That's the Comfort money.' He brought the statements across and held them out.

Brian Mackie, who was closer than Skinner, followed Ainscow's pointing finger, examined the paper for a few seconds, then nodded his head. 'The amounts seem to tally, sir. Looks like it is.'

'Bugger,' said Skinner. 'Seems like I'll be taking some police work on holiday with me after all!'

22

'You know, Bob. Every time I close the door behind me as we leave for Spain, I say a little prayer that everything'll be okay at the other end. But never more so than this time.'

Sarah slammed the heavy front door of the Fairyhouse Avenue bungalow, and turned the key in the double-locking Chubb. Her husband smiled as she joined him on the pathway, where he stood holding his son. 'Your prayer's been answered before you've even left. I called when you were in the shower, to check that everything was in hand. It is, so relax and enjoy the trip. Mary's fixed us up with a hired cot, as we asked. She says it's brand new, and you can be sure it will be.'

They strapped Jazz into his secure carrier in the rear of the big white BMW, with Sarah seated alongside him, and set off at ten a.m. on a dull grey morning, for the sun of Spain. Bob was as good as his word in the sedate pace which he set on the journey. They stopped every two hours to check on the baby, but Jazz was content to sleep the day away, made drowsy by the smooth movement of the car. They took the A1 south, bypassing the centre of Newcastle and skirting the ever-thronged MetroCentre, then heading on towards the curiously named Scotch Corner. After a stop for dinner, for parents and child, in a comfortable roadhouse on the outskirts of Newbury, they arrived at the modest Stena terminal in Southampton two hours ahead of their boarding time.

Their cabin was comfortable, the crossing was flat, and the pretty harbour of Cherbourg was bathed in morning sunlight as they disembarked in France. They waited for a while in an open-fronted waterside café, feasting on strong coffee and croissants and watching Jazz as his ears took in the sound of the gulls, and of vessels docking and making ready to sail. Eventually, they drove up the long hill out of port, and were soon into the open, undulating country of the peninsula. The sky was clear blue and, as the morning stretched towards noon and as they watched the rise, with the sun, of their car's external temperature read-out, they were grateful for its air-conditioning. Sarah, with the greyness of the drive through industrial

England fresh in her mind, was impressed by her first sight of the grand modern cities of Rennes and Nantes, and charmed by the rural communities beyond, in particular by one where the main Euro-route heading south wound through a paved shopping court.

Later they agreed that the highlight of their first day in France had been that encounter in the petrol station. They were just north of Niort, crossing rich flat country, when, uncertain of the distance to the next oasis, Bob decided that he would fill up the BMW's tank there, despite the ramshackle look of the place, with its ancient pumps. He drew alongside the museum pieces, then saw that the wooden hut was empty. He sounded his horn and waited for a good two minutes. As he stood there, in T-shirt and shorts, he realised for the first time the strength of the warm wind which was blowing across the plain.

He was about to drive on, when a sturdy, nut-brown old man, wearing oily blue overalls and a flat Breton cap, appeared from the side of the farmhouse which bounded the yard. The old man looked at the car and, as he drew near, made a swift, truly Gallic gesture, with a hand half-cupped over his lower regions, to indicate beyond any doubt the reason for his absence. Suddenly he caught sight of Sarah in the back of the car. He swept off his beret and bowed in profuse apologies. Bob grinned and pointed to one of the pumps on which a green *sans plomb* sticker had been affixed. Idly he wondered what else might be floating around in the tank beneath his feet, but took comfort from the Routier sign on the hut.

As the pump chugged laboriously, the old man nodded at the car. '*Angleterre?*'

Bob shook his head vigorously. '*Non! Ecossais. Edimbourg.*'

The old man's eyes lit up and he smiled, '*Ah! Edimbourg,*' he said, with evident if mysterious pleasure at the sound of the name.

Still the pump droned on. The attendant shrugged his shoulders and cast his eyes all around him. '*Eh, monsieur, le vent. C'est très fort, non?*'

Bob searched his French. '*Oui, mais c'est très chaud.*'

The ancient looked at him in amazement. '*Chaud, monsieur? Très chaud? Eh, monsieur, c'est comme l'hiver!*'

As they reached Bordeaux, Sarah was still laughing spontaneously at the memory of the old man, his gesture and his notion of winter chills. They spent the night in a small two-star hotel on the edge of the city, which Bob had found some years before on a trip with Alex, and had used frequently since. They ate early, before Sarah, seeing clearly that Nineties woman had not reached this part of France, retired to bathe and feed Jazz, and to bed him down for the night.

Next morning they took a leisurely breakfast, allowing Bordeaux's commuter traffic to clear before setting out on the last stage of their trip. Sarah dozed all the way to and through Toulouse, and so, when she awakened, the change in the texture of the countryside was suddenly and immediately apparent. 'Why, look, the hills seem almost, well, reddish.'

Eventually the road swept round a long curve, and there it was, like a huge tooth from a giant's mouth: Le Canigou, the great mountain, snow-capped almost all the year round – the high point of the Pyrenean skyline which dominated the view from their terrace in L'Escala.

'Yes!' Sarah squealed with delight, but quietly, lest she wake her sleeping child. 'My mountain. Now I know we're there!'

23

'So come on, Kath. Tell me what you know about Santi Alberni?' As he asked his sudden question, Bob gazed across the marina to the Pyrenees, fringed by the deepening red of the setting sun.

They were seated at a small rectangular table under a long yellow and brown striped awning, on the terrace of their favourite restaurant. Trattoria La Clota was quieter than it should have been at nine p.m. on a Saturday, but, even so, half the tables on the terrace were occupied. Conversations in French, Dutch, Spanish, and a language which Bob guessed might be Polish, went on all around them as they leaned back in their seats, the debris of their paella spread before them and an empty bottle of Torres Gran Vina Sol inverted in the ice-bucket.

A few seconds' silence made Bob turn to look again at their blonde companion. 'Who's asking?' she said. 'The property owner or the policeman?'

He smiled. 'Shrewd lady. It's Mr Plod that's asking. But don't worry, he never reveals his sources.'

Kathleen, their hostess, laughed. 'I've heard that one before from the boys here!' Even after twenty-five years in Spain, her tones were still almost as Scottish as his. She was about to answer him when her eye was caught by a movement at a table in the far corner of the terrace. 'Excuse me for a moment, please.' She bustled across the paved courtyard to answer the summons of the beckoning hand.

'Bob, you're terrible,' said Sarah. 'We're only just here and you're at work. Why don't you begin by telling her how good the paella was?'

'She knows that. Besides, if I did, Señor Carlos would probably put the prices up.'

Carlos Pallares and his Scottish wife were the Skinners' closest friends in L'Escala. For years their restaurant had been an unofficial advice centre. They had helped solve all types of problems for all types of people, and had been rewarded by a consistent custom the like of which most of the other restaurants in the town could only imagine. Bob and Sarah's arrival that evening had been anticipated. No sooner had they crossed the narrow roadway from the parking bays than the nutmeg-brown Carlos had come bounding down the four steps from the dining room and bar. 'Hola, my friends. Is good to see you. And this is the new arrival, yes?'

As they had anticipated, Jazz became the star of the show. Throughout their meal a stream of restaurant staff had ventured out, one by one, to peer into the buggy and go through the universal language of baby sounds.

Kathleen returned to their table. 'Everything all right up the road?'

'Yes,' said Sarah. 'No problem. Mary was as good as her word. The place was spotless, the water was hot, and the cot was there. It's brand new. We think we might buy it, rather than hiring.'

'Plans for more Jazzes, yes?'

Sarah winced. 'Give us a break!'

Kathleen laughed and, as she sat down, Bob poured her a glass of wine from a second bottle.

'So what do you want to know about friend Santi?'

'I want to know what you think about him. What sort of a bloke is he? You know just about everyone around here, and there's no one better for sizing people up.'

'Hmm. Thanks for the compliment. Is that why you phoned Carlos the other day?'

Skinner nodded. 'Yes. All he could say was that Santi isn't one of the local inner circle. But Carlos is a cagey character.'

'Hah, that's one way of putting it. He's right, though. No one here really knows too much about Alberni. He's been in the property business for a few years. Before that he worked in a bar down the coast somewhere. What sort of a man is he? Well on the surface he's everyone's friend. He's very showy, always well dressed. But nothing is Santi's. Flash car on the firm. Big new villa, with a swimming pool, mortgaged to the hilt. Having said all that, most people here like him. What's it all about, anyway?'

'Between you and me?'

'Course.'

'D'you know a bloke called Pitkeathly?'

'Greg and Jean? Sure! Nice couple. From Edinburgh, too, aren't they?'

'That's right. Well, they've had a wee problem. I hope it's all a mistake. I'm sure it is.'

There was a sudden bustle as a party of eight Germans converged on the restaurant. Kathleen jumped to her feet. 'Must go. Coffee, yes?'

Skinner nodded, smiling. '*Si, cortado, por favor. Y para la señora, Americano con poco leche frio aparte.*'

Kathleen scribbled a note in her book, and moved off to seat the Germans at a long table in front of the door.

Bob leaned over to look at his son. Jazz's eyes, caught and fascinated by the movement around him, sparkled in the silvery light of the street lamps. Then they fixed on his, and a tiny smile touched the corners of his mouth. A lump seemed to form in Bob's throat.

Sarah broke the moment by digging him in the ribs with her sharp knuckles. 'Hey copper, this piece of detecting that you brought without telling me – it is all a mistake, isn't it?'

'I'm not so sure about that, love. But even if it ain't, it'll be Arturo Pujol's problem. I'll brief him tomorrow, and that'll be it as far as I'm concerned.

'Honest!'

He turned back towards Jazz, and so he did not see her eyes narrow as she gazed at him, or her wry smile as she mouthed the word, 'Sure.'

24

'*Commandante, buenos dias! Que tal?*'

'*Muy bien, mi amigo, muy bien!*'

Skinner held the heavy wooden door of his villa open with his shoulder, and shook hands with his friend. 'Come away in, Arturo. It's good to see you again.'

'And you Bob. And you.'

Skinner led Commandante Arturo Pujol through the tiled hallway, into the living room, and beyond to the wide terrace of his villa, of which the greater part was flooded by the early afternoon sun. He offered him a blue cushioned seat beside a drinks trolley, on which four bottles of Damm Estrella beer sat chilling in a silver ice bucket. He uncapped two of them and handed one to Pujol, who took it with thanks, declining the offered glass.

'It's good of you to come round, Arturo. I'd have come to the barracks, no problem.'

'No, no, no, my friend. It is always a pleasure to come to the home of a colleague as distinguished as you. Assistant Chief of Police, government security advisor. Your rank dazzles this humble rural para-military.'

Skinner's laugh choked on a mouthful of beer.

'And also, it gives me a chance to meet once again your lovely wife, and to see your new son, who is already the talk of L'Escala. When Bob Skinner hires a crib from Mary, all of his friends learn very quickly. Where are they, anyway?'

'Here we are, Arturo.' Sarah emerged through the double door from the living room, pushing Jazz in his heavily shaded buggy. Pujol kissed her on both cheeks, then looked down to admire the baby. He leaned into the buggy and slipped a two-thousand-peseta note under the pillow. 'For a little gift, Sarah, yes?'

'Why, thank you, Arturo.'

'*You* choose something. I have no wife to do these things for me.'

'Okay. I'll buy him a toy from that nice shop in the old town – something tough that'll last for ever.'

She parked the buggy in an area of the terrace that was still in shade, and took a seat beside her husband and the Guardia Commandant.

Arturo Pujol was out of uniform, and no one at all would have taken him for a policeman. He was a stocky, bald man with a moustache, and the expression of someone who is anticipating a nasty surprise. But Skinner knew him in uniform and had noted, on his visits to the barracks, the respect in which Pujol was held by his men. He knew too that the Guardia's legendary toughness had not died with Franco, and that it was present in his self-effacing friend.

They made small talk for a while, in English, in which Pujol was much more proficient than was Skinner in Spanish. They compared notes on the standard of football in their respective countries, each looking back to the times when things had been very much better. Pujol asked Sarah about her new appointment, and bemoaned the lack of good medical support from which his own force suffered.

Eventually, halfway through his second beer, Pujol raised the subject which had led to his visit. 'So what is this problem that you bring with you from Scotland, Robert, and how does it relate to our friend Santiago Alberni?'

'Let me show you,' said Skinner. He picked up Greg Pitkeathly's folder, which he had placed in readiness in the lower shelf of the drinks trolley, and handed it to the commandant. Pujol took it without a word, and began to read through the dated documents in sequence. After a few minutes he put it down in his lap, and took another swig of Estrella.

'I see what you mean. This is why you asked about Alberni, and it is why your colleague Señor Mackie made his enquiries with our national records office.' He smiled at Skinner's reaction. 'Yes, I know about that. They sent me a copy of the request as a matter of form, and a copy of the result. Our friend is, as you say, quite clean. So what would you like me to do?'

Skinner shot him a look of surprise. 'Take it over, of course. Treat it as a complaint made against a Spanish national in Spain.'

'Mmm. *Si*, that is the proper thing for me to do.'

'Does that give you a problem?'

'Me, not at all. But it may be a little harsh for Alberni.'

'What d'you mean?'

'I mean that if I take this up officially, a record will be made. And even if Alberni has a perfect answer, and there is no problem, with him at any rate, that record will remain. Even a visit from the Guardia will be enough. Word gets around here, and it will cast a shadow on him in the future. It will mean that his record is not quite so clean. And possibly that will be through no fault of his. It could affect his credit rating. It could affect his business, if someone checks him out thoroughly enough. The papers which you have shown me still leave a strong possibility of a simple mistake. Do you want to cast such a shadow, if it is for nothing?'

'So you don't want to touch it?' said Skinner, surprised.

Pujol raised his hands in protest. 'No, no, no, Bob. If you feel it is necessary and if you insist, I will take it up at once. But what I would ask you to do is talk to the man yourself first. His English is as good as mine. Go to see him. Talk the matter over with him. See what he has to say. Once you have done that, if you still believe that there is a problem, then I will take it up. It is the fairest way, believe me.' He turned to Sarah. 'Don't you agree?'

Sarah grimaced. 'There goes some more holiday time. But yes, I think that's right.'

Pujol handed the folder back to Skinner. 'There. Perhaps you can call on him tomorrow. I happen to know that he is away today, with a client, but tomorrow, a Saturday, he should certainly be in his office.'

Skinner took the papers. 'Okay, if that's how you want it. Let's just hope today's client isn't being stitched up too!'

'If he is,' said Pujol, suddenly very serious, 'we will find that out. If you decide that there is something to be investigated, then it will not be this case alone that we will look into. I promise you, my people will turn InterCosta inside out. If this company is dishonest, then it is giving Catalunya's biggest industry a bad name. For that, we will come down hard, very hard indeed. If I find that Señor Alberni has been stealing from his clients, or from constructors, or anyone, he will go to prison not just for what he has done, but as an example to others. And now,' he said, pushing himself up from his chair, 'beautiful as the day is, and agreeable as my companions may be, I must go. How do you say it? Duty, she is calling. I like to go for a drive around the town while everyone is at siesta. Just to make sure that everything is quiet. And, of course, in beautiful L'Escala it always is.'

As Bob escorted their visitor to the door, Sarah pushed Jazz in his buggy through to the small bedroom next to their own and, without waking him from his afternoon slumber, laid him gently in his cot.

When Bob closed the front door and turned to go back to the terrace, she was in the hall, blocking his way. She wound her arms around him. 'As Arturo was saying, it's siesta time . . .'

He could feel the heat of her body through his T-shirt. He looked down at her, reading her agenda for the afternoon in her smouldering eyes. 'Hey, are you sure? It's only been a couple of weeks since Jazz.'

'Exactly!' she murmured. 'Nineteen whole days, and a while before that too. My darling, I'm just about as horny as I've ever been.

And just at this moment, from your significantly altered profile, you ain't going to persuade me that you ain't too!'

His laughter died in his throat as she pulled his head down and kissed him fiercely. He swept her off her feet in a single strong movement and carried her through the living room and into their bedroom. It was late enough in the afternoon for the sun to be flooding in through the brown-framed three-quarter-glazed doors which led out to the terrace, but not too late for it to have passed by the small square window to the side, above one of the two chests of drawers which flanked the white-quilted bed.

He laid her down, and in seconds they were naked, kissing and fondling, their fingers and tongues searching, exploring, reacquainting themselves with familiar regions. And then Bob's hand found Sarah's secret centre, the heart of her moistness, and she climaxed at once, suddenly, and quite unexpectedly, a bucking, thrusting, crying-out orgasm almost frightening in its intensity. As it peaked, she clamped her thighs closed on his fingers and twisted towards him, eyes shut, with a shout that was almost a scream. She lay still for a while, with her head resting on his shoulder. Occasionally, a small shiver ran through her.

Eventually she looked up at him, into his eyes. 'Bob, I'm sorry,' she whispered. 'That was so selfish. I don't know what happened.'

He nuzzled her auburn hair, laughing 'Selfish nothing. Don't be daft. Listen, love, if that's what happens when you have a baby, can I have one too!'

She chuckled with pleasure, a playful sound with more than a hint of promise. 'Okay, let's see what we can do about that.' As she spoke, she rolled over, straddling him, taking him deep inside her, and in a single movement pulling her knees up and sitting on him, bolt upright. She seemed barely to move, yet he could feel the honey grip of secret muscles, strengthened by childbirth, tensing and relaxing as they massaged him. He lay on his back, looking up, touching her only with his eyes. She started to sway more vigorously, rocking backwards and forwards upon him, tensing, relaxing, tensing again. Pleasure seemed to wash upwards and over him, starting from the soles of his feet, moving up through his ankles, his calves. He surrendered himself to the most powerful orgasm of his life, even though he expected that when the high tide of pleasure broke upon his groin he would die of its intensity. He was helpless beneath her. Someone in the room was shouting out aloud, and dimly he was aware that it was himself. Then the cries became a duet, and he knew that Sarah had climaxed also in the same moment. He saw her back arch and felt those secret muscles grasp tight and hold on as he pulsed and pumped into her, on and on. They held their frozen pose, neither breathing, each concentrating only on the other's pleasure, until eventually, with a last triumphant shout, Sarah relaxed, and slumped, shuddering, on to his chest.

A full five minutes elapsed in silence, as if each were printing every detail, every moment of the experience indelibly upon their memory. Eventually Bob wrapped his arms around his wife and kissed her on the forehead.

'Do you think it gets any better than that?' she asked. It was an entirely serious question.

'I think we should hope not, my love. If it did, I don't know if either of us could stand it. Think of it – that wee lad through there left an orphan because his parents humped each other to death!'

'Christ, imagine the postmortems!'

Sarah spluttered with laughter and, as she did, Jazz's hungry, wailing cry rang out, bang on cue through the baby-minder intercom, to rescue them from their jeopardy and to signal an end to their siesta.

25

TANCAT. CERRADO. FERMÉ. CLOSED.

Whether callers were Catalan, Castellano, French or English, the message was the same in all four signs hanging in the glass door. The office of InterCosta, on the ground floor of a high-rise block on the Passeig Maritim, a long promenade looking across the small, windswept Riells Bay to L'Escala's ever-growing marina complex, was very definitely *not* open for business. Skinner wondered idly whether it was company policy to leave German callers at a loss.

It was ten a.m. At such an hour on a Saturday morning, even the most indolent of Costa Brava property agents is normally to be found behind his desk. On the first day of June, the peak sales month, absence is unthinkable.

Skinner re-crossed the sun-washed road and climbed back into his car, which was parked in one of the angled bays opposite the high-rise, its nose facing the sea-wall. He sat there for ten minutes reading the sports section of *La Vanguardia*, watching the weekend windsurfers and looking occasionally in his rear-view mirror, checking for signs of activity at InterCosta. He saw several people stop at the office. One man, carrying a leather document case under his arm, pushed at the door without looking at the signs, and recoiled in surprise from the unexpected resistance. He peered through the glass for several seconds, and banged on the door with his fist in exasperation, before striding smartly back to a red Mercedes and driving off.

That bloke had an appointment, thought Skinner. Something up here.

He started the BMW's engine, reversed into the road and drove off, heading round Riells Bay to the marina and La Clota. Kathleen was on duty on the restaurant terrace when he arrived. She looked over as his car drew up, surprised to see him. 'Hello, Bob, you're early. Did you leave something last night?'

Skinner laughed. 'Aye, the baby. We're not used to having him around yet!'

Kathleen feigned horror. 'Och, that's terrible. How could yc forget a lovely wee boy like that!'

'No, seriously, Kath, I'm here to pick your brains . . . again. I know Alberni's new pad is in Camp dels Pilans, but do you know where, exactly.'

She angled her blonde head in thought. 'Yes. Come in and I'll show you.' She led the way into the unlit restaurant. Skinner's eyes had difficulty adjusting to the change from the bright morning outside. He peered in vain at the map which Kathleen held in front of him, until she led him into the neon-lit stainless-steel kitchen, where half a dozen staff were busy preparing the day's first meals. 'Look here,' she said. 'Take this turn here, and on round this road, up the hill. It's on top. You can't miss it: it's painted a horrible pink colour.'

'Thanks, Kath. I'll just nip up there and see what's keeping the boy off his work.'

26

The villa was, as Kathleen had said, a truly horrible pink.

It stood on an isolated site on the crest of a curving road which defined the limits of Camp dels Pilans, the only suburb of L'Escala to the west of the main road to Girona and Figueras. Set in the awful stucco, the two small windows on either side of the front door resembled, Skinner thought, hooded eyes looking northwards with embarrassment.

He pulled the BMW to a halt at the garden gate, and stepped out, picking up Pitkeathly's folder from the front passenger seat. He opened the gate and walked up the narrow path to the front door, timing his approach to avoid the sweep of a badly adjusted lawn-sprinkler, which seemed to be watering mainly the path and beyond it – to the right of the house – the driveway up to a single garage integral with the villa. Much of the spray was falling on a big Peugeot saloon, then running down the sides, creating zigzag patterns through the coating of reddish dust which the car had picked up since its last official wash.

To the left of the front garden, beside a path leading to the rear of the villa, a large mongrel dog was chained. As Skinner approached the door, a low growl in the animal's throat turned into a ferocious, snarling bark. It made towards him, but was pulled up short by its chain a good six feet away. Skinner shot the beast a glance which made it think again. Suddenly its ferocity was spent, and it slunk back to its place in the shade, beside empty food and water bowls.

A round brass bell-push was set in the centre of the studded door. Skinner pressed it and stood back, waiting for Alberni, or his wife to answer its call. But no one came. He rang the bell again. Another minute elapsed without a response. He pounded the door with his fist, but with no greater success.

Exasperation grew in him. 'Come on, you bastard,' he muttered. 'I'm supposed to be on my fucking holidays, and here I am chasing you around L'Escala.'

He abandoned his assault on the front door and walked around the

94

corner to his left, towards the rear of the house, past the dog, which gave another token growl, then fell silent again quickly.

The back garden was a shambles. Plastic poolside chairs were gathered around a small white table on which was scattered an assortment of empty beer and wine bottles and half a dozen empty glasses. A cigarette packet was floating in the middle of the pool.

'You've been on the piss last night, Santi my son'. Skinner spoke the thought aloud. He looked around. The sliding patio doors were wide open and pink curtains as hideous as the house itself flapped limply in the gentle breeze. He walked across to the doors and stuck his head inside. Despite its airing, the villa still smelled stale. He listened, but there was no sound other than, from another room, the soft buzz of a refrigerator motor.

'Señor Alberni! Señora!' He shouted loudly into the empty room, with unconcealed impatience. He waited and listened for sounds of human movement, but there were none. 'Señor, Señora!' he bellowed again, and waited once more, but the obstinate silence remained. He thought of searching the place, but decided that Pujol's brief did not extend that far. Angry and exasperated, Skinner retraced his steps through the untidy garden, to the front of the house.

This time the dog merely whined. The sound was so different to its earlier reaction to Skinner's presence that he stopped. The animal looked up at him and whined again. 'Come on, boy,' said Skinner. 'I'm not that fierce.' He knelt down and stroked the mongrel. It whined once more, and this time the sound turned into a keen of distress. He looked at it closely and realised that it was sniffing, its nostrils flared. He followed the direction of its gaze, towards the garage door. It was the type that opened up and over, and it was slightly ajar. Skinner patted the animal's head once more, then stood up. He walked over to the garage, grasped the door by its single, central handle, and pulled it up.

The sudden inrush of air made the body spin slowly round on the end of the rope.

'Sweet suffering Christ,' Skinner hissed into the garage gloom.

The man was hanging from a pulley set in the garage ceiling towards the far wall, and close to a heavy work bench. The stout yellow rope on which he twisted was fastened into a classic hangman's knot, and was tied securely at its other end to one of the legs of the workbench, which was bolted to the floor. His feet, in hand-stitched brown shoes, were well clear of the ground, and his arms hung limply, hands unclenched. One of the white plastic garden chairs lay on its side, on the floor.

95

Skinner stood in the doorway, frozen, for several seconds. Suddenly the thought came to him that the hanging man might not be dead yet, and he snapped out of his trance. He rushed over to the body, but as soon as he saw the face he knew that it was too late for any heroic rescue. The man was small and lightly built but, even so, the rope was cutting deep into his neck. His face was blue. His eyes bulged horribly, as if about to pop from their sockets. His tongue, black and swollen, protruded grotesquely between lips and teeth drawn back as if in a last, strangling snarl.

Skinner's stomach turned. He snatched a single deep breath to bring himself under control, and looked away through the garage window, in which was framed the beautiful, jagged, snow-crested skyline of Canigou and the high Pyrenees.

When he had mastered himself, he turned back to the body. He touched a hand. It was still as warm as his own. He looked again at the contorted face. The man had a small black moustache, but otherwise was freshly shaved. His thinning black hair was well groomed. He was smartly dressed in expensive blue slacks and a white, short-sleeved Dior shirt.

'All spruced up and ready for work, Alberni. I can picture the whole scene. The wife thinks it's business as usual. She goes off to her day job, then you step into the garage and jump into eternity. Very nice. Very thoughtful. A real considerate guy, eh. You stupid bastard!'

There was something about the suicides of otherwise healthy people that always angered Skinner. The determination and physical courage necessary for the act counted for nothing in his mind against the grief and the hurt that the victims, almost invariably, left behind. It was the sheer selfishness of the deed that enraged him.

He held the body with both hands to still its twisting on the rope, then turned and left the garage, closing the door behind him to hide the sight from any chance passers-by. Outside, he turned off the lawn sprinkler at its tap beside the garage door. Then on impulse he disconnected its hose, fetched over one of the dog's two dishes and filled it with water. The mongrel looked up at him, and Skinner could have sworn that it nodded its thanks.

He returned to the back of the villa, and entered the living area through the open doors. This time he searched without hesitation. He searched first for Señora Alberni, fearful lest her husband had decided – as he had seen others do before – that life for his beloved would be unbearable without him. He moved swiftly from room to room, but all he found were untidy relics of the previous evening, and signs of a rushed breakfast: an uncleared dinner table set for six, the remains of a selection of pastries set out on a dessert trolley, more glasses, more empty bottles, a single breakfast-sized coffee cup smeared with lipstick lying, with a cereal bowl, unwashed in the kitchen sink. In the Albernis' bedroom, the bed had been hastily made. The door of one of two fitted wardrobes lay open, revealing a rail of women's clothing hung inside. On the dressing table, a jar of make-up base lay uncapped.

Skinner, reassured that Señora Alberni was not in the house, returned to the living room. He found a telephone on a dark-wood sideboard, beside a number of framed family photographs. The largest showed a wedding scene. In this picture, the man now hanging in the garage wore a white tuxedo and black evening trousers. He smiled, looking youthful and handsome, and wore the same dark moustache; his hair, not so thin then, was immaculately groomed. The bride was a striking, dark-haired woman, perhaps a year or two older than her husband. Skinner would have described her as handsome rather than beautiful. Her eyes were her best feature: dark, oval, warm, and inviting trust. Beneath the pair, on the photograph's surround, the names *Santiago* and *Gloria* were inscribed in gold leaf.

Skinner picked up the telephone and retrieved the Guardia Civil number from his mental filing cabinet. The call was answered by a gruff-sounding man on the fifth ring. '*Commandante Pujol, por favor. Commandante Skinner, Escocia.*'

'*Si, Commandante.*'

A few seconds later, he was put through. '*Hola*, Bob.'

'Aye, hello Arturo,' he said, wearily. 'Listen, I'm at Alberni's. Not the office – the villa. You're in on this one, like it or not.'

'Why, won't he speak to you?'

'No. He's having trouble getting the words out, on account of he's hanging from a rope in his garage.'

'What!' Pujol's tone was incredulous. 'Is he dead?'

'If he isn't fucking dead, then he never will be! It looks like he topped himself as soon as his wife went to work.'

'Do you think he learned that you were coming to see him?'

'Could be. Let's see what we can find out. I've had a quick look round, but I can't see anything that looks like a "sorry" note. You and your guys better get up here right now.'

27

'Arturo wants *me* to help him?'

'Yes. Apparently his local doctor's off to Barcelona for the weekend, and the nearest alternative in Girona can't get along here for five or six hours. There was some sort of gypsy war there last night apparently. So our friend the commandant asked me to ask you if you, as a properly qualified person, could see your way clear to come up to Alberni's to state, for the medical record, the blindingly obvious: that the man is as dead as a fucking doornail. Because, apparently, until someone does that, the chief of the local police will not allow anyone to take the poor bastard down from his pulley.'

Sarah looked astonished. 'Why doesn't Arturo...?'

'Pull rank on him and tell him to piss off?'

Sarah nodded.

'He's got to live with the guy. Arturo knows he's an idiot, but he's still carrying the badge, and they have to work in harmony. Will you do it?'

'Of course. Will you stay with Jazz?'

'Sure, but I've got to go back up there too, once you've done your bit. I found the stiff, so I'll have to make a formal statement. Arturo wants me to hang around, too. They're going to fetch the widow back from the bank in Figueras where she works, and he'd like me there to explain how the body was found, if necessary. But, before she gets back they have to get him down off that rope.'

'Okay. Jazz is in his cot. He's out like a light. I'll be as quick as I can. Just don't go picking him up to talk football, or anything like that.'

28

The garage was full of policemen. Pujol and his Guardia were in immaculately pressed green uniforms. The local police, under the command of their impressively hatted chief, wore shapeless blue tunics which would have been unacceptable, Sarah thought to herself, on a garage forecourt.

Pujol introduced her to the local chief with impressive formality, referring to her as Señora Profesora Skinner. The man's heavy grey eyebrows bristled with scepticism, until she disarmed him by congratulating him in fluent Spanish on the efficiency of his local force.

Sarah never went anywhere, not even on holiday, without the basic tools of her trade. She stepped across to where the body hung, policemen moving aside deferentially as she did. She took hold of Alberni's right hand, which was already cooling. Her fingers moved quickly and expertly to confirm the absence of any pulse. She climbed up on the white plastic chair, which had been righted. She took a small torch from her shoulder bag and shone it in the bulging eyes. Finally she produced a stethoscope and, unfastening the second button of the Dior shirt, held it to the hairy chest.

She jumped down from the chair, and stepped back towards Pujol and the Policia chief. 'The man is dead,' she said formally, in Spanish, to the grey eyebrows. He nodded emphatically as if to confirm her finding. 'I'd say around two hours,' she explained to Pujol in English. She glanced at her watch. 'That would make it nine-thirty: about an hour before Bob found him.'

'How long would it take?' Pujol asked, wincing. He was pale; clearly, Sarah realised, unused or – odd for a policeman – unreconciled to violent death.

'Not long. He looks to have made a good job of it. That's a heavy knot, and the rope's been oiled to make the noose as tight as possible. I'd say he gave it some thought. Although he looks grotesque, all that facial stuff's reflex. He'd have lost consciousness in only a few seconds, not through strangulation but through pressure on the arteries, and he'd have been brain dead within five minutes. You can tell his wife, if she asks, that it didn't involve much pain . . . apart from the mental pain that drove him to do it.'

Pujol took Sarah's hands in his. 'My dear, you have been most kind. The Guardia Civil will, of course, pay you a proper professional fee for your services.'

She smiled and shook her head. 'Old Pals Act, Arturo,' she said. For a second the dapper commandant looked puzzled, until he worked out the meaning of the saying. 'In that case, perhaps I offer you something in return. Would it interest you, professionally, to attend the postmortem? To see how we do things here? We have a good pathologist in Figueras, and I know he would be delighted to meet you. It will be on Monday morning at ten o'clock.'

Sarah's eyes widened with pleasure. 'I'd be delighted, Arturo.' Suddenly a thought struck her. 'But what about . . . ?' She jerked a thumb surreptitiously toward the Policia chief, who had gone across to direct the untying of the knot and the lowering of Alberni's stiffening body from the pulley.

Pujol shook his head. 'No problem. As soon as that body crosses the L'Escala municipal limit, it's all mine. That clown has nothing to do with it from then on.'

'In that case, I'll see you tomorrow.'

'Excellent. I will collect you at nine-thirty. Let us hope that Bob does not mind.'

Sarah laughed. 'Don't worry. Minding the baby's still a novelty for him! Long may it stay that way!'

29

Skinner could barely believe what he saw when he returned to the Alberni villa.

There was movement in the garden as he came to the crest of the road. He drew the BMW to a halt a few yards away from the gate. Before him, as he stepped out into the street, stood a white ambulance, its back doors open wide. Closer to him was a police car from which a trim, well-dressed dark haired woman was emerging. And as she did, the local police chief led his men away from the garage, carrying the body of Santi Alberni, covered over, on a stretcher.

Skinner looked on, incredulous at the crassness of the man, as the Policia commandant signalled to the bearers to halt, and as he beckoned the woman towards him. Theatrically he drew back the sheet. *'Su marido, si?'*

The woman stared at the contorted face on the stretcher and shrieked. Her knees began to buckle but, before she could fall to the ground in her faint, Skinner stepped up behind her and caught her, his arm round her waist. She clutched him and leaned against his chest, sobbing.

'Dickhead!' Skinner roared at the policeman. 'If you were on my force, I'd have you making tea for the fucking traffic wardens.' He searched his limited Spanish. *'Tonto! Usted es tonto!'*

Arturo Pujol stepped between them. 'Bob, please. Look after Señora Alberni. I will deal with this.' He snapped an order to the stretcher bearers. The body was covered once more, and borne into the ambulance. He turned to the Policia commander and began to speak rapidly to him in Catalan. This time there was nothing placatory in his tone. It was quiet but ferocious. This was another side of Arturo Pujol, and Skinner could see at once from the fearful reaction of the Policia, and the silent, grim satisfaction of the Guardia officers, why his amiable friend was afforded such respect. This was old-style Guardia, and it made Skinner suddenly grateful that he had not been around in Spain during those former days.

Leaving Pujol to continue his dressing-down, he guided Gloria Alberni along the path and into her home. Inside, she sat down in a big chair in the living-room, and buried her face in her hands. Skinner left her to sob. He walked through to the kitchen, found coffee and a percolator, and made a fresh pot. When he returned to the living area, carrying the coffee in cups on a tray, Gloria Alberni's sobbing had subsided. She sat staring at the wall, expressionless, overwhelmed. Skinner fetched a small table, and put a cup of coffee close to her hand.

'Señora Alberni, do you speak English?'

She turned towards him slowly, taking in for the first time the kindly tanned face, the steel-grey hair, and the concern in his blue eyes.

'Yes,' she replied. 'I work in the National Westminster Bank in Figueras. Good English is required.' The vestiges of sobs tugged at her words.

'In that case, if we may, we will speak in English. I am a friend of Commandante Pujol of the Guardia Civil. My name is Bob Skinner. I am a policeman also. I am from Scotland, but I have a home in L'Escala.'

She nodded. 'What happened to my husband?'

'Has no one told you anything?'

'Nothing. The men from the L'Escala police, they just came to the bank and said I was to come. They said nothing at all on the way here. I asked but they said nothing. And then when I got here ...' She broke down again, as the awful memory of the face on the stretcher swept over her. She controlled herself more quickly this time, gathering her inner strength to fight off hysteria.

'What happened, Señor ...'

'Skinner,' he reminded her. 'Señora Alberni, it appears that your husband has killed himself.' He paused as his words sank in, final confirmation for her that this was not a dream, that the face on the stretcher had been real, that the body on the stretcher had been that of Santi, her husband.

When he was satisfied that she was ready to hear more, he went on. 'I came here to see him on a business matter. I called at the office but it was closed, and so I came here. There was no answer to the bell. I looked around, and found him in the garage. He was hanging. He was dead. I am very sorry.'

Gloria Alberni shuddered in her chair. She picked up her coffee and took a sip. She shook her head. 'I do not understand, Señor Skinner. You say he killed himself. He hanged himself. How can that be? Why would he?'

'Señora, the Guardia will ask all these questions of *you*, once you are ready.'

'I am ready now.' From long experience, Skinner recognised that this, the first moment after the shock of bereavement, might be the best time to interview the woman. Once the truth sank in, she would collapse again, and after that it could be days before she was able to talk sensibly about the morning of her husband's death. There was even a chance that her mind would reject the memory of it.

'If you're sure, I'll fetch Señor Pujol.'

'No!' she said vehemently. 'I do not like the Guardia men.'

'Señor Pujol is okay.'

'No. I would rather speak to you. You are a policeman, you said.'

Skinner thought for a second or two. Finally he nodded. 'Yes, okay. Arturo won't mind. I reckon he's got enough on his plate.' He sat down on a chair opposite the woman.

'So tell me, Señora. At what time did you leave for work this morning?'

She looked across at him. The tears had cut ridges through her make-up, but still she looked handsome; a classic Spanish face, Skinner thought.

'It would be around fifteen minutes to nine, maybe twenty to. I was late. We had friends visit us last night for dinner. We ate late, and the men had a lot to drink.'

'Your husband too?'

'No, not so much as the rest. Santi does not drink a lot. Wine, a little whisky, but not a lot.'

'Was he still in bed when you left?'

'No. He was up. But he said his first appointment at the office wasn't till ten, so he was not in a hurry. He made the coffee and heated the croissants, while I was getting ready. I remember I was worried by the mess. We went to bed last night without cleaning up. But he said it was okay: he would take care of everything.'

'Did you feed the dog?'

'No. Santi always does that. I don't like dogs much. That one outside, Romario it is called, after the footballer – that was Santi's.'

'What about the lawn-sprinkler?'

'Why? Was that on?'

Skinner nodded.

'Santi must have done that too. He is determined that the grass should be good from the start here. We got this house at a good price. Santi believes that once this area is fully developed we will be able to sell it and make a big profit.'

'How did he seem this morning?'

103

'Okay. As usual.'

'Did he say anything else to you?'

'No, only to hurry up and get to work. He shooed me out the door, but before I left he kissed me and told me he loved me. Then he patted my – how you say? – my bum, and pushed me out of the door.'

'Did he seem sad, preoccupied?'

Señora Alberni leaned back in her chair. She was silent for a few seconds, then she shook her head. 'No. He was quiet, that is true, but he has been that way for a few weeks now. He never talks to me about his business, and I don't talk to him about mine, but I think that there was something there that has been concerning him.'

Skinner stood up and strolled across the room. 'Señora, it looks to me as if, whatever it was, it worried him enough for him to kill himself.'

She shook her head again. 'No!' The word came out like a wail. Skinner thought that the tears would start again, but she held herself together. 'Santi would not do that.'

Skinner looked down at her sadly for a while, until she returned his gaze. He held her with his eyes, big, blue, kind, and full of concern. 'Señora, I have met very few people in your situation who are prepared to believe that their partner would choose to desert them in this way. It happens, though. I am very sorry, but that is the way it is. If I were you, I would try to come to terms with that. If you choose to believe the alternative – and there is only one alternative – then you will be headed for a load of grief. Pujol's people will investigate the business, and they will find whatever was worrying Santi. I hope that will put your mind at rest. I'll go and speak to the Commandante now, and tell him what you've told me. There will be no more questions, I think, but they will want to look around – and through Santi's papers. So far, they haven't found a note, but there might be one. Do you have a safe here?'

Gloria Alberni nodded. '*Si*. It is upstairs, in Santi's wardrobe.' She pointed to a bunch of keys lying on a low coffee table in the centre of the room. 'Those are Santi's. That little gold key is for the safe.'

Skinner picked up the bunch and slipped the gold key from the ring. 'Thanks. Señora, is there anyone you can ring? You should have someone here with you – a relative, a friend.'

'We have no relatives here. Santi and I are both from Tarragona. He has only his mother. I will call my father now, and ask him to tell her what has happened, then to come here if he can. My best friends are the people who were here last night, but if one of them came, it would only make me think of us all happy together such a short time ago.'

'When will your father arrive?'

'Tonight, I hope.'

'Well, until he gets here, I would be happy if you stayed with my wife and me. She's a doctor, and that may help you, too. Will you do that?'

She looked at him gratefully, and nodded. He picked up a pen from the sideboard, scribbled his address on a piece of paper from the memo pad beside the phone, and handed it to her. 'When you make your call, tell your father to come here.'

She took the paper from him, as she stood up, and walked over to the telephone. She was starting to dial, as Skinner left the room in search of Pujol. He found the commandant, his composure almost restored, in the kitchen. Through the small window Skinner could see only green uniforms outside. There was no sign of the local police, or of the ambulance.

'That man!' Pujol spat, as soon as Skinner entered the room. 'I say that I have to live with him. Well, no more. After that outrage, he has to live with me – and live very carefully.'

Skinner laughed. 'Don't worry about it. Every police force has a guy like that somewhere.' He explained to Pujol that he had questioned Señora Alberni, and the reason for it, which Pujol accepted readily.

'Of course, Bob, you were quite right. You are much more experienced than me in these matters, and perhaps to a Spanish person a little less intimidating than someone in a Guardia Civil uniform.' He looked around the kitchen. 'She said Alberni made the coffee, eh.' He pointed to a full cup lying on the work-surface. Alongside it a croissant lay, untouched, on a plate. 'It looks like he could not face his. I suppose he was only trying to behave as normal until she left, and he could then do what he had to do.'

'Mmm, maybe,' said Skinner. 'But maybe he didn't know he was going to do it until after she'd left. In my experience most suicides don't sit down and plan their end. It starts off with a worry, which gets a little worse week by week, then day by day, until full-scale depression sets in. They don't threaten suicide, they probably don't even contemplate it. The great majority of people who threaten to kill themselves don't do it. What they're really saying is, "I'm in trouble here. Will someone give a shit, please!" '

He glanced once more through the window, then continued. 'With guys like Alberni, the worry, the depression, deepens until, one day, it's there. The big idea. The urge to opt out. And they rush at it. It's very much a spur-of-the-moment thing. It has to be. If they thought about it, they wouldn't do it. They just swallow the pills, and half a bottle of gin, or they pick up the gun and go *bang!* right then, or they wander out to the garage, tie a noose in a rope, make it secure and kick the chair away. That's how it's done. Oh Christ, I've seen a fair few. A few too fucking many. They're rarely planned; almost invariably they come from a fatal urge which, for that short time, is just too strong to resist. That's how it would have been with Alberni this morning. She goes off to work, and he's left with only his nightmare, whatever it was, for company. And his time comes. His big idea. He goes into the garage, and out of this life.

'I have to admit that oiling the rope to make sure that the noose would run was a nice touch. I haven't seen that one before. Rivers of blood, yes. Brains on the ceiling, yes. But never an oily rope. That's a first. He's still a selfish bastard, though, to do that to her.' He gestured with his thumb towards the living room.

Skinner was unaware that his voice had risen, almost to a shout. Pujol touched his shoulder, gently. 'Hey, my friend, I think you care more than you like people to know. And I think that maybe you have seen too much of death by violence.'

The shout dropped to a whisper. 'Oh, Arturo, old son, you don't know the half of it.' Bob held up his big, tanned hands. 'See these things. I killed a guy with these once. Not so long ago, at that. I am a martial artist of the first rank, Commandante. With just one of these hands, I could put your lights out for good in about a second and a half. And that's not all. I am a fully trained and expert marksman, with experience. In doing my duty as a policeman, I have killed three people, and seriously wounded a fourth. Not one of them could have had any complaint about the outcome. They were all armed and offering violence, and I killed them all without a moment of hesitation. Because, in those circumstances, that's my job. Just as it's yours, my friend.

'You've never killed anyone, Arturo. Though you carry a gun, you've never used it. I can tell. Because it marks you, you see. You carry it with you like a piece of luggage you can't throw away, and when you meet someone with a matching piece, you *can* tell. You know you both belong to the same club . . . the AES, the Authorised Executioners' Society. My best friend's a member. He'll never get over his initiation. It's a club I hope you never join. So yes, Commandante, I have seen too much of death. And yes, I care. Thank Christ, I care. It's the caring that makes the difference between the likes of my friend Andy and me, and the guys on the other side of the argument. That's why, in the end, I get so angry with people like Alberni. When you've had to take life yourself, and know the hellish taste of it, the selfishness and the waste and the sheer bloody unnecessariness of suicide just makes you mad.'

He smashed his right fist into his left palm. Beside him, Pujol, struck silent by his friend's confession, jumped at the explosive sound.

'But life goes on, and all that. I've got a wife and son I want to see soon, so let's do what has to be done here, and I'll take Gloria away with me.' He held up the key. 'This opens Alberni's safe. Your guys still haven't found a note anywhere?' Pujol shook his head. 'Okay, let's you and I take a look and see if it's upstairs. Come on.'

He led the way up the curving, tiled staircase to the upper floor of the house, and into the Albernis' bedroom. The safe was where Señora Alberni had said it would be, but it was bolted to the floor. Skinner knelt beside it and unlocked it with the small golden key. Even with the doors of the wardrobe wide open, it was dark inside and difficult to see. He felt inside the safe, and lifted out two boxes, its only contents. He carried them across to the dressing table and set them down. One was a jewel box, secured by a clasp. Skinner flicked it open, and found not jewels but an assortment of documents. Pujol examined them one by one. 'Marriage certificate, birth certificates, life insurance, household insurance; all of these are personal documents. I see no letter from Alberni.'

'And no family jewels either. Maybe they kept them in the cigar box.' Skinner lifted the wooden lid of the second box. Pujol gasped with surprise, and muttered a Spanish imprecation. Skinner's reaction was confined to a slight raising of the eyebrows.

The cigar box was stuffed with Spanish banknotes. Pujol picked up a handful and flicked through it – then another, then another. 'It is in notes from one thousand pesetas to ten thousand.'

'How much d'you reckon is there?'

Pujol did not answer at once. Instead, he took out all of the cash from the box and arranged it in separate piles of one-thousand, two-thousand, five-thousand and ten-thousand peseta notes. He picked each bundle up in turn, flicking through it with his thumb, nodding continuously as he did, as if keeping count. Eventually he put the last bundle down. 'I'd say that there is a little over five million pesetas there.'

'In sterling,' said Skinner, 'that's twenty-five grand.'

'So Señor Alberni did not have the money problems of which we were told.'

'Maybe having all this money was his problem. It all fits together, Arturo. Alberni's a thief. He does Pitkeathly, then word gets to him on

107

the L'Escala grapevine that a Scottish copper's in town and looking for him. He panics – so much so that this morning he goes up the rope.'

'Who would know you were going to see him? I did not tell anyone.'

'You wouldn't have to. Scotland does a check on Alberni through your police national computer. A copy comes in for you. You come to see me. And you have to leave word with your office where you are. Yes?' Pujol nodded in confirmation.

'Okay, you run a police force, and police forces, regrettably, run on gossip.' Pujol smiled a wry smile of agreement. 'By yesterday afternoon it's bar talk wherever your people drink, maybe in that bar up in Avinguda Girona, that there's a problem with Alberni, and that a guy's come all the way from Scotland to see him, a guy so heavy that the Commandante goes to visit *him*. A friend of Alberni hears this and passes it on. Or maybe Alberni has a source in your building: someone who feeds him information. Don't be offended; corruption happens in many places, and stupidity is universal.'

'Professionally I hate easy answers. But this one is so fucking obvious that even I can't ignore it. We have to ask the lady about this cash. I'll do it. She'd probably still be frightened by that green uniform of yours.'

'*Si*, please do that. You take the money. I will lock the safe.'

Skinner picked up the box and went downstairs at a trot. Gloria Alberni had finished the phone-call to her father, and had resumed her seat. She was dabbing her eyes with a small white handkerchief. Skinner guessed that the first aftershock was heading her way.

'Señora, what can you tell us about this?' He showed her the box, and raised its lid.

The woman's tear-filled eyes opened wide with surprise. 'Where did you find that?'

'It was in your husband's safe.'

'I have never seen that before. How much money is there?'

'Pujol reckons five million pesetas.'

'Five million,' she gasped. 'What was Santi doing with five million in his safe?'

'Could it have been cash he was holding for a client?'

'No way. Santi always banked clients' cash as soon as he received it. He banked with Banca Catalana, here in L'Escala. I know he had a special arrangement with them, so that he could make deposits even when the bank was closed.'

'Pujol will want to find out where it came from. You understand?'

'*Si. I* want to know where it came from! Five million pesetas! Almost under my bed!'

30

'Boss! What can I do for you?' Brian had been expecting a call from a friend to confirm a golf tie. Instead he heard Skinner's voice, crystal-clear, via satellite.

'You can listen and do what I ask. It'll keep my phone bill down if it's arranged at your end. I want you to contact Paul Ainscow and get him on the first plane out here. He's needed here *now* to go through the accounts of InterCosta. But you'll have to break some bad news to him. His partner Alberni hanged himself this morning. We found twenty-five grand's worth of used notes in his safe. It looks as if Pitkeathly's just the tip of the iceberg.'

Brian Mackie whistled. 'Tough on Ainscow. Is there anything else you want me to tell him?'

'No – other than that he should probably have legal advice handy, and a good accountant. We'll want to go through those books with a fine-tooth comb.'

'That's twice you've said "we", boss. Are you helping out there?'

'Yes. Arturo Pujol's asked me to give him a hand because of the UK interest. Sort of unofficial liaison.'

'What's Sarah saying to that?'

Skinner laughed. 'He's cute, my friend Arturo. He invited her to observe their pathologist at work on Monday, knowing she'd jump at the chance. So she can hardly dig me up. Anyway, we're both keen that this is cleared up as quickly as possible, for the sake of Alberni's widow. Nice woman. Sarah's looking after her now. She's given her a sedative from the *farmacia* ... sorry, Brian, that's chemist to you! Okay, go on, get a hold of Ainscow. Tell him *first* available flight tomorrow, without fail! Tell him to let me know, through you, what flight he's on, and I'll have the Guardia pick him up from the airport. So long.'

He hung up and went out to join Sarah on the terrace. He found her in a bikini, walking Jazz up and down in her arms. He was awake and as bright as the day, taking a greater interest than ever in his surroundings, and in the things going on about him. Sarah had dressed him in a pale-blue sun-suit, and a wide brimmed sunhat fastened under his chin.

'Here, gimme a shot,' said Bob. Sarah passed the wriggling baby to him and sat down on a cushioned sun-bed. She unclipped her bikini top, picked up a yellow bottle of Delial factor four, and stretched out on her back to prepare herself for the sun.

Shielding him from the sun with his body, Bob turned the baby to face the Bay of Rosas. The bite-shaped expanse of blue water seemed to be alive with windsurfers. 'Fancy some of that, Jazz boy?' The baby wriggled and gurgled in his arms. 'Never done any myself, but I'm sure it'll become second nature to you.'

He felt the wriggling subside. 'Time to go back to the buggy, is it? Come on, then.' He laid the unprotesting baby in his mobile crib and, stripping off his shirt, settled on a recliner alongside Sarah.

'Is Gloria out for the count?' he asked.

'Yes. I found a good strong sedative down there. It isn't really over-the-counter stuff, even here, but I flashed my stethoscope and ID at him, and used Arturo's name to back them up. He came across without an argument.'

'How long will she be out?'

'Let's see. It's three now. I'd say till seven, anyway. I've got some Librium for when she wakes up. When did she think her father would get here?'

'She hoped he'd make it for eight. Where will they stay?'

'At her place. I asked her if she wanted them to be booked into the Bonaire or the Nieves Mar, but she said no. I suspect she was worried about cost, but she didn't say so – just that she'd have to face it some time, and it might as well be now.'

'She's a brave lady.'

A thought struck Sarah. 'God, I wasn't in the house, but didn't you say that it looked as if a bomb had hit it. I really hate the thought of her going back to the debris of last night's party with Santi and their friends and all.'

'No, that won't happen. Arturo set half a dozen of his finest to making the place look spotless. I told him he should have used the Policia for that, but he said he didn't want any breakages.'

'Yes! That man with the hat, wasn't he awful! Gloria told me about the stretcher. She said she thought you were going to hit him.'

'The thought did cross my mind. Arturo's too. What a bollocking he gave the guy – Chief of Police or not.'

'You'd better not park on any yellow lines in L'Escala for a while!'

Bob laughed. 'The only line I'd like to park on is the one round that

110

pillock's hat.' He propped himself up on an elbow, and picked up the sun cream. 'Want your back done?'

'Nope. It's not too comfortable lying face-down right now. The D cups are still pretty tender, thanks to the milk monster over there!'

31

'I must say, Mr Skinner, the thought of an airport welcome by the Guardia Civil had me worried all the way across. It was quite a relief when their driver turned out to be in plain clothes!'

Skinner smiled. 'Even the Guardia have men in suits, Mr Ainscow.'

The two Scots shook hands on the pavement of the Passeig Maritim, outside the office of InterCosta. Ainscow thanked his driver, and the black car which had delivered him pulled away from the kerb and headed off in the direction of L'Escala's old town. It was 4:30 p.m., and even on a Sunday the few shops along the Passeig were in the process of reopening after their afternoon break, in the hope of gathering in a few more pesetas from the weekend visitors.

'You made good time,' said Skinner.

'Yes, I took the quickest option available: Air France from Edinburgh and on to Barcelona from Charles de Gaulle. Bloody expensive, though. Not the way I'd choose to travel. I take charters to Girona from Glasgow when I can, and look for deals on schedules to Barcelona in the winter months, when Girona's shut. How do you come down?'

'Varies. Quite often, like on this trip, I drive down. Look, shall we go inside?'

Ainscow nodded. Skinner pushed open the door of the small office, and the two stepped inside. Ainscow dropped his flight bag on the floor and placed his briefcase on one of three desks in the room.

'That's the desk you use normally, when you're here?' Skinner asked.

'Yes. That's . . . that was Santi's over there, and the other's used by a part-time secretary.'

'Right. Nothing's been touched here since yesterday. Everything is exactly as it was the last time Alberni locked up. What I want you to do, or more precisely what the Guardia want, is to go through the books of the business, and try to locate all the funds transferred under that crazy blank-cheque system of yours. Have you called the InterCosta accountant?'

Ainscow looked at him a shade sheepishly. 'We don't have one. We have a book-keeper over here, and I have one in the UK. We operate as a partnership, so there's no need for filing of accounts anywhere. However, I have located an independent accountant in Girona. She'll be here tomorrow.'

'Good. What about a lawyer?'

'I'll call one if and when I need one. There's a bloke in Torroella that I've used in the past. But I've got nothing to hide. It was Santi who had the five million in his safe, not me. Do you want me to begin today?'

'No. Wait till your accountant gets here – and the Guardia man. They're sending someone up from their fraud department.

'Have you met Pujol, the local Commandante?'

'No.'

'Didn't think you would. Not too many people seek out the company of the Guardia. He's coming down here this afternoon to meet you.' Skinner looked out of the window, peering through a chink in the mass of posters which covered most of its surface and darkened the room. 'In fact, here he is now.'

As he spoke, Pujol, out of uniform, appeared in the doorway. Skinner made the formal introductions.

'I am glad to see you here, Señor,' said the Commandant. 'I think that there are matters with your company which have to be looked into: things that happened here in Spain.'

Ainscow broke in. 'Look, I want you to know that apart from this Pitkeathly business, and let's hope that still turns out to have been a mistake, there has never been a single complaint to me in Scotland by any client about any transaction. Ask around town and you will find nothing but satisfied people.'

'We *shall* ask, Señor. In fact we are asking already. Tell me, how long have you been in business with Señor Alberni.'

'Nearly ten years. I was in the estate-agency business back home. I built up a chain in central Scotland, then sold to an insurance company at the height of the boom. I did well – well enough to buy my place in Punta Montgo, and to spend some quality time out here. That's when I got to know Santi. He was working as a salesman for a big promoter-developer. He had sold me a couple of apartments as investments. I was looking for a manager, and the thought struck me: why not set up Santi in a business of his own, combining estate agency with property management, and all the other add-ons that brings? Then I thought that a business like that should have a UK outlet on the estate agency side. I looked at the restrictive covenant attached to my sale, and discovered that I was clear to deal in overseas property. So

113

InterCosta opened in Scotland as well. Initially I ran it from our house, but when the Stirling Business Centre was built, I liked it and moved in there. Gives clients a better impression, you understand.'

'You said you were partners,' said Skinner. 'What was the profit split?'

'I put up the development capital, so I had seventy-five per cent. Santi had twenty-five, but he still had a good package, by Spanish standards.'

'Has the business been profitable?' asked Pujol.

'It's washed its face, I'd say. If I were to be completely frank, I'd have to say that it's under-performing. It's always made a profit, but somehow it's never come up to business-plan forecasts. Some years the profit has been so low that I've given Santi a fifty-per cent share just so that he'd have something worth having.'

'Where has the problem been? Sales?' Skinner quizzed.

'Not really. The way the thing is structured, we're not dependent on the market. Property management – and by that I mean looking after villas and apartments and providing a rental service – that's always given us a second income stream. The problem has always been that the overhead at the Spanish end was way over budget.'

'Why didn't you crack down on it? Put in an accountant?'

'In a business like this, it's not that easy to pin down the overhead. There are always things that you didn't budget for. Things like putting clients up in a hotel for a night or two because the maid forgot to renew the gas bottle in their apartment and you can't get one till Monday, unexpected trips to the airport with clients, people taking inspection flights over and ripping you off by buying from someone else. Loads of wee things like that can cut into your costs. I've always reckoned I'd just have to live with that. As I said to you in Scotland, Mr Skinner, I've been feeling a bit uneasy lately, but until Pitkeathly there's been nothing to go on. Now there's this five million.'

'How often did you see Santi Alberni?' Pujol asked.

'I'm over here about half a dozen times a year, in some years more. When I'm here, even apart from on business, I see Santi a lot. And Gloria, of course.'

'Are you married, Señor?'

'Was once – not now.'

Pujol sighed. 'Ah, yes. I can say the same. And so could Bob here, until recently. Now he has a wife and a new family to go home to, so we should let him do that. Señor, I shall drive you to your villa, and tomorrow we will begin the search for the origin of Santi Alberni's five million.'

114

32

'Gloria and her father called in while you were gone. To thank us for yesterday.'

'I hope you told them it was *de nada*.'

'Of course.'

'How's she bearing up?'

'Pretty well. She's got guts – and her father being here, helping her a lot too. Arturo's told her that he'll release the body tomorrow straight after the autopsy, all being well. They're fixing the funeral for Wednesday. Gloria asked if we'd go. I said yes, if Kathleen could find us a babysitter.'

'Wait and see: Kathleen'll do it herself. There'll be no stopping her.'

'Then she'll be Jazz's first official sitter. It's just too bad about the reason we need one.'

'Yes. Here, try this theory for size. Apparently Ainscow's footloose and fancy free. No current missus. Arturo was wondering if he and Gloria might have been having it off, then Santi found out and couldn't take it. What d'you think?'

'No way. She's a well-brought-up Spanish lady. She wouldn't do that. And Santi was a Spanish guy, remember. If Arturo's idea was right, Santi would have been more likely to kill her, and Ainscow, than himself. No way, no way, no way.'

'Yes, that's more or less what I said to Arturo as well.'

They were dining at home, on their wide terrace. The air had cleared with the cooling of the day, and the jagged skyline of the Pyrenees was etched sharply on the horizon. The sun had just fallen and the sky along the mountains had taken on the pinkish tinge that they knew would darken and turn purple with the breakthrough of the earliest of the evening stars.

Sarah raised her glass of Fonter towards the Pyrenees in a toast. 'To my big mountain. It's a dream here, Bob, isn't it?'

He looked at her and smiled; a smile from the eyes, a smile from the heart. 'Because of you, Professor Sarah, all because of you. The best night I ever had in this town was the night you said you'd marry me. I still dream about that – here and in Scotland.'

She smiled back at him. Their eyes locked, and the air between them seemed to grow warmer, in defiance of the gathering dusk. 'Ask me again,' she whispered.

He gave a tiny shake of his head. 'No. You might give me a different answer.'

'No chance of that, copper. You're stuck with me.'

He reached across the table and took her hand. 'Well, in that case . . .' His smile widened again into a grin which had only one meaning.

And then the telephone rang.

'Bugger.' Bob walked into the villa and picked it up. *'Hola.'*

'Hi, *hombre*. How goes it with you, and how's my kid brother?' Alex's timing has always been accidentally impeccable, Bob thought.

'It goes great with us all, and your kid brother is unstoppable. Eats, sleeps, shits and smiles; that just about sums him up. He doesn't stint on any of them, either.'

'Buy him a drink for me, then.'

Bob laughed at his daughter's obvious delight in her new sibling. 'Aye, I'll do that.'

'I hear you're busy out there, Pops. Andy said you'd fallen on some police work.'

'Andy said?'

'Yes. I'm at his place just now.' Before he could comment, she added, 'I'm staying at Fairyhouse Avenue tonight.'

'Yes, fine. How are the finals?'

'One to go, on Tuesday. Studying's over, though. You could say that quiet confidence is flowing down the telephone line.'

'Good. Keep your mind on Tuesday, and let's hope that confidence is not misplaced.'

'So what is this thing you're caught up in?'

'It's a mess, but we'll sort it out in the next couple of days, I reckon. Now go and give Andy's phone bill a break. I'll call you after your last exam.'

'Don't make it Tuesday evening, then. Andy's taking me out to celebrate. Bye.'

He went back to the terrace, and to Sarah. She looked at him, enquiring with her eyes.

'Alex. Asking after Jazz. She's at Andy's.'

'Mmm.' Sarah smiled a quiet smile.

116

Bob reached his hand across the table once more. 'Now Professor, as I was saying . . .'

And then, through the baby intercom, came the strident sound of Jazz's first waking cry.

Bob shook his head and laughed. 'That does it. I'm going to have a beer. I know whose needs come first in this house!'

33

'My God, Bob, I'm cooked. Stand back, man, and let me get out of this shirt. Why did I choose to wear this spring gear? Why didn't I just put on a blouse and shorts, like every sensible woman I've seen today?'

'How's Jazz?'

'Fine. Good as gold. What does a Spanish postmortem look like then?'

'Messy, just like everywhere else. Dr Martinez, the pathologist, was first-class, though. We could use one or two like him back home. Nothing unnecessary. Straight to the point . . . Back in a minute.' She ran off towards the bedroom to change. When she reappeared in the kitchen a few minutes later, she was wearing a Lycra swimsuit and shorts.

Bob handed her a coffee 'What's the verdict, then?'

'Exactly as you'd expect. Death by asphyxiation, due to hanging. All vital organs okay, brain normal. Santi was as healthy as a horse, so you can rule out terminal illness as a motive. Slight alcohol level in the blood, but no more than you'd find from three or four beers the night before. No unusual marks on the body, apart from horizontal bruising on each upper arm. The pathologist suggested – and it's as good an explanation as I can think of – that the short sleeves of his shirt tightened on him as he struggled, after kicking the chair away. There was an oily mark on the chair by the way, and oil on the sole of Santi's left shoe.'

'How do you know he struggled?'

'Martinez found yellow hemp fibres from the rope under his fingernails. His proposition was that, after Santi kicked the chair away, he thought better of it and clawed at the rope. That fits too. It's a common finding in autopsies on hanging suicides.'

'So that's it then. Suicide officially.'

Sarah nodded. 'Yes. Arturo said he's completely satisfied. He's going to put the papers before a magistrate, but that's what they'll say, and that's what the magistrate will rule.' She paused, looking suddenly gloomy. 'I wish it was otherwise, for Gloria's sake. I looked in to see her on the way back, to let her know what had happened. She still refuses to believe that her husband could have done something like that. You couldn't do some clever detecting and prove otherwise, could you?'

A wry expression twisted Bob's face for a second. 'Much as I'd like to help the lady, and much as I hate pat answers, there are times when a responsible investigator has to accept the obvious and leave it at that. You know me. I've been gnawing away at the scene in my mind, looking for something that might argue against the suicide explanation. But if there is anything, I'm stuffed if I can see it. Anyway, that's enough shop for today. I phoned Ainscow. He won't be through until tomorrow, he reckons. He, Arturo and I are meeting in the afternoon. Also, while you were out, I managed to begin work on this great treatise on detecting that I came down here to write. But that is it. Enough, the sun is calling. So why don't we attend to Jazz's needs, and then we can all go out for lunch. Between you and me, my love, there's quite a lot I'd do for a pizza!'

34

It looked more like a business meeting over coffee by the beach, in true Costa style, than the culmination of a criminal investigation.

The three men sat around a table on the pavement outside La Caravel, Skinner with a *cortado* – a Spanish version of expresso with a little milk – Pujol and Ainscow with *café con leche*. Just across the way, the pocket-sized town beach was thronged with its usual late-afternoon mixture of mothers, infants and shoppers gathered together in a summer ritual of sunbathing and gossip. Some, from the bags which they carried, had come straight from the Maxor supermarket, less than two hundred metres away in one of the old town's narrow streets.

Pujol sampled his coffee, replaced the small white cup in its saucer, and picked up his briefcase. He opened it and withdrew a neatly typed document, which he placed in the centre of the table.

He looked at Skinner then at Ainscow. Finally, he said, 'That is a report prepared by my agent, after going through the accounts of InterCosta with Señor Ainscow's accountant. It is of course in Spanish, and I have not had the opportunity to have it translated. However I will summarise it for you. It seems that, for some time, amounts of money have been disappearing from the company account. They have been between three hundred thousand and two million pesetas. Each, shall we say, withdrawal has related to a sales transaction. It has not come from the property management side. That has been going on for years. It will take much time to identify every one of the thefts, but my *hombre* and yours, Señor Ainscow, they are agreed that the total missing could be as much as two hundred million pesetas.'

'A million sterling!' said Skinner in surprise. Ainscow said nothing, but looked grim.

'*Sí*. Over a number of years, but it is still a lot of money.'

'So how was it done?'

'Very simply. Señor Ainscow has told you of the way in which money was moved from Scotland to España. I know that you may think it irresponsible, Bob, but in fact it is quite a common practice in our property business. The banks have only themselves to blame. It is very expensive to move money from country to country by official transfer. Because of this, many people use blank cheques made out for cash, drawn on accounts in foreign countries. It is as effective as official transfer, it is often quicker, and it is not expensive.

'What has happened with InterCosta is that some of those cheques have been diverted. Señor Ainscow's records in Scotland show that they have been completed and honoured, but they have not all been paid into the InterCosta account in Banca Catalana. Some have been cashed somewhere else, with money-changers. Many of them here will accept ordinary cheques for a higher commission.

'It is so simple. The theft was not from the client. It was from the company itself, from the profits of InterCosta.'

'Yes,' said Skinner, 'I understand. I assume that, every time, the sum stolen was always within the level of commission due on that sale.'

'*Exactamente!* The sellers of the properties concerned were always paid in full. The buyers, they pay their money, they get their apartment, everybody is happy. The only person who does not get his money is Señor Ainscow. It seems that Alberni's great mistake was to forget, until it was too late, that Señor Pitkeathly's apartment was to be sold without commission being charged.'

Skinner looked across the table at Pujol. 'The InterCosta records confirm Alberni's guilt?'

'Bob, the cheques are cashed in España. The theft is of the profits from the company. Señor Ainscow here is entitled to seventy-five per cent of these profits. Why would he steal from himself?'

Skinner nodded in acceptance of the point. 'Yes, why indeed.' He looked at the other man. 'Seems like you've been stuffed all right, Mr Ainscow. What are you going to do about it all, Arturo?'

The commandant shrugged his shoulders. 'God, he knows. We have asked all the banks. Alberni has very little cash in his personal account. There is no trace of any other among his papers. He has simply made it disappear. There are many things he could have done here. For example, he could have set up dummy companies, with other people as administrators, and used them to buy property. That would be untraceable. Or he could have buried it in his garden. Or he could have given it all to the casinos. Many Spanish people, even more so if they are Catalan, are big gamblers.'

'What action will you take?'

'I have been giving that much thought, and I have spoken to Señor Ainscow about it. What I intend to do is . . . nothing. There will be no hearing. What would that achieve? Gloria Alberni knew nothing of this: of that we are both certain. She will have to live in L'Escala. It will be kinder if it is without disgrace. There is another reason too. What I have done so far is more or less unofficial. If I do any more, it will mean a full-scale investigation, by other people, of the company's business. If that happened, then our Ministerio de Hacienda – our taxman, you would say – might decide to look also at some of the declarations which have been made to the Notary of the prices paid for properties on which the tax is calculated. You know, Bob, that often the price which is declared is not the real price. It is much less. If our tax authorities took an interest, it could be catastrophic for many clients of InterCosta. And maybe not only InterCosta, too. They might then decide to investigate other companies in L'Escala.

'If that were to happen, how would it be for relations between the town and the Guardia Civil? My people live here. I live in Albons, not far away. We would be outcasts . . . *leprosos!* It is unthinkable. So if you agree, and Señor Ainscow agrees, I will do no more. I will bury this business with Santiago Alberni.'

Skinner shrugged his shoulders. 'It's your investigation, Arturo, I've got no problem with that outcome. Pitkeathly might, but then he's got to live here too.'

Ainscow broke in. 'I'll take care of Pitkeathly, Mr Skinner, don't you worry. That twenty-five grand in Santi's safe belongs to the company, clearly. I'll have that back, and I'll pay the Pitkeathlys this missing half million pesetas from it.'

'That's fair,' said Skinner. 'What will you do about the business?'

'Now that I see how profitable it could be, I'll probably look for new people out here. Two probably: one Spanish, one British. I'll let them buy in for twenty per cent each, in profits. That way they'll be watching each other. And from now on my accountant will be looking out for me.' For the first time that afternoon, Ainscow smiled. 'How about it, Mr Skinner, fancy staying here as a partner in InterCosta?'

Skinner, leaning back in his chair and finishing his *cortado*, smiled too. 'Bugger off!'

35

'Oh, Bob. Poor Gloria, there are so few people.'

'That's the way it is when they bury a suicide. Folk are embarrassed, they disapprove, they don't want to be involved. There's no church service either, no requiem mass for the sinner. I'm glad the priest's turned out, though. Sometimes they refuse.'

Sarah spotted a familiar face wearing a look of unfamiliar grimness. 'What's Carlos doing here?'

'The UBET asked him to represent them. You know, the local business organisation. Santi was a member. Kath said he'd be here when she arrived to baby-sit.'

They were about to join their friend when the cortège – the hearse and a single car – swung into the little walled cemetery on the road from L'Escala to Villadamat. Gloria's father was in the front seat of the black Mercedes. When the car came to a stop not far from the new grave, he jumped out first, opening the rear door and holding out his hand to assist his daughter as she emerged. Two other women, both middle-aged, rose with dignity from the other side. One bore a striking resemblance to Gloria. The other, Bob and Sarah each assumed correctly, was Santi's mother.

The graveside service was mercifully brief. Although Bob could not follow much of it, he was aware that the priest had little to say, and suspected that he had never met the man he was burying. He offered a few words of comfort to Gloria, pronounced the rites, and the coffin was interred in a silence broken only by the sobbing of three women.

The small congregation began to disperse at once. Carlos had not noticed the presence of Bob and Sarah, and when they turned to look for him again, they saw him hurrying off. They were about to follow when Gloria's father approached. 'Señor, Señora, you will join us at the villa to toast Santi?' He spoke to Sarah in Spanish.

'Thank you, Señor Gomez, but we must go back home to our baby.'

Bob cut in. 'Why don't you go for a while? I'll drop you off and then I'll relieve Kath. I'm sure Señor Gomez will run you home.'

'Okay. Maybe Gloria could use seeing someone her own age today. To cope with the aftermath of this, she'll need all the friends she can get.'

36

'Do these *really* come from Scotland?'

'Razor shells? Yup. There's every chance that these came from our west coast. We ignore them, and the Spanish treat them as a delicacy. But that's my fellow countrymen for you. If you can't serve it with chips, salt and vinegar, or roll it in breadcrumbs and call it scampi, they're not interested.'

It was mid-evening, late enough for *buenas tardes* to have become *buenas noches*, but far too early for *adios*. Bob and Sarah were finishing a tapas supper in the marble-lined bar of El Golf Isabel, one of their favourite old-town restaurants. Jazz was asleep in his buggy behind them – two hours away, Sarah estimated, from his next feed. On the next day, she had determined, she would begin to supplement his diet with rusks.

Apart from Navajos, the distinctive Spanish name of Scotland's secret export, the plates spread before them included small portions of mountain ham, meatballs, small green peppers fried in olive oil, and a delicious spicy chicken dish. Finally they were finished, and Romeo, the olive-skinned Italian waiter, appeared to clear their table. As they had noticed earlier, he seemed to take his name to heart, and his excessive attentions to Sarah, and her cleavage, pushed Bob's annoyance level close to breaking point. She, seeing the gathering frown, laughed as her admirer retreated to the kitchen to fetch two Creme Catalan desserts. 'Don't worry about him, Bob. It's good for a girl's morale, especially when she's just had a baby.'

'I'm not worried about him. Not one bit, but he should be bloody worried about me!' He spoke just loudly enough for his words to carry across to the kitchen area.

She laughed again at his annoyance, until eventually Bob's resolve cracked, and his grin returned.

'That's better. I'm sure he's got the message. This was a really nice idea of yours, darling, after the gloom of this afternoon.'

'How was it at the villa?'

'Grim. Poor Gloria; that's a really bad scene, you know. Her father

125

had to give her some bad news from Santi's insurance company. They're not paying out on his life policy.'

Bob shook his head sadly. 'To be expected with a suicide. Some do, depending on the circumstances; some just point-blank refuse. Sounds like Santi was with one of the latter kind, for them to have reached that decision so quickly. There'll be no chance of them changing it either.'

'I know. It'll mean that Gloria will have to sell the villa as fast as she can, and in a buyer's market too. She may not even get what they paid for it. She's got very little money, and she already has a spare-time job keeping books for a man who owns a few shops. She thinks that, until the villa's sold at least, she'll have to take a third job, at weekends. Bar work, cleaning, anything she can find. She'd like to go back to Tarragona, but she can't do that until the villa is sold.'

'Yeah, it's a damn shame. Too bad the selfish bastard didn't think about that before he topped himself.'

'Maybe he did, and it was still too much for him to face. A million pounds is a lot to have stolen. He'd have done twenty years.'

'Then that's what he should have done.'

Sarah changed the subject. 'Did you call Alex to ask about her last exam?'

'Yeah. Answerphones were on at her place, and at ours, so I left a message on each. You know our kid – she'll be out on a shopping binge to celebrate.'

Sarah smiled. 'Yes. Something like that.'

As Romeo returned with their desserts, Bob looked up, raising an eyebrow as if to say 'Just try it, son'. But the Italian's ardour was stilled. They ate in silence for a minute or two. Eventually Sarah paused, putting down her spoon.

'What makes it even tougher in a way is that apparently Santi's policy had one of those double-indemnity clauses in it. Suicide, zilch – but if he died by accident or some other violence, it would pay out twice the value. Forty million pesetas: two hundred thousand pounds.' She wrinkled her nose. 'Are you *sure* you couldn't prove he was murdered, Bob?'

He shook his head. 'Sarah, love, much as I'd like to help poor Gloria inherit some big bucks, if I could do that, then at the same time I could turn that *agua minerale* of yours into Gran Vina Sol. There is nothing, but nothing, for me to go on, and I am not here to waste our time.'

37

The weather held, as their holiday resumed its normal course.

The weaning of Jazz took place successfully, and quickly he developed an appetite for rusks to equal that for the natural element of his diet. And as his input became more varied, so inevitably did his output, introducing Sarah – and Bob once more – to those joys of parenthood which call for a little dedication.

With the Pitkeathly affair and Santi Alberni's suicide behind them, they began to do some of the things which had been on their original agenda. On the Thursday, as their first week at the villa drew to an end, Bob wrote productively in the morning. Later they visited Pals and its ceramic shops, and called for a late lunch at Mas Pou, a celebrated *Catalan Tipique* restaurant in the distinctive circular village of Palau Sator. Next morning, Bob did something which even a few months earlier would have seemed unthinkable. He telephoned Proud Jimmy and secured his chief's agreement to the proposition that, since much of his first week had been spent effectively on police work, he would write it off as holiday, and so would delay his return to Fettes by a further seven days.

'Of course, man,' his grizzled boss had said. 'Get to know your new son. Mackie tells me you got a good result in that business.'

'Good for whom, Jimmy? Pitkeathly's got his few quid back, Ainscow's down a million, Alberni's done himself in, and his widow's penniless. Apart from that, everyone's laughing.'

'Aye, well, that's the job sometimes, Bob. You know that. Now enjoy yourself!'

38

'You know Bob, my friend, in the work I do with the Spanish tourist industry I have been all over the world. America, Sri Lanka, Roma, South Africa, I have seen them all. But, of all the places I have seen, this here, in L'Escala, on the terrace outside our restaurant, looking across the marina to the town and to the mountains, this is my favourite place of all.'

Bob leaned back in his seat and took a deep mouthful of his beer. 'I can see why you say that, Carlos. It's beautiful all right. But, you know, you're really saying something else. Nowadays I have three homes. One here that I bought with – and for – my daughter. One in Gullane that I bought with, and for, my first wife. And one in Edinburgh that I bought with, and for, Sarah. And I'll tell you what's my favourite place. It's the terrace in Puig Pedro, looking out at the same mountains as you do. Or it's Gullane beach frozen solid on a bright cold January morning. Or it's the tree in our back garden in Edinburgh, where Jazz's swing is going to be. It's wherever they are,' he pointed behind him, over his shoulder with his left forefinger, to where Sarah stood in the shade of the awning, holding Jazz to her brown shoulder, and speaking with Kathleen, 'those two; here, there or anywhere, that's my favourite place. And when you sit here in the sun and look out, you're really looking over your shoulder, too, at Kathleen and the boys. That's your favourite place: the one you have with them. And for all you'd admit it, suppose it wasn't here, but in some back street in Girona – that's still how it'd be.'

The two men sat in silence for a while. Then Carlos turned and smiled, a sly smile filled with fun. 'Yes, and I suppose I can see a day when I will *be* here, but only in an urn behind the bar, and the place will still go on without me!'

'That's right, but it won't be just any old urn. It'll be shaped like the European Cup, and draped in Barcelona ribbons!'

The howls of their laughter startled Jazz, and drew an insistent 'Sshh' from Sarah.

'Ah, we mus' keep down the noise,' said Carlos. 'Tell me, that Alberni business. Is all finished now, *si*?'

Skinner nodded. 'Yes, it's a suicide, and that's how it's been put away in the box.' He offered no detail on the investigation, nor even hinted that one had taken place.

'Suicide. That is very bad, very, how you say, un-Catalan. Even from Tarragona, Alberni was still Catalan. We are not suicidal people. We are excitable, yes. We are happy and sad like others. But suicide, that is not the way with us. Your Scandinavians, they are so cold they kill themselves all the time! Your French, they are so miserable and always in love. You British, not *you* but you know what I mean, you are so discontented. But we Catalans, we are happy people, not suicidal. We support the greatest football team in the world, we have a beautiful warm country, we love our wives, we spoil our children. And, when we are not eating them, we are even kind to animals.'

Skinner took another mouthful of beer as he considered the point ... and choked. Wide-eyed, he sat bolt upright in his chair, and slammed his glass back on the table. As Sarah, Kathleen and Carlos stared at him in alarm, he jumped from his chair and clasped his hands together as if in triumph.

'Carlos, that's it! That's what was wrong. Alberni – he didn't feed the dog! Sarah,' he called out, 'he didn't feed the bloody dog!'

She looked across at him, bewildered. 'Yes, but—'

'Look, he was thoughtful enough to make his wife breakfast. He cared enough for the grass to switch on the lawn sprinkler. But he died and left his dog – Romario the footballer, *his* dog, not Gloria's; she told me how much he cared for it – left it howling, with licked-clean, bone-dry food and water dishes. That doesn't fit. That's what's wrong with Alberni's death. *Now* I've got a reason to look into it some more! That guy was done in, and I *will* prove it. Gloria's insurance company had better get its chequebook out.

'And *you*, Carlos, can buy in a few litres of *agua minerale*, and look for a saving on the wine bill!'

39

'Where did you put those notes?'

'They're in the *escritura*. You bring Jazz in, I'll go fetch them.'

Skinner unfastened the straps of his son's car cradle and carried him, asleep, through to his cot. As he went through to the living room, the motorised shutters were rising slowly, and light was advancing into the room from the patio doors towards the centre. Sarah stood waiting for him, a notebook in her hand.

'Good job you took those.'

'Come on, Bob, it's a reflex with me at autopsies. It helps keep my mind on the job. Do you think I never get squeamish over some of the things I see. Remember that time in Advocates Close?'

Skinner looked at her in silence. 'Then you do a hell of a job of covering it up, my darling – even from me. The boys and girls all think you're superhuman, the way you've kept your cool, especially among some of the messes we've had to clear up.'

She flicked the notepad open. 'Here they are. Don't know what good you expect they'll do, though. Just an hour ago we were both agreed it could only be suicide. Are you sure you aren't just grasping at this dog theory like a straw, to humour me?'

'Come on, girl, what sort of a copper do you think I am? Listen, I was there. I saw that dog. It's a big friendly mutt, but when I got there it seemed terrified – of me. Barking, snarling, all the rest. As soon as it saw I was a friend, it was fine. It more or less pointed me, believe this or not, towards the garage. And those feeding bowls were bone dry.'

'Couldn't they have dried out in the sun?'

Skinner shook his head emphatically. 'They were well in the shade. Believe me. That was a friendly, well-fed, well-groomed animal, treated kindly, just like Carlos said. And it was Santi who treated it that way. Gloria doesn't like dogs. Believe me, he thought as much of the mongrel as he did of his grass. If he switched on the lawn sprinkler, he'd have fed the dog too ... unless someone stopped him. So, Professor, my forensic genius of a wife, since what I'm saying *is* what happened, I want you to work out, from those notes, a picture of

130

how it was done. Once you've done that, we'll get around to finding out who did it, and why.'

Sarah looked at him doubtfully. 'Christ, you don't want much. You want me to make bricks, give me some straw. There ain't none in here that I can see.'

'Nonetheless, let's go for it.'

'Okay. Let's go outside.' Sarah led the way outside to the patio. Bob made a diversion via the kitchen to fetch two beers. They sat side-by-side at the white table, facing the mountains. Sarah read through her notes, then read then again.

'Cause of death,' said Bob. 'Is there any chance that he was strangled manually by someone, and then hung up there as dead meat.'

Sarah shook her head. 'Absolutely no indication of any other ligature being applied. Remember, too, the strands of rope under the fingernails.'

'That's true. And there was that oily footmark on the chair, matching the smear on Alberni's shoe. So let's take that as certain: he died by hanging. So someone strung him up. How many would it take?'

'At least two, obviously. To control him, and to hoist him up on to that chair.'

'Alberni wasn't very big, but he'd have put up some sort of a struggle. Surely they'd have had to pop him one to keep him quiet. There were no other signs of injury, no bruising, no bang on the head?'

'No, absolutely none. We looked, believe me. If he'd been hit, anywhere, between his toes even, that guy Martinez would have found it. The only unusual things we found were, as I told you, those funny marks on his upper arms.' She picked up her Estrella and took a swig. 'Bob. Go. Vamoose. Have a swim. Change a diaper. Anything at all, but just go and leave me here for a few minutes to try and figure this one out. Go. Scoot!'

Thus bidden, Bob stood up, slipped off his shirt and the shorts which he wore over his trunks, sauntered around to the side of the house, and plunged into the small pool. He swam its short length, backward and forward, until he lost count, then floated for a while on his back in the sun. 'This time next year, maybe Jazz'll be in here with me.' They had decided that the baby would be taught to swim naturally, even before he could walk. Already, Sarah, a college swimming blue, had introduced him to the pool, and he had reacted with delight, taking his own buoyancy for granted, and splashing and kicking like a cygnet trying to fly.

131

Sarah broke into his daydream with her shout. 'Copper! Get back here!'

He hauled himself out of the pool at the deep end, and rejoined her at the table where she sat, hands clasped together on the closed notebook. There was an expression of satisfaction on her face which fell only a few points short of smugness.

'I think I've got it. Think I've built you something you can fly in. Sit down. I'll be back.' She disappeared into the house, and returned a few seconds later carrying a ball of string.

'Those marks on his arms could have been made by a rope.'

'How?'

'Like this. Stand up again. Ohh, you're still dripping!' She stepped round behind him with the string. The two guys; let's say they're waiting in the garage with their rope – which Gloria said *she'd* never seen before. She leaves. Santi comes out. They hear him turning on the lawn sprinkler. Then one of them makes a noise, maybe accidentally, probably deliberately. Santi goes into the garage. They grab him, and before he can do anything, they do this.'

She took the string and slipped it under and around Skinner's left arm, then across behind his back and around the right arm. She pulled sharply on the string, and he found that his arms were pinioned to his side.

'Okay, so far,' she continued. 'He's helpless, and they frog-march him over to beneath the maintenance pulley, where they've already set up the hanging rope and the chair. With this rope, they hoist him up on to the chair. He realises what's going to happen by now, and he's probably screaming bloody murder, but the villa is empty and isolated and there's only the dog to hear him. One of the guys holds him helpless; the other one slips the noose over his head, and kicks the chair away. They pull the other rope out from behind his back, then stand back and watch the poor man claw at the noose until he blacks out and dies. They take the other rope and they leave. Bingo.'

'How did they get there? How do they leave?'

'Very early, across the field behind the villa. They'd leave by the same way. Well?'

Skinner smiled at his wife. 'God, you're clever. With an instinct for planning like that, I hope you never get mad at me.' He nodded 'Yes, I'll buy it, all right. I want another word with Gloria. I'll do that this evening, then I'll take it to Arturo in the morning.'

'You'd *better* buy it. It's all you're gonna get.' She grinned at him wickedly. 'You could say your whole case is hanging on it!'

40

There was no answer to Bob's ring on the doorbell. A car, this time a battered Renault 5, stood in the driveway. The lawn sprinkler was on. A momentary shiver of apprehension rippled through him.

He walked around to the back of the house, treading softly. 'Gloria?' he called.

The area around the pool was neat and tidy, a far cry from the shambles which Bob had found on his first visit six days earlier. A single empty glass lay on the poolside table.

And then he saw it: a dark shape submerged below the sunlit shimmers of the pool, near the deep-end ladder. He took three long steps forward and readied himself to dive . . . only to pull himself up sharp as Gloria's head and shoulders broke the surface. She trod water and shook her hair loose from the side of her head, sending spray across Skinner's feet. Her eyes, previously squeezed tight together, opened first, then widened in surprise.

'Bob, how good to see you.' She caught hold of the poolside ledge with both hands, bracing her feet against the tiles beneath the surface. 'Would you like to swim?'

He smiled and shook his head. 'No, thank you. I've had some of that today. No, I just wanted another word about Santi. Come on out and I'll explain.' Suddenly he realised that she was wearing only a bikini bottom. 'Oh, I'm sorry. Look, I'll . . .'

She smiled at his momentary confusion. 'Bob, this is Spain. Just imagine that you're on the beach.' She swam over to the ladder and climbed out. 'Sit down, please. Would you like a drink?'

He nodded. 'Beer would be nice.' He looked after her as she walked towards the house. Dark-skinned, high-breasted, slim-waisted, moving with a natural elegance. Yes, he thought, a man's mind would have to be seriously unbalanced to leave a woman like that behind. He took a seat beside the table.

When she returned, she was wearing a short, pink towelling robe. Her wet black hair was pulled back and tied in a pony-tail. In her left hand she carried a bottle of Blanc Pescador, opened, and in the other a litre bottle of Damm Xibeca beer, glistening from the fridge, with a long glass upside down over its neck.

She handed the beer to Bob and refilled her glass on the table, as he unscrewed the Xibeca and poured himself a drink.

'So,' she said, settling into her chair. 'What was it that you wanted to ask me?'

He was about to answer, when a thought struck him. 'Hey, where's the dog?'

She smiled. 'Was that it? My father took Romario back to Tarragona with him. He likes dogs, too; he'll give him a good home.'

'That's fine. But, no, that wasn't my worry. Gloria, without being critical of my friends in the Guardia, because I understand the reasons for it, I'm still a bit concerned at the speed with which this whole thing has been put to rest.'

She nodded vigorously. 'So am I. Santi didn't kill himself and, however it looks, I can't believe he was a thief. That money in the safe, that Ainscow has been allowed to keep. Can anyone say that it ever came from InterCosta? Could I not have said that it was mine, that I had won it in the Casino?'

'Not if you didn't. In any case, that's history now. The Guardia have given the cash to Ainscow, and you won't see it again. What d'you think of Ainscow?'

'I have nothing against him. Santi always got on well with him, in business. Officially they were partners, but Ainscow was the boss. A few times we went to dinner with him, and once or twice he had ladies here, from Scotland. Except I did not think they were ladies. I thought they were more like *putas* ... what would you say?'

'Tarts,' said Skinner. She nodded.

'*Si*, that is the word. Then I did not like Paul ... But, no, with InterCosta they had no problems that Santi ever spoke of, although he never spoke to me much of InterCosta – or any of his other business.'

'Did he have other business?'

'Well, that may be too big a description for it. There were one or two friends that he would help, or advise. Not buyers, not holiday people.' She paused. 'You do not take offence at that, Bob?'

He smiled. 'Not at all. I *am* a holiday person, and for a while longer, too. What sort of friends?'

'Local people looking for homes, looking for places to rent. Tony and Maria who were here a week ago, they were two of them. Santi found them an apartment when they were getting married. There are people who come here and buy property, then prefer to rent it out long-term, through local agents to local families, rather than to put it

on the holiday market. Okay, the weekly rent for holidays is high in the summer, but in the winter there is nothing. Overall, renting to local people is more solid income. They take better care of your property, too. Santi knew many of these owners, and people used to come to him. He never took money for helping them. But if they owned a bar, then there would be free drinks; or if someone's father owned a restaurant, then there would be a big piece off the bill; or if someone was an electrician . . . A favour for a favour, you would say.'

'There's no chance that Santi might have seen himself as a Robin Hood, and have been helping some of these people with InterCosta money?'

'No. I know most of these people. They wouldn't have taken it – any more than he would have taken money from them.'

'How about the other side: the property owners?'

'There were a few; most of them had only one or two apartments. The rental agents here are mostly interested only in holidays. It was known that Santi could place local people, and so some investors would ask him to manage their properties, through InterCosta, because of the good long-term renters he could find.'

'Does anyone stand out among these people?'

She thought for a second or two. 'Well, the biggest would be Nick Vaudan, but he is not an InterCosta client. He manages his own properties. He has a company, Montgo SA, to actually own them.'

'Do you know anything about him?'

'I've met him a few times. Friendly guy, *machismo* sort of guy. He's half French, and I think the other half is Greek. He lives in the south of France, when he is not here. Property is not his main business, according to Santi. The rest is something to do with boats. Here he owns maybe twelve, maybe fifteen, apartments and small villas. Santi used to give him advice on properties he was thinking of buying.'

'Was that on a professional basis?'

'No, no. Santi was very honourable. He would never do anything for money outside InterCosta. Nick did him favours, though. The biggest was getting us this place.'

'How did he do that?'

Gloria paused to refill her glass, and Skinner poured himself another glass of Xibeca, before screwing the cap tight on what was left in the bottle. Beyond the villa, the sun was beginning to sink towards the hilly horizon.

'The man who built this house was greedy. We made him an offer that we thought was fair, but we needed a mortgage. So he said, "No, you take loan, so someone else take bigger loan. I get my price." That's the Catalan way with property. Tony mentioned this to Nick, and Nick goes to the builder. He shows him cash. The developer can't resist. Nick buys the place next day, for cash, at less than the price we were offering, but still way above the declared value, so the builder can maybe, if he wants, cheat on his income taxes. The day after that, he sells it to us at the same price. We pay the *notario* fees and the IVA on both sides, so Nick isn't out of pocket. Then Montgo SA buys our previous villa, a little one, at the price we ask, as an investment property.'

'Sounds like a very decent guy.'

'He is. He was at the funeral. In fact he was here, afterwards. I think I saw Sarah speak to him.'

'Is he still in town?'

'As far as I know. He came down for the funeral, and I think he said he was staying for another two weeks.'

'Where does he live?'

'Punta Montgo, but I don't know which house. He has an office, though. A very small one. Somewhere off the Riells road, near the beach.'

'Okay,' said Skinner, finishing his beer. 'I'll try to persuade Pujol to talk to him. To see if he can think of anyone who might have had a major grudge against your husband. Cause, just between you and me, Gloria, I agree with you. I don't think Santi killed himself, either. But don't build your hopes up because, between what we think and what the Guardia Civil will accept as true, there lies a gap as wide as that blue bay over there! Now, you'd better get inside, and I must be off. It's drying time for you, but it's bathtime for Jazz!'

41

'Grgrgrgrg!'

It was a small squeal. Bob and Sarah looked at each other across the bath, mouths slightly agape with surprise. Bob filled the soft sponge with water, held it over Jazz and squeezed once more, directing the water towards the centre of his long soft belly.

'Grgrgrgrgrgrgrgrgrg!' As the stream splashed into his navel, the baby kicked his legs furiously, splashing water over the side of the plastic bath and on to the floor of his bedroom. And his mouth opened wide in unmistakable delight, showing an expanse of toothless gums.

'He's laughing! Look he's smiling. Sarah, should he be laughing out loud at this age?'

She grinned. 'Why the hell not? He obviously finds you pretty funny.'

Bob beamed at the sudden development of his son's vocal range, and he sent another stream of bath water cascading over his midriff.

'Grgrgrgrgrgrgrgrgrgrgrgrg!'

Bathtime for Jazz had become an essential part of the Skinner family's daily ritual. Sarah and Bob had agreed, in considering their parenthood, that, however busy each might be professionally, it would be their cardinal rule that father and mother would do all in their power to be at home every evening, if only for that special time.

As Bob lifted him out of the cooling water, the baby gave a small whimper of annoyance. But as Sarah took him, wrapping him in the folds of a soft yellow towel, the smile returned. She dried him gently, rocking him in her arms and speaking softly to him. The child nuzzled, contented, against her shoulder.

Bob watched her from a chair in the corner of the room, as she completed the process of drying, dusting, oiling and dressing for the night. 'Okay, chum,' she said eventually. 'Let's you and Mom take a walk on the terrace while Daddy makes up those rusks.'

Half an hour later they were seated in the living room. Bob held the baby, fed to the point of contentment, and rubbed his back very gently between the shoulder-blades, until he heard the soft rumble of breaking wind.

'That it?' asked Sarah.

'Yes,' Bob said, quietly. 'Let's give him a minute, then I'll put him to bed.'

Sarah left the room and returned with two flutes of pink *cava*. She put one on a small table within Bob's reach, holding her own glass as she settled on the couch alongside him.

'So how was your talk with Gloria?'

'Worthwhile.' He paused. 'So who was this bloke who was chatting you up at the villa after the funeral, then?' He glanced down at her.

For a second she looked puzzled, until recollection came. Bob saw to his surprise that, for an instant, she flushed.

'The amorous Monsieur Nicolas Vaudan, you mean? I didn't realise that Gloria had overheard us.'

'She didn't. I was joking. D'you mean the guy really was chatting you up?'

She nodded. 'Yes. Why not?' she said slightly defensively. 'Most men take it as a compliment when someone else finds their wife attractive.'

'Within reason. Was the guy out of order?'

'Not really, for a Frenchman. Sexually aggressive, Alex would say. Par for the course, really.'

'Not with my wife, it isn't. Anyway, he's only half French, so he's nowhere near par. What'd he say?'

She smiled, self-consciously this time. 'Nothing much. He just came up and introduced himself. I didn't say who I was, and he clearly didn't know. The usual small talk, then the usual "Madame, even in black *vous êtes tres belle*." Then he told me I had beautiful eyes, and bet me they were bedroom eyes.'

A heavy frown gathered on Bob's forehead. 'So what did you say?'

'You know me. I said "How perceptive. Come on!" No, I said, "If I do, Monsieur, then I flash them only at my husband." And then I told him how I came to be there, the story of how you found Santi. I told him that you were a policeman from Scotland – a very senior policeman, I said; a very large and strong policeman, I even added for good measure – but he was well under control by that time. The guy had the decency to act embarrassed, and to become apologetic. After that he couldn't have been nicer.'

Bob was mollified. 'You didn't tell him why I had gone to see Santi, did you?'

'I said you were enquiring about a property for a friend: a small lie, but not too far from the truth. Why d'you ask that?'

'Because I'm going to ask Arturo to visit him, and go along with him myself, if he'll let me. What language did you use?'

'English. His was better than my French.'

'Not Spanish?'

'No. He told me that he spoke five languages fluently, but that Spanish was his one blind spot.'

Skinner grunted. 'Know what he means.'

Jazz, still on his shoulder, made a soft sound.

Sarah looked at him. 'He's out. Here, gimme him. I'll put him to bed. While I'm doing that, you can make a start on those desperately ugly fish that you bought.'

'The monkfish? You love monkfish.'

'Yes, but off the bone. You always buy them whole. Those faces, those mouths, those teeth, those eyes. Uggh!'

'Yeah!' Bob grinned. 'Hey!' he called to her retreating back. 'Wonder if lady monkfish have bedroom eyes, too!'

42

'Bob, my amigo. I know of your reputation as a policeman and as a detective. I have heard of some of the things you have done. But this idea of yours – if I were to reopen the investigation of the death of Alberni on that basis alone, it would stir up a nest of hornets.'

'Come on, Arturo. I've told you how it was done.'

The Commandante was seated in uniform behind a file-covered desk in his small dark office at the rear of the five-storey yellow-brick Guardia Civil building on the crest of Avinguda Girona. Slowly and deliberately, he shook his head.

'No, you have not. You have told me what you think. And Sarah, very clever also in her field, has produced an explanation to fit your theory. You and I have discussed the matter. You agreed with my reasons for taking it no further. Those reasons have not changed.'

'But, man, if we're talking about murder now—'

'*You* are talking about murder, Bob. I am not. The Guardia has said it was suicide. The magistrate has said it was suicide. I cannot argue with him without a very good reason, and you have not given me one.'

Pujol paused. 'You have to allow me to be selfish, Bob. I have my career to consider. My superiors would look at me in a very strange way if I did as you ask.'

Skinner shrugged his shoulders in resignation. 'Okay, Arturo. I hear all of that. I won't press you further.'

Pujol smiled. 'That is good.' He paused. 'Of course, if you were in a position to offer me more conclusive information . . .'

Skinner's eyes narrowed slightly. 'And how would I come by that?'

Pujol shrugged in his turn. 'Well, you are a private citizen. I cannot stop you from asking questions of anyone. But I cannot be seen to be lending you authority, you understand.'

Skinner nodded, a light smile flicking the corners of his mouth. 'I understand.' The smile widened. 'In that case, there are one or two things I'd like to ask you!'

'Hah! The investigator is at work already! Very well, what can I tell you?'

'D'you know a man named Nicolas Vaudan?'

Pujol thought for a moment. '*Si*. I know him as I know most people with business interests in L'Escala. He is an *extranjero* from France. I know of him rather than knowing him in person.'

Skinner cut in. 'The south of France, or so I'm told. But go on. What d'you know about him?'

'Not very much. He has a company which makes investments in *immobiliara* – apartments and villas – and rents them to local people at very reasonable cost. One of my officers is his tenant, and I have never heard him speak badly of him.'

'Where's his company based?'

'Montgo SA? It has a small office in the *edificio* in the marina which looks towards L'Escala. Close to the Café Navili.'

Skinner nodded. 'Yes, I know where you mean. Does Vaudan have many associates in L'Escala?'

'He has a secretary who looks after his business here: collecting rent from tenants, and dealing with any problems they have. Her name is Veronica. She is Belgian, I think, and she is very nice. Also there is Paco – Paco Garcia. He is from L'Escala, and he does small things – odd jobs, you would say – for Señor Vaudan around his properties. He paints, fixes the water pipes when they need to be replaced, mends broken tiles, things like that. Paco is a simple fellow: big, clumsy. When Señor Vaudan is here, I often see them together, Paco following after him like a big dog.' From nowhere an image of Tony Manson and Lennie Plenderleith swam into Skinner's mind. He pushed it away and concentrated on Pujol.

'Is Vaudan married?'

'Yes, I think so. I don't know for certain, but I did hear it said once that there is a Madame Vaudan – but that she is very grand, very much of the Côte d'Azur, and does not like it here.'

'Apart from business, does he have many friends here?'

'None come to my mind. Sometimes, when he is here and I drive past, I see him sitting on the terrace of the Club Nautic, but apart from that I do not know what he does or who he sees.'

'D'you ever see him with Santi Alberni?'

Pujol shook his head emphatically. 'No.'

'Or hear of any links between them?'

'Never.'

'I take it that Vaudan and his people aren't known to you officially, so to speak.'

'Señor Vaudan and Veronica, certainly not. Paco Garcia is slightly different. In the past we have suspected that he might be involved in minor crimes, mostly smuggling. When he was younger, he was a bit . . .' Pujol struggled for the English expression.

'Wild?'

'*Si*. But now now he is harmless, I judge.'

Skinner leaned back in his chair and stretched himself. 'Well, thanks for that, Arturo. I think I'll go for a stroll in the sun. And who knows, it might take me down past the Café Navili.' He stood up and gestured with a thumb at the files heaped on the small desk. 'I'll leave you to get on with that lot. I sympathise with you. Back home I have an intray too.'

'*Si*,' said Pujol, showing him to the door. 'And you will have someone to empty it for you also. Here, I do my own dirty work. Good day, my friend, and good luck with your theory. But as you try to prove it, please try not to make too many splashes!'

43

Skinner almost walked past the man. He was seated on the terrace of the Café Navili, in a cane chair in the shade, looking out across Riells Bay as it glistened in the morning sun. He was alone; a black Americano coffee and a croissant lay before him on the marble-topped table.

The tall policeman glanced at him, then looked ahead, searching for the Montgo SA office. He saw what he thought might be it, just before the walkway took a right turn, and was about to lengthen his stride when the memory came back to him. A slim, sleek man, immaculately suited, with gold-framed spectacles, jet-black hair and a neatly-trimmed moustache, standing a little way from him at Santi's funeral, quite close to Carlos.

Skinner stopped and turned towards the figure and, as he did so, the man picked up a newspaper from beside his chair. Skinner saw that it was French. He stepped up to the table.

'Monsieur Vaudan?'

Surprised, the man looked up. Skinner had a flashing impression of cold, cruel, dark eyes – threatening eyes, dangerous eyes – but then they blinked and, in that instant, softened.

'*Oui.*' The response was cautious.

'I thought I recognised you from Santi Alberni's funeral. I'm Bob Skinner.'

Vaudan sprang lithely to his feet, extending his hand.

Skinner shook it and felt a strong grip testing his own. He returned it with equal, but no greater, force. The man was, he guessed, around forty, but he moved with the ease of one who made a point of maintaining maximum fitness. He stood around six feet tall. He wore tan slacks and a tailored cotton shirt which gave emphasis to powerful shoulders.

'Monsieur Skinner, I am pleased to meet you. I spoke with your wife after Santi's funeral, at the villa.' His expression seemed to be probing, trying to establish whether his new acquaintance might have intentions which were other than friendly. 'Perhaps she told you.'

Skinner smiled and looked the man straight in his dark eyes. He nodded. 'Yes, she told me.'

A silence hung between the two men for a few seconds. Skinner supposed that Vaudan was trying to guess whether Sarah had told him of his clumsy pass, and whether he should offer an apology. Bob decided to let him off that hook. 'You're from the Côte d'Azur, she said.'

Vaudan relaxed appreciably. 'Yes, that is my home now. But I have lived in other parts of France – and in Greece. My mother was from Athens. Come, sit down, please.' He pulled one of the cane chairs up to his table. 'You will have coffee? Croissants?'

'Coffee, yes, thank you. *Cortado*. Croissants, no. I make it a rule to eat only one breakfast a day.' He sat down at the table as Vaudan leaned through the service hatch to the bar and called for the waiter. Skinner's *cortado* ordered, he returned to join him.

'I understand that you had the misfortune to find poor Santi hanging in his garage. I know from your wife that you are a policeman, but that must have given even you a great shock.'

Skinner nodded his grey mane. 'Normally, when you walk into a garage, you expect to find a car. But in my time I've seen a few people end up like that, and in other violent ways. It's always ugly.'

Vaudan nodded. 'It is not something in which I am experienced, but I can imagine. Did you know Santi well?'

'No, I'd never met him. I went looking for him on business that same morning. Gloria tells me that you were a good friend of theirs, though. She told me how you helped them with their villa.'

Vaudan's smile seemed genuinely self-deprecating. 'One does what one can to help a friend.'

'You were that close?'

'I'm a nice guy.' Vaudan smiled, but Skinner this time did not return it.

'You have a company here, don't you?'

'*Oui*. Montgo SA. Just a little property investment. It brings me some nice rental income.'

'Is that your main interest?'

Vaudan shook his head. 'Oh no. Far from it. This is just a sideline, something to cover the cost of maintaining my villa here. In everything I do, Mr Skinner, I am a businessman. My main activity is in boats, luxury vessels. I am a broker: I buy and sell yachts and cruisers of all sorts. I have a number of dealerships in Monaco for major manufacturers. Big, big, money – international money. For such an operation, Monaco is the ideal base. As well as buying and selling, I have a number of cruisers which are available for charter.'

'Around here?'

'No. Frankly there is not enough money here to make such an operation pay. I do some brokerage in Spain, but my chartering is done out of Monte Carlo, and in the Aegean and eastern Mediterranean.'

'That's very interesting.' A white-coated waiter arrived with Skinner's *cortado*, always served at the Navili in a cup rather than in the usual small glass. He took a sip, and tasted its sharp bite.

'Did you know much about Santi's business?'

'InterCosta? No. Why do you ask?'

'Gloria hasn't said anything to you?'

'No. What would she say?'

Skinner looked the man in the eye once more. 'In confidence, yes?' Vaudan nodded. 'The thing I went to see Santi about wasn't just a property matter; it was police business as well. A man came to see me in Scotland, complaining that he had been involved in a deal with InterCosta, and that some of the money had disappeared. It looked like a clear case of fraud by the company. I interviewed Santi's partner, Ainscow. He showed me certain evidence which pointed to Santi, and I was going to interview him, with the approval of the Guardia, when I found him dead.

'Since then the InterCosta accounts have been examined and it seems clear that Santi was ripping it off for years. The trouble is, it was done very simply but very cleverly. We found *some* money, but we don't know where the rest is. My continuing interest, as a policeman, is that this business is half-British, and that a British subject has been defrauded. Maybe there are others. Ainscow's prepared to forget about it but, as a policeman, if I see a crime I have a duty to investigate.'

Vaudan nodded. 'Of course, of course.' Skinner felt an edge of concern in his companion. He decided to turn on a little heat. 'Apart from your friendship with Alberni, how strong were your business links?'

'Monsieur, what business links? We were friends.'

'That's not what Gloria told me.' He leaned towards Vaudan, his right forearm resting on the table. 'Look, I'll be frank. I didn't just happen past here this morning. I was on my way to your office. I'm the sort of copper who doesn't put an investigation to bed with lots of questions still unanswered. And, believe me, there are many questions unanswered about the death of Santi Alberni. For example, I'd like to know how come, if Alberni had ripped off a couple of hundred million pesetas from InterCosta, he still died heavily in debt. I'd like to know where all that money went to, because no one has a fucking clue. And, Monsieur Vaudan, I'd like to know, without being fed any more nice-guy crap, what sort of a link there was between you and Alberni to make you risk, I'd guess, around twenty million pesetas of your own to help him buy his new house. Why, for God's sake, if he had stolen all that cash, did he need your help in the first place?

'When I have good answers to all these questions, and a few more, I may start to believe that Santi Alberni strung himself up in his garage. Until I do, I'm inclined to the view that he had some help. Now, my new friend, what do you have to tell me to ease my troubled mind?'

For almost half a minute the Frenchman sat silent, staring out across the sunlit bay towards the high-rise blocks of the Passeig Maritim. And then he turned to face Skinner, and in the dark eyes the coldness and the danger showed once more, with something new: a strange smugness emphasised by the man's confident smile.

'All right, Skinner. All right. I could make you jump through a few hoops for your answers but, hell, it's a nice day and I have better things to do. I'll give you some answers. But I do not think you will like them. I'm going to say all these things just once, with no one but you and me to hear them, and then I will never repeat them. Have a beer while you listen. You may need it.'

He rose and walked back over to the hatch. 'Juan, *deux bieres, si'l vous plaît. Pression.*' He waited while the barman poured two glasses of St Miguel from its ornate tap, and carried them back to the table, one cupped in each hand.

'This is a wonderful place, L'Escala, is it not?' He settled back into his chair and took a generous mouthful of St Miguel. The creamy head left a white shadow on his moustache. He wiped it off with the back of his hand.

'I came here for the first time around ten years ago. I had sold a cruiser to a man in Monaco, and had agreed to deliver it to L'Escala, where his brother would berth it and look after it for him. I brought it across myself, and spent a day or two training the brother in its ways. I took to the place at once. I had been looking for a second home, somewhere outside France, and when my client told me of a building plot for sale at Punta Montgo, I was interested in it. Santi Alberni was the agent for the owner. He was very young. It was a prime site, perched on the hill, but difficult to build on. Because of that I was able to beat Santi down on the price. I bought it there and then for cash, for less than half the profit on that one cruiser deal. I was paid for the boat on delivery, in dollars, and I gave the rest of the money to Santi to find me an architect and builder. He did a good job, and less than a year later my wife and I took over my new villa. I have to say that she hated L'Escala as much as I love it. However, I bought her an apartment in Rome, and she was happy. Now she has hers, I have mine, and we have *ours* near Cannes.'

He paused for another swig of beer. 'Santi and I would bump into each other when I was here, but we were not what you would call close friends. Then one day, around seven years ago, he came up to the villa and put a business proposition to me. He told me that InterCosta was making very good profits, and that it tore at his heart to have to give any of them to the taxman. He said that his accountant had advised him that if he converted his share into cash and reinvested it somewhere else, the taxman would never catch up with the money. It would simply be written through the company books as disbursements, and both company tax and income tax would be avoided.

'He asked me if I would act as the front man in a new company through which this cash profit from InterCosta would be laundered and turned into long-term investments in property. He said that, as a foreign national, I would be less likely to be asked to explain where the cash had come from. I asked him who would own the new company. He said that officially it would be in my name, but that there would be a letter of agreement between us confirming Santi's ownership of the shares. I asked him what would be in it for me, and we settled on half the net rental income. The idea was that the properties would be held for not less than ten years from the date of acquisition, and indefinitely if they were good enough.

'We shook hands on the deal, and Montgo SA was formed, in my name, with no traceable link to Santi. Straight away Santi began to deposit large chunks of cash in the company safe. He would bank them at intervals, or sometimes he would buy properties for straight cash. Gradually, as Montgo SA's portfolio built up, so did its income. We took office costs out of that, and kept back an amount for property maintenance and other contingencies. The rest we split between us.'

'How much?' asked Skinner.

'At first, hardly anything. Then it began to build up. It has never been big money though. Montgo SA is a good landlord. We charge on average around eighty thousand pesetas per month in rent for good-quality accommodation – no rubbish. In the summer people will pay more than that here for a week's rental. Take off office costs, which are peanuts, and our contingency funding, and I would say that over the years Santi and I have split around twelve million pesetas between us.'

'What did you do with your slice?'

'I kept it in cash, and used it to pay for the maintenance of my villa here.'

'How big is the contingency fund?'

'Eighteen million. We used the contingency money to do the deal on Santi's villa.' Vaudan grinned. 'Well I *was* a nice guy. I agreed to it, and half that cash was mine! What if his mortgage had fallen through?'

'How much has been laundered through Montgo in those seven years?'

'Roughly around one hundred million pesetas.'

'Half a million sterling. Are you sure?'

Vaudan nodded. 'Certain. I don't make mistakes about money. Why?'

'Because that's maybe half of the cash that's been stripped out of InterCosta. Are you involved in any other companies with Alberni?'

'No, thank you. One was quite enough; an amusement, and a neat source of peseta cash-flow. Two would begin to resemble hard work.'

'Did you know of any other money laundries that he might have set up?'

Vaudan hesitated. 'Once or twice he mentioned an Englishman named Eensh.'

'What?'

'Eensh. I-N-C-H. Alan Eensh. I believe he works in Torroella as a property salesman. Santi spoke of him once and said that he had another interest, a company called Torroella Locals. It was like Montgo, only it didn't buy houses. It bought shops along the Costa at knock-down prices, and let them for high rents to short-term businesses – ice-cream parlours, video arcades, sports clothing, fashion. Santi never said, but I always suspected that he might have been funding Monsieur Eensh also.'

'Who does Inch work for in Torroella?'

'A general agency called Immobiliara Brava. It has an office in the old town near the square.'

Skinner nodded, noting the name mentally. 'How well d'you know Paul Ainscow?'

'Not at all. Earlier you called him Santi's partner. That is not what Santi told me. He said that Ainscow was not more than an employee, or an agent, working on salary and commission, and that all of the profit that he was diverting from InterCosta belonged to Santi.'

'You believed that?'

'Why not? Santi was my friend. Why should I think him a liar?'

'And you didn't have any scruples about being involved in a scheme that you knew was set up for tax-evasion purposes?'

'Monsieur Skinner, this is Spain. One of the blackest economies in Europe. Tax evasion in business is a way of life. As for me, I do not do business in Monaco so that I can pay high taxes. Rather the opposite. Think of it, man, *I* am not a burden to anyone else in this world, therefore why should I work to pay the salaries of people like you, and the millions like you on the public payroll.' The suddenness of Vaudan's contempt took Skinner by surprise.

His eyes flashed in anger, but he checked himself. 'What makes you so fucking special that you shouldn't?'

Vaudan laughed softly. 'Friend, I pay my dues. I simply make sure that they are as low as possible. Check me out. You won't get your hands dirty.'

'I may take you up on that,' Skinner said evenly.

'Now, about Ainscow. You're telling me you didn't know he was the major partner in InterCosta?'

'*Oui*. As I said, I've never met the man. He means nothing to me.'

'Now that you do know, what will you do with Montgo SA?'

'Why should I do anything?'

'Because what you've told me means that seventy-five per cent of it belongs to Ainscow, and the other quarter to Gloria Alberni.'

Vaudan shook his head. 'Oh no, *monsieur*. The record says that I am the owner and administrator of Montgo SA and all its assets.'

'What about the letter you mentioned earlier? The one which confirms Santi's legal ownership?'

Vaudan's smile was at its widest, stretching the moustache and revealing an expanse of white teeth. 'Did the Guardia find a copy among his papers?'

'No, not that I know of. What about *your* copy?'

'Hah. Life is strange. A few weeks ago, on my last visit here, I was arranging some papers on my terrace. My copy of the letter was among them. I have never known a *tramuntana* to spring up so quickly. A few seconds, that was all it took, and they were gone on the wind, all of them, the Montgo SA letter among them. Gone and never seen again.'

Skinner looked at him. Now he understood his air of confidence.

'Let me guess, because of the nature of the thing, it was a private letter prepared by a lawyer, but not signed before the notary.'

'*Exactement*. And so, my friend the policeman, if Ainscow or anyone else wants to talk to me about the legal ownership of Montgo SA, they had better come with Santi's copy of that letter.'

He picked up his glass from the table and drained it. 'But what letter would that be, anyway? One of which I have never heard. I meant what I said earlier. I will never speak of this again, to you or anyone else. Poor Santi, I am sorry that he chose that way out of his problem with Monsieur Ainscow. But that is life's way: it is filled with winners and losers. Santi lost, but out of it Nick Vaudan seems to have won.'

He made to rise, but Skinner grabbed his arm, and held him in his chair.

'Sit down, pal. If what you've told me is true, it also says to me that Nick Vaudan had a first-class motive for helping Santi – proactively, you might say – to commit suicide.'

Vaudan shook his hand away. 'If you check you will find that at the time of Santi's death I was in Monaco selling a very large yacht to a very well-known oil sheikh.'

Skinner nodded. 'Maybe, but some people have long arms.'

'Not me, my friend.' Vaudan looked him coolly, disturbingly, in the eye as he spoke. 'If you think that someone killed Alberni, you'd better look some place else. I didn't do it. That is my word on it, and you can take it to the bank. Now I have no more to say to you. Ever.'

Skinner stood up. 'I'm all talked out too, Vaudan. There is just one other thing, though.' He picked up his beer which lay untouched on the table. 'A poor public servant like me couldn't be seen taking a drink from a guy like you. Corruption is all too easily alleged.' With a flick of the wrist, he emptied the contents of the glass into Vaudan's lap.

The man started from his seat, his expression suddenly twisted into one of anger. He seemed ready to spring.

'Yes?' Skinner hissed the word as he stood waiting for him, a smile on his face and an invitation in his eyes; an invitation which Vaudan decided it would be much better not to accept. Lazily Skinner reached out with his left hand and pushed him back into his chair. 'Stay cool, Nick. And, by the way, if you ever make a pass at my wife again, your interest in sex will become academic, very suddenly. See you again.'

150

44

'Brian? Skinner here. I've got a job for you. I want you to run a check with the French police on a man named Nicolas Vaudan.' He spelled out the name. 'He lives on the Riviera with his wife. They also own an apartment in Rome, possibly in her name. He's in the boat business. Deals in high-value yachts and cruisers, and also runs charters. I want to know everything about him and about his business. Has he any convictions, has he ever been arrested, has he ever been investigated for any crime, does he pay his parking tickets quickly...? Everything they can dig up on him. I want to know about his business too. Ask them to check all filed accounts, and to look in particular at his tax affairs.'

He paused to listen. 'Yes, the Guardia could do this, Brian, but they have their reasons for not wanting to get involved. So you use your international contacts to get it moving, and fax me a report as soon as you can . . . Yes, I said fax. The way things are going here, it'll be an asset. I'm taking Sarah and the baby to Girona this afternoon to buy one.'

'Bob?' Sarah's voice sounded from the living room as Skinner replaced the phone in the hall.

'Yes, honey, it's me.'

'I didn't hear you come in. I was dozing on the terrace. Who were you talking to? What were you saying about a fax? What's the time? God, you've been ages.'

'Question one, Brian Mackie – and question two, get ready for Hipercort. We're going shopping.'

'Okay, but first tell me what you've been up to. Did you see Arturo?'

'Yes, and then I had a long talk with your admirer, Vaudan. Smart bastard – or he thinks he is.'

Quickly he related Vaudan's account of Santi's involvement with Montgo SA, and of the missing letters.

'He's a cute operator, is our Nick. And very confident. I need to talk to Gloria about that document.'

151

'Then you'll get your chance tonight. You and I are going to La Clota for dinner, *à deux*, and Gloria's baby-sitting. Now, if we're going to Girona, let's get ready.'

45

The Panasonic tele/fax with integral answerphone was installed and tested by eight p.m. when Gloria arrived to baby-sit. It stood, white and gleaming, on a table in the living room. Gloria looked at it in surprise.

'Keeps me in touch with the office,' offered Bob. 'Come on through, why don't you.' He led the way through the living room to the terrace. 'Sarah's got the wee fella plugged in in the bedroom. He's all groomed and ready for bed, so with a touch of luck you won't see any action. Have a seat. While we're waiting, there are a couple of things I'd like to ask you.'

Gloria turned a chair round to face the sun, and sat down. It was just after seven-thirty. The customary evening clouds were building on the horizon, but the day was still warm. Bob handed his guest a glass of white wine from a bottle in the ice-bucket and offered her olives from a wide, flat dish.

'I went to see Nick Vaudan today. Gloria, did you ever have any reason to believe that Santi might have had a stake in Montgo SA, or that he might have been the beneficial owner of the company, with Vaudan as a nominee shareholder?'

She looked at him, incredulous. 'Whoever told you that?'

'That's Vaudan's story. He says that the Montgo property portfolio was bought with cash stripped out of InterCosta by Santi.'

'That's crazy. Santi died with hardly a peseta to his name.'

'What about the five million in the safe? According to Vaudan's story, that could have been his share of the profit from Montgo.'

Gloria lowered her eyes, bit her lip and shook her head.

'All right,' said Skinner gently. 'Let me ask you, when you went through Santi's papers, did you find a letter referring to Vaudan, or to Montgo, the company? It would probably have been drafted by a lawyer and would have been on his stationery.'

'No. Nothing like that.'

'Did Santi ever talk to you at all about Montgo SA.'

The woman's face brightened. 'Yes. Yes, he did once. He told me that he understood from Vaudan that the money which he used to buy those properties came in cash from boat sales in Spain. It was so that he would not have to pay tax anywhere. He said that when he sold Nick the site for his villa, then found him a builder, that was how he paid.'

'Yes,' said Skinner, 'that at least squares with Vaudan's account. When Santi told you this, did you feel that he believed it to be true?'

Gloria looked hurt. 'Bob, Santi never told me a lie in his life. Of course he believed it. Santi trusted people. If someone told him something, he would naturally accept it as true.'

'Okay. Let me ask you something else. Have you ever heard Santi mention a man named Inch.'

'*Que?*'

'Inch. I-N-C-H. From Torroella?'

'No, never.'

'Or a company called Torroella Locals?'

She shook her head. 'Never.'

Just then Sarah emerged from the villa. 'Hi, Gloria. Junior's just dropped off to sleep. He should stay under till we get back. If you do need us, the number's on the pin-board in the kitchen. We'll be as quick as we can.'

Gloria stood up from her chair. 'No, no, no, you enjoy. Jazz will be fine with me.'

As Bob and Sarah turned to go, Gloria called after them. 'Bob. What I told you, does that help?'

'I hope so, Gloria. But to be honest, even assuming that Santi has been framed, it's been bloody well done. Vaudan won't crack, that's for sure. It's about time for a touch of luck.'

46

At La Clota they were shown to their customary table under the awning, to the front of the terrace. Skinner looked across the roadway to Club Nautic. Vaudan was seated among a group scattered around the tables of the outdoor bar. Bob caught his eye, smiled and waved. The Frenchman, grim-faced, turned his chair around and set his back towards them.

'What went on between you two this morning?' Sarah asked. 'I thought you just had a chat with him. He looked at you there as if he'd like to kill you.'

'He probably would, but he's much too smart to try.'

'You didn't say anything about . . . ?'

Bob flashed her a sly smile. 'Who, me?'

They chose, as a starter, piping hot onion soup with an egg poached in its liquor, finally deciding on roast duck as a main course, in spite of the counter-attractions of the chef's special *fidua* – delicious but laden with garlic.

Bob was mopping up the last of his orange sauce with bread when Sarah asked him about his discussion with Gloria.

'How does it look?'

'To tell you the truth, love, it looks bloody awful. Vaudan's a smooth, opportunistic bastard, but his story is very plausible. Santi rips off InterCosta and washes the dough through Montgo SA, and through this other company. The twenty-five grand we found in Santi's safe could have been part of the profit split from one of those. Originally the idea is that Vaudan acts as a front, no questions asked, but now he finds himself in the box seat, with Santi gone, as the legal owner of a hundred million peseta property company. The thing that would prove it would be Santi's copy of the letter Vaudan talked about: the one confirming his ownership. But there's no trace of that and, of course, Vaudan says he's trashed his copy . . . as he would. More than that, if the letter existed – and if Vaudan's story is true – it's a cert that he's got hold of Santi's copy too, or he'd never have mentioned it.'

'Could Vaudan have . . . ?'

Skinner shook his head. 'No. He's got some sheikh as an alibi. I'm afraid that Santi, guilty or innocent, is well in the frame, and I can't see a way round it.'

Sarah sat silent for a while, while Bob ordered coffee. As the waiter disappeared back into the restaurant, she reached across the table and grasped her husband's hand. 'No, Bob. He didn't do it. Look, who understands a man better than his wife? Know what Gloria said to me about Santi? She said, "He was a great salesman, one of the best, but as a book-keeper, one of the worst." She looked after all the household accounts, and their family banking. Santi handled it when they were first married, but he was hopeless. Their affairs were a shambles. Does that sound like a clever and devious fraudster to you?'

'Depends how clever and devious he was. All that could have been an act – part of an elaborate cover.'

'Come on! You think that, you've been out in the sun too long. Santi was not a thief, and if he wasn't who was?'

'Paul Ainscow. But there's one big hole in that proposition. Ainscow had seventy-five per cent of the action. Why would he steal from himself? Also there's no link between Vaudan and Ainscow; there is between Vaudan and Santi. Sorry.'

'Ahh!' Sarah threw up her hands in exasperation. 'Look, I *know* Santi was murdered. Your heart tells you that's so. Maybe there *is* a link between Vaudan and Ainscow. Maybe Ainscow *had* a reason to steal from himself. You're the detective, so find out. Go the extra mile, Bob!'

He smiled at her persistence. 'Okay. But not the extra mile, the extra Inch. Alan Inch to be exact, of Torroella Locals. Tomorrow I'll pay him a visit. Let's see if he can help the cause.'

47

The new fax rolled out its first incoming message soon after eleven next morning, just as Bob and Sarah were about to leave for Torroella de Montgri. They heard the ring, and Bob was on his way to pick up the phone in the hall when the fax recognition system kicked in.

The message took only a few seconds to arrive, and was contained within two A4 pages. As always with Brian Mackie's communications, it was to the point. Its content came as no surprise to Skinner. Nicolas Vaudan had no criminal record of any sort, not even a speeding conviction. He had never been arrested or interviewed in connection with any crime. He was regarded with respect in the Monegasque business community, and included among his clients several members of European and Middle Eastern royal families. While his company was based in Monaco, he and his wife lived in Mougins, an exclusive suburb of Cannes, which boasted several major entertainment and sporting personalities among its residents.

His business record was equally pristine. There had once been a complaint that a used boat had been offered to a buyer as new, but that had been revealed to be the malicious work of a frustrated rival. Scrupulous accounts of Vaudan Marine were filed annually. Invariably they showed all stock accounted for, no long-term creditors and no bad debts. They showed the company to have been consistently turning in adequate, although not excessive profits, and that most of these were being invested openly in pension funds for Vaudan and his wife.

Both as a private citizen in France and as a company director in Monaco, Vaudan's tax affairs were similarly as spotless. He paid his taxes promptly and without complaint, and his returns were filed by the Monte Carlo office of one of the world's major accountancy firms.

Sarah watched Skinner's face as he read the fax, seeing a look of resignation settle in.

'No use?' she asked.

'No. Just as I expected. The guy's as clean as a whistle. He seemed far too confident for it to have turned out any other way. Whatever Santi may have been told, there was no way that this fellow was siphoning off profit, not recently anyway. Every deal, everywhere, is logged and accounted for, as I thought. A bloody dead end. Let's get along to Torroella and see if there's more joy to be had out of Mr Inch.'

48

They sat in the sun, on the new white plastic chairs outside Bar Isidre, in Torroella's town square, oblivious of the Sunday bustle around them, as they watched the sun creep westward to flood the old street at the foot of the sloping quadrangle. Outside a watchmaker's shop in the narrow thoroughfare, an LCD readout displayed time and temperature alternately.

They sat patiently waiting for the sun to have its effect on the device, to see how high the temperature would climb from its shade level of twenty-three degrees. 'Five hundred pesetas says it tops thirty-three,' said Sarah.

Bob licked a finger and held it up. He shook his head. 'No, there's a breeze. My five hundred says thirty-one.'

The thermometer soared. Each time the clock gave way to the centigrade reading, it had risen by another degree. Five minutes after the bet was struck, Bob fished a five-hundred-peseta piece from his pocket and slapped it on the table in front of Sarah. She punched the air, and cheered as the figure rose. Eventually it topped out at thirty-six degrees.

'Okay,' said Bob. 'Now that you've cleaned me out, I'm off to find Inch. Coming?'

Sarah shook her head. 'No. I like it here, and Jazz is fine in the shade of this awning.'

'Okay. I'll be as quick as I can.' Skinner headed off down the narrow street, passing under the temperature sign as it dropped to thirty-four degrees with the passage of the sun. He took the first turning to his right and found, much sooner than he had hoped, the office of Immobiliara Brava. He looked through the glass and saw three people inside: two women, one sitting at a desk and the other behind a counter, and a wiry, balding man with a deep walnut tan.

Skinner pushed the door open and stepped inside. '*Habla usted inglés?*' he asked, tentatively.

The little man turned, a professional smile settling on his face. 'You're in luck, sir. I don't just speak English, I am English. How can we help you?'

159

'Well, it was about property.'

'You've come to the right place. We have the finest register around here, and it's all on our wonderful computer programme. Complete details on two hundred villas and apartments at the push of a button. Fantastic technology.'

'Actually,' said Skinner quietly, 'I was more interested in shop properties. Owned by a company called Torroella Locals. It is Mr Inch, isn't it?'

The smile lost its warmth in an instant – it stayed in place, but seemed to freeze on the little man's face. Skinner had seen fear in another human ten thousand times before; it was unmistakable. Inch went pale beneath the tan as he nodded dumbly.

'That's good. I was told I would find you here. Can we speak in private?'

Inch nodded again and led the way behind the counter and into a small office. The smile was gone completely as he closed the door. 'How can I help you?'

The big detective looked down at him. 'First, let me introduce myself. My name's Bob Skinner. I'm a policeman, from Scotland. I've been investigating an allegation of financial impropriety made against a company called InterCosta by one of its clients. In the line of that, I'm talking to all known associates of the late Santiago Alberni. I'm led to believe that you may have been acquainted with him, and that you may have had common interest in an investment company called Torroella Locals. Before I ask you anything, I must emphasise that I am acting entirely unofficially. On that basis, are you prepared to talk to me?'

Inch nodded again.

'Good. Can I begin by asking if my information is correct, and that you are the owner of record of a company called Torroella Locals?'

Inch looked at him sidelong. 'Yes.' It was scarcely more than a whisper.

'And was Santi Alberni a sleeping partner?'

'Yes, he was.'

'When was the company set up?'

'Six or seven years ago.'

'To do what?'

Inch coughed, and his voice seemed to strengthen slightly. 'To reinvest profits from InterCosta in empty shop properties in good locations.'

'Around here?'

'No. Further south, in the busier resorts. They were the sort of properties where we could pull in high rents through the summer season from short-term operators.'

'Whose idea was it to set up the company?'

'Alberni's.'

'Who owns it?'

'Officially I do, but Alberni has a lawyer's letter signed by me confirming that he is the legal owner.'

'You don't have a copy?'

Inch shook his head vigorously enough to make his remaining hair fly up.

'How much in total did Alberni salt away in Torroella Locals?'

'About ninety million pesetas. Four-fifty grand.'

'And you assumed it was kosher money.'

'That's what he said.'

'What about Ainscow? Didn't he have any say in it?'

'I don't know Ainscow. Who's he?'

Skinner looked at him. 'Come on, you're in the agency business, aren't you? For how long?'

Inch nodded again, alarmed by the new toughness in Skinner's tone. 'For ten years.'

'All you boys know each other around here. You're telling me you've been here since the mid-Eighties, as Paul Ainscow has, and you've never heard of him?'

'I haven't!'

Skinner stared hard at him for several seconds. Eventually he grinned. 'Okay, so you haven't. Let me ask you something else. What's the current valuation of the shops?'

'They're in the books at one hundred and thirty million. That's a professional valuation,' Inch added hurriedly.

'And who holds the deeds?'

Inch looked up at Skinner leaning relaxed against the wall. The corner of his mouth twitched, but he stayed silent.

'Come on, Inch. It's an easy question. Who holds the deeds?'

The little man shook his head, 'No, I'm not saying any more – not without legal advice. You said you were unofficial. I don't have to talk to you at all.'

Skinner straightened up. 'That's right, you don't . . . yet. But you take that legal advice, and make sure that it's sound. This is one step away from being a murder investigation, and you could be bang in the middle of it.'

Terror flared in Inch's eyes. 'Murder! What do you mean murder? I had nothing to do with any of it!'

'Any of what, wee man?' asked Skinner quietly. Leaving Inch

standing, mouth slightly agape, in the middle of the small room, he turned on his heel and walked out of the shop.

He found Sarah still at her table outside Bar Isidre. She was rocking Jazz gently back and forward in his buggy, making soft shushing noises as she did.

She looked up as Bob approached. 'Well; find him?'

'Sure did.'

'And?'

'He was primed, for certain, warned that I was on my way. The wee bugger didn't even ask my name. He knew exactly who I was and what I was there for. I'm bloody certain that he was following a script. I know, because eventually we got to a bit that wasn't in it, and he was lost. Come on, love. Let's get back to L'Escala. I've got a fax to send.'

49

The transmission signal changed pitch, then stopped, as the connection was made. The machine lay still and silent for a few seconds, causing Skinner to wonder whether, after all, it was faulty, until, with a low hum, the single white sheet began to roll through.

Half a minute later it cleared the transmission gate, and fell to the floor.

Sarah, who had come into the room half-way through the process, picked it up and read its contents, aloud.

Confidential
DCI Mackie from ACC Skinner.
Please put the following into effect.
I wish total surveillance placed on Paul Ainscow immediately. Its purpose is to establish who are his associates, whether any have criminal connections, and in particular whether there is any link between Ainscow and Nicolas Vaudan, and one Alan Inch.
Using all available sources, check for any available information on Alan Inch. Currently employed as a property salesman by Immobiliara Brava of Torroella de Montgri. Search for information should pay attention in particular to convictions/arrests for fraud. I will seek to arrange here for a watch to be placed on Inch.
Finally, use international connections to have a watch placed on Nicolas Vaudan in France. I have just been advised by his office that he returned to Mougins this morning. Purpose is again to ascertain who his business contacts might be, and to establish any possible link between Vaudan/Inch/Ainscow.
Please confirm as soon as all arrangements are in place, and report regularly.

'Mmm,' said Sarah. '*Not* very policespeak. No "aforementioneds" or "thereafters"!'

Skinner grinned. 'Sorry, I must be slipping. You know, back home

163

sometimes I still receive the odd report that's "respectfully submitted", even although I tried to ban the phrase on the ground that if I need to be told that I had the respect of my officers, then I don't deserve it!'

'Where do you go now? Back to Arturo?'

'Yes, but I can't do that until tomorrow. Even *he* takes Sunday off.'

'You've really latched on to this one, my darling, haven't you?' Sarah smiled. 'International surveillance; I mean that's pretty heavy. What if Vaudan's letter turns up and proves that Santi was guilty and that he did kill himself? Won't you be—?'

Skinner interrupted. 'Won't my arse be hung out to dry, you mean? Trust me, my love. If that letter turns up, Santa Claus will bring it down the fucking chimney! I have no doubts. Not since smelling Inch sweat in an air-conditioned room. Not since he lied to me all the way through our chat – I know when I'm being lied to, Sarah. Not since I threw the word "murder" at him.'

'You did? How did he react?'

'You could say that the bottom dropped out of his world . . . or maybe it was the other way around.'

50

The tall yellow Guardia Civil barracks seemed to reflect the early afternoon sunshine as Skinner walked towards it. The day was even hotter than its predecessor, and there was a heaviness in the air which hinted that somewhere, maybe still a day or two distant but with gathering strength, a storm was brewing.

He turned into the building. At first the officer on desk duty looked sternly at the tall figure in T-shirt and shorts framed as a black shadow in the light of the doorway. But when the shadow said, '*Commandante por favor,*' recognition dawned and the man sprang to his feet, snapping a salute.

The officer left his post to advise Pujol of his visitor, and returned a few seconds later to escort Skinner through to the small office.

'*Buenas tardes, Bob,*' said Pujol, rising. 'How are your conversations going? Is your "dog theory" any nearer proof?'

Skinner said nothing, but took from his bumbag, which was slung over his left shoulder, his fax to Brian Mackie of the day before, and the DCI's response, received three hours later, confirming that all arrangements were in place.

Pujol's eyebrows climbed skywards on his forehead as he read. 'You seem to be covering quite a bit of ground. When I see that you can sit in your villa and call up the resources of Interpol, I have to say that not even I realised how long is your arm. It frightens me a little. You are so sure that Alberni was murdered, and that he was innocent?'

Skinner lowered himself into a chair facing the commandant. He nodded. 'Let me tell you why.'

He recounted in every detail his conversation with Vaudan and Inch, describing the latter's panic when murder had been added to the agenda of the investigation. 'Can you tell when someone is lying to you, Arturo? Course you can, you're a good copper. So take it from me, Santi was innocent. I believe that he was killed to prevent him finding out about something that's been going on under his nose for years, and to me it's inconceivable that Paul

165

Ainscow wasn't involved. I've taken care of Scotland and France. I'd like you to look after this end. I don't care whether it's formal or not. I want Inch watched round the clock. If you can manage it, I want his phones tapped, office and home. Stick as close to him as possible.'

He looked across the desk. Pujol was smiling, but his eyes were heavy with irony. At once, Skinner was gripped by a sense of foreboding.

'I am ahead of you, Bob. I have Inch under close surveillance already. As close as it could be. Come and I will show you.'

He led the way from the small room, and along the corridor. At its end, an officer stood guard over a heavy brown-stained wooden door. He stood aside as Pujol and Skinner approached. In the centre of the small, windowless, air-conditioned room stood a narrow table. Something lay on it. Something covered by a white sheet. Something – Skinner guessed – that was around five feet six from end to end, with a walnut tan.

Pujol drew back one end of the sheet.

'Shit!' Skinner spat the word out. 'Son of a bitch!'

Inch's face was unmarked, but his tan had taken on an odd yellowish tinge as death had drained the blood from beneath the skin. His head lay at an odd angle on his shoulders, and Skinner knew without asking that his neck had been broken. Another death, he thought. How many more?

'What happened?' he asked, wearily.

'Señor Inch lived in L'Escala,' said Pujol, 'which makes it even less likely that he did not know Ainscow. He was a keen wind-surfer. It was his sport. Every Monday – you know, Bob, that the property people all take Monday as their holiday – you would find him in Riells Bay, usually far out from the beach. It was the same today. Only today, at around eleven this morning, a man in a Sunseeker powerboat stolen from the marina, a man who appeared to be drunk, ran him down at full speed. He was killed instantly.'

'Where is the man now?'

'I have just sent men to take him to prison in Barcelona. He will be interrogated there and charged, no doubt, with everything we can think of.'

'Who is he?'

'I do not yet know. As I said, he seemed to be drunk. He wouldn't tell us anything, other than what we could do with our mothers. But he did tell us in German.'

'When can I see him?'

'Too soon to say, Bob. But I'll try to arrange a visit for us both as

166

quickly as I can. And,' he added, with emphasis, 'I will arrange for the investigation of Torroella Locals. The Guardia is involved now ... whether I like it or not!'

51

'What d'you call a thousand lawyers chained together at the bottom of the sea?' asked Skinner.

'A good start,' said Pujol.

'So it's the same in Spain, then.'

'Even more so, my friend. Even more so. And shortly this one here, who clearly speaks no English, judging from his bewildered expression, will wish that he *was* at the bottom of the sea. This one thinks that he can play dumb with me and get away with it.'

Josep Albert, the lawyer of record listed on the company registration of Torroella Locals, was as unprepossessing as his seedy backstreet office on the third floor of a tumbledown Girona building. Lank, wavy black hair was plastered to the sides of his head by too much oil, and his pinched yellow face looked overdue for a meeting with soap and water. Thick-lensed spectacles made his eyes seem huge, and served only to accentuate their shiftiness. But perched on a swivel chair, behind a huge desk which seemed to be designed at least in part as a barricade, he presented a wall of resistance to Pujol's gentle questioning.

Since Albert had insisted on speaking in Catalan, the content of their exchanges had been a mystery to Skinner from the start. He could follow the general drift of most conversations in Spanish, but was completely lost when the guttural regional tongue was used. However, from Pujol's translated summaries, he knew that Albert was being deliberately obstructive, denying knowledge of the operations of Torroella Locals, and claiming no involvement in its management.

'This man,' said Pujol to Skinner, 'he would not admit to knowing his own mother if a policeman asked him. "Señor Inch? He was a minor client. Of course he has no idea where the money invested in the company came from." And "Santi Alberni? He has never heard of him."' Pujol glowered at the little man perched on his swivel chair, but Albert sat there, smug and defiant. 'Paul Ainscow? "Oh no, Commandante, I do not know him. Scottish you say? I know no Scottish people."'

'So introduce him to this one,' Skinner murmured.

'Okay,' said Pujol. 'You don't speak his language, but you can't get any less out of him than me!' He turned back to face Albert, and spoke rapidly to him in Spanish. Skinner picked up enough to know that he was being introduced as a very important policeman from Great Britain, who was in Spain specially to investigate property fraud. The introduction completed, Pujol leaned back.

Skinner pulled his chair close to Albert's massive desk and leaned forward, his forearms resting on the scratched wooden surface. He smiled. Nervously, the little lawyer smiled back. And then Skinner's smile faded and, with it, all of his customary warmth and amiability. It was as if another Skinner held Albert in his gaze: a cold, dangerous gaze full of threat and menace. He sat in silence for a full minute staring across the desk at the untidy little man, as if he was probing him, trying to read his mind.

As Pujol looked on from the side, he saw first bewilderment, then panic, then fear gather in Albert's hugely magnified eyes. He began to shift uncomfortably in his seat, fidgeting, working the swivel from side to side, glancing down occasionally into his lap, but always drawn back by the magnet of Skinner's hypnotic stare. Once, then again, he opened his mouth as if to speak, but closed it each time, helpless.

Eventually, after three full unblinking minutes, Skinner said quietly, 'Arturo, ask him where the deeds to the Torroella Locals properties are held.'

Pujol put the question, and saw a look of almost pathetic gratitude sweep across the man's face at the chance to break free from his silent inquisitor. The words poured out, in Catalan, as if the Commandante had become his confessor.

When Albert fell silent, Pujol turned to Skinner. 'He says that they are held by a bank in Amsterdam, as security for a loan of one hundred million pesetas in US dollars. He says that he did not arrange the loan. He was simply instructed to inspect the agreement, and to pass on the deeds to the bank. He does not know to whom the money was paid, or what happened to it. He says that if it was used to buy more property, then it was for another company, one of which he knows nothing.'

'Ask him who arranged the loan.'

Pujol translated the question. Again, the response was instant. Even in Catalan, Skinner recognised one word, a name – confirmed by the Commandante's translation. 'He says it was Nick Vaudan.'

'Not Inch?'

'No. He says that Inch was simply, how you say, a puppet. He was the name on the record, but the orders came from Vaudan.'

'Ask him again about Alberni and Ainscow, and about the money coming into Torroella Locals.'

Again, Pujol translated. Albert's reply was insistent, almost beseeching.

'He swears that he has never met Ainscow, although he knows of him, and that he had never heard of Alberni until Vaudan called to tell him that you would probably come to see him, to ask him about the company, and about the deaths of Inch and Alberni. Of the money, he knows nothing.'

'When did Vaudan call?'

'Around one o'clock. He said that he was calling from Monaco, and that is true. I had my people check on him after you left my office yesterday afternoon. He flew home on Sunday.'

'He's good at not being around when suicides and fatal accidents happen, isn't he? Yet, two hours after Inch is killed, he calls our man here to tell him about it and to warn him about me.'

'*Si*, and he told him that you were a very dangerous man. He said something else, too. He said that you were maybe too dangerous for your own good.'

Skinner flashed a look at Pujol which made the Spaniard feel suddenly very glad that they were on the same side. 'Did he indeed! Tell you something, my friend. Before this is over, Monsieur Vaudan is going to find out just how fucking dangerous I am. Now please ask Ratso here whether he knows of any connection between Vaudan and Ainscow, and tell him that unless I am personally convinced that he is telling the truth, you will take a walk outside for five minutes.'

Pujol smiled, and put the question. Skinner saw Albert's mouth drop open and terror flare in his eyes behind the magnifying lenses. As he answered, he held out his hands in supplication. As he finished, Pujol nodded gently, calming his hysteria.

He turned back to Skinner. 'Our friend swears on the lives of his family that he knows of no such connection. I believe him, for he believed me when I said that I would take that walk.'

'Okay, he can do one more thing, and he's off the hook. Tell him to give you a letter of authority to the Torroella Locals bank. You should look into that account, and trace the source of all payments made into it. Tell him something else, too. Tell him, whether you mean it or not, that his telephones, office and home will be tapped from now on, in case of calls from Vaudan or anyone else. And tell him that if Vaudan does call, he's to swear blind that he never told us about Amsterdam. One whisper, tell him, and I'll be back. Alone.'

52

The instant Bob stepped into the hall, he sensed that something was wrong. He paused, listening for alien sounds, only to realise that it was the absence of noise that was unusual. Normally, during the day, the cries of gulls and the breaking of waves drifted in from the terrace. But on this blazing afternoon, the patio doors were closed.

'Sarah?' He called from the hallway, fearful.

'Bob! I'm in here.' She called to him from the living room, her voice edged with tension. He found her sitting at one end of their long sofa, facing the glass doors, with the sleeping Jazz cradled in her arms. As he came into the room she looked over her shoulder towards him, and he saw a small cut on the right side of her forehead, just below the hairline. Lying on the coffee table, within her reach, was the long, sharp-pointed, jagged-edged carving knife from their kitchen set.

'Honey, what the hell . . . ?'

'It's all right. We're all right. Stay cool. Just go and look in the kitchen.' She sounded calmer than before.

Skinner did as she asked. He crossed the hall, and opened the kitchen door. 'Bloody hell!' he hissed. Of the room's single window only a few wicked shards of glass remained in the frame. The rest, shattered, was spread all over the work surface and all over the floor. In the midst lay a large red building brick. A huge boiling rage welled up in Skinner as he remembered words he had heard only an hour before. 'Too dangerous for my own good,' he snarled into the room. 'Vaudan, if this was your doing . . .'

Mastering his fury he returned to Sarah. 'Are you sure you're okay?'

'Yes, I'm fine, and Jazz is oblivious to it all.'

'So tell me what happened. But can I get you a drink first?'

She looked up at him and shook her head. He noticed that the blood on her forehead was dried and crusted.

'It was just after you left. Oh, only a couple of minutes. I went into the kitchen and there was this man. He was standing outside the kitchen window and he was holding a brick. I don't think he was waiting for me, or anything like that. For a second or two we both just stood and stared at each other. And then he threw the brick. I flung my arms up in front of my face. But I got this . . .' she pointed to her forehead 'and this . . .' she held up her right forearm to show another small cut 'and my hair was full of glass, but otherwise I was all right. But, Bob,' she whispered, 'suppose I'd been holding the baby.'

'Don't. Just tell yourself, for ever more, that he wouldn't have thrown the brick. What happened after that?'

'Well, when I looked again he seemed to be edging towards the window, as if he was going to climb in. So I picked up the biggest knife I could find, and I said to him, in Spanish, "Come here, motherfucker and I'll stick this right in your guts." And, boy, did I mean it. My baby was in this house. If that man had come in here, I'd have put that knife right through him and worried about the Hippocratic Oath later. So he stayed outside, and eventually he ran off. But before he did, he said something in bad English, something all jumbled up and confused, about it being a message, and him being a messenger to you.'

Bob nodded his head. 'I understand. Describe this guy for me.'

She thought for a second or two. 'He looked to be late thirties or early forties, and quite tall for a Spanish man of that age. Heavily built, with black curly hair and dark eyes. Hadn't shaved for a couple of days. He wore a dirty check shirt, and jeans, and I could see workboots when he ran.'

Bob sat down beside her and put his arms around her. 'You are a very brave lady. I am so glad for that guy that he didn't climb through the window.' He gave her a gentle hug. She laid her head on his shoulder and began to cry. He comforted her until she quietened down.

'Did you call the police?'

'No. I decided to wait for you. I was pretty sure he wouldn't be back, but I kept that thing close just in case.' She nodded towards the knife on the coffee table. 'What did he mean, about being a messenger? You said you understood.'

'He meant that he had been sent to warn me off.'

'Who would send him?'

'Nick Vaudan, or Ainscow, or both. I'm starting to ask the wrong questions. There's a big operation of some sort going on here, using laundered money, and I'm starting to unravel it. Alberni and Inch were both killed, I'm quite certain, as part of a cover-up. That hasn't worked, so now they revert to Plan B, which presumably means scaring me off. Vaudan's a smart guy. He knows that everyone has a weak point, and he knows that you and the baby are mine.'

He looked down at them both, and kissed Sarah on the forehead – on the wound. 'Maybe I should just back off and let Arturo take it as far as he can.'

She nodded. 'Yes. Then Santi can stay in the books as a suicide, and Gloria'll be broke, and this big operation of theirs, that's big enough to have two people killed for, that can go on too. Maybe, with you out of the picture, they'll decide to get rid of poor old Arturo. I mean Guardia Civil people are killed every week in Spain. It wouldn't even make the national news.' She snorted. 'Back off? You don't know how, Skinner.'

He kissed her again, and pushed himself up from the couch. 'Well, if that's so, there's *one* thing that's going to happen. You're going home, by air, tomorrow. Vaudan's right. You two are my weakness. But as soon as you're safe back in Edinburgh, then he and Mr Ainscow – for I can smell him in this now – are in the deepest shit of their lives.'

He walked out into the hall, picked up the telephone, and punched in Pujol's direct line number. 'Arturo, hello. Who am I describing? Around forty, tallish, heavily built, dark curly hair, badly dressed, usually needs a shave.'

'Paco Garcia.'

'Thought so. Where can I find him? Bastard tossed a brick through my kitchen window, courtesy of Vaudan. I wouldn't mind, but Sarah was in the kitchen at the time.'

Pujol growled at the other end of the line. 'Leave Paco to me. I know where to find him. Come and see me in an hour. Meantime, I send someone to mend the window.'

'There's something else you could do for me. You could make sure that there's a seat for a woman with a baby on tomorrow's Iberia flight from Barcelona to Manchester. I'm sending Sarah and Jazz back to Scotland.'

'*Si*,' said Pujol. 'That may be wise. I will arrange it. And if you are in Barcelona tomorrow, we can go to the prison and talk to the German. He should be sober by then. But, for now, let us deal with Paco.'

53

'Señor Commandante Skinner, may I introduce Señor Don Francisco Garcia, who is our guest at this time.'

There was one chair only in the small interrogation cell, and it was bolted to the floor. Paco Garcia stood behind it, grasping its back with strong hands, as if wishing to tear it loose and use it as a weapon.

'*Buenas Tardes*, señor,' said Skinner evenly. 'I think you owe me a new window.' Garcia stared back at him. 'How much English does this pig speak?' The man did not react in any way to his question to Pujol.

'Not much. His French is okay.'

'Sarah did say that he sounded mixed up. What's he told you so far?'

'Nothing. He called your wife a bad name and said she was a liar. You know, Bob, it is very stuffy in here without windows. I am feeling a little faint. I think I will take that walk of which I spoke this morning.'

'That's good,' said Skinner, smiling at Garcia. 'About five or ten minutes' worth should see you all right. You might want to bring something to write on when you come back.'

As the door closed on Pujol's back, the smile left Skinner's face. '*Pourquoi*. Garcia, *pourquoi?*'

The man pulled himself up to his full height, puffing out his chest. '*Vous n'êtes pas policia ici. Ici vous êtes rien.*' He spat on the floor.

Slowly Skinner walked towards him. '*Rien? Je suis rien?*' Lazily he reached out his right hand and slapped Garcia lightly across the face. The man looked back at him in astonishment.

Skinner reached out again, and the big man seemed to offer his cheek to the slap – but one never landed. Instead it changed into a flashing, smashing, cutting-edge blow to the base of the jaw, just below the left ear. With a loud click, the joint dislocated. Garcia's mouth opened with the force and the pain of the blow, but before he could scream, Skinner pivoted and drove his left hand, straight-fingered, into the pit of his stomach, just above the diaphragm. The air hissed out of the man's lungs in a low moan. He slumped forward, catching hold of the back of the chair, instinctively, as support.

In no particular hurry, Skinner moved round behind him and, impacting with the first joints of his fingers rather than the tips or the knuckles, struck him two downward blows, right-handed, one to each kidney. Garcia's back arched with the pain. His legs seemed to bow under him, but he stayed on his feet, bent forward over the chair.

'*Celà, il était pour ma femme, Garcia, et pour mon petit.*' Skinner paused and took a pace back, then went on in a whisper. '*Celui ici, il est pour mes vacances!*' He kicked the man between his spread legs, square on the testicles.

At last Garcia screamed, and crumpled to the floor. He lay there, clutching himself and moaning for perhaps three minutes. Eventually, Skinner bent over, grabbed him under the armpits, and hauled him to his feet, before dropping him into the bolted chair. The man began to double over again, but Skinner pushed him upright.

'Oh,' he said. 'I see you've hurt your jaw. We must fix you up so you can talk to the Commandante.'

The man looked back at him uncomprehending, his eyes still crossed with pain. Skinner threw a punch: a short, powerful boxer's left hook. It landed on the right side of the jaw. There was a second click, as loud as the first, as the joint snapped back into place. This time Garcia howled with pain, and tears streamed down his face.

Skinner grabbed him under the chin and pulled his head up, forcing the man to look into his eyes. '*Oui, monsieur,*' he said softly. '*Je suis rien, mais ma femme et mon enfant sont tout le monde.*'

At that moment, there was a soft knock on the door. Skinner opened it, and Pujol stepped back into the room, looking anxiously at Garcia in the process, as if checking him for visible injuries, and brightening up when he saw him sitting in the chair, unmarked and seemingly none the worse for wear.

'D'you feel the better for your stroll, Arturo? Paco and I got on great when you were away. I think you'll find he's quite keen to answer your questions now, starting with who told him to heave that fucking brick through my window!'

Pujol stood in front of Garcia and put the question to him in Spanish. The big man looked up at him, tears still shining in his eyes, then sneaked a fearful glance across at Skinner, and answered, 'Señor Vaudan.'

'*Por que?*'

Garcia blurted out his answer almost before the question was out. He paused, then leaned forwards conspiratorially towards Pujol and muttered something else. The Commandante turned to Skinner. 'He says that Vaudan told him you had become a problem, and that he was to give you a message by frightening Sarah. He says that she frightened him. When he broke the window, he thought that she was going to cut his heart out.'

'If he'd made a move for her she would have.'

'Bob, Paco also says that he would speak much more readily if you were not here. He seems to think that you wish him harm. I think perhaps that it is—'

'Sure,' said Skinner. 'Wouldn't want to upset the poor chap. I'll wait outside. But don't piss about with him. As soon as I'm through that door, you ask him who was with him when he murdered Santi.'

Pujol nodded. Skinner opened the door and stepped out into the corridor.

Ten minutes later, he heard a buzzer sound. When two uniformed officers marched past him along the corridor, and into the interrogation room, he realised that it had been a signal from Pujol. As Garcia was led away, still doubled over and clutching his groin, the commandant signalled him to come back into the room.

'Well?' asked Skinner.

'I put your question to him as you asked. It was amazing. Twenty minutes ago he knew nothing. Now, in here he would have told my fortune if I had asked him. What did you do to him, Bob?'

'I'll show you sometime. What did he say?'

Pujol smiled. 'When I put your question to him, he went as white as a ghost. Then he said, "It was Serge Lucan, Señor Vaudan's man from France. I was with him. But we did not kill Señor Alberni."'

'Oh, yes?'

'That's right. He said that he was there, at Alberni's villa, with Lucan. They were there before you. Vaudan sent them to put money in Alberni's safe. Santi had shown him around the house, so he knew where it was. They thought that Alberni would be at work and that they would have to break in, but when they got there, the garden door was open and Santi's car was still there. They were going to go away and come back later, but when the dog barked at them and no one appeared, they decided to take a look around. Paco said that he looked through the window of the garage, and saw Santi hanging there. He called Lucan over to show him. He said that Lucan just laughed, and said, "That's saved me a messy job." When Paco asked him what he meant, Lucan said that his orders were that, once the money was in the safe, Santi was to suffer a fatal accident.'

'How did Garcia react to that?'

'He said that he was terrified. He said that he did not realise until then what sort of a man Vaudan is.'

Skinner snorted. 'So how come he's still doing his dirty work?'

'He is afraid not to. He heard about Inch's accident, and he thinks that it would be easy for him to have one also, if he crossed Vaudan.'

'I suppose so. Anyway, how did his story go on?'

'There wasn't much more to it. They went into the villa, found the safe, found Santi's key so they didn't have to pick the lock, and they put the money inside. Paco said that Lucan had locksmith's tools with him.'

'Did you ask him if they took anything from the safe – a letter, for example?'

Pujol nodded. '*Si*. I asked him that. He thought I was going to accuse him of robbery as well as all the rest. He said to me – he gave me his solemn promise – that they did not take anything. They put the money in, and then they left. From the time he said, they can only have been gone a couple of minutes before you arrived.'

Skinner cast his mind back to that Saturday morning. He recalled a battered old green van, with two men inside, waiting to pull out of the Camp dels Pilans road as he had swung in from the highway. 'Does Paco have a car?'

'*Si*. A very old Renault, green, but not a car, a . . . oh, what is the word?'

'It's all right. I remember. I saw them. He's told you true, about the time, at least. That doesn't mean they didn't kill Santi, though. They could have taken their time about it.'

Pujol's expressive face became mournful. 'No, my friend. I am afraid not. I am a policeman like you, and like you I have an idea when a man is telling me lies. I have an idea about people, too. Paco may be stupid, and ready to do things like he did today, at your house. He is someone you would send out to frighten a woman, but not a man. He is certainly not someone that you could send out to kill.'

Skinner sat down in the bolted chair and looked up at Pujol. 'You're a good copper, Arturo. You have good instincts. You're right about him. I found that out when I was . . . having my talk with him. Sarah scared him with that knife far more than he scared her. A lioness with her cub, right enough.' He laughed softly.

'Yes, Bob, and whatever you, mm, said, to him, he is now far more afraid of you than of Vaudan.'

'That could come in handy.'

Skinner folded his arms across his chest and leaned back in the chair. 'So what have we got? We know that Vaudan had that money planted in Santi's safe. We know that he was planning to kill him. Except Santi seems to have beaten him to it. It looks as if, whatever my friend Carlos says about the Catalan character and your kindness to animals, the guy killed himself after all. Yet the money in the safe

177

indicates that Vaudan was trying to frame him. That was done to fit in with Vaudan's story.'

'Perhaps,' Pujol said tentatively, 'Vaudan had frightened or blackmailed Santi into taking the money from InterCosta.'

Skinner shook his head. 'No, that would require Santi to have a partner who was so fucking stupid that he wouldn't notice a missing million – or one who was scared along with him. You've met Ainscow. Is he that fucking stupid? Is he the type who would scare easily? Sorry, Arturo, that's another bit I find hard to swallow. Ainscow's in this, I can feel it. He and Vaudan have been smart in covering up any link between them, but there has to be one. That makes it still my business, even after Pitkeathly's been paid off. That's why I'm using my force resources on this business. What we've got here is a very clever money-laundering operation. Cash ripped off, salted away in property to make it legit, then turned back into cash again. We know about the loan on the Torroella Locals shops. You can bet that if we looked, we'd find that the same had been done with the Montgo properties. So there's a million in funny money, carefully built up over a period of years. Where is it, and what's it doing? Those are the questions I want to answer. Santi topping himself, that's just confusing, and bad luck for Gloria, but in this business it's no more than a sideshow.'

Pujol leaned on the steel door of the dingy, sweat-smelling room. With head pressed back against the metal, he closed his eyes, considering what Skinner had said. Eventually he looked down at his companion, still in the interrogation chair. 'Yes, you are absolutely right, my friend. All of that, simply put. But it is a million miles above the head of Paco Garcia. What do you want me to do with him? I could throw him in jail for quite a long time.'

Skinner shook his head. 'Your jails are full enough already, man. Why don't you just let him go? We won't press charges. Before you kick him out, though, tell him that when Vaudan gets in touch, he should say that I've got the message, and that I'm flying Sarah and the baby home tomorrow morning, then driving back myself. Tell him, too, that if I ever find out that he told Vaudan anything different, then the next time we have a talk there won't be anyone else around, and he won't walk away after it.' He pushed himself powerfully out of the chair. 'Now I'm going home to spend some time with my family, and to send another fax. We need to know all about Mr Serge Lucan, and we need to watch him very carefully from this day on.'

54

'You are sure the baby'll be okay on the plane?'

'Hey, I'm not just his mother. I'm a doctor, remember. Everything in his life is a new experience. This will be another. They've given us a front-row seat, so we'll have plenty of space, and we'll be well in front of the engines, so it'll be quiet, or as quiet as you can get on a Spanish airplane!'

They were standing at the end of the long straight concourse of Barcelona Airport. Behind them it stretched back almost a kilometre, looking more like a high-quality shopping arcade than a major international terminal. Arturo Pujol's Guardia uniform had whisked them round a long queue at passport control. As Bob and Sarah said their farewells, he sat across in the cafeteria, among passengers and air crew, sipping his first coffee of the day.

'Okay,' said Bob, 'I'm convinced. Anyway it's a short flight. Alex will be well on her way down to Manchester to meet you by now. Alex and Andy, that is. It was nice of him to offer to keep her company.'

Sarah smiled, 'Mmm, wasn't it. He must be keen to see his new godson again.'

'Yeah, that'll be it. Single guys in their mid-thirties do tend to get broody. Time he got himself sorted out in that area.'

'He will. Don't you worry. He'll probably take you completely by surprise one day.'

'Not him. I know him too well. Listen, when you get home, do one thing for me. Call Jimmy and tell him what's been going on here. Tell him that, since all this started from a complaint made in Scotland, and since there's a possibility that Ainscow's involved, I'm staying on here at the request of the Guardia to help their investigation.'

Sarah nodded. 'I'll call him soon as we're settled in. If he's free I'll invite him down for coffee, late afternoon. How long do you think you'll have to stay out here?'

'A few days, probably. Until we establish a link with Ainscow, or until the thing just stalls completely. When the time is right, I'll just jump in the car and drive up.' He glanced across at Gate 44. The queue for embarkation was down to its last few passengers. 'You'd better get on board now. I love you . . . both.' He kissed her, long and tenderly. 'Now, safe home. And while you're in the air, Arturo and I'll be in jail!'

55

Just as there is something unmistakable about the look of a prison from outside its walls, so also it is distinguished on the inside by its unmistakable smell.

'Bad cooking and piss; it's the same the world over,' Skinner muttered to Pujol, screwing up his face, as the latest in a series of barriers was slammed shut behind them, and the key turned in the lock. A uniformed jailer led them along one more dark corridor, before showing them into a small room furnished with a table and four chairs. With a few words to Pujol, he withdrew, leaving the door open behind him.

'He says he's going to fetch Gruber.'

'Gruber,' said Skinner. 'They must have made some progress. Yesterday you said that he wouldn't even tell you his name.'

'*Si*, that's right. When he was arrested, all he did was curse in German. He seemed to be drunk, and he made no sense at all.'

'He *seemed* to be drunk, but are you sure he was?'

'No, not now. Now, like you, I think it was an act. When he was arrested, all he had on him was money and a set of keys. Nothing else. Then yesterday one of our sea patrols spotted a Kawasaki motorcycle on the shore on the old army land between L'Escala and Montgo. It had camping equipment strapped to the saddle, and two panniers. They alerted us and we picked it up. Those keys fitted it. In the pannier we found a passport identifying him as Hansi Gruber. There was also more money, in French francs.'

'French? No D-Marks?'

'No, there were none.'

'Okay, Gruber is a biker. He comes in from France, parks his machine on a deserted piece of coast, gets drunk, makes his way to the marina, hot-wires the biggest, fastest boat he can see, takes it out into the bay, and just happens to run over Inch. Is that the picture? No, I think not.'

Skinner paused and looked at Pujol. 'This is how it was. Gruber is sent down here. He's shown a picture of Inch, told where he lives, where he works, and what his habits are. Then he's told to kill him.

181

He works out the best way to do it, probably keeps Inch under observation all the way to the beach, then drives over the hill and plants his bike. His idea would be to take the boat round there after he's done the business, dump it and get away on the bike, maybe cross the border somewhere quiet and be in France within an hour. How come you caught him?'

'He was unlucky,' said Pujol. 'When he ran down Inch, the sail of the surfboard, and sadly, the right foot of Señor Inch were drawn into the engine of the boat. It seized up and stopped. Several other wind-surfers, members of the same club as Señor Inch, saw what had happened, then sailed over and held on to Gruber. They pulled Señor Inch from the water and on to the boat, but he was dead.'

'I take it you've run checks on this guy in Germany and France.'

'*Si*,' said Pujol. 'There is nothing in France, but in Germany he has a record of violence. He is from Bremerhaven. He was a sailor, but five years ago he was sent to prison for attacking a man with a knife. He cut him up very badly. He was released over a year ago, and that was the last that the German authorities heard of him.'

'Does he know that *we* know who he is?'

'No. I instructed that that information should be kept from him.'

'Good. When he comes in, speak to him in French. See what reaction you get. Then I suggest you tell him my story of how he killed Inch, ask him to admit it, and to confirm that Vaudan sent him.'

Pujol nodded. Less than a minute later, the jailer returned with another officer. Each grasped an arm of the stocky blond, handcuffed man whom they escorted. At a signal from Pujol they unlocked his manacles, and pressed the prisoner down into one of the four chairs, to face his two visitors across the table.

'Good morning, Gruber,' said Pujol in French. The man's eyes widened in surprise, but he said nothing. Pujol reached into the left breast pocket of his uniform shirt and produced a German passport. He threw it on the desk.

Gruber looked at it and shrugged.

'Listen to me, my friend, and look at me while I am speaking to you,' said Pujol. He began to spell out in detail Skinner's scenario for the murder of Inch. A few seconds into the story, Gruber affected a yawn, and looked away from Pujol, staring up at the ventilator fan in the ceiling. Pujol's back-handed slap seemed to echo round the four corners of the room. 'I said look at me when I am speaking.' A vivid red mark showed on the German's cheek as Pujol completed his account.

'Now my friend, you have a simple opportunity. You will admit to me that you were sent to do this thing by Nick Vaudan, and I will see

182

to it that your case comes to court quickly, and that you are charged with something less than murder. What do you say?'

Gruber leaned forward, his forearms on the table. No emotion showed in his eyes. He nodded his head, very slightly, then spat, full into Pujol's face. The Commandante jumped from his chair, his moustache twisted by the snarl on his face. The two officers grabbed their prisoner and hauled him upright. Wiping the spit away with his left hand, Pujol bunched his right into a fist and set himself to swing a punch across the table.

But Skinner caught his arm and held it. 'No Arturo. You'd only hurt your hand.' He spoke in English, looking away from Gruber. 'You won't beat anything out of this guy. He's got a deal, and he'll protect it. Next thing you know, he'll have a good lawyer too, and he'll bargain the charge down to something not much worse than drunk driving. If we want him to finger Vaudan, we have to find out what his deal is, and try to put a spoke in it. Okay?'

With an effort, Pujol controlled his anger. 'Yes, I agree.'

He turned to Gruber and spoke again in French. 'You, my friend, have just made a bad choice. Whatever you may have been told, there will be no reduced charge. Your case will take for ever to come to court, and once it does, you will be sent to jail for ever and a few more days. And some of our jails are very bad places, my friend. Not like this one. You may think you are tough, but in there you will be some monster's sweetheart within a week. Look forward to it, because I will make it happen.'

He glanced at the escorts. 'Now take this insolent piece of shit away, before I forget my friend's advice.'

56

The emptiness of the villa washed over Skinner as soon as he opened the door, bringing with it a pang of sudden loneliness so strong that it carried him back to his youth, and to the days after the death of Myra, his first wife, Alex's mother.

He glanced at his watch. It was ten minutes after five o'clock. To free their nostrils of the stench of the prison, he and Pujol had taken time out in Barcelona. They had visited the Sagrada Familia, Gaudi's epic, if impossible, cathedral with its melted-icing towers, and its cranes soaring above the most visited building site in the world. Then they had eaten a tapas lunch at one of the pavement tables of a Ramblas bar, where Pujol's green uniform had attracted the deepest respect of the waiters. Finally, with Skinner at the wheel of his white BMW, they had headed northward out of the hilly city, spectacular even in its occasional seediness, with its forests of medium- and high-rise buildings flanking traffic-thronged highways.

But now, back in L'Escala, there was nothing to stave off the blues brought on by the departure of Sarah and Jazz. Bob walked into the living room, and looked at the new fax. Its LCD read-out told him that the answer machine held two messages.

He pushed the replay button. The mechanism whirred for a second or two, as the tape rewound. Then there was a whistle, before, suddenly, the room was filled with Sarah's voice. 'Hi, darling. Just a call to say that we're home okay. The plane was fine, and Jazz was great. Alex and Andy were there waiting. I think there's something—'

'Here stepmother, let me say hello.'

Bob smiled as his daughter's effervescent tones cut across Sarah's light New York drawl. 'Hi, Pops. That brother of mine's a wee heartbreaker. You know, maybe I'm biased, but you do real good-looking kids. I've got some good news and some better news. The good news is I got my finals results this morning. The better news is I got a first. So get used to it. Your kid's a lawyer. Now, Pops, don't hang about too long out there. Get that thing sorted and come home. Sarah's missing you already – and it's only been six hours.'

There was a click and a buzz as the message ended. Then a few seconds later, a whistling sound prefaced the second message. When a voice came on the line, it was that of Brian Mackie. 'Boss, hello. Could you call me back as soon as you get in. I've had feedback from France that you should know about. It's three forty-five BST at the moment.' The message clicked to a halt.

Curious, Skinner pushed the hands-free button on the tele-fax console and keyed in 07. Within three seconds, the second tone sounded, and he dialled in a direct-line number.

'Mackie.'

'Brian, Skinner. What's the story?'

'The man Lucan, sir. The associate of your fellow Vaudan that you asked us to tag as from yesterday. He's been on the move today. The French watchers had only just picked him up, when he headed for Nice Airport and caught an early flight to Hamburg.'

'Yes?'

'The French faxed a photo to Germany while the plane was in the air, and the locals in Hamburg got on his tail. He took a taxi to a hotel, had coffee and strudel with the receptionist, then took another taxi, back to the airport and caught the first plane back to Nice. What d'you think of that?'

'I can think of one or two things, but I don't want to get ahead of myself. What do we know about the girl?'

'Leggy redhead with big knockers, so the German watchers said. Name of Hilda Braun. They stayed clear of her, though.'

'Good. When I go to see her I want it to come as a surprise.'

'You're going to Germany?'

'Yeah. There's fuck all to do here now. All the leads are dead, dried up, or staying silent. But Lucan's visit to this girl – I don't want to get too excited, but that could be a break for us, and I want to interview her. Fix it with the German police. And get yourself booked out, too. If there's any chance that this might wind up as evidence in a Scottish prosecution of Ainscow, then there must be two of us at the interview. Arturo Pujol's serving that purpose here, but I want you in Germany.'

'You're still sure that Ainscow's involved, then?'

'Bloody certain, and I'm not letting up till I prove it. Brian, this is a big scam with one, probably two murders thrown in. It's been set up to accumulate, over a period, a pile of laundered cash. Once I find out what that's going to be used for, and once I can show that Ainscow and Vaudan are acting in concert, then I can pull the whole thing down.'

'Where's this cash pile lying now, boss?'

185

'That's a bloody good question, my son. Once we've done the business in Hamburg, we'll try to answer it. And to do that we'll need to go to Amsterdam.'

'Amsterdam?'

'That's right. The vice capital of Europe. Maybe I should take Andy Martin on that instead. That's more his line.'

There was a silence at the other end of the line.

'No, *you* make the arrangements and the bookings. Get me on a plane from Barcelona to tie in with your arrival, and then book me back to Edinburgh with you from Amsterdam. Tell Ruth what you want, and ask her to make it happen.'

'Okay, sir, will do.' Mackie paused. 'Wait a minute. What about your car?'

'I'll leave it here in my garage, and get a cheap tourist flight out to pick it up once things have settled down.'

'Okay, I'll get things moving at once,' said the Chief Inspector. 'I'll send you a fax to let you know the arrangements. Can I leave that until tomorrow, though?'

'Sure. But why? You got a date?'

'Aye, sir. With Maggie Rose. She's kicking her heels with you away, so I gave her a stint in Stirling keeping tabs on Ainscow. She called me in around half an hour ago to say that he's on the move. He's heading down the M9 towards Edinburgh. I told her to call in when he stopped, and I'd meet up with her.'

'He's probably heading for Safeway. You can grab a trolley each and tail him through the aisles! Let me know if it's anything more significant. Otherwise I'll see you in Hamburg.'

'Cheers, boss. I'll be in touch.'

Mackie replaced his receiver, then picked it up again immediately and called Skinner's secretary. He relayed the ACC's instructions and asked her to make travel arrangements. Next he called in the Special Branch typist and dictated a fax to the Interpol contact in Hamburg, advising him of their visit to interview Hilda Braun, and asking that they be met by an English-speaking officer who could interpret if necessary.

'Check the ETA of the flights with Ruth. Once you have them, send it off.' The typist, a middle-aged woman of formidable demeanour, nodded. Even after only a short time in his new post, Mackie knew that there was no need to check her work.

She had barely left the room before his phone rang again. He picked it up. 'DCI Mackie.'

'Brian, it's Maggie Rose. Our man Ainscow's reached his

destination. Believe it or not, he's at Tony Manson's sauna in Powderhall. Pulled right up to the door and walked in.'

'Eh! Bit early in the day, isn't it?'

'I don't know. Maybe he really has gone for a sauna.'

'Come on, Maggie. *Nobody* goes to one of those places for that!'

'You're just a cynic. Anyway, I've got a small complication. Andy Martin and Neil McIlhenney are parked right across the road from the place. We seem to have crossed wires with another investigation. What do I do if they decide to go in? You remember the boss's orders on Ainscow. "Look, but don't touch."'

'Shit, yes. Listen, have they seen you yet?'

'No.'

'Right. Sit tight where you are. I'm on my way.'

57

'Like a fucking CID convention,' Mackie muttered to himself as he pulled his car into a parking space in Powderhall Road, around a hundred yards away from the red-painted shop-front of the Hot Spot sauna and massage parlour.

As he looked along the street, he could see a flash of Andy Martin's blond head and the bulk of McIlhenney in the front seats of an anonymous blue Sierra. They were parked around twenty yards beyond the Hot Spot, with a clear view of the entrance. Fifty yards further on, Mackie recognised a red Metro GTi, and saw the outline of a figure in the driver's seat.

Mackie was almost level with the Sierra before Martin spotted his approach. He looked up, surprised, but reached round at once and opened the rear door. Glancing around to make sure that he was unobserved, Mackie slid quickly into the back seat.

'What are you doing here?' Martin asked sharply.

'Sorry, sir,' said Mackie, 'but we've got a wee situation. You weren't thinking about raiding that place, were you?'

'No,' said Martin, shaking his head. 'We're just keeping it under observation for now. It seems that Tony Manson hasn't left a will. In the absence, wee Cocozza's appointed himself administrator of the estate. We've had no word of any drugs action for a while but, as far as we can see, Cocozza's still running the girls in the saunas. I want to put a stop to that, so we're building up a photograph album of his punters. Once we've got enough, I'm going to give him a straight choice: pack it in or I go to the Law Society. I tell you, we've got some crackers already. Bankers, lawyers, accountants, even a certain deputy Fiscal. The professions are well represented at the Hot Spot saunas, that's for sure. But today . . . today could be very interesting indeed. Cocozza's in there himself, and four other guys have gone in while we've been watching. Once of them we recognised.'

'Tall, well built, smooth-looking guy, late thirties, went in about fifteen minutes ago. Yes?'

'Him? No. Never seen him before in my life. No, I was talking about Eddie Gilhooley. You've heard of him, haven't you? The

Godfather of Glasgow. Tony Manson's opposite number through in the west. A premier-league drug baron, if ever there was one. So who's this other guy? And what's your problem?'

Mackie took a deep breath. 'Paul Ainscow. Maggie Rose followed him here from Stirling. She's back there.' He gestured over his shoulder with his thumb. 'We've got him under round-the-clock watch for the boss. He thinks he's—'

Martin interrupted. 'Yes, Sarah told me all about it. So that's Mr Ainscow. He keeps some funny company, then. Wonder what the hell he's doing here?'

'Aye, and the boss'll wonder too. You don't know who the other guys are?'

'No. We should have some pretty good mug-shots though. We'll get them processed as fast as we can, and run them through the PNC. Could you take the film back to the lab for me?'

'Sure. I'll tell them it's a SB rush job. I'll do the PNC check, too.'

'Thanks,' said Martin. 'Meantime I'll go along and say hello to Maggie. Odd job for a woman, isn't it, sitting all evening in Powderhall Road waiting for your subject to get his end away!'

58

'You on your usual, Brian?'

'Aye, thanks, Andy.'

Martin turned back to the barman. 'That's another pint shandy, please.' He waited while the last drink was poured, paid the barman, and carried the round across, on a tray, to the corner table where Maggie Rose, Mario McGuire, Alison Higgins and the newly arrived Brian Mackie were waiting. Ryrie's, the famous Haymarket tavern, was a regular meeting place for police officers. It was only a few hundred yards away from the Torphichen Place Divisional HQ, and coincidentally, from Andy Martin's flat.

'So Neil's taken over the Ainscow surveillance?' asked Mackie.

'Yes,' said Martin. 'He volunteered. Said he'd take him home and put him to bed. Apparently his wife's having her pals round tonight, so he was glad of something to do. You okay with that, Brian?'

'Sure. Glad to be of help.'

'Okay. So how d'you do with our snapshots? Anything back from the PNC scan? I thought you were looking a bit pleased with yourself when you came in.'

Mackie grinned. 'I've got every right. And so have you, Superintendent. We've got results on both your mystery men. Tell me, did you see them leave?'

'Yes. They went not long after you. A taxi stopped at the sauna. Gilhooley and the two unknowns went off in it. Then wee Cocozza came out and drove off in his GSi.'

'What about Ainscow?'

Martin shook his head. 'No. He was still inside when Maggie and I left. Maybe he had nothing to do with the rest of them. Maybe he *was* only there to get his leg over.'

'Be a blow if he was. The boss would just love to tie Ainscow in with Gilhooley and those other two. I think it could be a hell of a big piece in the jigsaw he's putting together.'

'So who *were* these guys?'

Mackie smiled again round all the faces at the table. They looked back at him, curious, as he savoured the moment of his disclosure.

'Okay. You ready? One's called Peter McAteer. He's from Newcastle. The other one is Terence Michael Bennett. He's from Manchester. According to the PNC, each one is to his own city what Eddie Gilhooley is to Glasgow, and what Tony Manson was to Edinburgh – Mr Big in the drugs business. You, Superintendent, in what I am sure you will describe later as a brilliant piece of detection, have stumbled upon a drug dealers' convention.'

Martin looked at him, his green eyes wide with surprise. 'Je-sus Christ,' he whispered. 'And Cocozza was there. Not only that, he was the host. God, but the wee bugger's getting above himself, playing with the likes of them. He must really fancy taking over Tony's seat at the big table. But what the hell was your man Ainscow doing there?'

'Beats me. As you said, maybe that was just a coincidence.'

Martin nudged him with an elbow. 'Look out that window, thin man, and you will see a pig in a Hibernian strip flying over Haymarket. Coincidence, my arse. You've been around big Bob long enough to know what he thinks of them. Coincidences of that sort are like miracles. They happen very rarely, or not at all. I'd love to hear what the boss says to this.'

'I'll hear that the day after tomorrow. I'm meeting him. The Big Man's taking me on a tour of the fleshpots of Europe.'

'What?' said Maggie Rose. 'When did all this happen?' There was a tinge of annoyance in her tone, as though she felt slighted at not being the first to know of her boss's return.

'S'all right, Maggie,' said Mackie. 'It all came up while you were out following Ainscow. We're going to Germany – to Hamburg – to follow up a lead that the Ainscow inquiry threw up today. Then we're off to Amsterdam. Don't know what that's about, though, other than that it's all part of the same investigation.' He leaned back in his chair and took a deep swallow of his shandy. 'After that, he's coming home.'

Beside him, Martin was lost in thought. He shook his head. 'I still can't get over that meeting, or Cocozza being the host. The nerve of the bastard. Those hooligans on my patch. Christ, I'm going to have him. From tomorrow morning, Cocozza's on twenty-four-hour cover. He yawns – I know it. Just like Ainscow. Let's see if they meet up again.' He looked across the table. 'Alison, I'm going to be tight for people. I don't suppose . . .'

Superintendent Higgins grinned at the big figure on her right. 'Sergeant McGuire's bloody useless, I know, but you can have him if you like.'

'That's good. Thanks.' He glanced to his left. 'Maggie, would you make up the numbers till the boss gets back?'

'Of course. Be just like old times.'

Martin glanced at his watch. 'Right, that's fixed. My office eight o'clock tomorrow. Now I've got to go. Dinner must be nearly ready.' He finished his Beck's and stood up.

Brian Mackie looked at him curiously. 'You not doing your own cooking any more, Andy?'

Martin returned his gaze with a bland smile. 'Brian, my friend, you're letting Special Branch go to your head. You should leave the detecting for the office, not the pub. G'night all.'

59

The blonde girl's pale blue eyes sparkled a welcome as Pujol – with Skinner following behind – walked into the offices of Montgo SA.

'*Buenos días, señores.*'

'*Habla Inglés, por favor?*' asked the Commandante, explaining, '*Por mi amigo.*' He was dressed as casually as Skinner, in light slacks and a pale blue shirt.

She smiled. 'Yes, and French also.'

Pujol was charmed. But he began to feel a pang of concern over the purpose of their visit.

Skinner had received his call on the heels of Mackie's fax advising him of his flight and arrival times, and briefing him on the merging at Powderhall of Mackie's surveillance with that conducted by Andy Martin. As he read the message, a long slow grin of satisfaction had spread over Skinner's face, as he had grasped the possible implications of Ainscow's presence at the meeting. But before he could dwell on the message any further, the phone had sounded its single repeating tone.

'Bob? This is Arturo. My people have reported something positive from the check on the Torroella Locals bank. They have found the pay-in records from the account. Some are rents, but there are many others. The Director of the bank remembered that they were large amounts in sterling paid directly into that account, by a special arrangement agreed with Señor Inch. The records show that on each occasion the cheques were paid in by one Veronica Chaumont.'

'And she is?'

'The secretary of Nicolas Vaudan. You now have your first link between him and Ainscow. Meet me at the Montgo SA office in ten minutes, and we will talk to this lady.'

The girl was utterly charming. She looked to be in her mid-twenties. The pale eyes were set in an oval face with a light golden tan. Only slightly irregular teeth stopped her short of cover-girl perfection. She smiled up at Pujol and Skinner like someone with nothing in the world to hide.

Forcing himself to the business at hand, Pujol coughed, and

introduced first himself, then Skinner. She nodded to each in turn, not appearing flustered in the slightest. 'Veronica Chaumont,' she responded, offering each a chair.

'You are Belgian, yes?' Pujol asked, as he sat down.

She nodded her head. *'Oui!'*

'How long have you worked for Señor Vaudan?'

She shrugged. 'Since the company was started.'

'This company, Montgo SA?'

'Yes. I do not work for any other.'

'No?' Pujol paused and looked at her a little less kindly than before. 'Are you not involved also with a company called Torroella Locals?'

She shook her head. 'No, I am not. I know of it, of course, but I don't work for it.'

'But we know that you have made payments into its bank account.'

She paused. 'Yes, that is true, but only on the instructions of Nicolas.'

'Can you describe how the payments were made?'

'Yes. Every little while, Nicolas would give me a number of blank cheques. They were made out for cash, and they were for a bank in Scotland. It was called the Clydesdale.' She pronounced the name slowly and with difficulty.

Skinner spoke for the first time. 'Do you remember the name of the account?'

Veronica nodded. 'Yes, it was InterCosta UK.'

'Were you told when to pay each one in?'

'Yes. Nicolas would call me and give me instructions. He would tell me the amount in sterling that the cheque should be made out for, and where it should be paid.'

'Where?' said Pujol, surprised.

'Yes. Sometimes I would pay into the Torroella Locals account, and other times into our own account here.'

'Did the cheques always have the same signature?'

'Yes. Mr Paul Ainscow.'

'Never Santi Alberni?' asked Skinner.

It was Veronica's turn to look surprised. 'Santi? No never. Why would he sign? He only worked for InterCosta, didn't he? That's what Nick said.'

Skinner shook his head. 'No, he had a piece of it. How well did you know Santi Alberni?'

'Not very well. He was a friend of Nick's. Occasionally the three of us would have coffee in the Café Navili, but other than that he didn't come around here much.'

194

'Did you know much about him as a businessman?'

'He was a great salesman. The best in L'Escala, everyone said. InterCosta did very well, thanks to him. Sold a lot of properties, and some of them were very big ones. But he used to make jokes about how bad he was with money. I remember him saying once that it was just as well that he did not have to do the accounts for InterCosta, otherwise they would be in trouble.'

'Were you surprised when he killed himself?'

'I couldn't believe it. He never seemed like a sad guy.'

'What about Paul Ainscow? Did he come around here much?'

'Never. I have never met Mr Ainscow. I have never even spoken to him on the telephone.'

'Have you ever seen him at all; with Nick Vaudan for example?'

'No. I often think that it is odd. Sometimes I wonder if he exists.'

'Is there any correspondence anywhere between him and Vaudan.'

Again, Veronica shook her head. 'No, there is nothing I can think of. The only time I have ever seen Mr Ainscow's signature is on those blank cheques.'

'Tell me, señorita,' said Pujol. 'Did it not strike you as strange, to be paying this money from one company to others in this way?'

'Why should it? Many things much stranger than that happen in Spain, as you must know, Commandante. Nicolas told me that Paul Ainscow wished to invest money in two businesses: Montgo SA and Torroella Locals. He had agreed to run Montgo, and that Alan Inch – poor man – was looking after the other one. He said that Ainscow was never quite sure until the last moment how much each investment would be, and that blank cheques were the simplest way of going about it.'

'Were you surprised by the amounts of money being transferred?'

'Not when I saw how good a salesman Santi Alberni was. The other parts of the business – property management and holiday rentals – seemed to do well also.'

Skinner shifted in his chair. 'The Montgo properties, Miss Chaumont. Do you know where the deeds are?'

'The *escrituras*? Nicolas keeps them himself. I never see them. There is no need. My job is to collect the rents, fix the problems, keep the books, and make sure that everyone is happy. That's all.'

Pujol coughed again. 'Señorita Veronica, there is one other thing I must ask you. Your relationship with Nicolas Vaudan. Is it purely one of business?'

A light pink flush showed beneath the girl's tan. 'Certainly! Señor Commandante, you must know that Nicolas is a happily married man.' She stared boldly across the desk, a sparkle still in the pale eyes

195

and a smile toying with the corners of her mouth. 'So what possible reason could you have for asking me such a question?'

Beneath his tan, Arturo Pujol blushed bright red.

60

'What do I think? I think you fancy your chances with Mamselle Veronica, that's what I bloody think!'

Pujol smiled, replacing his beer on the Café Navili's marble-topped table. 'You know what I mean. Did you believe her?'

'Implicitly. Every word she said was true, or at least she believed it was. That girl has never told a lie in her life. There, does that satisfy you?'

'*Si*. I am glad to hear you say it.'

'Think of it. What purpose would there be in getting her involved? Wide-eyed, totally honest, totally innocent. Her job, as she says, is to keep everybody happy – and who could be better at it? She's perfect. And, yes, for what it's worth, I think you might have scored there.'

Pujol grinned even more broadly. 'Do you think she will keep her word not to say anything to Vaudan about our visit?'

'I hope so. Let's just keep our fingers crossed that he doesn't ask her a direct question. I wouldn't like that to be her first lie. With any luck at all, though, Vaudan still thinks that his thing with the brick worked, and that I'm off the pitch. I'm bloody sure Garcia would do as he was told, and report mission accomplished. He'd better. He's got his testicles in a sling as it is. If he crosses me on this one, he'll have them for paperweights!'

Skinner reached into the left breast pocket of his shirt, and produced two folded sheets of fax paper. 'But enough of him. I've got serious news on the Ainscow front. Take a look at this. You should be able to understand Edinburgh police jargon!' He handed over Mackie's fax.

Pujol scanned it quickly, then reread the second section, his eyes widening.

'But this is incredible. You are watching this man Cocozza, and all this happens.'

'Yeah. We clock these three big dealers, then Ainscow walks slap bang into the middle of it. Arturo, if I'm reading this right, we haven't just got our link between Ainscow and Vaudan through those cheques. We know *why* they've been building up their cash mountain over the years. It's a bankroll for one of the biggest drugs buys ever made in Europe, enough to keep four cities high for years, and to make some people very very rich. This is a classic deal. A straightforward supply chain leading from manufacturer to customer. Those three hooligans in the sauna, and Cocozza who'd like to be one of them, they're the retailers. Ainscow, he and Vaudan, they're the wholesalers. And somewhere, if they haven't done it already, they're going to touch base with the manufacturers. And I don't need to tell you what the product is.'

Skinner's eyes gleamed with excitement. 'If I can find out from the man in Amsterdam where that money is, and keep a track of it, wherever it goes, then follow what it buys to its destination, then there's a chance that we can wrap up the whole supply chain in one go. And that would be some outcome, from a minor property fraud. I wish I was going to Amsterdam first tomorrow. Fuck it, I wish I was going today!'

'Can't you change your plans?'

Skinner shook his head. 'No, Brian'll have lined it all up by now. But what I can and will do, once I've seen the girl, is get to that bank in Amsterdam as fast as I can, even if the local law has to drive us.'

'Will you come back here?'

Skinner shook his head. 'No, I think this investigation's moving back towards my patch. You've still got to tie Inch's accident, and Alberni's dodgy suicide, to Vaudan, if you can. But me, I'm off down another trail!'

61

It was a very smart hotel located in the heart of Hamburg's main business district, with the well-polished look of private ownership rather than the glitz of a major chain. Its furnishings were opulent, and its staff had the air of people who knew that they were there not simply to serve, but to care.

Skinner and Mackie sat in the coffee shop and waited for Hilda Braun to join them. A German detective, who had met them at the airport, sat alongside. However, they had already discovered that his interpretative skills would not be needed. Not unexpectedly for a big-city hotel receptionist, the woman turned out to be multilingual.

They rose as she approached. She fitted the shorthand description which Skinner had been given. Busty, and with a crest of soft, well-groomed red hair, she came to the table still wearing her receptionist smile, but with curiosity and concern showing in her eyes.

The three men continued standing as she reached the table. The German moved round and drew out for her the fourth chair. As she sat down, he poured her coffee from a large chrome Thermos pot.

'Thank you for joining us, Miss Braun,' said Skinner. 'Let me explain why we are here. My colleague here on my left and I are involved in an international investigation of what could be a very big crime indeed. This gentleman,' he nodded to his right, 'is from the police in Hamburg. He is helping us today.'

'I see. And why do you need to talk to me?' Her smile had gone. Only the concern remained.

'In the course of our investigation, we are watching a number of people. A couple of days ago, one of them made a trip to Hamburg: a very short trip. He flew here, he met with you, and then he flew away again. His name is Serge Lucan. We'd like you to tell us what you talked about.'

The girl took a sip of coffee. Skinner noticed that her hand was trembling slightly. She sat silent for a few seconds, as if considering her reply. Then she looked up and across at Skinner.

'I have a boyfriend,' she began hesitantly. 'His name is Hansi. We have known each other for many years. We are both from Bremerhaven, quite near here. Hansi was ... had a little trouble a few years ago. When it was over, he decided that there was no future for him in Germany, and we agreed that he should go somewhere else to try to make a new start. We agreed that when he was established I would join him. Hansi was a sailor, on inshore boats mostly, so he decided to go to the south of France to look for work crewing on private yachts. He was only there for a few weeks when he called me to say that he had found a job with a man named Vaudan, as a crewman on yacht and cruiser charters around the Mediterranean. The pay was good, and he said that Vaudan had told him that there might be opportunities later for other work, with even better money. That was a few months ago. He has written regularly, but I have not seen him since then.'

She took another sip of coffee. The tremor was still there.

'The man you are talking about – Lucan. He called me one morning earlier this week. From the airport, he said. He said that he too worked for Monsieur Vaudan, and that he had a message for me from Hansi. I told him to come to the hotel. We met here. He said that Hansi had asked him to come. He gave me a letter from him, and he gave me twenty thousand Deutschmarks.

'Hansi's letter said that he had been given an even better job by Vaudan as a crewman on a big yacht which some man from the Middle East had chartered, but that the cruise was not just the Mediterranean; it was around the world, and could take up to two years. He said that the man from the Middle East was paying the crew directly, and that the money was crazy. Hansi asked me if I would bank some of it for him, and use any I needed for myself. He said that, as well as the twenty thousand, every six months while he was away I would receive another fifteen thousand. It would come through Monsieur Vaudan, by bank draft. Hansi asked me to give this man Lucan a note confirming that I had received the money. So I did. He said that I could write to him through Vaudan's office in Monaco.'

She took a third sip of coffee. Her hand was now steady. 'That's all there was. Lucan finished his coffee and his strudel, and left. Does that help you?'

Skinner nodded. 'Yes, it helps me a lot. Do you still have Hansi's letter?'

She held up her handbag. 'Yes, in here.'

'And what did you do with the money?'

'I opened a bank account the same day. Now, what is this about, please?'

Skinner held up a hand. 'I'll tell you, Miss Braun, but first I want you to give me Hansi's letter. My German colleague here will give you a receipt if you wish one.'

She looked at him with a touch of fear in her eyes, seeming to clutch her bag tighter than before.

'Miss Braun, you haven't told us Hansi's surname. So I'll tell you: it's Gruber. I've met him. In a prison in Barcelona. He's being held there in connection with the death of a man in Spain. I expect that he will be charged with murder. The money that he is being paid is to keep him quiet while he's inside. But I don't imagine they'll pay it for too long. It'll be cheaper to arrange for him to have an accident in jail, or to commit suicide in his cell. I know Vaudan, too. He's very good at arranging accidents and suicides.'

Hilda Braun seemed to sag back in her chair. Tears ran down her face. She held a hand to her mouth, shaking her head slightly as if to deny the truth of what Skinner was saying.

'I'm sorry to have to hit you with this, but there was no way I could edge up to it. Look, do you want to help Hansi?'

She nodded.

'Well, there might be a chance. But I want you to give me that letter, and to write me another one.'

62

The oriental girl spread herself against the window, beckoning to Skinner and Mackie as they walked past. Her tiny bra and G-string were almost the same yellowish colour as her skin. Mackie, in spite of himself, looked towards her. The beckoning grew even more insistent.

'Want me to wait for you, Brian?' Skinner asked with a grin.

The slim detective shook himself theatrically and forced himself to move on. 'Christ, sir, are they all like that?'

'From what I remember, most of them just sit there in their Marks & Spencer bras and knickers, looking bored. That lass must have been working on her sales technique.'

'I once had a girlfriend,' said Mackie, 'who had one of those big Garfield cats stuck halfway up her bedroom window. That's what that one there reminds me of, pressed against the glass like that.'

'You'd be a lot safer shaggin' Garfield than her,' Skinner muttered grimly.

'You been to Amsterdam often, boss?' Mackie asked.

'Once,' said Skinner. 'About fifteen years ago. I'd been a good boy or something, and my boss fixed it for me to be liaison man with the local police on a football trip. The local lads gave me the grand tour of the canal district. And before you ask, the answer's "Mind your own business".' He grinned at a sudden memory. 'Actually, to tell the truth, there was this Dutch lady detective in their squad. I really fancied her, so the last thing I was going to do was let her see me taking any interest in the women in the windows!'

'How did you do there, then?' asked Mackie, amused by this sudden burst of frankness from his boss.

Skinner smiled again. 'The answer's still "Mind your own business". It was a long time ago. Don't know what I'd do if I met her here today, though.'

They walked on down the narrow street, which at the end opened out into the first of the notorious canals of Europe's legal red-light capital.

The German police helicopter which had flown them from

Hamburg to Schiphol had made excellent time. Mackie, having ascertained that there would be no language difficulty at the Nederland Property Investment Bank, had declined the offer of an official reception. Instead they had taken the short taxi trip from the airport to central Amsterdam, where their driver had been disinclined to drive through the narrow canalside streets, and had dropped them off to walk the remaining half mile to their destination. Even in mid-afternoon, the city's most famous industry was in full swing. As Skinner had recalled, the canals were lined with window after window of bored prostitutes, largely ignoring their potential clientele. Some were smoking, others renewing their heavy make-up. One or two were knitting. Eventually they left the canals behind and turned into another narrow street, where every business establishment was either a bar or a sex-shop.

Mackie stared at the implements on sale and shook his head. 'What in Christ's name would anyone want with one of those?' His Calvinist upbringing asserted itself. 'I can't be doing with all that. I don't know if I've ever told you, sir, but my lifetime hobby is model railways. Everywhere I go I like to buy a set for my collection.'

Skinner's shoulders shook with sudden laughter. 'You could probably do that here, too, Brian. Only thing is, the engine would be a funny shape!'

Less than a minute later, they emerged from their seedy surroundings into the wide pedestrianised courtyard towards which they had been heading. Skinner looked around and saw, on a building on the far side, a large brass plate bearing the letters 'NPIB'. He tapped Mackie on the shoulder and led him across the paved central area, between tubs of multicoloured flowers. He opened the high, heavy, half-glazed door. The name of the bank was spelled out in gold leaf on the opaque glass panel. Inside, a stern, tweed-clad receptionist-secretary was stationed in the centre of the walnut-panelled entrance hall, barring the progress of visitors. Her eyebrows were pencilled on, and her grey-flecked black hair was pulled back in a bun. She reminded Skinner of a memorably intimidating primary school teacher of his childhood.

Mackie introduced Skinner and himself. 'We are here to see Mr van Troost,' he added.

'Wait here, please,' said the forbidding woman. She withdrew through a door at the end of the hall. A few seconds later it opened once more, and her head and shoulders reappeared. 'Come this way,' she ordered. The two detectives obeyed without a word. She led them into a room panelled in the same style as the hall, with a desk in matching wood behind which sat a trim man with a narrow face and a long nose, crested by gold-framed spectacles. He wore a grey suit made of a shiny fabric, and a white shirt with a 'fresh from the wrapper' look.

Van Troost did not rise as they approached, nor did he smile. The secretary-guardian beckoned them to two uncomfortable wooden chairs, then retreated from the room.

'So,' said van Troost without preamble. 'What is the purpose of this mysterious visit?' His clipped tones seemed laden with hostility. 'You said that your enquiries relate to a fraud investigation, but not more than that. I must tell you that, as Director of this bank, I recoil from the very mention of the word fraud. Our reputation in Europe is impeccable.'

'I don't doubt that for a second, sir,' said Skinner, 'and no one is impugning it. We know that the transactions which we want to discuss are quite legitimate – on your part at least. We are looking into a certain loan, and most probably a second, which we believe you have made against the security of some properties in Spain. We know of one loan of around seven hundred and fifty thousand US dollars, arranged by or on behalf of a French national named Vaudan, possibly in association with a UK national named Ainscow. The loan of which we are sure is secured against a number of shop properties in the Spanish province of Girona. The second, if it exists, will be covered by a residential portfolio in the same area.'

Van Troost knitted his fingers together, and stared across the desk at Skinner over the top of his gold-rimmed glasses.

'Suppose I knew of such loans. Why should I break the trust of my clients by telling you about them?'

Skinner smiled. 'To help us with our enquiries, of course.'

'But if I do not choose to do so?' said Van Troost evenly, looking Skinner straight in the eye.

The big policeman's smile did not waver for a second as he returned the banker's stare. 'Mr van Troost, you *will* tell me, please believe that, if not on this visit, then on the next. I have the power to ensure that you do. That is not a threat; it is a simple statement of fact.'

Van Troost looked at him for several seconds more, as if weighing his words. Eventually he unclasped his hands and leaned back in his chair. 'I believe you, sir. You are not a man to say such a thing without meaning it, or being able to bring it about. Very well. There are two loans. Each is for seven hundred and fifty thousand US dollars. One is to Nicolas Vaudan and the other is to Paul Ainscow. They are secured in the way you described.'

'When were they negotiated?'

Van Troost thought for a second. 'Arrangements were completed

204

around six weeks ago. We took some care over verification of title to the security. It was impeccable in every case.'

'What are the terms?'

'The loans are repayable in full within one year, although Monsieur Vaudan did say that he expected them to be cleared within six months. Interest is at two per cent over base rate per annum. Very generous of us, I believe. Of course, if the loans are not repaid as agreed, the rate will increase retrospectively to ten per cent over base.'

Skinner smiled. 'Can't expect you to be *too* generous.'

Van Troost grinned in turn and nodded.

'Have the loans been drawn down?'

'Yes, that was done two weeks ago, on joint instructions. All of the money was transferred to a numbered account in a bank in Monaco: an obscure private concern named Sneyder et Fils.' Van Troost leaned forward once more. 'That is all I can tell you. The loans were granted in good faith, against sound security which we now hold. I have no idea what the money was for. If every bank such as ours asked the purpose of loans such as these, we would do little business. There must be a place for trust in this world, no?'

Skinner nodded. 'Of course there must. You've been a great help to us. I will make sure that is known here. If I can give you some advice in return, this is it. Don't let the deeds to your security out of your sight. You may need them.'

63

'Arturo? Hello, it's Bob here. I'm at Schiphol. Sorry, Amsterdam Airport. Listen, I've just put a package on the 19.10 KLM flight to Barcelona. It's marked for you, strictly personal, so have one of your lads pick it up from the purser. The flight's due in at 21.20, so you've got plenty of time to get someone down there.'

Pujol's voice echoed back up the line. 'What is in this package of mystery?'

'Two letters. They're in German – so set up a translator. It'll be worth it, I promise you. The girl we went to see was Hansi's girlfriend. Lucan visited her to pay her off. One letter's from him to her, spinning her some bullshit about a long sea voyage. The other one she wrote to Gruber after we put her wise. You're going to love it. She's got a fertile imagination, that girl. Once you've read them both, you'll know what to do. Have fun.'

'You seem to have done well in Hamburg. How about your other visit?'

'There, too. At first I thought we might have trouble, but fortunately Mr Van Troost was a realist. We were right. There are two loans, for one and a half million dollars in total, transferred already to a very secretive-sounding private bank in Monaco – not the sort of place where we'll be able to walk in and demand information. We must keep track of that money, though – assuming that it isn't too late already. I've got an idea on that score.'

Pujol laughed. 'I'll bet you have. So where do you go now, my friend? Monaco?'

'Sod that for a game. So far I've been in three countries today, with a fourth to come when we touch down in Edinburgh. That'll do me for this week. If I got home, then buggered off straight away to Monaco, Sarah'd kill me. Anyway, I couldn't take the slightest chance of Nick Vaudan spotting me, or of him hearing I was there. He thinks he's free and clear, remember, and that I've been scared off and run back to Scotland. If your girlfriend and Paco Garcia did as they were asked – and they will have, each for a different reason – he thinks he's in the clear. That's what gives us our chance of closing down this whole operation.'

'*Si*, I know. Good luck, my friend.'

'Good luck to you too, when you have your talk with Gruber. Somehow I don't think he'll gob on you this time.'

Skinner hung up and left his booth, which was one of a semicircle of twenty, and went to the cash desk to settle up for his call. As he signed his credit-card slip, Brian Mackie stepped up to his shoulder. 'Get through okay, sir?'

'Okay. My Spanish mate'll send someone to meet the plane and pick up those letters. It's up to him after that. How d'you get on?'

'Fine. There's a fax waiting for me, reporting something from the Vaudan surveillance. Seems he had a visitor from Scotland yesterday. I thought you'd want to see it as soon as we got back, so I've asked for it to be sent down to your house. I didn't think you'd want to go into the office tonight.'

'Too bloody right! D'you arrange for a car to pick us up?'

'No need. Mine's at the airport.'

'Good. Drop me off and come in for some supper, so we can have a look at it together. When do we land?'

'Quarter to eight. We board in ten minutes.'

'Right. Gives us time to hit the shops. I've got to buy an Amsterdam T-shirt for Sarah. We've got this deal. If I get to go somewhere on my own, I bring her back something to prove I've been there. She's done okay today, and that's for sure!'

64

Jazz's windy howl came to an abrupt halt the moment that Bob appeared in the nursery doorway.

He gave one loud burp and forgot his discomfort as recognition showed in his tiny eyes. Sarah stood up from her chair and held the baby out to his father.

Bob took him, arms outstretched, and raised him high above his head. 'Hello there, wee man. If you've missed me one-tenth as much as I've missed you these last couple of days, then you've still missed me a lot.' Jazz smiled down at him, a dribble starting at the corner of his mouth. Bob cradled him to his shoulder, leaned over and kissed Sarah.

'Hello, love. The same goes for you, too.'

She squeezed his arm. 'Mmm. I'm just glad you're back so soon. How were Hamburg and Amsterdam?'

'Interesting and very useful. We're hot on Ainscow now. He's tied right into Vaudan through that money.'

'Where does that put Gloria? Does it help you prove that Santi's death wasn't suicide?'

'Not yet. Paco Garcia's statement still gives us a big problem there. If it were discounted, Gloria would probably have enough doubt on her side now to challenge the insurance company in the civil courts. But with that on the record, she's stuffed.'

'But couldn't Garcia be lying?'

Skinner shook his head. 'No chance, love. Garcia would have given me the PIN number to his granny's cash card if I'd asked him. He was telling the truth, no doubt about it. It looks as if I was wrong about Santi. That dog theory was just the great detective's imagination running away with him. The guy must have had a brainstorm. *Suicide while the balance of his mind was disturbed*; that's how it goes. The fact that Vaudan *was* going to kill him won't soften the insurers' hearts.'

'Dammit!' said Sarah. 'I feel so sorry for that woman.'

'Yeah, so do I, but we've done all we can. Anyway, enough of that. Brian's downstairs. He's stopping for supper ... if that's okay. Has Fettes dropped off a paper for me?'

Sarah gave him a longish look. 'Of course it's all right for Brian to stay. I was half expecting him anyway. As for the fax, couldn't it wait until tomorrow morning?'

'Maybe not. Things are moving fast on this one.'

They walked downstairs – Jazz still nestled happily on Bob's shoulder, drooling quietly on to his shirt – and joined Brian Mackie in the living room. 'Your envelope's on the coffee table,' said Sarah. 'I'll get supper under way while you two see what's in it.'

Skinner nodded toward the brown manila envelope. 'Open that, Brian, will you.'

The Chief Inspector picked it up and tore it open with his index finger. He took out a sheet of paper, scanned it and passed it to Skinner, who took it from him, left-handed.

The report was a day in the life of Nicolas Vaudan, compiled in secret by his watchers. It listed everyone with whom he had been in contact while Skinner and Mackie had been in Hamburg and Amsterdam: some by name, others unidentified and simply by description. One section was underlined.

Skinner read aloud. '"Caller arrived at Vaudan's waterfront office just before midday. White male, aged around fifty, stocky, of medium height wearing denims. Heavy moustache, black-framed spectacles. Drove a Ford Transit van, UK registration L 254 DQT, with trailer attached. Spent twenty minutes in Vaudan's office before Vaudan himself showed him to the door. Left his vehicle parked in Vaudan's yard and left in a taxi."'

He looked across at Mackie. 'Has anyone . . .' The question was answered with a nod before it was complete.

'Yes, sir. This was in the envelope too.'

He handed across a second sheet of A4 paper. Skinner read once more. '"Caller subsequently identified provisionally from van registration as Norman Melville Monklands, age forty-nine, of 7 Dalziel Terrace, Whitburn, West Lothian. Monklands has no record of convictions or arrests. He is DSS registered as a self-employed delivery driver, specialising in the transportation of light motor-boats between Spain, Portugal, France, Italy and the UK. He maintains a small office at Inverkip Marina, near Gourock, and employs two other drivers on a casual basis. Monklands is known, on a social and business basis, to the police in Whitburn, where he and his wife also operate a small fleet of vehicles as licensed taxis. Whitburn officers provided the information that his main social interest is golf, and that he is a member of Dalmahoy Golf Club."'

The note was signed by Maggie Rose.

'Interesting,' said Skinner. 'Maybe this guy is a complete innocent. Maybe he's in Monaco to pick up a boat.' He paused to shift position in his chair as Jazz, falling asleep, slumped against his neck. 'But in a deal like this one – if we are on the right trail – there has to be a courier. And if you didn't have someone like Mr Norman Melville Monklands, you'd have to invent him. Tomorrow, Brian, while I'm arranging to have a look in that Monaco bank account without anyone knowing about it, you do some more checking. Find out everything there is to know about this guy. What kind of perfume his mistress likes, the whole damn lot. But that *is* for tomorrow. For now, I am going to put my son to bed. Then you, his mother and I are going to eat. So far today, I've had a Spanish breakfast, a German lunch, and a Dutch tea. It'll be nice to end it with a plain Scottish supper!'

65

'You need to get details of a numbered account in a small private bank without anyone knowing you've done it?'

'That's right, Maggie, and I need them today if possible. See to it, will you.'

Maggie Rose shook her red locks and smiled. 'Too tall an order for me, sir. I think I'll have to decline.'

'I was afraid you would. Looks like I'll have to get on my Superman cape. And I'm knackered after yesterday, too. Okay, Mags, sit down and learn something. What I'm going to do is cheat a bit and call in the resources of my other job.'

The young inspector nodded and sat down. By virtue of his 'other job' as part-time Security Adviser to the Secretary of State for Scotland, Skinner was recognised as a senior member of a service which, while it had become less 'secret' over the years, could still call on facilities and cut corners in a way of which no police force could dream. Now, he picked up a black scrambled telephone on his desk and punched in a short-coded number. The telephonist answered with a number, not a name.

'Morning. This is Skinner in Scotland. I know it's Saturday, but is Angie Dickson in? Good. Let me speak to her, please.'

The extension rang twice, before a bubbly voice answered: 'Dickson.'

'Ms Dickson? This is Bob Skinner, the Five man in Scotland.'

'Good morning, Mr Skinner. How can I help you?'

'By showing off your skills. Remember the lecture you gave at that seminar in Yorkshire last winter? "Armchair Spying" you called it. I found it fascinating, but I have to admit I was sceptical at times. Can you really do all those things?'

'Sure. Given a fair wind, I can do everything I told you. I even managed to hack into the CIA last week. We thought they were holding out on us over a deal in the Middle East. We were right. Now the negotiations have taken a whole new turn, and the Americans can't figure out why.'

Skinner laughed. 'Then what I've got for you should be plain sailing. I'm involved in an international investigation. It's a police matter rather than a security job, but something's come up which calls for skills that simply don't exist in that network. I need to know details of a numbered account in a small private bank in Monaco, called Sneyder et Fils. But I have to tap in with absolute secrecy, and leave no trace. You said in Yorkshire that you can do that.'

'That's right, I can, in theory. Assuming that Mr Sneyder and his son have computerised records and a modem in their system.'

'Yes,' said Skinner, 'that's the chance I'm taking. But I'm pretty certain they will have, though, for transferring credit. What do you need, to get in?'

'Nothing other than the number of the modem. Once I've got that, I'll squirt my little gizmo down the line, and it will persuade Sneyder's system to cough up its access code. Once I'm in, I can go where I like, get what I'm after, and get out again. Then another little gizmo will persuade their computer not to log the search – and that's that.'

'So will you do it?'

'Natch. Anything for a brother officer. What's the account number?'

Skinner dug a small piece of paper from his pocket. 'C 159480.'

'Got it. Leave it with me. I'll be quick as I can. I'll get you all the info I can. Balance, account owners, signatories – all that sort of stuff.'

'That's the game. When will you be able to do it?'

'Right now, I should think.'

'Although it's Saturday?'

'Yes. If they have a system, it'll be accessible to receive electronic transfers even when the bank is closed.'

'How long'll it take?'

'Will you be there all morning?'

'For you, as long as it takes.' He gave her his direct number. 'Thanks in advance.'

He replaced the receiver. 'There you are, Maggie. Did you pick up enough from one side of the conversation?'

'Yes, sir, I get it. I'm going to have to start calling you God. You surely move in mysterious ways!'

Skinner snorted. 'Hmph. D'you think God's got an in-tray as big as that one?' He pointed to the small mountain of files, memos and letters heaped on the big desk, close to his left hand. 'If I was the Almighty, you'd see a miracle done right here and now and that lot'd disappear. I take it this is what's left after you've filtered out the nonessential stuff.'

'That's right, sir. I spared you as much as I could. I even farmed some of the punter correspondence out to Alan Royston, and told him to sign himself "Head of Public Affairs" instead of Media Relations Manager.'

'Hope he doesn't come after me for a rise! Right, then. Let's get to it.'

His hand was almost on a memo, balanced precariously on top of the heap, when there was a knock on the door and Brian Mackie burst into the room. 'Can I have a minute, sir?' The thin detective could barely contain his smile. Even the top of his head, which during the previous few months had moved beyond its balding phase and now could be described only as dome-like, shone red with excitement.

'You can have as many minutes as you need, Brian. Grab yourself a coffee.'

Mackie filled a mug from the pot in the corner, then took a seat beside Maggie Rose. He was still smiling. 'Took a detour on the way in, this morning, boss. I dropped into Dalmahoy Golf and Country Club, just for a look around. I went into the club-house. I found a bloody great noticeboard covered with competition charts and results. One of them was the club foursomes. Mr Norrie Monklands is doing very well this year. He's in the semi-finals. Know who his partner is?'

Mackie's grin broadened, until it infected Skinner. A smile spread across his face.

'So tell me, Brian. You've earned the pleasure.'

'Only Mr P. Ainscow, that's all. D'you think there's more than one?'

Behind his desk, Skinner punched the air with his right fist. 'You – pardon my French, Maggie – fucking beauty! The whole thing fits. Vaudan, buyer; Monklands, courier; Ainscow, distributor. We've got them by the jewels. We follow Monklands home, let Ainscow make his contacts, and there won't be a court in Edinburgh that's big enough to hold all the drug-dealing bastards we'll pull in. Too bad for Monklands and Ainscow. Somehow, I don't see them making the foursomes final!'

213

66

They were in the same small room in the Barcelona prison.

Two guards stood in the corner, only a small step away from Gruber. The German's left eye was puffed and blackened. Pujol wondered if his escorts, after their previous meeting, had taken it upon themselves to instil in their prisoner a little respect for the Guardia Civil uniform. If that was the case, it seemed to have worked. Hansi Gruber seemed altogether more circumspect as he looked across the small table.

The Commandante enjoyed his advantage. 'You are surprised to see me again?' he asked in French. 'Don't be. It's just that I was asked to deliver something to you, and being an obliging fellow by nature, well, I said "of course." Actually, I was asked to deliver two things to you. The first, you have seen before.'

He took from his right breast pocket the German's letter to Hilda Braun, and threw it on the table. 'Sure, you have seen it before. In fact you wrote it, didn't you? When you did, you never thought it would need to be delivered. You didn't imagine you'd be so stupid as to foul your engine on Mr Inch and his sailboard. That letter, it was just to cover you against a million-to-one chance. You left it with Vaudan, to be delivered only if you were caught.'

Gruber grunted. 'No, everything in that letter is true. I was going away on that cruise, but I had the accident with that poor man, and now I am here.'

'That *accident*, after you planned your escape, then stole a boat.'

Gruber spread his hands wide in a theatrical gesture. 'I do crazy things sometimes, when I am drunk.'

'Okay,' said Pujol. 'That is of little importance for now. The second thing I have for you, here it is.' He produced a second letter, folded, from his left breast pocket and waved it in the air. As he did so, he fished in the same pocket with his left hand, and found a further piece of paper. He threw the letter on to the table with a broad smile.

'That is for you, from Hilda. It is written in German, but I have had it translated into Spanish. Let me read it to you. Our friends in the corner will enjoy it too. She says:

' "Dear Hansi

' "How big a fool can you be? Your friend Lucan came to me with your letter, your story, and your money. Then two policemen arrived and told me the truth, that you are lying in a stinking jail in Spain on a murder charge. What have you done? You went away to find a new life for us, one free of trouble, and all you have done is throw away the little that we had. Your friend Lucan, some friend he is. He told to me that your trip might last much longer than you thought, and that the money might not be as good as you had been led to expect. He even said that if I needed comfort while you were away, then all I had to do was call him and he would come back to Germany just for me. Your friend is a pig, Hansi.

' "The two policemen who came to see me said that, the way things are for you, you will go to jail for ever. But they also said that if you were to tell the truth – that you were paid to kill this man – and that if you gave evidence against the man who paid you, then you could go free. Be sure of this, Hansi, I will not grow old waiting for you. If you continue to protect these people, I will not be outside the prison gates when you come out, old and bent and leaning on a stick. If you ever want to see me again, and to feel free air in your lungs while you have the strength to enjoy it, then, for the first time in your stupid life, do something sensible. Tell the Spanish police what they want to know, and give evidence against this man. Otherwise, rot in there; at least until they eliminate you as a risk to them by arranging another accident – for you this time.

' "Hilda" '

'Some love letter, eh, Hansi.'
As Pujol had read aloud, Gruber had been following Hilda's words in her original letter. He now re-read it in silence, then dropped it on the table and buried his face in his hands.
'Nice man, that Lucan, isn't he, Hansi,' said Pujol sympathetically, 'offering to look after your girlfriend for you while you're inside. He could get to look after her for a long time. Now, are you going to do the sensible thing? Here is the deal. You give evidence, and when Vaudan is convicted you walk free. Otherwise ... well, you can forget about the sound of birdsong, the surge of the sea, and the smell of a woman for a long time, maybe forever. You going to do it?'

Gruber's eyes seemed beaten as they looked up and across the table. He nodded briefly.

'Good,' said Pujol. 'Now I want to hear you say it. You were paid to stage Inch's accident, yes?'

'Yes,' said the German hoarsely.

'By whom?'

'By Nick Vaudan.'

'He gave you your orders in person, yes?'

'Yes.'

'Was anyone else there?'

'Yes. That filthy bastard Serge Lucan.'

'All very good. Now I am going to bring in a secretary who is fluent in German. You will dictate your story to her, she will type it up, and you will sign it. Then we will have copies made in Spanish, French and English. In whatever language you say it, Señor Vaudan will be cooked!'

67

'Nice little bank, Sneyder et Fils. I had a good rummage while I was there. I looked at a dozen numbered accounts, as well as the one you gave me. Two were held by terrorist organisations, one by a Mafia don, and a third by a company which is known to us as a CIA front. Once I can set aside some more time, I'm going to take a longer look. Congratulations, Mr Skinner, you're a hero of the Service.' Angie Dickson's voice sounded even more effervescent than before.

'Don't think I really want to be,' said Skinner. 'Don't think I want to know too much, either, about what you can do to banks. As a policeman, it'd make me feel too uncomfortable. Apart from that rogues' gallery, what have you got on the account you went in to look for?'

'All there was to know. Opened a couple of weeks ago. Joint holders: Nicolas Vaudan, French national, and Paul Ainscow, British. The day after the account was opened, a deposit of one and a half million US dollars was made by EFT from a lending bank in Holland.'

'And it's still there?'

'No, I just missed it. It was pulled at eight thirty this morning. French time.'

'Bugger!' Skinner snapped. 'All of it?'

'The lot,' said Angie Dickson. 'One-point-five mil. In greenbacks. It would have to be on the signatures of the joint holders.'

'Would both need to be there?'

'I don't know. I wouldn't have thought so, though. The Red Brigade are hardly going to turn up in person to pick up their cash.'

Skinner grunted. 'No. Silly question really. I know that one of the signatories is in Scotland. Anything more to tell me?'

'No, that's it. Glad to have been of help, though.' She added, 'That's assuming I have been.'

'Oh yes, Ms Dickson,' said Skinner. 'You surely have.'

'Good. I love being given the chance to show off! Bye.' There was a click and the scrambled line went dead.

Skinner replaced the black phone in its cradle. He looked across at

Maggie Rose. 'There you are, Mags. An electronic bank job, by request, and it isn't even lunchtime yet.'

'What did she have to say?'

'Enough. Let's go see DCI Mackie, international liaison officer.'

As they walked the short distance from the Command Suite to the Special Branch office, Skinner briefed his assistant on Angie Dickson's report. 'That money's on the move, Mags. I want to follow it to wherever it's going.'

He threw open the door of the DCI's office, calling out as he did. 'Brian, get on to your French friends and—' He stopped short when he noticed Mackie was hunched over his desk with the phone pressed to his ear.

He looked up and cupped a hand over the receiver. 'They're on to me, sir.'

As Skinner and Rose watched, he nodded, grunted, muttered the odd '*Oui*' into the phone. Suddenly, quite unexpectedly, he sat upright in his chair, and slapped his palm on the desk in frustration. '*Oui, oui, oui, je comprends. Au revoir à vous aussi.*'

Mackie put the phone down and looked up at Skinner.

'Go on, Brian,' said the big ACC. 'Tell me whatever it is. I know all this was too good to last.'

Mackie stood up. 'The French have lost them. Vaudan and Lucan. They're off.'

'How?'

'It went like this. Vaudan's in his office around nine. Then Norrie Monklands shows up, carrying a hold-all, and goes inside. Meanwhile the guys watching Lucan see him playing about with a big, fast, sea-going cruiser. They think he's just turning the motor over, when he slips the cable and eases out of the berth. He's on his own, and they don't think for a minute that he's gong to take the thing out to sea, but he does. He drifts out of the marina, and he guns the bugger.

'Back at Vaudan's place, the watchers suddenly see Monklands and Vaudan in a speedboat. They can't see the boathouse exit from where they are, and you can enter it from the office, they said, so they didn't see them getting in. It was just a wee boat, they said, like you'd use to tow a water-skier. They know it can't go far, so they're not too worried. In fact they decide that they're probably test-driving the boat Monklands will be taking back on his trailer. But half an hour later Norrie Monklands comes back alone.'

'So he must have transferred Vaudan to Lucan's cruiser?'

'Yes. D'you think they've twigged they were being watched?'

'Shouldn't think so. They've got one and a half million dollars with them. They're just being extra careful.'

Mackie looked at Skinner in surprise. He nodded, 'Yes, pulled from the bank at sparrow-fart this morning. That's what would have been in Monklands' bag. So what did the French do?'

'They called in the coastguard. Or they tried to. The coastguard told them to go through channels. They wouldn't even put a single helicopter up without an order from Paris. But by that time . . .'

Skinner finished the sentence. '. . . they'd have been long bloody gone.'

'I asked the French what the range would be of a boat that size,' said Mackie. 'They said it could go anywhere in the Mediterranean with maybe just one refuelling stop.'

'Yeah,' said Skinner. 'They're off with their cash pile to meet their supplier, and we can only guess where *he* might be. Sicily, Morocco, the Lebanon – any-bloody-where. Bang goes our chance of shutting down the whole supply chain.'

He looked up and grinned. 'Still, the ball's not burst yet. That's only part of it. We've still got Vaudan and Ainscow by the nuts. As long as we don't lose sight of Monklands, we're still in play. We can assume that he brought down Ainscow's signed authority for the dollar withdrawal. But he's still there, with his empty trailer, so let's add the assumption that he's taking a delivery back with him. Brian, you're on your travels again. I want you to get out there now, or maybe sooner. Join up with the French watchers, and wait for Vaudan and Lucan to get back from wherever they've been with whatever they've bought. Then, once Monklands leaves, tail him every centimetre of the way. As soon as you see which channel crossing he's going to take, call ahead so that I can fix it with the customs at his landing port.'

Maggie Rose looked at her boss in surprise. 'I thought we'd follow him *all* the way home.'

Skinner nodded. 'We will. I want to make sure that he *doesn't* get stopped by the customs.' He turned back towards Mackie. 'You all right with that, Brian?'

A shaft of sunlight shone through the window and glistened on Mackie's bald head, as he smiled back at him. 'Sure, boss. But don't *you* want to go. I mean, Sarah could always use another T-shirt. You only brought her back three last night!'

Skinner laughed. 'No, you just be a good boss, and bring back the duty-free for your squad! Right, Detective Inspector Rose. Let's go up and see how Mr Martin's getting on, keeping tabs on Ainscow and that wee shit Cocozza.'

He led the way from the Special Branch suite up the single flight of stairs to Andy Martin's Drugs and Vice team. The outer office was empty save for a typist, hard at work. She was wearing transcription headphones.

Andy Martin, seated at his desk signing correspondence, looked up as they entered. His blond hair was tousled, and his green eyes shone. The breadth of his shoulders stood out beneath his tight-fitting, short-sleeved shirt. His tie was loosened and the top button was open. Skinner noticed that he had a fresh red scratch on his neck, but before he could comment Martin greeted them, brightly. 'Hello, sir; Maggie. I thought you two would be up to your fetlocks in paper today.'

'Aye, we were, but we found an excuse to drag ourselves away.' Quickly, Skinner explained the events of the previous twenty-four hours: the discovery of the cash-pile and the Monaco bank, Angie Dickson's electronic break-in, the withdrawal and, finally, the evasion of surveillance by Vaudan and Lucan.

'Christ,' said Martin, 'that makes my poor life seem dull and humdrum. I've just spent the last few days supervising a team watching two guys do sweet eff-all out of the ordinary.'

'All quiet on the Ainscow front, then?'

'Yes. Church-mouse. And Cocozza too. He's been doing the rounds of the former Manson empire. He's spending a lot more time there than in his law practice.'

'He never really had one,' said Skinner. 'Tony Manson was always his biggest client. I heard that Tony knew Cocozza's old man, and that he more or less set the son up in practice.'

Martin leaned back in his chair. 'There is one thing on Ainscow, boss. I asked Alison Higgins' guy, Ogilvie, to pull the record of his old estate agency from the back files in Companies House – remember, the one he cashed in back in the Eighties – and have a look at them. He gave me his report last night. He said that anyone who paid big money for that business must have been off his head. He said the last couple of years' accounts were bloody ropy. I've arranged to see the managing director of the current parent company first thing on Monday morning, through in Glasgow. Want to come?'

Skinner thought for a moment. 'Yes, I think I will. I want to know as much as I can about Mr Ainscow, even if I have to go to Glasgow to find out. Will you pick me up from home?'

Before Martin could reply, Ruth appeared in the doorway, clutching a fax. 'Excuse me, sir. I thought you'd want to see this right away. It's just come in, from Barcelona.'

Skinner took the paper from her. As he read Pujol's account of his second meeting with Hansi Gruber, then the English translation of the German's statement, a broad smile spread over his face.

'Good news?' asked Martin.

Skinner nodded. 'Mmm. But very bad news for Nick Vaudan. A life sentence, I'd say, on top of what he gets for complicity in fraud and for drug dealing.' He chuckled. 'That'll teach the bastard to proposition my wife!'

68

Bob Skinner never visited Glasgow without being struck by the differences, architectural, climatic, cultural, social and emotional, between the former Second City of the Empire and Edinburgh, Scotland's capital.

There exists in many ordinary Glaswegians a bitter contempt for their compatriots forty-five miles to the east. Skinner, brought up on the city's outskirts, had managed to escape its influence, but could feel it hanging, almost palpable in the air as soon as he set foot in the city.

'It's like another world, Andy, isn't it?' he said to Martin as the younger man locked his red sports hatch, parked in a bay found unexpectedly in Blythswood Square, where the solemn classic frontage of the staid and ultra-conservative Royal Scottish Automobile Club – 'Jurassic Park' as Skinner had once christened it – looked out across a leafy garden which once upon a time had turned after dark into a red-light district of national renown.

'Yes, I suppose it is. Nothing wrong with it, though,' said Martin defensively.

'No, but the Glasgow folk think there is. They don't just have a chip on their shoulder, they've got a whole bagful – with salt and vinegar. They're jealous of Edinburgh, and they feel inferior to it, so instead of just being content to be different they go in for all these daft civic slogans that cost big money and don't mean a fucking thing. Glasgow's got some of the most distinctive architecture of any city in Europe. It's got its galleries, its concert hall, three universities, two of the biggest football clubs in Britain, all sorts of things going for it, yet it's still got this inferiority that makes it stick out its chest and shout challenges along the M8. People in Edinburgh don't understand Glaswegians, because they don't have that aggression in their blood, but they don't resent them either.' He paused. 'At least that's how I see it. What about you?'

'I don't know,' said Martin. 'You're right about the differences, and about the aggressive streak through here. That's probably the effect of the Scots-Irish element in Glasgow. But this place, it's got far more life to it than Edinburgh. Some of the people I know through there – I don't mean in the job. Other people . . .'

'You mean women?'

Martin smiled, 'Aye, okay, women. They're very shallow. They're only enjoying life up to a point. Whereas, through here, people are more, more . . . I don't know how to say it really. Well, look, take Alex as a classic example. She's lived in Glasgow for the last four years, virtually all her adult life you could say. And she's the most alive person I know. I realise she was only a youngster when she went through, but she's blossomed and taken on a depth to her personality that I've never encountered in anyone else. Not even . . .'

The name died on Andy's lips as the memory flooded back. A memory which, even close on a year after the event, still thrust a pain like a red-hot spear into the pit of his soul. As they turned the corner from Blythswood Square into West George Street, Skinner decided that it was time to change the subject.

'To business, Andy,' he said gently. 'Remind me, this guy we're going to see. Who is he again?'

'Bernard McGirk. He's the head of the estate-agency division of the General Alliance insurance company. He's the bloke who bought Paul Ainscow's business. I've told him that I want to ask him about it purely as background, but that our investigation doesn't touch him or the business in any way.'

'As far as we know.'

'True.' They crossed West George Street and headed down a steep hill into St Vincent Street. The General Alliance headquarters was a tall marble and glass edifice built during the property boom of the 1980s, a modern structure which blended well, for all that, with its refurbished sandstone neighbours. A uniformed commissionaire greeted them with impressive formality, snapping to attention even more rigidly at the mention of Skinner's rank. He directed them to a lift.

'Mr McGirk's office is on the second floor, gentlemen.'

Bernard McGirk was a small, friendly man, with an efficient secretary who brought in a tray laden with coffee and biscuits almost before Skinner and Martin had settled into their seats at a low, round table. While the coffee was being poured and handed round, they made small talk about the depth of Skinner's tan and the unpredictability of the weather, leading inevitably to the weekend's golf.

Eventually, McGirk looked across at Martin. 'Well Superintendent. You wanted to ask me about my purchase a few years back?'

Martin glanced sideways at Skinner, who nodded, happy that his subordinate should ask the questions.

'Before I do that, I ought to tell you why we're here. We are involved in another investigation, in which Mr Paul Ainscow may be caught up. We're building up as much information about him as we can, and that includes his financial health. We've been led to believe that he did well out of the sale to you of his estate-agency chain.'

McGirk smiled. 'I suppose you could say that.'

'On the other hand,' Martin continued, 'we've pulled some back accounts which don't look too clever. We hope that you'll be prepared to tell us how much General Alliance paid for the business, and how much of that would go to Ainscow.'

'Do either of you have a General Alliance policy?' McGirk asked, looking from Martin to Skinner and back again.

'Yes,' said Skinner, 'I have an endowment policy, and I've just taken one out for my son.'

'Fine. In that case, since we're a mutual, you're a member of the company, and as far as I'm concerned reasonably entitled to information on its business. So, where do I begin? At the end I suppose. Ainscow didn't pocket a hell of a lot from the sale. AREA, it was called. That stood for Ainscow Residential Estate Agency. It had high-street shopfront outlets in Stirling, Perth, Falkirk, Dundee and Edinburgh, opened in that order. Ainscow founded the business when he was in his mid-twenties. In those days any idiot could sell a house, and so he did well. Stirling prospered, he went to Perth. That did well – and so on. He lived a very full life, did the young Mr Ainscow. Bought himself his Porsche, obligatory in those days, a very nice house in Dunblane, and eventually a villa in Spain, and a couple of apartments for rental. He stuffed his pension fund too, for all he could.'

McGirk paused. 'Terrific while it lasted. The man was one of Thatcher's children, a youthful entrepreneur. Something of a business celebrity for a while, in a small way. The trouble was, like many of these boys, while he could sell in a boom market, when things turned down he didn't know what to do. Actually he was in trouble even before the slump. He could afford his various premises while things were rosy, but when the market began to edge south, his overhead caught up with him very quickly. He was tied to very long, very expensive leases, with no breakers, and he had ripped out so much of the profit in the boom years, without leaving anything for a rainy day.

'He went from boom to potentially bust in two years, as you no doubt saw from those accounts. Eventually he approached us. We were diversifying into estate agency at the time, and we were his landlords in Dundee and Perth. The location of his premises fitted our expanding portfolio, so we did a deal. We bought AREA's goodwill, basically, and its debt, and that, believe me, more or less cancelled out the cash value of the goodwill.'

'So what did he walk away with?' asked Martin.

'In cash terms? Virtually nothing. Maybe twenty thousand out of the net fifty we paid him for goodwill. His properties, and the Porsche, were all owned through a subsidiary of the main business. He separated that company out and kept it. There was about thirty thousand in borrowing there, which he flattened. He asked for a consultancy as part of the deal, but I didn't see that he had anything to offer, so I said no. However, I did tie him to a restrictive covenant which kept him out of business in the UK for three years. I heard that he had gone into the Spanish property market, and that didn't surprise me. Presumably he's an agent for a promoter-developer over there.'

'No,' said Skinner. 'He's the principal shareholder of a solidly capitalised business. We were told that he had funded the start-up with some of the money he got from you.'

McGirk shook his head. 'No way. His lifestyle wouldn't have left him with the cash to do that. I'm not saying he was broke after he sold out, but he wouldn't have any investment capital. Unless he borrowed on his house.'

Martin shook his head. 'No, we've checked. There's nothing secured on it. What about his pension fund?'

'Locked up tight, and can't be used against borrowing.'

'And he didn't win the pools as far as we know. So, yet another mystery. Where the hell did he find the fifty grand it took to start InterCosta?'

69

At first the ringing of the telephone was part of Skinner's dream. He was in L'Escala on the terrace, with Sarah on the sun-bed beside him, and he was dreaming of home. In the living room, the phone was sounding . . . except that its ring was different from the usual Spanish single tone.

His mind was fuzzy with confusion as the dreamscape blurred. Then suddenly the sound from the bedside table snapped him into wakefulness. As he snatched the phone from its cradle, Sarah lay beside him, oblivious.

'Skinner.'

'Boss, it's Brian. Sorry, did I wake you?'

'Mmm. It was my turn on the early shift with Jazz. Never mind.'

'Sorry to call so early, your time. I realise it's only seven forty with you, but I thought you'd want to know: they're back. Docked an hour ago. They sailed the big cruiser right into Vaudan's boat-house. Monklands just turned up, too.'

Skinner sat upright in bed. 'Any guesses as to where they've been? That's *how* long? This is Tuesday, so just under three days for the trip. Where could they have reached in that time?'

'The boys who know here say possibly halfway down the Italian coast, to one of the small islands offshore, maybe Elba. Definitely not Sicily. The best guess they're giving me is the north-west coast of Sardinia. There's some pretty wild stuff there, and no Coastguard cover, so it would have made a good meeting point.'

'Right. Maybe we'll let the Italian police know later but, for now, are you ready for action?'

'Yes, the French are being very helpful. Their national drugs agency has put two cars on the job. The drivers sound as if they know what they're doing. They have a lot of this type of surveillance over here. Wherever Monklands goes, and whenever he sets off, we'll be after him.'

'Where are you now?'

'In an apartment straight across the road, about two hundred yards away. I can see the yard . . . Hey, there's some action right now.

226

Norrie Monklands and another bloke—' He broke off for a second. 'The lads here say it's Lucan. They've unhitched the trailer from Monklands' Transit, and they're wheeling it into the boathouse, out of our sight.'

'Okay, Brian, that's good work. You stick to it. Let me know once he leaves, then check in whenever you can, on the road. Speak to you later.'

Beside him, Sarah rubbed her bleary eyes. 'Whwsat?' she murmured.

'Brian Clouseau calling in from France. I think our game's about to kick off!'

She reached up and pulled him down beside her. 'Well, before it does,' she yawned, 'how about one final training session?'

70

As Skinner's morning unfurled and moved towards midday, his mood grew more and more tetchy. He had given Ruth instructions that he would take no calls other than from Brian Mackie, but as time passed the silent telephone on his desk disrupted his concentration. He could barely read a single page without his attention wandering as he eyed the receiver, urging it to ring.

The mountainous in-tray which he had faced on the Saturday morning of his return had been largely weeded out. He was reduced to reading routine reports from the various divisions on the containment of petty crime, when Ruth buzzed him through. He flicked the intercom switch.

'Sir, if you've got a few minutes, the Chief wonders if you'd join him for coffee. He's just back from his conference in Birmingham.'

'Aye, sure. I'd welcome it. Can't get used to having my backside stuck in a chair again.'

Sir James Proud's office was on the opposite side of the Command Corridor from his own. Skinner preferred his perch over the main driveway, from which he could keep an eye on the traffic to and from the headquarters, to his boss's outlook over the force's modest playing fields.

Mary, the Chief's new secretary, was arranging three cups and a jug on a tray. 'Morning, sir. Go right in, please.'

The unspoken question prompted by the third cup was answered as soon as he stepped into the long, spacious office. Proud Jimmy was sitting in an armchair facing his coffee table. Beside him was Chris Whitlow, the force's Management Services Director. Whitlow was a professional administrator who had been recruited from local government to take responsibility for establishment tasks, and to manage the force's budgets. To make way for him, one of the authorised Assistant Chief Constable posts had been removed from the establishment. Before the appointment had been made, Skinner had expressed private reservations over the principle of appointing a civilian to such a senior post in a disciplined service. 'Theory's great, Chief, but what about the practice? How long will it be before a guy like this starts questioning command decisions and policy on grounds of cost? It could be the thin end of a wedge. Before you know it we could have a chief executive, with powers, slotted in between us and the police board.' Nevertheless he had welcomed Whitlow to the team on his appointment, and had co-operated with him in every way, even suppressing slight feelings of alarm when the new broom had taken over the office next to Proud's own, made vacant by the retirement of Eddie McGuinness, the former Deputy Chief.

Sir James jumped to his feet as Skinner entered the room.

'Bob, good to see you. My, you're looking brown!'

The ACC grinned at his boss. 'So they tell me. I'm thinking about putting in for a transfer to the Guardia Civil. After the last few days I feel like an honorary member anyway.'

'Yes. Some holiday you've had. Roy Old told me about that business with Sarah and the man with the brick. That was bad. Did they get him?'

Skinner nodded, a gleam in his eye. 'Oh yes, I got him,' he said quietly. 'He said he was sorry and he won't do it again. Now I'm going to get the guy who sent him. He's going to be sorry too.'

'Sounds a mite personal, Bob.' If Whitlow's tone was jocular, it was lost on Skinner.

'It *is* fucking personal, Chris, but it's professional too.' He turned back to Proud. 'So how was the ACPO conference, Jimmy?'

The Chief pulled a face. 'Ponderous as usual. A sea of silver braid gathered together for the sole purpose of being lectured by civil servants and politicians. Here, sit down while I pour.' Mary had followed Skinner into the room with her tray. Proud Jimmy thanked her, picked up the jug and poured coffee into the three cups. They faced each other around the low table.

'So tell me about this business, Bob. Maggie Rose has been keeping me broadly up to date. Your simple fraud investigation seems to have taken wings.'

'Wings and jet engines, Chief.' Quickly, Skinner explained the sequence of events which had stretched the investigation over five countries and half a continent.

'So where are things now?' asked Proud.

'Waiting for the phone to ring. Something's happening in Monte Carlo. Our target's getting ready to leave, and it's our bet that he's bringing more than a boat back with him.'

'But it is no more than a bet, Bob, isn't it?' said Whitlow.

Skinner looked at him coldly. 'Maybe, but it's odds on. We've got a million-odd quid in laundered cash disappearing into the Mediterranean. That cash isn't a fucking donation to Oxfam. We know it's been used to buy something, and given Ainscow's encounter with Cocozza and the three wise men in the Powderhall sauna, our belief is that it's drugs.'

'But what if you're wrong? What if it's not? What if this man Monklands isn't bringing anything back with him. What if Skinner's trail goes cold? You've had Mackie flying all over Europe . . . and you yourself for that matter. At the end of the day, if there's nothing to show for it, how am I going to explain those costs to the police board?'

Skinner flashed a look at Proud. 'What is this, sir? Am I on the carpet here?'

The Chief shook his head emphatically. 'Chris voiced some concerns to me. I told him he'd better put them to you directly.'

'Okay.' Skinner, mollified, turned back to Whitlow. 'Right, Chris. I think it's time I spelled out the rules of engagement around here, because you seem to have misunderstood them. This is an active operation, and I'm in charge. I've been taking command decisions in this force for years and I back my own judgement on what is reasonable and what is not. If I think I'm into major cost, I'll tell you; otherwise I won't.

'As for this so-called bet of mine, we have reason to believe that smack worth one and a half million dollars nett is about to be imported into this country. Do you know what that will be worth on the street? Easily over ten million sterling, maybe much more, depending on how it's cut. Do you know something else? It'll sell like hot-cross buns at Easter. Get your accountant's mind round this. Try putting out a rights issue for ten million to private shareholders in your average public company. The odds are that the underwriters will be left with a good chunk. Not with this issue. It'll be fully subscribed within weeks of going on offer. Thousands of people with dependencies will be exploited. Their addictions will be fed and prolonged. Some will overdose and die. Few of these people earn enough to feed their habits. So as soon as this stuff becomes available in Edinburgh, Glasgow, and wherever else it goes, there will be an outbreak, in each of those cities, of petty and not-so-petty crime: burglaries, muggings, the odd armed robbery and so on. All the work of junkies needing readies. The public will be added to the list of victims and police resources everywhere will be stretched. Now, you weigh all of that against a couple of plane fares.

'Through all of this, a few people will get very rich. Vaudan and Ainscow will pick up maybe half the total take. They'll be able to pay off their seed capital loan, set aside more cash for the next buy, and still split a couple of million sterling in profit. The dealers will be awash with surplus cash, ready to invest in whatever other villainy they're into. You follow that, and do you appreciate all the consequences?'

Whitlow nodded, but said nothing.

'That's good. Because it's important that we all operate in harmony along this corridor. So that we can do that, let me spell out a couple more of Skinner's rules for you. The first is that *you* don't answer to the police board for my actions. I do. You're here to service the force, not run it. The second is that if you've got a concern over any aspect of my operations, the first person you speak to about it had better be me.'

Whitlow nodded again. He coughed. 'Yes, Bob, I hear what you say. I should have come to you first, and I will in future.' He stood up. 'Now, if you will excuse me, Sir James.'

'Of course, Chris. Glad we've cleared the air.'

Skinner was still fuming quietly as the door closed. Proud Jimmy smiled at him. 'Thought it was better to handle things that way than simply come across the corridor and tell you about it. I know you. You'd have kicked his bloody door in! Anyway, that's him calmed down now. Wish I could sort people out the way you can.'

'Aye, maybe,' growled Skinner. 'We'd still better tell Ruth and Mary to keep a running tally of the paper-clips, though.'

Proud laughed. 'That's the future, Bob. It'll all be yours when you're behind my desk.'

'You're forgetting the regulation, Jimmy. No promotion to Chief without experience of command rank in another force.'

Proud's smile grew even wider. 'Didn't I tell you? I've fixed that with ACPO and the Scottish Office. That other job of yours – Secretary of State's security adviser? That'll be counted as outside experience when the time comes. I've told you before, even if you're kicking and screaming, Bob, I'm going to make certain that you succeed me.'

The surprise was still on Skinner's face when the phone rang.

Proud moved to his desk and picked it up. 'Yes. Put him through.' He held out the receiver. 'For you. Mackie.'

Skinner took one long step across to take the call. 'Brian, yes.'

'They're on the move sir. Two of them. Neil Monklands and Lucan. They've just pulled out of the yard. My first car's gone with them, and I'm off next. There's a speedboat on the trailer. Quite a big thing, it is, with two heavy outboard engines on the back.'

'So Lucan's gone as well. Not surprised. If they're carrying what we think, Vaudan'll want his man there all the way. There's neither honour nor trust among criminals, is there, Brian? Okay, you get on your way, and let me know progress as you can. Meantime I'll start to set things up this end.'

He hung up. 'That's it, Chief. Our courier's on the move. With a minder, and, though he doesn't know it, a police escort.'

'What do you do now? Sit and wait?'

'More or less, once I've briefed the Customs, to make sure that those people are waved through, wherever they land. I want them filmed, too. I want to be able to show the court a video of every stop that consignment makes in the UK, from the docks to the dealers. If you'll excuse me, I'll go and take care of that. Then I think I'll check on the surveillance of Ainscow and Cocozza.'

71

Skinner opened the door of Andy Martin's office, and collided heavily with the detective superintendent as he stepped into the room. Martin was zipping up his brown leather jacket.

'You off, Andy?'

'Yes, boss. We've got action from our targets. I've got Neil McIlhenney tailing Cocozza, and McGuire watching Ainscow. Mario called in nearly an hour ago to say that Ainscow had left his office in Stirling. He followed, and phoned in to say that he's heading for Glasgow. Meantime, Neil called in to say that Cocozza seems to be on a pub-crawl. He's been to three of the Manson places so far. Stopped for about twenty minutes at each one. That's unusual behaviour for him. He checks up on them, sure, but we've never found him making a round of visits like this before. At one stop, a bloke arrived at the same time as him. They started talking on the street and went inside. Neil thought he recognised the guy as someone known to us. He took a couple of photos of the two of them together. I'm off out now to meet up with him. Neil's last call put him at the top of Leith Walk, probably heading for that pub near the foot, where big Lennie used to work.'

'What's your guess about what he's doing?' asked Skinner.

'Same as yours, I reckon. That he could be putting word around the network that there's a ship coming in. Fucking idiot if he is, getting personally involved in it like that.'

'Aye, you're right there. In Manson's day, if you saw signs on the street that there was a new supply around, you could bet that Tony would be on holiday at the time, somewhere far away. He was brilliant at distancing himself. He ran his show on the basis of one word to one person, and letting his orders filter out from there. Wee Cocozza doesn't have that authority, y'see. A message from Tony, even at third or fourth hand, and it was as if it had come from the Burning Bush. This wee chap, he'll be having to say "Please". Out of his depth. What about Ainscow, then Andy? What's your guess there?'

Martin shrugged his shoulders. 'He could be going to Ralph

Slater's for a new suit. But given what Cocozza's doing, I wouldn't be surprised if he's off to Glasgow to see Eddie Gilhooley, then to Manchester and Newcastle, and the other two Wise Men, to let them all know that the buy's made, and the stuff's on the way.'

Skinner nodded. 'Yes. Ainscow didn't strike me as the Ralph Slater type. Hope big McGuire's got plenty of petrol and film in his camera. I think he's in for a long day. Make sure he keeps me informed as it goes on.'

Skinner paused. 'As for you, don't bother teaming up with McIlhenney. Get on the line and tell him to get back in here. I want you two to draw a diesel-engined vehicle with a big fuel tank – the sort that'll let you go at least five hundred miles without having to fill up – and head off down south. Make for somewhere on the M25 south of London, from where you can reach any port or terminal within two hours, and wait for further instructions. Wherever Monklands and Lucan make landfall, they're going to have a reception committee: you, big Neil and me. Then, once the Customs boys have closed their eyes and waved them through, you and McIlhenney are going to stick to them like glue all the way home. Okay?'

'Yes, boss.' As Martin nodded in response, Skinner caught a pensive gleam in his eye.

'Am I buggering up your social diary, Andy? You got a new lady?'

Martin smiled softly. He opened his mouth as if to reply, then changed his mind. He shook his head. 'That's okay Bob. She understands all about the job.' The distant look came back into his green eyes.

72

This time, Skinner was wide awake when the bedside phone rang, ten minutes before eleven p.m.

He was propped up on his pillows, holding Jazz as the baby settled to sleep. He smiled and winced simultaneously as tiny but strong fingers wound round his chest hairs and tugged. The muted ringing of the phone did not disturb the child, nor did Skinner's whispered 'Hello.'

'Boss, sorry again, but this is the first chance I've had. Our targets have been sharing the driving, and making good time, sticking to autoroutes all the way. These French police drivers are very good. They've been doing a team job, keeping in touch by radio. The Transit's pulled into a service area for now. It looks as if they might be bedding down for the night.'

'Where are you bound? D'you know yet?'

'All I can tell for now is that we're headed for Paris. We just passed the fork in the road that leads to Reims and directly to Calais, but they took the other option. That means we still could be heading for any port in France. There is one clue, though. Monkland's van has a Brittany Ferries sticker on the back. That doesn't tell you much either. They have four terminals in France and three in Britain.'

The line was silent for a moment. When Mackie spoke again it was with a question. 'Which route would *you* choose boss, in their shoes?'

Skinner paused as the baby sighed and moved on his chest.

'I've been thinking about that,' he said quietly. 'I'd avoid Calais, Dunkerque, or the Channel Tunnel. The Customs there are always on the look-out for vans with big quantities of booze. They tail some too, to see if they can catch the owners selling their cargo. Other than that, getting on board a vessel is no problem. The danger is at the other end. Plymouth, Poole, Newhaven are all small. You'd be more obvious there, with a higher percentage chance of a random pull-over. On balance, I'd go for Portsmouth or Southampton. With a bit of luck, you'll be having supper in Cherbourg tomorrow.'

'With a bit of luck, boss, I'll be having a shower and a shave! I'll call you again soon as I can.'

73

'Morning, Maggie. What time did big McGuire get in, then? Or is he still out on the tiles?'

DI Rose scowled. 'Don't ask, sir! He followed Ainscow all the way, like you guessed, from Glasgow to Manchester, then to Newcastle. Finally he tailed him back up the A1 to Edinburgh. But does Mr Ainscow go home? Oh no. He goes to the Powderhall sauna for an hour and a half. Mario, thoughtful as ever, called me – woke me from a sound sleep – at one o'clock in the morning to tell me he was sitting in Powderhall Road, waiting while the guy got his executive relief. By the time he had seen him home to Dunblane, as per standing orders, it was five o'clock when he got in.'

Skinner smiled. 'Very quietly, I hope.'

'Not bloody quietly enough.'

'Ouch!' He paused. 'Who's picking up Ainscow and Cocozza this morning?'

'Superintendent Higgins' people are handling it.'

'That's good, 'cause we're getting to crunch time. Once the consignment gets to wherever it's going, we mustn't let either of those bastards out of our sight. We've got to catch them up to their elbows in the stuff.'

Skinner hung up his overcoat, still wet with the heavy morning rain, and went to sit behind his desk.

'Do you want me back on surveillance duty, sir?' asked Rose.

'Yes. When it gets vital, I want all my best involved. But for now I've got a few tasks for you. I want you to make contact with the chief regional officer of HM Customs and Excise in the south of England, and brief him on what we're involved with. Tell him that we expect our subjects to make landfall in the UK within the next twenty-four hours, at a port as yet unknown, but possibly Portsmouth or Southampton. Give him details of Monklands' van and trailer, and ask him to make absolutely certain it gets clearance without trouble. No one is to stop it, or do the slightest thing to arouse suspicion.'

Skinner paused. 'That's top priority. Eventually Brian Mackie will confirm the destination. Once he does, contact the local police force, and tell them what's happening. Make sure that, whatever reason might arise – dodgy brake lights or anything else – no one approaches the van. Then put the word around all the forces on all routes back to Scotland. Find out the number of the car that Andy Martin's in too, and circulate that. I don't want this operation blown through him and McIlhenney being pulled for speeding by some over-zealous plod in a motorway car. Finally, get me a return ticket on the shuttle. Leave the flight details for now. I'll wait as long as I can for Brian Mackie to call in.'

74

'Sorry if I startled you.'

He had been walking through the security gate at Edinburgh Airport when the sound rang out. The strange tone threw the duty officer into a state of sudden confusion, until Skinner produced his mobile phone from his pocket, apologising at the same time. He stepped to one side and pushed the *receive* button.

'Boss, it's Brian. They're crossing Caen to Portsmouth, Brittany Ferries, midnight sailing. They just got here. Monklands bought a ticket at the gate. It's not their biggest vessel, but it seems quiet. He must have known there'd be no problem getting on a night sailing.'

'Good lad. You book yourself on, too. Check that they board, then your job's done. Get yourself a cabin and crash out. We'll handle things from the landing point on.'

'Where are you just now, sir?'

'Edinburgh Airport, about to board the eight o'clock shuttle. Andy and McIlhenney are picking me up at Heathrow. We'll head straight down to Portsmouth from there. What time do they dock?'

'Six a.m. UK time.'

'Okay. We'll be there to see them through safely, then Andy and Neil will tail them up the road. You and I'll fly back. I'm going to board this plane now, so you call Fettes and get Maggie or someone to pass on the details to Kevin Cochran, my contact in the Customs. This has got to go like clockwork, and at the moment they're the mainspring of the operation.'

75

There is something inherently unattractive about all customs halls. None are beautiful, thought Skinner, but the building at the Portsmouth ferry terminal, was exceptional in its drabness.

Skinner, Martin and McIlhenney were seated along one side of a long refectory table, in a long narrow room lit by neon tubes. A series of windows ran along the wall behind them. The glass in each was one-way, allowing a clear view of all of the arrivals hall, but allowing nothing, not even the faintest glimmer of light, to show from the observation room.

Facing them across the table was a group of eight men and women. Seven were wearing white short-sleeved shirts with epaulettes. The eighth, like the three policemen, wore a lounge suit. The table was strewn with white mugs and the scraps from a large platter which, only a few minutes earlier, had been piled high with bacon rolls.

The customs officer in the lounge suit turned to a colleague. 'Is the *Duc de Normandie* making good time?'

'Yes, sir,' one of the women replied. 'In fact it was well ahead of schedule, so it laid up for a while. It'll be docking in ten minutes.'

'Right, you'd better all think about taking up position. You've all heard Mr Skinner, and so you know the form. For once we *don't* want to catch someone. This is a quite unique situation, in that not only do the police know of a suspected shipment coming in, but they believe they know also where it's heading. If our colleagues here can follow this consignment all the way, they can do some real damage. So no slip-ups. Normal treatment for these two, quick passport check, and wave them on.'

Skinner broke in. 'Kevin, there is one other thing you might be able to do for us. We're going on the strongest supposition that this is a drugs deal, but we failed to track the French end of the operation to the buy, and so we haven't *seen* the stuff yet. How good is your sniffer dog?'

'Harry,' Kevin Cochran called to a man at the back of the room. He was holding, on a short leash, the biggest golden Labrador bitch that any of the policemen had ever seen. 'How good is Thatcher there?'

'She's brilliant, sir. Old Mags could sniff out a spoonful of heroin in a hundredweight of sugar.'

'In that case,' Skinner asked, 'would it be possible to walk her past the Transit and trailer while Monklands and Lucan are in the passport queue, to see if she reacts?'

'Sure.'

'We mustn't alert the suspects, though.'

'No problem, sir. Just you leave it to me.'

'Okay,' said Cochran. 'Places, everyone.'

The white-shirted officers left the room, and reappeared a few seconds later on the other side of the viewing windows. Cochran and the three policemen gathered around one window. 'What's the normal route north out of Portsmouth, Kevin?' asked Martin.

'If you're going north, the usual way is to head towards Southampton, then pick up the A34 and head on up through Newbury, towards Oxford. You take the M40 from there, and then choose whether to go up the M1 or the M6.'

'Good. Neil, you and I had better get to the car. Will you call me on the mobile, boss, once they're about to clear?'

Skinner nodded.

'Okay, then. See you in Scotland. Come on, Neil.'

The two detectives left through the door at the other end of the long room.

'How are we doing, Kevin?' asked Skinner.

The Waterguard chief regional officer glanced at his watch. 'Any minute now. The Brittany Ferries crews are very slick.'

'Will we have a good view from here?'

'The best. I'm only opening one passport-control channel. They'll pass by right under our noses.'

The first vehicle, a Renault Twingo with French plates, swung into the long hall less than two minutes later, leading a line of assorted cars and vans. The lady in the passport booth was a model of efficiency, checking each document without appearing to rush, but clearing the line in double-quick time.

Eventually the first of a series of caravans joined the end of the queue. 'Your guys, with their trailer, ought to be in this lot.' Cochran pressed against the window, looking to his left to see as far as possible down the line. 'Yes. That's got to be them. Navy blue Transit, UK plates; and there's a boat on the back.'

He took a two-way radio set from the pocket of his jacket, and pressed the *send* switch. 'Okay, Sandra, they're in the line now. Two cars, four vans, then our target. Skinner saw the woman in the booth acknowledge the message with a brief nod of her head. He took out

240

his mobile phone and dialled Andy Martin's number. It was answered on the first ring. 'Okay, lads, ready for the off. Three or four minutes, no more.'

One by one, at the same brisk pace, the officer in the booth cleared the vehicles in the line, sending each on its way with a smile, until at last the Transit drew to a halt at her window, and Skinner had his first clear view of Norrie Monklands and Serge Lucan. Monklands, in the driver's seat, leaned down and handed two passports to the woman. She accepted them with a broad smile, responding – Skinner assumed – to a casual piece of small-talk. She glanced at the first passport, then looked up at Monklands in the Transit. As they chatted, Skinner saw the dog-handler walk the huge Labrador behind the boat trailer, to the far side of the line. He could not be sure but he thought that, as the dog passed the boat, its handler gave a sharp tug on the short lead to keep the animal moving.

As the handler passed out of sight behind the boat, the woman glanced at the second passport in her hand. She spoke up towards the van, and Lucan leaned forward suddenly in the passenger seat, into her line of vision. As he did, the handler walked his dog briskly back across the line and back down the shed, away from the Transit. Still holding the passports the woman smiled and said something else to the two men. Whether she spoke in French or English, both Monklands and Lucan threw back their heads in laughter.

'Come on, now girl,' the big policeman muttered to himself. 'That's great, but don't drag it out. Get them to hell out of there.'

As if she had heard him, the woman, with a last smile, handed the two passports back to Monklands. The man, stocky even in the driving seat, accepted them with a nod, wound up his window, and drove off slowly and carefully to the exit from the shed. He took a sharp left turn and, in a second, Transit and trailer had passed out of sight.

'Okay, Andy and Neil,' said Skinner, once again to no one in particular. 'You've caught the pass. Now run with the ball.' He turned to Kevin Cochran. 'That was excellent. Your lady out there is a star.'

The man smiled. 'She's well used to it, is our Sandra. She's a specialist. I get a job like this every so often. Whenever I do, I bring her along. She doesn't panic, and she never gives a flicker of what's going on.'

'How about Harry and Thatcher?'

Cochran nodded. 'Yes, they're on my flying squad, too. Terrific dog, that. She's the best in the business . . . and Harry Garden's not too bad either. Let's go and find them.'

He led the way out into the main shed. Sandra had been relieved by one of the regular officers, and a second line had been opened up. She and Harry stood chatting; Thatcher lay idly at her handler's feet.

'Well done, you lot,' shouted Cochran as he and Skinner approached. 'No problems that we couldn't see?'

Sandra shook her head. 'No. That Monklands thinks he's made another conquest. He's the god's-gift type.' She had a mellow voice with a slight West Country accent. Listening to her reassuring tones, Skinner understood at least one reason why she was so good at her specialist role. She went on, 'Lucan, the Frenchman, doesn't seem to speak much English, but Monklands' French is very good. I cracked a joke for Lucan, and the Scots fellow picked it up even before he did.'

'Good,' said Cochran. 'Harry, how about you? Did Thatcher have anything to tell you?'

'Did she just, sir. Did she just.' The big man smiled broadly. 'First time I walked her behind the boat, she nearly took my arm out its socket. Had a hell of a job keeping her going on past. I took her back again to make sure, and it was the same. Even on the trot, she was wanting to climb on that trailer.' He looked at Skinner. 'When you nick 'em, sir, don't waste time with the boat. Just go straight to those outboard motors. It's in there and, judging by the way Old Mags acted, there's a hell of a lot. You got a bonanza there. Bloody good work by whoever tailed 'em.'

Skinner looked past the dog-handler. 'Speak of the devil. Here's that very guy.'

Even after a night on the *Duc de Normandie*, Brian Mackie still looked worn and dishevelled. He carried bags of tiredness under both eyes, and his few remaining wisps of hair were flying about untidily.

Skinner smiled as he approached. 'Brian, you look bloody awful. I send you off to France on a cushy job and you come back like a death's head. Didn't you get a cabin?'

Mackie nodded. 'Sure. Right over the engine, I think. I've had better nights sleeping on the floor! Please, boss. Can we go back to plain, boring old Edinburgh? And can I get to stay there for a while?'

76

'Christ, sir, have these boys got a toilet in that Transit, d'ye think? It's been four hours since we had those mugs of coffee. Don't know about you, but my bladder's beginning to get annoyed. A bit pissed off, y'might say.'

Andy Martin, in the passenger seat of the Peugeot, laughed softly. 'That's what they teach us on the Senior Command course, Neil. Self-discipline and iron-hard bladder control. But, seriously, they'll have to stop soon. The Transit must be eating up the fuel, with that trailer on the back. They have to be due a fill-up.'

They had made steady progress since leaving Portsmouth. Kevin Cochran's prediction of Monklands' route had been accurate. They had followed their quarry westward to Southampton, before striking north towards, and through the centre of the pretty town of Newbury. Even at that hour of the morning, the traffic had been sufficiently heavy for their pursuit to be unobtrusive, while keeping the target always in sight. From the start, Monklands had driven steadily, and within the speed limit, as concerned, possibly, that he give the trailer a smooth ride as with ensuring that he did not attract the attention of the motorway patrols.

Eventually, around three and a half hours after setting out, and with McIlhenney's fidgets behind the wheel becoming more and more frequent, the van's orange indicator flashed at the approach of the Leicester Forest East service area. 'Thank Christ for that,' the detective sergeant muttered. 'Look, sir, if they're only stopping for petrol, will you take the wheel and let me nip off for a Jimmy Riddle?'

Martin nodded. But in fact, rather than heading directly for the pumps, the Transit pulled into the main car park. Keeping two cars between them, McIlhenney followed. He parked several rows away, and turned to look at Martin with an unspoken appeal. Smiling, the detective superintendent nodded; the big man jumped from the car and headed off briskly towards the single-storey service building.

Alone in the Peugeot, Martin eased down in his seat. While keeping his eyes on the van, he became aware, for the first time, that the forecourt was unusually crowded. Several coaches were parked in their designated spaces, and throngs of Asian men were milling about, many carrying brightly coloured flags which fluttered in the fresh morning breeze. For a moment he was puzzled, until he remembered the Test Match, due to begin that morning. The crowds were boisterous almost to the point of rowdiness. He glanced around, and took in a heavy presence of uniformed policemen, with several dog-handlers among their number.

'More like football supporters every year,' he whispered to himself. 'It's an all-year-round job for the crowd-control squads now.'

Movement from the Transit reclaimed his attention. The driver's door opened, and Monklands jumped out. He emptied the remaining contents of a plastic cup on to the ground, then looked back into the van and spoke to his passenger, before heading off towards the shops and toilets.

Must be peeing in turn, one on guard all the time, thought Martin; just like us, if they only knew. He settled down again, to await McIlhenney's return.

At first he thought little of the dog's insistent bark. There's always some idiot who gets brave when he sees a dog safely on the lead, he mused. But then it barked once more, the sound turning this time into something approaching a howl. He looked round, and saw the animal at once. Even by German Shepherd standards, this was a powerful dog. It was pulling its puzzled handler along gradually, inexorably, in the direction of the blue van and the trailer.

'Oh shit!' Martin cried aloud this time. 'It's a sniffer!'

As he watched, the handler loosed his grip on the leash, allowing the dog to follow its nose. It pulled him at a trot across the last few yards, straight to the twin outboard engines, canted up at the back of the boat, jumping up as it reached them and pawing at the engine casing. Martin could not see inside the van, but he knew inevitably what would happen. He did not have to wait long. The passenger door of the Transit slid open, and Serge Lucan jumped out, running full-tilt away from the dog.

'Oh shit!' Martin roared once more, as he threw open the door of the Peugeot and sprinted towards the Frenchman. Lucan recognised this new threat almost at once, and veered away from his approach. But he was too late. Martin was already too close, and had an edge in speed which enabled him to run the man down in only a few strides. He launched himself in a rugby tackle, taking the man around the knees and bringing him down, heavily. Lucan kicked out fiercely, in his grip, and made to rise. He swung a punch at his pursuer's blond head, but his arm was trapped expertly and twisted up behind his back. Swiftly, brutally, Martin kicked his legs out from under him slamming him once more into the tarmac, face-down and helpless.

He looked over his shoulder, and saw McIlhenney returning with a look of pure bewilderment on his face.

'Neil!' he shouted. 'Monklands is in the building somewhere! Nail him!' He glared across at the dog-handler, who was approaching uncertainly. 'Police! Drugs Squad. Don't ask, just give my sergeant assistance!' The helmeted constable, who recognised authority when he heard it, obeyed at once.

The bulky McIlhenney was halfway across the car park when Monklands appeared in the wide doorway. Panic flooded his features as he saw Lucan on the ground with Martin on top of him, his knee driven into his back. Then he, too, took to his heels. McIlhenney, who was built for endurance rather than speed, began to give chase, but stopped in almost palpable relief as the dog, unleashed, shot past him. It caught Monklands in eight strides. Launching itself, it seized the man's forearm and knocked him to the ground. The man screamed. 'Get it off me, for Christ's sake!' Detective and handler arrived together. As the dog obeyed a command to release and come to heel, McIlhenney took his prisoner by the collar and belt, hauled him to his feet and marched him off to join Martin and Lucan.

As the two pursuers stood beside the Transit, their captives restrained firmly, a uniformed inspector marched across, bristling with indignation.

'What are you people? What is this? Why wasn't I told?'

Piercing green eyes fixed upon him and silenced his outburst. 'Superintendent Martin and Sergeant McIlhenney, Edinburgh Drugs Squad. We'd show you our warrant cards, but we've sort of got our hands full.'

The uniformed man stiffened with respect for rank. 'Yes, sir.'

Martin gave him a resigned smile. 'It's not your fault, Inspector, but I've got some bad news for you – then some worse news. The bad news is that RinTinTin here has just fucked up the biggest drugs round-up in the history of British policing. The worse news is that, until I can calm him down, there's a certain Assistant Chief Constable who's going to want to tear your heart out with his bare hands, and probably the dog's too!'

77

'I'd like to tear their fucking hearts out, Andy – with my bare hands!'

On the other end of the line, Martin winced. 'Aye, sir, I know. But it wasn't their fault. These guys had their own operation on, and our target just landed in the middle of it. We briefed all the traffic departments to keep out of our road, but we couldn't warn every copper in Britain. It was luck, sir. Rank bad luck.'

There was a long silence. Eventually Skinner sighed. 'Yes, I suppose so. Where did you say you were now?'

'Back in Leicester, boss. The Transit and the boat have been brought here, and the local drugs boys are about to take the engines apart. Monklands and Lucan have been cautioned and detained. We've got no claim on them either.'

'No,' said Skinner, 'we won't have. They never made it north of the Border, so it'll be an English prosecution. What a bastard! There's no way now we'll lay a finger on Gilhooley and his two mates: probably not on Cocozza either. We can only hope to lean on Monklands and Lucan, and get them to incriminate Ainscow and Vaudan. That'll still be quite a score, but when I think of what we might have done . . . Bugger!'

Silence returned to the line until it was broken by Martin. 'There is one bright spot. Since I told them what they'd blown, the boys down here are being very co-operative. While you're right about this being an English prosecution, they've said that, if it helps tie in Ainscow to a conspiracy charge in England, we can borrow Monklands and Lucan for questioning if we like. What d'you think?'

'No!' Skinner's response was swift and vehement. 'Don't do that. If we're going to salvage anything from this, Ainscow and Vaudan have got to think that this has been a pure accident. On the face of it, that shipment could have been going anywhere. They don't know we were tailing it, but as soon as I take those guys over the Border, then, in effect, we've told them. Surprise is the only small advantage we have left, so let's keep it if we can. I want to interrogate Monklands, sure, but I'll come down there to do it. And, one other thing, when they go public on the seizure, I want no mention made of you and McIlhenney, or your parts in it.'

'Okay, that's how it'll be. When'll you be down?'

'I'll get a flight to Birmingham or East Midlands tomorrow morning. You wait for me there – even if it does screw up your love life. I tell you, Andy. Once this lot's over, suppose I never see another aeroplane...'

78

'Aye, so what if I know Paul Ainscow? Paul's got fuck all tae do with this. He just gave me an intro tae Vaudan. Towin' boats is what I do for a livin', and that's what the job was – towing a fuckin' boat.'

Police interview rooms have the same uniform drabness wherever they are, thought Skinner, recalling Pujol's hospitality suite in L'Escala, with its single chair bolted to the floor. The Leicester model had movable furniture, but the paint on the walls had a depressing similarity.

Local officers had begun the interview with Monklands, who had received their insistent questions with a stoic silence. After half an hour, Skinner, frustrated beyond endurance by the man's lack of response, had driven his rank through the formalities of territorial jurisdiction and had taken over.

'Look, pal. This is the scene. Paul Ainscow's your golf pal. He has a drug deal with Vaudan in France. He sends you down with a piece of paper to unlock the funds, and a trailer for smuggling back the stuff that it buys. I know that, as sure as you've got a hole in your arse. Now you make a statement confirming it, and it'll save you a right few years in Parkhurst, or Dartmoor, or some other nice hotel down here.'

Monklands' reply was accompanied by a defiant stare. At once, Skinner knew in his heart that the man would not be broken.

'Interview suspended.' He glanced down at his watch. 'Eleven twenty-two.' He reached over and switched off the tape-recorder, then leaned across the table. 'Okay, Norrie, we've nailed you fair and square with the narcotics equivalent of Santa's sledge on Christmas Eve. Not even the stupidest jury in England is going to let you off. You're going down for fifteen years, yet you won't give us Ainscow and Vaudan even though it would take ten years off that stretch, maybe more. I'm not going to lose my voice or bloody my knuckles trying to make you, 'cause I know I can't. So, tell me off the record. Satisfy my inquisitive mind. Is it money, or is it fear?'

Monklands glanced across at the tape-recorder, as if to verify that it really was switched off. He looked up at Skinner. 'If I did what you

248

ask, how long d'you think I'd last. See that man in Glasgow? Any jail you like to name, he's got someone in it that would do me in for five hundred quid tae his wife on the outside. So you're right, mister. You and these Brummies can kick the shit out of me all day, and all I'll tell you is that Serge and I did the deal ourselves, off our own bats. The same goes for Lucan too. Bet on it.'

Skinner stood up and shrugged his shoulders. He looked across at the detective who had begun the interrogation. 'You lads might as well charge them and take the rest of the day off. You heard what he said, and he's not kidding. Come on, Andy, Neil.'

Martin and McIlhenney stood up from their seats in the corner of the room. McIlhenney held the door open for Skinner. As the ACC left the room, he beckoned for the local officer to follow.

The man obeyed. Looking to see that the door was securely closed, Skinner leaned close to him. 'Listen, I don't care how you do it, but I want those two kept incommunicado. Use the Prevention of Terrorism Act, rabies regulations, anything you need, but keep them under wraps for as long as you can. When you do have to let them see lawyers, make sure that you hear every word of the conversation. I don't want any messages sent anywhere by either of them.'

He turned back to Martin and McIlhenney. 'Come on, lads. Let's drive on up the road.'

79

'No, Arturo, believe me, there's no way these boys are going to cough. The Leicester fellas did their best. They went at them all week-end. No contact with the outside or with each other, sleep deprivation, the whole works. No use at all.'

Skinner paused to take a sip from the coffee on his desk.

'Each of them trotted out the same story, word-perfect, over and over again. Paul Ainscow told Monklands about Vaudan's business, then he got a few jobs from him. He got to know Lucan, and between them they cooked up the drugs idea. Vaudan knew nothing about it, they say, and Ainscow, he knew even less. They questioned them all through Friday and Saturday, right up to last night. Eventually they gave up. They charged them last night and released the story to the press. They said that it was pure luck that a police dog, at the service area on other business, was alerted by the scent of heroin from the boat. It's all over the English press today.'

Pujol's voice echoed down the line. 'So what about Vaudan and Ainscow? What can you do there?'

'The French police have already done it. They went to see Vaudan yesterday, and told him that Lucan and Monklands had been arrested. He must have known by then, of course, but he kept a straight face, apparently. He looked shocked, and of course he denied all knowledge of the stuff. He even said that he knew Lucan was a bit of a suspect character, but he was good at his job, so he had kept him on. As far as Ainscow's concerned, we've got nothing to gain by going anywhere near him, so we've left him alone. He's still under close surveillance, although he hasn't twigged.'

'What about the joint bank account, and the cash withdrawal? Does not that give you grounds to arrest them?'

Skinner hesitated. 'It would, except we've got a wee problem there. That bank is not going to say a bloody word to the police about the ownership or the business of a numbered account. If it did, given the nature of its clientele, it would lose all its best accounts overnight, and its owners would probably wind up face-down in the Med. And without their co-operation, we're stuffed.'

Pujol was puzzled. 'But how did you know about the account?'

'That I can't tell you, my friend, on an open telephone line, and I most certainly couldn't discuss it in open court. If I did, a life would be at risk. I'm afraid that's the way things stand. All we've got from that shipment, and from all that work, are the two humphers – that's carriers to you. The thinkers, the planners, the money men are all in the clear. It's a bastard, and I hate it, but that clever fucking dog in Leicester blew the lot.'

Pujol sighed. 'That is too bad, Bob. I know how much it all meant to you.'

'Maybe it meant too much. Maybe I was getting too wrapped up for my own good in that one investigation, big as it was. It didn't help when Vaudan made it personal. You know, I've been tied up all weekend by a nice juicy axe murder on my patch. Blood, bone and brains all over the place. It was almost a pleasant relief to be investigating a nice simple uncomplicated crime again.'

'Did you solve it?'

'Yeah, no problem. My deputy led the team; he wrapped it up in a day and a half. It was a fall-out among thieves. There are two of them up in the Sheriff Court this morning.'

'You make it sound like a second prize.' Pujol's laughter echoed down the line.

Skinner interrupted. 'Hold on a minute, mate. I haven't given up on the other yet! You're forgetting something. We can't do Vaudan for the drugs, but we do have him bang to rights for Alan Inch's killing. You've still got Hani Gruber shut up tight, haven't you?'

'Yes,' said Pujol hesitantly. 'But that would mean extradition from France. That would be very difficult, maybe impossible. For sure it would take a long time.'

'That's right,' said Skinner. 'That's why you've got to arrest him in Spain. And I'm going to be there. There's a cheap flight from Newcastle to Girona tomorrow night, and I'm coming over on it to pick up my car. It's the last time I'll be on a plane this year, I swear. But while I'm there I'd like nothing better than to be around for the arrest of Mr Nicolas fucking Vaudan.' He paused. 'Now this is what I suggest you do.'

80

'Oh honey, did it have to be this week?'

Bob saw the depth of Sarah's disappointment, and hung his head, feeling as guilty as Roy Old's two axe-murderers. 'I'm sorry, love, but I really find it awkward being without the car. The flight costs peanuts, and it ties in with this ploy that Arturo and I have got on the go.'

'What's so important about that?' she asked.

'I'll tell you once it works out. I know we've been living like gypsies lately, but I'll only be away for a few days, and then we'll be back to normal. Why the long face, anyway, as the barman asked the horse?'

'Is it just that you'll miss me, or did you have something planned?'

Coyness sat uncomfortably on Sarah. 'We–ell. It's a bit of both, actually. I've invited these people for dinner on Friday. Nice couple. They've only just got together, and I thought it'll be nice for you to meet them and have dinner with them. With one thing and another, Friday was the only day we could fix up over the next few weeks.'

Bob took her in his arms and pressed her to his chest. 'I'm really sorry, love. But the ticket's bought and paid for, and Arturo's plans are laid. You'll just have to go ahead with it, and be host and hostess in one. Or maybe Andy could come along.'

'Mmm. Maybe. So when do you expect to be back?'

'The flight leaves Newcastle just after midnight, and gets to Girona at about half-three. Arturo's having one of his lads pick me up, but even at that it'll be half-four by the time I get to the villa. So Wednesday'll be a "sleep on the terrace" day. Arturo's arrangements could fall into place either Thursday or Friday. Once the business is over with, I'll drive up to Cherbourg. So look for me Sunday at the latest. Promise. And that'll be the last time. So you can rearrange your dinner party.'

'Copper, it had better be! As for the party, that might not wait.'

81

'She sent it exactly as we discussed?'

'Precisely. Word for word.'

It was almost six p.m. but it was still hot on the Town Beach. Skinner had been true to his word to Sarah, and had slept away most of Wednesday on a lounger on the terrace. Now he sat, wearing only shorts and trainers, on the low wall at the edge of the sand. Arturo Pujol sweltered uncomfortably beside him, even though clad in light slacks and a cotton shirt. Each man drank from a can of Seven-Up acquired from one of several dispensers around the promenade.

'I have a copy here,' said the Commandante. He fished in his shirt pocket and handed a folded piece of paper to Skinner.

The photocopied fax was printed on Montgo SA letterhead. Skinner read through it, translating the French laboriously. 'Señora Alberni has asked me to contact you. She is forced to sell her villa because of problems with her late husband's insurance, and she wonders whether Montgo SA would consider acquiring it as an investment, at no more than she and Señor Alberni paid for it. The matter is urgent, since she is being pressed by her husband's bank. She asks if you will come to L'Escala this week, on Thursday or Friday, to discuss it with her. She decided to contact you through me, rather than directly, since she felt that Madame Vaudan might not appreciate your having calls from strange women.'

Skinner handed the creased paper back to Pujol. 'You told Gloria, I take it, in case he decided to phone her.'

'*Si.* But he has not.'

'Has Veronica had an acknowledgement?'

'Yesterday. Vaudan says that he will arrive on Friday afternoon, that he will go straight to his villa, and that he will see Señora Alberni once she has finished work, at six p.m. at his office.'

'Ace! One minute past six and he's nicked.'

Pujol shook his head. 'No. If he goes to his villa, we will arrest him there.'

Skinner frowned. 'What d'you want to do that for? The villa's built on the hillside up in Punta Montgo. He knows its layout – you don't.

253

Wait till he gets to the office, and arrest him there. Much easier. You don't want to underrate this guy, Arturo. You're going to arrest him for ordering at least one murder, and maybe two. Don't assume that he'll just hold out his hands for the cuffs. And never give a man like that anything that might be an edge.'

'*Si*, Bob. I understand that, but if we go into the office . . .'

Skinner nodded. 'I get it. The lovely Veronica'll be right in the middle of it!'

Pujol flushed.

'Get her out of there. Tell her to go to the ladies at two minutes to six, and lock herself in! When you go in, don't advertise yourselves. Your guys don't have to wear their green suits and their funny hats. You have heard of plain clothes, haven't you?'

'No, Bob. That is not the way we do it. We will take him in uniform, at his villa.'

'Fuckin' 'ell, I don't know! Just as well that you'll have me along.'

Pujol looked at him sideways and shook his head. 'No, I am sorry. I am grateful, Bob, for all your help, but I think that now I have to follow the rules. This is a murder case in my jurisdiction. If I allowed you to take part in the arrest, my superiors would take – what is it you say? – a dark view.'

Skinner sat upright on the wall. 'Come on, man. You can't keep me out of it now!'

The Commandante's round, sallow face wore a pained expression. 'I am sorry, but if you were there and there was an . . . accident. No, it is not possible.'

'Arturo, this probably will be a straightforward arrest. But on the off-chance that it isn't, I've got experience you haven't. I've dealt with people who'd make Vaudan piss his pants.'

Pujol shook his head. 'Much as I would be comforted by having you at my side, I cannot allow it.'

Skinner saw that he would not win the argument. 'All right. Let me be a spectator. Give me field-glasses and a radio, and I'll keep watch on the villa and call you once he's inside.'

The Commandante considered this request for a few moments in silence. Eventually he smiled. 'Okay. That I will allow. After all, I cannot keep you from going to the top of the Garbinell, can I? But, to be proper, one of my men will go with you. He will have the radio and the binoculars. I *will* do things by the rules.'

82

'There can't be many finer views than this in Europe,' said Skinner in faltering Spanish, to his uniformed companion. He added in English, 'The seventh tee of my golf course maybe, but damn few others.'

It was just after three on a shimmering afternoon. He stood on the flattened top of the Garbinell, the crest of Punta Montgo, and looked across the Golfe de Rosas, to the north. The Pyrenean skyline, fringed with wispy cloud and, incredibly, with traces of snow still clinging to the peak of Canigou, was much the same as that which faced his own terrace, but below him the whole bay stretched out in a wide circle, from the wooded Montgo campsites, to the sprawling town of L'Escala and beyond. Kilometres of beach extended like a thin golden smile all the way to Ampuriabrava, tapering off only shortly before the rise of the northern headland. It was dotted with white houses built into the hillside above Rosas, the town with which the great bight shared its name. The 'Stormy Bay' was almost still, too calm for windsurfers or sail-boats. The water shimmered and glistened under the high sun.

Skinner hauled his attention back to the business of the afternoon. Their vantage point was little more than a hundred yards away from Nick Vaudan's sugar-white, castellated villa, but thick foliage growing from the rocks offered complete cover. The house was built into the steep hillside on three levels, topped by a wide three-sided terrace with stylised mock battlements, which surrounded the shuttered upper apartments. Skinner guessed that these would be the main reception rooms, with sleeping accommodation on the lower floors.

He unrolled a rush mat and threw it on the ground, handing a second to the young Guardia private. They settled down into their hide, looking down towards the villa and the twisting approach road. The young man placed his machine-carbine between them and handed the field-glasses to Skinner.

'*Gracias.*' The big Scot spun the focus wheel and took a closer look at Vaudan's mock castle. An impressive alarm box, with an orange light above, was fixed to the wall above the window on the east side of the terrace. The shutters were of steel, and Skinner guessed that they were motorised. To the rear of the house, a short concrete driveway led from black-painted, wrought-metal gates to a single garage. 'I'm surprised he doesn't have a fucking drawbridge!' muttered Skinner.

The young policeman at his side looked at him, bewildered.

They had been in position for a little less than an hour when they heard the throb of a big engine labouring up the hill. Seconds later, a red Jaguar XJS convertible, its top down, swung awkwardly round the bend. Skinner recognised Vaudan at once. The Frenchman drew the car to a halt, and pointed a small black box at the gate. Moments later it began to slide open, disappearing from sight behind the perimeter wall. Vaudan parked on the driveway, jumped from the car and, carrying a briefcase, trotted down a stairway which led from the drive, passing out of sight.

Less than two minutes later, the steel shutters on the terrace level of the villa began to roll up slowly. As the light flooded in, Skinner could see that the upper floor comprised one large sitting room, furnished with leather sofas and armchairs and a long coffee table. In one corner of the room stood a huge television set, near which, silhouetted against the western window, were a twin-pedestal desk and low-backed chair. Vaudan sat down in the chair, his briefcase on the desk before him with lid upraised. Then, flipping it closed, he moved across to the north-facing patio doors and threw them wide, allowing him to roll out two white plastic loungers and a matching refectory table. With the terrace furniture arranged to his evident satisfaction, the Frenchman stripped off his shirt and settled on a lounger.

Skinner lowered the field-glasses and nodded to the man at his side. The young policeman picked up his radio and muttered a few words of Spanish into the mouthpiece.

The green Nissan Patrol made even more noise than the V12 Jaguar, as it hauled itself up the steep hill. As it approached and swung round the bend, Skinner trained the binoculars on Vaudan on the terrace. At first, the man did not react to the sound. Then, as it drew closer, he propped himself on an elbow to look over the mock battlements and the perimeter wall. As the vehicle drew to a halt, Skinner saw a frown crease the Frenchman's forehead. The man stood up, grabbed his shirt, and slipped it on.

Pujol, in full uniform, his gun in its holster by his side, stepped from the front passenger seat. Three other officers each carrying a machine-carbine identical to that which lay beside Skinner, followed his lead. The Commandante spoke to one of the three men, who remained beside the vehicle. Then he led the other two down the driveway and through the small gate to the terrace.

Vaudan stood waiting for them, the frown still lining his face. Although Pujol had his back to Skinner, the latter knew at once when he had spoken and, from the sudden widening of the Frenchman's eyes, what he had said. Through the glasses, the scene was that of a silent movie. He saw Vaudan's lips move, but caught not even the faintest sound. Then the Frenchman threw his hands wide, as if in appeal. A few seconds later he saw Pujol nod his head briefly. The Frenchman turned and walked back into the villa, moving across to the desk.

Skinner focused the glasses as sharply as he could. As he watched, Vaudan raised the lid of the briefcase very slightly and very swiftly, and took out a small dark object. Then he closed the case, spun its locks, and picked it up . . . with his left hand.

Instinct made Skinner call out. 'Arturo! Gun!'

For an instant, Pujol looked back over his shoulder. Then, trusting what he had heard, he reached for the safety buckle on his holster. His gun was drawn as Vaudan stepped back on to the terrace. Skinner saw it move up to cover the Frenchman, but realised at once that it was too late. From the doorway, Vaudan fired a quick shot from a small automatic pistol.

'No!' Skinner shouted in anguish as Pujol fell backwards.

The Frenchman gestured urgently with his gun to the two other officers on the terrace. At once they threw their carbines over the mock battlements, and clasped their hands together, behind their heads. Vaudan gestured again, and they retreated into a corner of the terrace. As they did, he turned and sprinted through the gate to the driveway. Pujol's third officer was waiting, his gun raised, but stiff and frozen. Vaudan snapped off two shots. The young man spun round and fell face-down.

Skinner looked at the private by his side, and saw the boy's face transfixed and white with shock. He grabbed the machine-carbine, and looked quickly at its mechanism. He found the safety and flicked it off.

The Frenchman had reached the Jaguar. He tossed his case into the back and reached awkwardly, left-handed, for his keys.

The bellow from the hill-top froze him in his tracks. 'Vaudan! Drop the gun on the ground *now*, and raise your hands.'

The Frenchman looked up towards the sound of the voice and, as he did, Skinner realised that the sun was shining on the barrel of the carbine he held. Vaudan did not drop his pistol. Instead he swung it up towards the glint of light.

Skinner's single shot took him square in the forehead. For a second he stood stock-still; then, like a discarded marionette, he collapsed sideways against the car, his left shoulder wedging between the side mirror and the sloping windscreen. Thus jammed, he hung there, head lolling, eyes glazed, and blood trickling slowly down his nose from the hole just above its bridge.

The carbine hung loosely in Skinner's hands. He lay still on his mat, his face suddenly as bloodless as that of his young companion.

Eventually the green-uniformed private prodded him, gently. 'Señor?' He pointed towards the grotesquely trapped Vaudan. '*Es morte?*'

Skinner looked at him in silence for a few seconds, feeling his colour return. 'Oh yes, son. He's dead. He points a gun at me and he's fucking dead all right. That's the way it is.'

A slow smile crept over his face. He patted the young man on the shoulder, and pressed the carbine into his hands. 'That was a fine shot of yours,' he said in pidgin Spanish. He patted him again. 'Hero.'

The private looked back at him blankly.

The smile left Skinner's face. He stood up and motioned to the man to follow him down the hillside towards the villa, where nothing moved and a funereal silence hung in the air.

83

'The Commandante will be okay, *si*?'

'Yes, Carlos. He'll be fine, thank Christ. It was a flesh wound. The bullet went through his side but missed all the organs. An inch or so to the left and it would have taken a kidney out. He's a lucky fellow, Arturo is. He's not cut out to be a gunfighter, though.'

'How about the other Guardia? How is he? Alive too, I hear.'

Skinner nodded. 'Yes, but not so lucky. He's paralysed. One of the bullets is lodged in his spine. The surgeons hope to remove it once he builds up some strength. He lost a lot of blood.'

The two friends sat side-by-side on high stools at the end of the bar in La Clota. Carlos looked at Skinner's reflection in the big mirror which formed virtually the whole back wall.

'You know, Bob,' he said softly, 'That must have been some shot by young Joaquim. Hit him bang in the forehead, yes?' He made a sign with his extended index finger touching the bridge of his nose.

Skinner nodded silently towards the mirror.

'It's a funny thing,' said Carlos. 'My sons, they know Joaquim. In fact sometimes they go rabbit shooting, in a crowd. Only Joaquim, he never takes a rifle. He says it's because he doesn't want to shoot anything, not even a rabbit for the kitchen. My sons, they say that the other reason is that he is a lousy shot.' He looked sideways at Skinner. 'I guess they were wrong, eh.'

'*Si, mi amigo*. I guess they were.' As Bob picked up his beer and drained it in a single swallow, Carlos thought he saw a very slight tremor in his hand.

He slapped him on the shoulder. 'So what's it to be? You come here just to drink, or you eat? I get you a menu?'

'Don't bother with the menu. I'll have the duck. In honour of old Arturo – who forgot to. Meantime, Paquita, another beer, please.'

The duckling and the telephone arrived at the table at the same time. As the elegant waiter was serving Skinner's meal, Kathleen appeared at his side, holding out a small black cordless telephone.

'Bob, this is for you. It's Maggie somebody.' She smiled. 'Who's this we don't know about?'

Skinner took the phone with a smile. 'Maggie, hi. What's up?'

'Nothing vital, sir, but it's the sort of thing I thought you'd like to know about, so hope you don't mind. Sarah gave me the number. She said it'd be all right to call.'

'Mmm. No problem, but make it quick or my meal'll get cold.'

'Okay. Leicester called this evening. There's trouble between Monklands and Lucan apparently. It seems they were allowed exercise today, and Lucan attacked Monklands. Took a punch at him and broke his nose. They've had to separate them. They're due in court tomorrow, so apparently they're going to send them in separate vans.'

'Do they know what it was about?'

'No, sir. Apparently, when they ask him, Lucan just swears in French. And when they ask Monklands, he just holds his nose and says it was an accident. Any idea what the problem could be?'

'No ideas, only guesses. Has anyone told them about Vaudan yet?'

'Not as far as I know.'

'Well, get back on to Leicester and ask them to break the bad news to Lucan, then watch his reaction. They should be sure to have a French speaker handy when they do, just in case he lets something slip that we can use. And now, if you'll excuse me, this duckling needs my full attention. See you Monday.'

84

He was cruising around the western outskirts of the city of Bordeaux when the shrill tone of his car phone mingled with the Latin rhythms of the David Byrne CD.

'Bloody hell! Is there no peace?'

He stopped the player and pushed the phone's *receive* button. Brian Mackie's voice boomed out of the hands-free speaker. 'Hello, boss. How's the drive going?'

'Fine, until about five seconds ago. Making these things international was the worst telecommunications advance ever. What is it this time?'

'It's Lucan, chief.'

'Yes, I know,' said Skinner impatiently. 'Maggie called me last night.'

'No, sir. This is today. Lucan's escaped. We've just had a flash from Leicester. They were taking him to court. Apparently the van was stopped at traffic lights, when he banjoed his guard and kicked the back door open.'

''Kin' 'ell!' Skinner shouted into the small microphone clipped above the sun visor. 'Let me know developments.'

He pushed the *cancel* button and drove on in the sunshine, across the bridge over the wide river and on towards the north. As the kilometres unrolled, he recalled his outward journey with Sarah and Jazz. It seemed as if months had gone by, yet he knew that his son was still a day under seven weeks old.

He was striking out along the N 175, at the base of the Cherbourg peninsula and with the Autoroute network far behind him, when the phone rang again.

'Boss, it's Brian. No sign of Lucan, I'm afraid. He was in his own clothes, and he made it into a busy shopping centre, so they just lost him in the crowd. There was a report of a mugging in the area not long afterwards by someone answering his description, so they think he's now got some cash for the road.'

'Aye, but which road? He doesn't speak the language. His best chance would be to hitch a lift on a French lorry, I suppose. Did the Leicester people break the news about Vaudan?'

'Yes, first thing this morning. Lucan went ape-shit apparently. Burst into tears, but all he would say was "Bastards!" in French, over and over again.'

'Wonder which bastards he meant. Do we know any more about his dust-up with Monklands?'

'I was coming to that. The Leicester guys had another go at Monklands this afternoon. He told them to get stuffed. Said he would only speak to you, no one else.'

Behind the wheel, Skinner frowned. 'Didn't think I'd made that much of an impression. Okay, Brian. Ask them to have him ready to see me at police headquarters in Leicester tomorrow morning. I'll call in on my way up from Southampton. I'll bet he just wants to sell me a deal, though!'

85

'I hope Lucan did that, and not one of the boys here.'

Norrie Monklands sat at the table in an airless interview room in the main police station in Leicester. The left side of his face was disfigured by a huge yellow and purple swelling around the eye, which was closed to a slit. He nodded, wincing as he did.

'Aye, it was him, all right. Fuckin' nutter that he is. They brought us out of our cells in that remand unit, and as soon as we were alone in the exercise yard he wallops me. Down I go and he starts kickin' the shit out of me, till the warders came and hauled him off – eventually. They didna' seem too bothered, I have to say.'

'They've seen it all before, pal. You don't like the jail much, do you?' Monklands and Skinner were alone in the room. The tape-recorder on the desk was switched off.

'So come on then,' continued Skinner. 'What's so important that you hauled me all the way here? If it turns out that all you wanted to do was to show me your black eye, you'll be lucky not to wind up with a matching pair. Why did Lucan whack you? When I was here last you were all pals together?'

Monklands leaned back in his chair. 'Aye, that's right. But he's got a slow-burning, suspicious, vindictive mind, that bastard. Typical fuckin' anglophobic Frenchman. When he was layin' into me on the ground, he was shouting in French. What he was saying was that we'd been set up by . . .' Monklands paused. 'Here, before I go any further, I'm talking off the record here, right? I'm not admitting that anyone else was involved in this. I'm just telling you what Lucan thinks.'

Skinner shrugged. 'Sure, if that's how you want it. I know who was involved, anyway. I probably know a lot more than you do. You're just a poor fucking gopher who's going to jail, without being able to do anything about it. If you're thinking that there's a deal here, on the basis of no evidence offered, you can forget that.'

'No, I'm not looking for anything. I've got a good lawyer. He reckons he can get me off with three or four years.'

Skinner smiled. 'He'll need to be the bloody goods to do that, Norrie. But never mind that. Go on with what you were saying.'

'Okay. So Lucan's locked up by himself, away from me. And his suspicious French mind starts to work. Even though his spoken English is shite, he knows accents, and he understands words. He realises that the guy that flattened him, and the one that collared me, were Scottish, and that they'd been following us all the way up from Portsmouth, and maybe further. So he figures out that the operation's sprung a leak, and that it happened in Scotland. He convinces himself that Paul and I got cold feet and tipped you guys off.'

'Oh aye,' said Skinner, 'and in the process you get arrested and half eaten by a police dog!'

Monklands shook his head. 'No, he'd worked out that we were supposed to get to Scotland, and that one we were there he'd get nicked and I'd give evidence. He thought that Paul and I were working for you lot, to nail him and Vaudan. Now he's escaped, he can hardly get at me again. But Paul could be in real bother, if he can find him.'

Skinner looked long at the man with the yellow-and-purple eye. 'Got some news for you, Norrie. Nick Vaudan's dead. He was killed on Friday in a shoot-out with the Spanish police. Lucan was told not long after it happened. How'd you think he'd react?'

Monklands stared back at him in disbelief through one and a half eyes. 'Serge? He'd go crazy. You do know that Vaudan was his brother?'

It was Skinner's turn to show surprise.

'That's right. Half-brother, to be accurate. Apparently, Vaudan's old man had a few mistresses around the Côte d'Azur. One of them got pregnant, and Serge was the result. He was a secret for years, until Nick's father got cancer. Just before he died, he told Nick about Serge, and where to find him. He made him promise to look after him – and he did. If somebody killed Nick, then Serge'll kill somebody else. Where did it happen?'

'L'Escala.'

'Where Paul had his Spanish business? Then he's got to be bookie's favourite. Look out for him, will you. He's my mate.'

'Man, we haven't taken our eyes off him in weeks. Have you tried to get a message to him?'

Monklands shook his head. 'No.'

'Good. Don't, otherwise we'll let Serge – if he shows up – walk right through the front door.' He paused. 'What's your theory, Norrie? D'you think you were set up?'

'I haven't a fuckin' clue. My best guess is that you guys got lucky, found out about the buy, and were trying to follow us all the way home, so that you could tie in . . . whoever was waiting at the other end.'

'That's not a bad guess, except we know who was waiting. What d'you know about Cocozza?'

'Who's fuckin' Cocozza? Wait a minute. Lucan did shout something that I didn't understand when he was kicking my ribs in. It could have been something about someone called Cocozza.'

Skinner paused. 'Okay, if you've never heard of Cocozza, what d'you know about Tony Manson?'

'Only two things for sure. One, that he's dead; and, two, that he bank-rolled Paul when he started his Spanish business.'

A fist of excitement gripped Skinner's stomach, but he managed to keep his reaction from showing on his face.

'I thought Ainscow made a few quid when he sold his estate agency.'

Monklands smiled. 'That's what he let people think. He was a wee bit of a gambler in his early days. That's how he met Tony Manson. He didn't get a hell of a lot when he sold out; the casinos had had a lot before that.'

'Did he and Manson keep in touch?'

'Aye, as far as I know. Paul cut out the casinos a while back, but he was partial to a sauna – if you know what I mean. In fact there's a bird in one of Manson's saunas that he fancies. He sees her quite a bit. He's got a stake in a couple of pubs around Stirling. He's never said as much, but I think Manson's got – or rather had – money in them, too.'

Skinner shrugged. 'That's history now. Okay, Norrie, we'll keep an eye out for your mate, as best we can. And when we get Lucan back, we'll try and arrange for him to be in the next cell to you. Would you like that?'

Monklands fingered his swollen eye. 'I'd like never to see that crazy bastard again as long as I live.'

Skinner laughed. 'I'll see if I can help there. Meantime, I hope this lawyer of yours is as good as you think. But if you can summon up a few remorseful tears for the judge and jury, that might come in handy too!'

86

'God, Jazz, but you're getting bigger by the day!'

'Bigger every time you see him, you mean,' said Sarah with a sideways glance along the top of the living-room sofa to where he sat holding his smiling son high in his outstretched arms.

'Yes, okay, don't rub it in. I missed you two every moment – most of all sitting on that hilltop.'

She slid along the leather couch and nestled beside him as he lowered the baby to his shoulder. 'Want to tell me about it?'

He shook his head, as much to clear his mind of a sudden vision of Vaudan's dying eyes, as to answer her question.

'You're sure Arturo's going to be okay, though?'

'Yes, absolutely. He'll be home by now, maybe even in the care of the fair Veronica. As bullet wounds go, I've done worse while shaving.'

'Not Vaudan's though,' she said softly. 'Just as well that kid was a crack shot.' She looked at him: their eyes met, and she knew for certain what she had really known all along. She squeezed his arm. He nodded. They were silent for a time as the room lost the sudden chill that had crept in.

Eventually Bob looked down at her once more. 'You rescheduled that dinner party yet?'

'No. There's no chance for weeks. They're going off on holiday next Sunday night.'

'Sometime, though?'

'Yes, sometime.' Skinner nuzzled Jazz. 'How about our other kid? How's she been?'

'I've never seen her happier. She wants to see you.'

'What's this? A new guy in her life?'

'That's for Alex to tell you.'

'I tried to call her from the road, in Glasgow, but all I got was the answering machine.'

'Yeah, you would. She isn't in Glasgow. She's staying through here for a while, with a friend.'

Skinner gave his wife a curious look. She held up a hand. 'Don't ask. Alex's business.'

'Christ, you women. Samson had no bloody chance, had he.'

87

'Okay, troops. It's good to be back together with so many of you.'

Skinner stood in the main briefing room at Fettes Avenue. He smiled around the assembled faces. They included Roy Old, Alison Higgins, Andy Martin, Brian Mackie, Maggie Rose and a number of junior officers from the Drugs and Vice Squad, and from Alison Higgins' divisional team.

He looked at Martin. 'Who's baby-sitting?'

'McGuire's got Cocozza, and McIlhenney's with Ainscow.'

'Good. I want our most experienced people covering them from now on. I had an interesting visit yesterday. It seems that there might be a new player in the game.'

He described in detail his detour to Leicester, his meeting with Norrie Monklands, and the story of Lucan's paranoid rage.

'This guy is not to be pissed about with. He and his late half-brother were peas from the same pod. Killers. Sometimes they hired help, like the German in L'Escala, but Nick was capable of doing the job himself, and we can assume that Lucan is too. So, if this guy is headed up here, then we aren't simply keeping Ainscow and Cocozza under surveillance. We could be keeping them alive.'

Roy Old raised a hand. 'Couldn't we just lift them, Bob?'

Skinner shook his head. 'That'd be the easy answer. But what grounds do we have? Monklands is too scared to go on the record, so we've nothing but our assumptions to rely on. Listen, I still want these guys – don't be in any doubt. If it hadn't been for that bloody dog in Leicester, we'd have them right now. We'll keep watching them in the faint hope that they make a wrong move, and that we can save something from that wreckage. They've ridden their luck so far, and as far as Lucan's concerned they can ride it some more. If we see him, we nick him. If not, then we keep Monklands' information to ourselves.'

'Do you think Ainscow knows about Vaudan yet?' asked Andy Martin.

'It's possible. The way he's most likely to find out is by calling his secretary in InterCosta – it's still trading – or if he contacts Gloria

Alberni for any reason. If he does, then he'll get the official version, which is that the Guardia Civil went up to question Vaudan about a series of thefts of high-value boats along the Costa Brava, and that he panicked, pulled out a gun and started shooting. Nobody down there, other than my friend Pujol, knows what the real story is.'

Skinner looked around the room. 'All sorts of things could happen in this one yet. I think that our best chance of getting a result is through Cocozza. He's out of his league. He's a wee man who's suddenly got big ambitions. If we can find a reason to put the pressure on him, he might crack and give us the extra witness we need to wrap up Ainscow. So let's just carry on with what we're doing, and see what turns up. Andy, this is a drugs operation, so you carry on co-ordinating operations. Keep me informed if the cork pops out of the bottle.'

He glanced across at his personal assistant. 'Come on Maggie. Let's get back to that bloody in-tray.'

The gathering stood up as he did. He preceded Maggie Rose from the room and along the corridor which led to the stairs to the Command Suite. As they turned the corner, they barely avoided collision with a young woman officer who had come rushing down the steps.

She looked up and flushed bright scarlet. 'Sorry, sir. Excuse me, but is Mr Martin still along there.'

Skinner nodded. 'Yes, he is. And he can only get out this way, so you've got him cornered. You can take it a bit easier from now on.'

Back in his office, Skinner and Rose sat on either side of the desk and began to work their way through the great pile of folders, reports and correspondence that had accumulated in Skinner's short absence. They were only on the third item, a report from the Borders division on a recent increase in cattle-rustling, when there was a heavy knock on the door.

'Yes!'

The door swung open and Andy Martin came into the room. A slight frown line creased his forehead.

'Could be the cork's out the bottle already, boss. I've just spoken to Neil McIlhenney. It looks as if Ainscow's disappeared.'

'What! How the hell did that happen?'

'Sounds like the night-shift. Neil took over at half-eight as usual. Ainscow's car was still in the driveway, so he didn't think anything of the curtains being closed. But then the postwoman turned up with a parcel that was too big for the letter-box. She rang the bell for two or three minutes, but there was no answer. So Neil called Ainscow's telephone, meaning to say "Wrong number" if the call was picked up.

Still no reply. So he went in. He hadn't heard about Lucan, remember. He just didn't fancy the feel of things. Anyway, he went round and tried the back door. It was unlocked, so he went in and searched the house. There was no sign of Ainscow, but in the main bedroom the shirt drawer and wardrobe were lying open, as if someone had packed some kit in a hurry. The bed hadn't been slept in.

'He went back outside and looked in the garden. There's a back gate from the property that we didn't know about, which leads to a lane. It looked as if the gate wasn't used very much, because leaves and stuff had gathered around it. They were scraped back, as if the gate had been opened recently. Neil looked at the lane. It leads down to the main street, and right there is a twenty-four-hour taxi office. He checked. A man with a small suitcase walked in last night around ten thirty and took a taxi to Stirling station. There are still four trains after then, including one that feeds a London overnight service, with seating accommodation. So he could be anywhere!'

Skinner stared at Martin, stone-faced. 'Magic. A back gate and we didn't know about it!'

'Boss, it was overgrown.'

'So bloody what. We're policemen Andy, not spectators.' He slapped his hand, palm down, on the table.

'What d'you think might have happened? Did he call L'Escala and get the wrong story about Vaudan?

'I told you, no one knows the truth there except Arturo. Anyway, he'll still be recovering. No, there's a likelier explanation.' Skinner pressed his hands-free intercom. 'Ruth, get me the Leicester remand centre. I want to speak to the guy who was in charge, yesterday afternoon and last night, of the floor Monklands is on.'

Skinner, Martin and Rose sat in heavy silence for just under three minutes. When the phone sounded, Skinner snatched it up on the first ring. 'Yes.'

'Senior Officer Morgan is on the line, sir.'

'Thanks.'

Ruth switched the call through.

'Mr Morgan, you had Norman Monklands under your care yesterday. Did he make a phone-call?'

The voice on the other end had a heavy Welsh accent, 'Yes, sir, I'm afraid he did. I know he was supposed to be denied access to the pay-phone but, with it being Sunday and all, I had a couple of probationers on duty with me. One of them made a mistake, and let him make a call. I gave the lad a bollocking when I found out, mind you.'

'What time did he make this call?'

'Oh, t'would be about nine thirty in the evening.'

'I don't suppose your lad checked the number.'

'No, sir. Well, we can't, see.'

'Right. Have someone check with BT now, and get the number that he called, just to confirm our suspicions.'

'Very good, sir.'

Skinner hung up. 'That's the answer. Norrie Monklands couldn't stop himself. He had to warn his mate about Lucan. Christ, we'll be lucky if we ever see Ainscow again.'

Martin looked crestfallen. 'I'm sorry, boss. I've blown it. I'll take the flak.'

Skinner shook his head. 'Not alone, you won't. I'm to blame too. I should have put the fear of Jehovah into Monklands about what would happen to him if he made a call. And to make double certain, I should have repeated my instruction to the remand unit that he was to be kept away from the phone.'

He stood up. 'Only three things to do, Andy. Tell Neil to make sure that he hasn't left a trace of his presence in Ainscow's house, keep watching it – front and back – in case he comes back after a couple of days; and keep tabs on Cocozza everywhere he goes. I want a report on every step that wee man takes.'

88

Skinner hated the feeling of being becalmed. In his early days as a detective, a senior colleague had nicknamed him 'Jaws', not because of the voracity of his appetite but because, like a hunting fish, it seemed that he could only live if he were moving perpetually forward.

Now, as Monday stretched into Tuesday, and on into Wednesday, without a sighting of Paul Ainscow or a wrong move by Richard Cocozza, he felt a mounting frustration based on every detective's dread that an investigation, in which he requires only a single piece of evidence, had stalled. Skinner's trail had gone cold, and he hated the feeling.

He countered that by throwing himself into other work, at the office and at home. His in-tray was flattened in record time during what remained of Monday, and on Tuesday he went to Leith to begin what he intended would be a week-long tour of unannounced inspections of divisional CID offices. At home he joined Sarah in her tending of their minimum maintenance garden, where he began to build the walls of a sand-pit for Jazz.

On Wednesday morning, he had been about to leave for Hawick, when Ruth came into his office. 'Sir, the Chief called. He has a doctor's appointment this morning, and it's just been delayed by two hours. He's due to go to a civic lunch today as the guest of the Dean of the Faculty of Advocates, and he wonders if you would take his place.'

'Yes, sure. I've got nothing better to do. Where is it?'

'The Balmoral. Drinks at twelve forty-five.'

The Balmoral Hotel, which is still known to most of Edinburgh by its former name, the North British, is one of two great hotels which stand like bookends at either end of Princes Street, vying with each other constantly for the accolade of being Number One in the public perception. After a period of neglect, a multi-million-pound refit and a high-powered management team led by a Scots trouble-shooter with international experience, had restored the Balmoral to the point at which it could compete with its rival, the Caledonian, on equal terms. Its kilted doorman greeted Skinner with a professional smile, and directed him to the hotel's main banqueting hall, a long room with windows which looked westward along the length of Princes Street. He was still looking around the throng for his host, when he heard him call out, 'Bob! Over here.'

Archie Nelson was standing by the window with a glass of white wine in his hand. Skinner accepted a glass of red from the waiter at the door, and walked across the room to join him.

'Hi, Archie. Sorry Jimmy had to drop out. It's his six-monthly at the Murrayfield, and his doc was delayed. So I'm afraid you've got me instead.'

Nelson smiled. 'I suppose I can make do.' The Dean of the Faculty of Advocates, Scotland's senior practising lawyer, was a round, jolly man with prematurely grey hair and twinkling eyes which had beguiled many a witness, only to turn to gimlets as the serious cross-examination began. He had been in post for almost a year, elected in the wake of the elevation to judicial office of his predecessor, David Murray. He and Skinner were old friends, having been allies during Nelson's successful spell as a High Court prosecutor.

'I should know, Archie,' said the Assistant Chief Constable quietly, 'but what's the reason for this beanfeast?'

'Football, would you believe. The City Fathers, whom I represent on occasion, thought it would be a good idea to hold a lunch in honour of Heart of Midlothian winning the Scottish Cup. Thereby they caused outrage and alienated the two-thirds of the population who support Hibernian, Rangers or Celtic. The row gave the *Evening News* front-page banner headlines for three days on the trot. I'm surprised you didn't know.'

'I've been away a lot recently. Sarah and I went off on a holiday of sorts after the baby was born.'

Nelson's face was wreathed in a sudden smile. 'Oh, yes, I heard about that. A son, I heard. Congratulations. How's he doing?'

'Absolutely great. Sleeps a lot, smiles a lot, shits a lot. That just about sums up the boy's life at the moment.'

'That's quite a gap between your offspring. How is Alex, by the way?'

'Fine as far as I know. I've been trying to catch up with her all week. Haven't succeeded yet. She's got a new man, I think.'

'Yes, I heard a rumour. Was it a surprise to you?'

Skinner looked at him, slightly puzzled, but before he could respond he was interrupted by a diffident cough and a quiet familiar voice. 'Hello, Mr Skinner. Remember me?'

He turned to find Greg Pitkeathly at his shoulder.

'I haven't had a chance to thank you for sorting that matter out for me. Paul Ainscow sent me a cheque and a note of explanation. I'm glad I've got my money back, but that was a terrible thing about Santi Alberni. A major fraud, Ainscow said. How big was it, can you tell me?'

'About a million sterling.'

'Good God! No wonder he hung himself rather than face that.'

'Mmm,' Skinner muttered. 'Convenient all round.'

'You know, it was a bit macabre for me, that time,' said Pitkeathly. 'Death seemed to be following me around. I spoke to Tony Manson only a few days before I saw you, and then he was murdered. I go looking for Alberni, and he dies. They say that death comes in threes. I'm glad that hasn't been true in this case.'

'Don't be so sure,' said Skinner. 'You say you spoke to Tony Manson. How well did you know him?'

'Not very. I'm a curler. A member of his club. We used to pass the time of day, but I'd heard too much talk about him to want to be a close friend.'

'When you spoke to him,' asked Skinner, 'did you mention your Spanish problem?'

'As a matter of fact, I did.'

'Did he seem interested?'

'As a matter of fact, he did.'

'Did you tell him you were coming to see me?'

Pitkeathly thought for a second. 'Yes, I did. He asked if I wasn't going a bit over the top. I remember saying he should try telling that to my wife! Poor man. Whatever he may or may not have been, that was a brutal way to die.'

At the far end of the room, the toastmaster's gavel called the gathering to order.

'Must go,' said Pitkeathly. 'Thanks again for sorting it all out.' He slipped away into the throng.

'What was all that about?' asked Archie Nelson.

'I'm not sure,' said Skinner softly, as if he had been asking himself the same question. 'Maybe nothing at all. Maybe a hell of a lot. Either way, I'm going to have to find out.'

89

'Now isn't that interesting, boys?'

Skinner looked at Andy Martin and Brian Mackie across the low coffee table. He had fidgeted his way through the excellent Balmoral lunch, through the diffident speech by the Heart of Midlothian manager, and through the rather more fulsome address by the club chairman. But even before the applause had died away, he had called headquarters for a pick-up car.

Now, back in his office, Andy Martin caught his mood at once. 'Isn't it just, boss. It's just a wee thread, but who knows what it's tied into. Alberni and Inch, two of the very few people who either knew about the InterCosta fraud or were linked into it, have both wound up dead. Now we find out that Tony Manson, who bank-rolled the company in the first place, was told about it too – just before he died a violent death.'

'Spot on,' said Skinner. 'Maybe a pure coincidence, but it's something that makes alarm bells go off in our policemen's minds. So what are we going to do about it?' He glanced at Brian Mackie.

'There's only one thing left for us to do, sir, as I see it anyway, and that's to pull in Richard Cocozza. Ainscow's done his runner: we may never see him again. We've been waiting either for Lucan to show, or for some lucky break that might kick-start the investigation again. This may be all the luck we're going to get. We've found out that Manson knew about the fraud. Did it come as a surprise to him? Was he bothered about it? Did he talk to anyone about it? Wee Cocozza's the only person left for us to ask. Let's have him in.'

Skinner looked at Andy Martin. The blond head nodded.

'Right. I agree. Go and get him, lads. Bring him here, rather than taking him to Torphichen Place. Let's make the wee bugger feel important. Let's give him the Head Office treatment.'

90

'You are certain that he's in there, Mario?'

'Abso-bloody-lutely, sir. He left here at eight thirty-two, and walked to his office in Queen Street. I tailed him myself, and young John brought the car round. He left again at eleven fifty-three and walked back here. I tailed him again. Here he's been ever since; that's, what, three hours and a quarter. All that time I've been watching the front door, and John's been watching the garden gate.'

'Is there a Mrs Cocozza?'

'Not here, sir. They separated a year ago.'

Richard Cocozza's flat was on the ground floor of a converted grey stone mill-house on the banks of the Water of Leith, where the river wound its way through Dean Village, a city-centre enclave whose quaintness had been eroded by the attempts of various property developers to make it exclusive. The entry-phone system seemed to be in working order, but repeated pressing of the button alongside the name 'Cocozza' had produced not a sound from the intercom.

'Try another,' said Martin.

Mario McGuire began to press other buttons in turn, beginning with the other ground-floor flats, and working up the building. On the fourth attempt there was a response.

'Yes?' A male voice answered, sleep-sodden even through the tinniness of the speaker.

'Sorry to disturb you, sir, but this is the police. We have to call on one of the flats in this building. Could you come down and let us in, please.'

'Yeah, sure.'

Less than a minute later, a dishevelled young man in a blue towelling robe emerged from the lift, which faced the glass entry door. He walked barefoot across the hall, and turned the wheel of the Yale lock. 'I suppose I should ask to see—'

Before he could finish his sentence, McGuire held up his warrant card.

'Of course you should, sir. Sorry we had to wake you. Night-shift, are you?'

The man nodded. 'This week anyway. I work in the bakery in Leith.'

'Okay, you get back to sleep, then. We'll make as little noise as we can.'

'Which may have to be quite a lot,' muttered Martin, as the steel lift doors closed.

The entrance to Cocozza's flat was set back in an alcove off the hall. There was a second bell-push in the centre of the door. Martin pressed it for a good twenty seconds, but its buzz was the only sound from within the apartment. He took his finger from the button. 'Okay, I have reason to believe that there may be a person in this flat who is involved in the commission of crime. Mario, see if you can do it the quick way. If the thing's mortised we may have to send for the locksmith, but try the size elevens first.'

Obediently, McGuire kicked out with his right heel, once, twice, three times. With the third blow, they heard the keeper of the lock tear loose, and the oak door swung open.

Four doors opened off a central corridor. One, at the end, lay ajar. Martin led the way along the hall and stepped into the room.

'Oh Jesus. Not another.'

Cocozza was sitting slumped in a dining chair, with his back to the door. He was held in his awkward position by black insulating tape which secured his forearms and ankles to the frame of the chair. He was naked, save for a pair of badly soiled white underpants. On his back, shoulders and upper arms, large angry bruises stood out against the yellowness of his skin. The back of his head was a mass of hair, bone and gristle matted together by blood and brain tissue.

Slowly and hesitantly, the three detectives stepped around the body, being careful not to bump against it, or touch anything in the room. Martin crouched on one knee and looked up into Cocozza's face. It was covered in blood, not only from the cranial wounds, but from the nose and from a cut over the right eye, which was bruised and swollen. A face-cloth or small hand towel had been stuffed into the mouth, making the cheeks puff grotesquely.

'Look there, sir.'

Martin followed McGuire's pointing finger. A line of blue circular indentations ran up each shin. Each knee was swollen and distorted. On the stained wooden floor, between Cocozza's feet, a heavy metal-shafted hammer with a black rubber grip lay in a pool of blood and urine.

Martin shuddered as he stood up. 'Mario, did you see anyone go out – anyone at all?'

277

McGuire shook his head vigorously. 'No, sir. And John was told to call me on the radio if he spotted anyone.'

'Right,' said Martin assertively. 'Guard that front door. Brian, you and I'll search this place. Carefully.'

Splitting up, they moved swiftly through the flat, checking behind every door, in every wardrobe, in every cupboard, even in the shower compartment and the kitchen cabinets, but the house was empty.

'Andy.' Brian Mackie's call drew Martin back to the living room. The tall, thin man was leaning out of the window. For a second Martin thought that he was being sick, until he stood upright once more. 'I think this is how he got away. This window was open. From here he could have dropped down towards the river, and on to the walkway, without being seen by either Mario or young John.'

'How would he have got in?'

'With the postman, maybe. It must have been while Cocozza was at his office, and our two weren't here. There were stairs back in the hall leading to basement storage. He could have hidden there till everything was quiet, then picked Cocozza's Yale. From what the boss was saying, it looks like Lucan.'

'Maybe. Let's see what he thinks. I'll call him now. When he sees this mess he'll wish he hadn't eaten that lunch at the Balmoral!'

91

'Poor little guy. The last half-hour of his life doesn't bear imagining. Tied up and systematically tortured, then finally dispatched like an animal in a badly-run slaughterhouse.'

Sarah turned to the ambulance crew. 'Okay. If the photographers and technicians are finished, you can take him away now.' At a nod from Skinner, they set to work, noisily ripping off the tape which bound Cocozza's body to the chair.

He put an arm around Sarah's shoulders and led her from the flat, away from the scene and from its smell, which had grown overpowering. 'Thanks, love, for coming down. Let's get back.' As soon as he had digested Martin's call, he had rushed to Dean Village, calling at home to pick up Sarah and to drop off his beaming secretary as a very willing babysitter for Jazz.

They climbed back into Skinner's car. As he drove up the steep incline of Bell's Brae, out of the Village, he glanced towards her. 'Any idea from that back there as to whether our man was waiting for Cocozza inside the flat, or whether the wee chap answered the door?'

'It is essential that you know?'

'No. It's just a small detail but, if I can, I like to know all the answers.'

Sarah was silent for a few seconds. 'Well, don't stand me up in court and ask me to say this, but there was a single bruise behind the right ear that didn't look like all the rest. It was a different shape. I'd say that whoever it was had been waiting inside the flat already. When Cocozza came in, he stepped up behind him, slugged him, stuffed the towel in his mouth, ripped off his clothing and trussed him up. Then he picked up the hammer, and began to give him tender loving care. So do you think it was your runaway Frenchman taking revenge for his brother?'

As the BMW crossed the high Dean Bridge, Skinner gestured with his left hand. 'The picture fits the frame. Norrie Monklands said Lucan blamed the Scottish end for their being nicked. If Vaudan told him all the detail, who was who, and so on, he'd know who to look for, and probably where to go.'

Sarah looked across at him doubtfully. 'Even down to the address?'

He smiled. 'Research document number one: the telephone directory. There aren't too many Cocozzas in the phone-book. Once he got to Edinburgh, he'd have had no problem pinning down the address.'

She leaned back in her seat. Her smile was teasing. 'So why don't you believe it was him?'

He grinned back. 'Who says I don't? All the evidence points to Lucan, and I have to go on evidence, not hunches, don't I?' He gripped the steering wheel. 'Tell you one thing. I'm going to find Mr Ainscow, come hell or high tide, and when I do, he'll sing his heart out just to stay alive. Otherwise I might just let him go – to take his chances with Cocozza's unexpected caller.'

92

'Boss, since yesterday we've interviewed everyone we can find who knows Ainscow: his other golfing buddies apart from Norrie Monklands, the people in his business, both here and in Spain, bankers, lawyers, everyone. Since he disappeared, there hasn't been a trace of the man, not even a withdrawal from a cash machine. We've got nothing else to go on. There were no address books in his house or his office.'

Skinner and Martin, with Maggie Rose as their guest, were lunching in the senior officers' small dining room in the Fettes Avenue Command corridor.

'What about Lucan? What are we doing there?'

Maggie Rose leaned forward to answer Skinner's question. 'Just before we came here, I had a call from Crown Office giving us the go-ahead to release a photograph of Lucan to press and television, and to issue a "Do not approach" warning to the public. The ACC Operations has put every one of our traffic cars and pandas on the look-out, and he's arranged for every other force in the UK to do the same. We're watching ports and oil terminals, and we're trying to contact every major haulier in the UK, including companies with big in-house lorry fleets, to get them to warn their drivers. Once Alan Royston's press release appears, then the sightings are bound to come rolling in, although you know there's only a slim chance of a result there. Can't think of anything else that can be done.'

Skinner nodded in agreement. 'Yes, that covers it, all right.' He paused as a waitress served his salad. 'Thanks, Jessie.'

He waited till his companions had their main courses before them, then looked at Martin. 'About Ainscow, Andy. You said we'd covered all his contacts. Does that include the Powderhall Sauna?'

The detective superintendent looked up sharply. 'God no, it doesn't. Of course, we followed him there twice, and we've heard that he has a liking for rough trade, in the female department. I'll have it checked out this afternoon.'

'Do it yourself, Andy. Lean on the guy with your rank. And take Maggie along with you. You might find that some of the girls are

281

more likely to talk about a punter to another woman. It's probably just another piece of routine, but you never know.'

Martin nodded. He took a mouthful of steak and kidney pie, then glanced up at Skinner. 'How are we doing on a formal identification of Cocozza?'

'Not too well. He didn't have any partners in his practice – only a qualified assistant and a secretary. As far as we can find out, there's only one relative, a brother. He's an on-course bookie in the south of England. All the race meetings down there are being covered this afternoon. Once we find him, we'll fly him up to complete the formalities. Until then all we can say is that we're investigating the murder of an unnamed man. Officially, no one knows yet that Cocozza's dead!'

93

'You know how it is, Mr Martin. Punters come, and punters go—'

'So they say,' Martin interjected, with a slight grin. The manager acknowledged, feebly, his slip of the tongue.

'Aye, but the last thing you're going to do is ask their name, if you want them to come back. Paul Ainscow, you said? Means nothing to me.'

Martin shook his head. 'I don't buy that. This guy had a business connection with Tony Manson. We're certain he knew Cocozza. We followed him here twice, and on the first occasion Cocozza was here too. So were some other people whose names you sure wouldn't want to know. This wasn't any other punter, mate. This was one of the home team. Just to jog your memory: take a look at this.'

He handed over a blown-up photograph of Ainscow in a dinner jacket, copied from a group shot which McIlhenney had found in Ainscow's empty house. The manager took it from him, and nodded after barely a glance. 'Aye, okay. He's been here. Has he done a runner, then?'

'Never you mind. You just keep your mouth shut about this visit. Did he use the girls here, or was he only here for meetings?'

The manager glanced nervously at Maggie Rose, then back towards Martin. 'He spent time with the ladies.'

'Any favourites?'

'He used to like Linda.'

'Hah,' said Martin. 'You mean the one you told us you'd never heard of!'

The man flushed. 'What else could ah say? You know the score.'

'Forget it. Was it only Linda?'

'No. Sometimes he'd take on two or three at a time. A beast for his executive relief is Mr Ainscow.'

'Any of those girls here now?'

'Aye, most of them.'

'Right, send them in.'

'But what if they're workin'?'

283

'Then they'd better finish up whatever they're doing *now*, or we'll go and fetch them. I don't think their punters would like that.'

Five minutes later three sullen, dishevelled, stale-smelling women filed into the room. Martin felt Maggie Rose, seated beside him at the manager's desk, give a small shudder of distaste. The women pulled up chairs and sat opposite them.

'Good afternoon, ladies.' Martin introduced himself and Detective Inspector Rose. 'We're told that you've all – how do I put it? – provided services at one time or another to Mr Paul Ainscow. We're very anxious to speak with him on a number of matters, but we can't find him. He's vanished from his home and from his business, without trace. How well did you ladies know Mr Ainscow? We gather he was a fairly regular visitor.'

The three sat, heads bowed and impassive.

'Come on,' snapped Maggie Rose. 'This isn't for the record. Did Ainscow ever say anything about himself to any of you? Did he tell you anything about his life, his haunts?'

The biggest of the three hostesses, a redhead like Detective Inspector Rose, looked up from her contemplation of the centre of the desk. Slowly she shook her head. 'The only things that Ainscow ever says tae us is things that you wouldna want tae hear, miss. He's nobody's favourite punter, that man. Tells ye what he wants, does it, and he's away. Definitely no one for the chat.'

'When did you see him last?' asked Martin.

'A wee while back. Ah cannae really remember.'

'And you three ladies were his regulars.'

All three nodded. 'Aye,' said the self-appointed spokeswoman. 'Apart from poor wee Linda that is. Damn shame that.

'See men!' she added, with a sudden blazing vehemence.

'So that's all you can tell us? Nothing else, nothing personal?'

The redhead and the woman on her left shook their heads. But the third, a short fat peroxide blonde, looked across the table, hesitantly chewing on her lip.

'Yes?' said Maggie Rose.

'Well . . . ah don't think he jist came here.'

'Why d'you say that?'

The phony blonde hesitated again, glancing at her companions for signs of approval or disapproval, but seeing neither. 'Well,' she said, almost in a whisper. 'Once he was givin' me a hard time. He was hurtin' me and ah told him, but he said that he didna have this problem wi' big Jo down in Leith.'

'Big Jo?' echoed Martin, the green eyes flashing suddenly.

'Aye, there's a wumman works in the Leith place. Big girl fae

284

Glasgow, name o' Joanne. Ainscow seemed tae think that she could dae it every way he ever heard of.'

Martin smiled softly. 'Now, there's a thing. Maggie, I think we'll make it Leith next stop, to look up my old friend Big Joanne. From what I remember of her, she liked to know all about her punters. And if the big lass asked, they tended to answer. Let's head on down. Thanks for your help, ladies. You deserve the night off. Can't see you getting it, though. Must be tough being in a recession-proof business!'

94

'"Closed Thursday." Bloody magic! Imagine a knocking shop taking a day off.'

Martin's red sports hatch was pulled up at the door of the drab shop-front in Constitution Street, finished in the same livery as its stable-mate in Powderhall. The front door was secured with a bar and heavy padlock, emphasising the clumsily printed message which was taped to the door.

He pressed the accelerator in his impatience, revving the throaty engine. 'Let's dig the manager out, wherever he is. He dialled a short coded number on the mobile phone, resting in its car cradle by his side. The Fettes switchboard answered with its usual speed.

'This is Mr Martin. Sergeant McIlhenney, please.'

A few seconds later, McIlhenney's voice boomed out of the car-phone's speaker. 'Yes, sir. What can I do for you?'

'Neil, can you dig me out, from our list, the name and address of the manager of the Hot Spot sauna in Constitution Street.'

'Aye, sir. Hold on a minute.' The speaker made a rattling sound, as McIlhenney laid his phone down. His search took only a few seconds. 'Here it is, sir. His name's Ricky Barratt. He lives more or less over the shop, round in Queen Charlotte Street, number 279a.'

'Thanks, Neil.' Martin pressed the *end* button and, slipping the car into gear, drove the few hundred yards to Queen Charlotte Street.

Although a light showed through the glass front door to Number 279a, it was opened only on the fourth ring of the bell, by a sour-faced woman dressed in a dirty off-white top and faded denims.

'Mrs Barratt?' asked Martin.

She eyed him suspiciously, but eventually snapped, 'Aye!'

'Police. We'd like to speak to your husband, please.'

'Ye're in the wrang place, then.'

'Why's that, then?' said Martin, irritation in his voice.

'It's Thursday, 's it no'? Well the fat bastard'll be in Noble's round the corner as usual, fillin' himself up wi' beer. If he's no there, he's fuckin' deid.' Abruptly she slammed the door in Martin's face.

He glanced at Maggie Rose, a smile wreathing his face. 'Hardly blame the bastard, can you? Come on, let's see if Ricky's running true to form.'

They returned to the car. Martin spun it in a tight U-turn, and drove back to Constitution Street. Noble's Bar, one of Leith's most celebrated, was less than one hundred yards away from the silent sauna, on the same side of the street. They parked, and Martin shouldered open the swing doors, Rose following close behind him. Within seconds the detective inspector realised two things: she was the only woman on the premises, and Martin was the only man wearing a tie. The thronged saloon paid no attention to the new arrivals.

Martin pressed up to the bar, and beckoned to its middle-aged manager. 'Police,' he said softly. 'We want a word with Ricky Barratt.'

The manager nodded briefly towards a gross man of medium height standing near the door of the gents' toilet. No one else in the pub observed this exchange.

Martin and Rose stepped across the pub. Barratt was deep in conversation with three other men, holding court, the centre of attraction. Martin tapped his shoulder and he turned towards him, an imperious look on his face.

'Who the fuck 'r you?'

The detective superintendent smiled. 'We're the fuckin' polis,' he said, 'and we want a word with you about one of your ladies.'

The man gave him the sneer of a barrack-room lawyer. 'Ah don't have to talk to you, or the bird. Piss off, the pair of ye.'

Maggie Rose saw the sudden tensing of muscles at the base of Andy Martin's short neck. For a moment she thought that, for the first time in her life, she would see him lose his temper. She recalled a remark by Bob Skinner that he and Martin made a great team, not least because his occasionally short fuse was counterbalanced by the younger man's impenetrable calm. And, now, in the crowded bar, Martin continued to smile at his insolent, fat protagonist.

'Wrong, Mr Barratt. We are involved in a murder investigation and you *will* talk to us. We can either do it quietly outside, or loudly, very loudly, right here. By the time I'm finished, everyone in this pub will think you're our best friend in these parts. Fancy that, fat man, do you? If not then get your arse outside, now!'

Barratt's three companions were looking awkwardly at their feet, each one desperate to be somewhere else. The man struggled for a few seconds more to maintain his truculence, but finally his head dropped, and he rolled his great body in short strides towards the door.

Outside they stood on the pavement, as if they were three acquaintances having a casual conversation.

'Right, Ricky. To complete the formalities, I'm DS Martin, head of the Drugs and Vice team, and this is Inspector Rose. We know what your job is, and what sort of a place you run, so don't let's have any more theatricals. What can you tell us about a man called Paul Ainscow and one of your ladies, Joanne?'

Barratt stared downwards, at the endless folds of his stomach. 'Ainscow? He was some sort of pal of Tony's. He'd been gettin' too keen on a lassie up at Powderhall – one of Tony's favourites, I think – and Tony sent him down here tae see Big Joanne, tae sort of take his mind off her, ken. Big Joanne's good at that. She's heid girl in there.' He glanced seedily at Martin. 'In every way.'

'When was this?'

'A right few months ago now.'

'How did they get on?'

'Like Tony meant them to. I told you, she's good, is Big Joanne.'

'How often does he come to your place?'

'He doesnae, any more. That place isnae one of the nicest. One night when he was in, his car was damaged. He kicked up hell's delight. Since then he's phoned up, and the big yin's seen him at her place. She's got a wee flat in King's Landing, round by the Waterfront pub.'

'That's an unusual thing for a working girl to do, isn't it?'

Barratt nodded. 'Aye. But the big beast was quite keen on the boy, too. The rougher they are, the better she likes them and, from what I can gather, Ainscow's a rough type. Pleasant on the surface, but once the doors were closed, a cold hard bastard. Right up her street.'

'Has he called in for her lately – like this week?'

The man shook his great head slowly. 'Naw. No' this week. He'd have been wasting his time, onyway. The big yin phoned in sick on Monday. Havnae seen her since then.'

95

'You've checked out the address?'

'Yes, sir,' said Maggie Rose. 'It's a one-bedroom flat on the top floor. She's on the board at the door – and you won't believe what her surname is.'

'Try me,' said Skinner.

'Virtue.'

He grinned. 'What's so odd about that? I know at least two traffic wardens called Good!'

The Fettes Avenue building wore the quiet feel of evening. Skinner, Rose and Martin sat in the detective superintendent's office.

'Did you have a look at the place?'

'Yes, for a while,' said Martin. 'No sign of movement.'

'Okay, let's pay the lady a call, and see if she's got a house guest. I want it done by the book. Maggie, dig up a Sheriff and get a proper search warrant, in case it's needed. Take someone else with you when you go, a bit of extra muscle in case he is there and doesn't feel like being reasonable. Big McIlhenney's wife can always use the overtime pay. Take him.'

Rose nodded. 'Yes, sir, I'll tell him. Aren't you coming, though?'

Skinner smiled. 'Maggie, I'm a family man again, and I've missed too many of my small son's bath times lately. I intend to spend my evenings at home from now on, whenever I can. Privileges of rank, and all that, as both of you will find out some day.'

'Does that mean,' asked Martin, with a show of innocence, 'that if we nick Ainscow we don't phone to tell you, but wait till you come in tomorrow?'

'No, son, if that happens, you phone me, but if Sarah answers you'd better disguise your voice!'

'What do I put down as the purpose of the search warrant?' asked Rose.

'Investigation of a conspiracy to import controlled substances. It's all we've got that's solid enough. Although, maybe—' Skinner paused. 'No, forget it. That's enough: it lets us nick him. Once we've done that, we'll just have to catch our man and persuade him to talk, to make it stand up in court.'

'When do we go in?' asked Martin.

'Normally you'd say dawn, wouldn't you. But this time let's make it late evening. Let them get settled down for the night, then go up and thump the door. Say eleven o'clock. If Ainscow's there, it'll be all the easier if his pants are hanging over the bedroom chair!'

96

King's Landing was peaceful in the Scottish summer gloaming. The block, one of the first built during the revival of Leith as a living community, was framed against the deepening blue of the northern sky.

'Thank Christ, there's no entry phone this time,' muttered Martin as they approached the entrance. He pushed the door open and led the way up the twisting stairs. On the top landing there were two doors, facing each other. He glanced at each, and on the one on the left, read the name 'Virtue' on a small brass plate set just above a glass spyhole. Beckoning to Rose and McIlhenney, he strode towards it. There was a bell push, but Martin ignored it, and thumped the surface with the side of his closed fist.

'Joanne!' he called. 'It's the police. Mr Martin. Open up, please.'

He stepped back so that he, and his companions, could be seen clearly through the viewing glass. He listened, and eventually he heard the creak of a floorboard from within the flat. The door swung open slightly, as far as its safety chain would allow. Joanne Virtue peered around its edge. Her blonde hair was tousled, and held back by a band, and she wore no make-up, yet she was still striking. But there was something in her eyes that Martin had not seen before, an expression that was far from her usual cheerful self-confidence – something that he would not expect to see on a woman of her profession, even when receiving a visit from the police. Martin looked at her and saw fear in her face.

Nevertheless, she tried to stick to type. 'What is it, Mr Martin? Some bloody time this! An' three of yis, an' all!'

'Is he here, Joanne?'

There was a flicker, a momentary tensing around those eyes. 'Who?'

'You know who. Paul Ainscow?'

'Naw! Paul's no here. Why should he be?'

'Because he's been missing for about the same time that you've been away from the sauna. Your spell off must have done you good.

291

You look pretty healthy to me. Now open up and let us in. We want to interview Ainscow in connection with serious offences, and we've got reason to believe that he might be here. We've got a Sheriff's warrant to come in, so let that chain off the door.'

'Look, he's no' here. Why don't y'all just fuck off!'

Martin's jaw tightened. 'Sorry, Joanne, I'm not kidding. Either you let us in or that door comes off its hinges.'

The woman opened her mouth as if to argue, then all at once gave in. The door closed, its chain rattled as it was released, and then it swung open fully.

'Right,' said Martin. 'That's sensible. Listen, we're not here to hurt you or lift you or anything else. It's Ainscow we want.'

'But ah tell ye—'

'We have to see for ourselves. Now, you wait out here with DI Rose, while Neil and I search the place.' He brushed past her into the flat, McIlhenney on his heels.

'Careful, Neil,' he warned. The first of the three doors off the hall was ajar. He turned back to Joanne Virtue. 'Bedroom?'

She nodded reluctantly. 'Aye. And the bog on the right, and the living room at the far end. The kitchen's off that. Mind ye don't break anything.'

Martin pushed the door open and stepped quickly inside, tensed and ready for action. The room was empty, yet full of signs of recent occupancy. The musky smell of sex hung in the air. The bed was rumpled, and both pillows were crushed. There were night tables on either side, and on each lay a mug. Martin picked one up. It was half full of what looked like coffee, and it was still slightly warm. He checked the other. It was almost drained, but the dregs had not yet dried to a stain. He stepped back into the hall, signalling to McIlhenney to open the bathroom door. An aerosol can of shaving gel and a razor lay on the shelf above the basin. Quickly they checked the living room and kitchen. They too were empty, but further signs of a guest were strewn all around.

'Okay, ladies,' Martin called. 'You can come in now.'

A few seconds later, Joanne Virtue stepped hesitantly into the room, with Maggie Rose close behind her.

'Okay, Joanne,' snapped Martin. 'No crap. How long has he been here? Since Monday?'

'Sunday night, late,' she said softly.

'And when did he go?'

'About twenty minutes ago.'

'It must have been a sudden decision, judging from those mugs in the bedroom. What happened? Did that fat bastard Barratt tip you off? I promised him that if he did, I would rip his balls off. He should have believed me.'

Big Joanne shook her head. 'Naw, it wisnae Ricky. We had this call a wee while ago. Just after ten. We've been screening all the phone-calls – no' that there've been many – leaving the answer machine on all the time. So we taped it.'

'That makes a change,' said Martin. 'A wee bit of luck for once. Play it back for us.'

She stepped over to a low sideboard on which the combination phone and answering machine sat, and pressed the *replay* button. There was a whirr as the tape rewound. Joanne turned up the volume.

Suddenly the rewind stopped and replay began. After four or five seconds, there was an intake of breath and a voice filled the room: a strange, strained voice, as if the speaker was concentrating very hard on something very important. 'Don't say anything. Just listen. I need to see you right away. It's about Tony's will. It's turned up. Go to the Botanics now, get in the back gate, and meet me at the entrance to the big glasshouse at eleven. Get moving.'

The line clicked as the phone at the other end was replaced. There was a whistle for a few seconds, before the machine switched itself off.

Martin and McIlhenney looked at each other in astonishment. 'Jesus!' whispered the detective sergeant.

'Do you know who that is?' Martin asked Joanne.

'It sounded like that wee lawyer chap, Cocozza – him that was Tony Manson's message boy. Paul knows him. He sounded funny, though.'

'No bloody wonder, Joanne. He's been dead for a day and a half!'

97

Skinner leapt to the phone and picked it up on the first ring. For one of the few times in his short life, Jazz had been difficult about sleep. Eventually he had succumbed to the cajoling of his parents, and now lay upstairs, fitfully, in his cot.

'Hello.' Skinner was unusually curt.

'Bob, sorry, did I wake you?'

'No, but you'd better not have wakened the baby. What's the score?'

'I'm calling from Joanne's. Ainscow was here, but he's gone. Called by telephone, half an hour ago, to a meeting at the big glass-house in the Botanics at eleven. Right this minute, in fact.'

'Who called him?'

'Would you believe, Richard Cocozza?'

'That's a bloody good trick. A tape.'

'Yes. That must have been why he was tortured. To force him to tape a message setting up Ainscow, and to get Joanne's telephone number out of him.'

'Clever bastard, right enough,' said Skinner, almost to himself.

'Yes,' agreed Martin. 'Lucan's English must have been a lot better than he let on. And his brother must have given him chapter and verse on everyone involved at this end. We're heading off there now, boss. Will you call in back-up?'

'Bugger that! I'm your back-up.'

Martin laughed. 'So much for the family man. See you at the Inverleith Row gate.'

Skinner hung up. He turned, to find Sarah standing in the doorway.

'What was that?'

'Andy.'

'What's up?'

'Ainscow. Someone's got to him before we did. He's walking into a trap. I've got to go – and I could be a while.'

She crossed the room and kissed him. 'Okay, but be safe.'

'Don't worry, love. This one's just a walk in the park. Literally.'

He picked up the sweater which he had discarded earlier while cradling Jazz, and pulled it on as he went out into the cool night air. The garden was flooded by the light of a full moon as he walked to his car, reversed out into Fairyhouse Avenue, and headed towards Inverleith, and Edinburgh's famous Royal Botanic Garden. He was driving fast up East Fettes Avenue, past the headquarters building, when his car-phone rang. He pushed the *receive* button.

'Bob, my friend. It is Arturo Pujol. I know it is late, but Sarah said it was okay to call you with my news. We have had a great excitement again in L'Escala. The man you are looking for in Britain: Lucan, the brother of Vaudan. He is here in Spain, in jail.'

Skinner smiled to himself in the dark of the car, a satisfied smile – the sort that comes with the final piece of the jigsaw.

'What happened?' he asked.

'It was this afternoon. Young Joaquim – the officer who was with you and whose shot killed Vaudan – he was leaving the Gala, the bar across from my barracks, when he was attacked by a wild-eyed man with a knife. The man was dirty and had been days needing a shave. It was Lucan, and he had in his pocket a page torn from our local newspaper, the *Empordan*, describing Vaudan's death, and with a photograph of the man who shot him. Joaquim was cut, but he fought him off, and was able to stop him with two shots in the leg. He said later that he had been aiming for his head.' Pujol paused. 'It seems that Joaquim's shooting has returned to its normal form. Does all that interest you?'

As Pujol finished his tale, Skinner drew his car to a halt beside the side entrance to the Botanic Garden. 'Arturo,' he said, 'it's fascinating. I'm a bit busy right now, but I'll call you back tomorrow. We'll talk further and, who knows, I may have an even stranger story for you.'

98

Martin took the roundabout at high speed, and swung back towards Ferry Road, the shortest route from Leith to the Botanic Garden.

The colourful sparkling of the moonlight on the petrol spill gave him advance warning of the hazard, but far too late for him to take any evasive action. He hit the slick as he exited from the roundabout, and the car went into an uncontrollable spin. He steered into it, but with absolutely no effect. McIlhenney, in the front passenger seat, braced himself for the impact which he saw coming, but which Martin did not, as he fought for control.

The off-side of the car slammed into the base of the solid iron lamp-standard, wrapping itself around it like a sleeping lover in the night. Maggie Rose, in the back seat, was held in place by her retaining strap. McIlhenney was pulled up short by his belt, as it cut into his chest and side. But Andy Martin, taken unawares, slammed sideways into the arch of the driver's door, his head hitting the tightly padded metal with a definitive thud. He rebounded back against McIlhenney, unconscious, and with blood beginning to trickle from a cut above his right eye.

The engine stalled. Rose and McIlhenney sat in the shocked silence, until Martin's weight against him triggered the sergeant into action. Gently he straightened the other man on his seat, with his head against its restraint.

'Sir,' he said urgently. 'Andy?'

Martin gave a faint groan, but that was all.

'He's spark out,' said McIlhenney to Rose, over his shoulder. 'See if the phone's still working.'

The inspector obeyed her subordinate's order and took the instrument from its cradle between the front seats. Its dial showed that it was still operational. She keyed in the Fettes number. 'This is DI Rose. I'm at the foot of Ferry Road at the Leith end, in DS Martin's car. There's been an accident. One injured: unconscious. Get an ambulance here fast.' She ended the call and searched her diary for Skinner's car-phone number. She dialled it in and waited.

'I don't believe it,' she said to McIlhenney. 'The boss's car-phone is engaged!'

She dialled another number: her own. A sleepy-voiced Mario McGuire answered. Thirty seconds later he was wide awake and calling Brian Mackie.

99

'Come on, people, you should have been here first!'

Skinner voiced his exasperation in the darkness of his car as he sat at the end of the short roadway off Inverleith Row, which led to the smaller of the two gates into the Royal Botanic Garden. He glanced at the computer-set time display on the LCD panel of his cassette player. It showed seven minutes past eleven.

He shook his head. 'Can't wait any longer,' he muttered to himself. He stepped out of the car, and clambered over the gate with surprising agility for a man in his mid-forties.

The Botanics, as the people of Edinburgh know it, is one of the world's great gardens, set in seventy acres in the heart of Scotland's capital. Every day, save Christmas and New Year, it offers free access to thousands of visitors who walk its leafy paths among the trees, plants and shrubs, admiring and sometimes feeding the pigeons, ducks and impertinent squirrels who animate the scene.

The centrepiece of the Botanics is its great glasshouse. As Skinner emerged into the wide open space of the garden, he saw it three hundred yards away, silhouetted massively against the northern skyline. To prevent any chance of his being spotted in the moonlight, he hugged the trees to his right as he ran towards the building, taking extra cover from their darkness, but occasionally leaving the grass and cutting through the planted beds. Soon, he had reached the steps which led up towards the scientific study centre. He looked along the length of the Glasshouse, but saw no figures, no shapes, no movement. Pressing himself against the glass wall, he crept silently along towards the main entrance.

The flash of moonlight from the slivers of glass on the ground caught his eye before he reached the doorway. He froze for a second, listening, but heard nothing. Very slowly he advanced towards the entrance, moving lightly on his feet. When he had almost reached it, he broke away from the wall in a wide sweep and flattened himself against a tree opposite the doorway. One of the double doors was wide open, allowing him a clear view into the reception area. It was empty. Taking a deep breath, he pushed himself off from his tree and reached the door in a few strides, taking care not to step on the broken glass lest he make a sound. Inside the small hallway, a corridor led off to the right towards offices and to the scientific centre. To the left, another door led to the glasshouse itself. He stepped past the reception desk and tried its handle. It opened silently, and Skinner slipped into the first gallery of the great glass structure.

The door closed automatically behind him and, as it did, he looked around. Moonbeams shone through the higher branches of the trees and bushes, casting weird shadows on the paved walkways which led visitors through each section of the exhibition. He listened again, but still the silence was total. Then, through the foliage, he caught a flash of artificial light. He moved towards the source, almost on tiptoe, until he came to a second door. Through its glass, he could make out, to his left, a series of illuminated panels in which floated an assortment of aquatic plants, their fronds moving in the tanks' continuous aeration. He opened the door and stepped into the expected darkness beyond.

At once, he knew that he had arrived too late for Paul Ainscow.

The thick glass panel on his right was around ten feet wide and five feet high. It was back-lit and offered a view of the lily-pond which was the centrepiece of the upper area of the glasshouse. Ainscow's body was still settling on to the round stones and pebbles which made up the bed of the lily-pond – settling down to an eternal sleep. The corpse lay close to the glass, facing Skinner as he looked on in resigned horror. The eyes stared, wide and round. The normally sleek hair drifted, Afro-style, in the water. The head lay at an odd angle, strange enough to tell Skinner at once that drowning would not feature on the death certificate. The body lay on its side, the right arm thrown up and over the head, palm and wrist pressed against the glass. Skinner stepped forward and looked at the wrist. There, at the base of the thumb, vivid against the whiteness of death, he saw three small, pink semicircular scars.

'Knew it,' he whispered, softly, to himself.

Suddenly, his eye was caught by movement above and beyond the body, above the moonlit surface of the pond. There was a figure framed there, bent over as if peering into the pond to make sure that Ainscow was not about to resurface.

Moving as if his life depended on his silence, and imagining that it might, Skinner slipped back out of the aquarium room and looked up. The pathway to the lily-pond gallery was ten feet above his head. The steps leading up to it were at the far end of the area in which he stood. He paused for a moment and looked around, until his eye lit upon a strange, long tree-trunk, similar to a palm, but with deciduous leaves. It reached up to and over the path above his head. He grasped it and began to climb, monkey-style, hands and feet digging for purchase into the rough, thick bark, sweeping small twiglet branches aside, scrambling up and up until the trunk began to curve and he was straddling it, perched above the walkway.

He sat and stared at the door to the lily-pond gallery, trying to decide his next move. But it was decided for him.

The glass door opened, framing a figure, silhouetted black in the moonlight – a huge figure.

Skinner jumped down from the tree. The man froze, then moved back into the pool gallery. Skinner followed, watching him through the glass panel as he backed away. He opened the door and stepped through. The gallery was lit by the moon, and by its reflection from the surface of the pool.

The man had stopped his retreat. He stood there waiting, a great dark slab, towering and vast. Skinner was six-two himself, but this giant stood almost a full head taller, straight-backed, wide-shouldered, and built like a bulldozer.

Oh shit, Skinner thought, of all the times for the cavalry to go missing!

'Hello, Lennie.'

He had forgotten just how *big* Lennie Plenderleith was.

He felt eyes boring into him, even in the dark. Eventually the mountain spoke.

'It's Mr Skinner, isn't it?'

It was possibly the most incongruous voice that he had ever heard. While its owner was huge and threatening, the voice was soft, slow and gentle, almost soothing in its tone. It struck Skinner that it might just have been that of a telephone Samaritan. 'You sound as if you were expecting me.'

'I was. Officially we've been setting traps for a Frenchman, but I was pretty certain that it would be you who turned up. I did some private research on you, Lennie. You're not the big thick muscleman that you and Tony wanted us to see, are you? You were going to nightschool classes even when you were working in that pub in Leith Walk. And while you were inside you were never out of the library. Correspondence courses in – what were they? – business admin, economics and Spanish. Who paid for them? Linda?'

Plenderleith shook his massive head. 'You're joking. No, Tony did.'

'He was grooming you, Lennie, wasn't he? You were going to be his right-hand man when you got out, weren't you? His adopted heir?

What was that about a will in Cocozza's message? He had told us he couldn't find one. Was that just a way to get Ainscow here, or does it exist?'

There was a gleam in the dark as the big man smiled. 'Oh yes, Tony left a will all right. He gave it to me when he visited me in Shotts just before I got out. He thought it would be a long time before it was needed, though. He didn't think anyone could touch him.' Lennie gave a soft tinkling chuckle. 'He reckoned even God would think twice about having a go at him. Tony took me under his wing years ago. I was giving some trouble to the manager of one of his launderettes. Back then, I thought I could make it big in the protection racket. I read *The Godfather* and thought that was for me. So I went into this launderette, and told the manager it was ten quid a week or his windows were in, and after that his face. And then the real Godfather came to the launderette to see me: Tony Manson. He was younger then, and not quite as smooth as he was later on. The hardest man I'd ever seen. It just radiated off him. He never said a word, just looked at me, and I knew that this man could kill me, and would if it came to it. So I said, "Sorry, I didn't understand. I won't bother this place again," and Tony said, "That's good. I like a quick learner. Sit down." And he talked to me. He asked me about myself, and I told him. We sat there for about three hours, cracking a few beers and talking, and at the end of it Tony offered me a job. He said he fancied making me his secret weapon.

'Most folk, aye even someone like you, look at a big guy like me, and all they see is size and muscle.' Lennie tapped the side of his head. 'They can't cope with the idea that there's anything going on in here. Tony wasn't like that. He realised that I could think as well as punch people's lights out, but he knew that I needed control. So he put me to work where he could keep an eye on me, and he began to teach me. Gradually he told me more and more, till I knew almost everything about his business. He even began to ask what I thought about things. It was a sort of test, I suppose, but once or twice I'd suggest ideas that he hadn't thought of, and he'd accept them. When you folk got lucky and I went to jail, he was gutted, but I said "What the hell. I'll put the time to good use." And I did.'

'Did he tell you about Ainscow's operation?' Skinner queried.

The great head nodded in the dark. 'Aye. He asked me what I thought.'

'What did you tell him?'

'I said "Do it. It sounds okay." I said that it was a clever way of generating a pile of black money from a clean source, and that if Ainscow wanted a few quid to get started, he should give it to him.

301

But I told him that, if it was ever tumbled, he should cut his losses and get his dough back. Tony's great secret was in keeping the money separate. Too many guys like him pump money from legit business,' again, the giant laughed softly in the dark, taking Skinner by surprise, '—or more or less legit, like knocking-shop saunas – straight into the other side. He never did that. He lived well from the pubs and the casinos and the rest, and he put the profits back into that side of the business, or into the stock market. If he'd used a penny of it on a drugs buy, you guys would have had a chance of tracking it down. All the drugs money was black, from armed robbery, extortion, stuff like that. When Ainscow came along with a long-term scheme for generating a million in funny money, it was a natural for him.'

Skinner shifted from one foot to the other. 'How did Ainscow know to come to Tony?'

'He was a casino punter. And he used to deal in a small way. Tony's organisation supplied him.'

'Mmmm. Did Tony have anything to do with the Spanish business?'

'Absolutely not. He gave Ainscow the money and told him to get on with it. Dick Cocozza was the only link. He was supposed to check on it occasionally. But there was never anything in paper. No correspondence. The cash that Tony gave him came from the black side.'

'Where did he keep that sort of money?'

'Switzerland. Tony used to go there every year, with a party from the curling club. He'd run a bus, and every year he'd just take it out in a suitcase and stick it in a bank account. Then, after a couple of years, he'd move it into a private investment trust in Liechtenstein. Guess who owns that trust now?'

'So that's what was in the will,' said Skinner. 'That's your legacy, Lennie?'

'That *was* the will, Mr Skinner. A document transferring the trust to me in the event of Tony's death. It's worth millions. The pubs, and all the other stuff over here, they didn't matter. As far as we were concerned, they could pass to the Crown, like with any death where the estate's unclaimed. Wonder how the Queen'll take to living off the earnings of a string of dodgy saunas?' The big man chuckled again. 'My name's not Plenderleith any more, of course. I'm somebody else now, and now that I've tied off all the loose ends here, that's who I'll be from now on.'

'There's one big obstacle to that, Lennie.'

'Not too big, though, Mr Skinner. There's room in that pond for two.'

They stood there in silence in the silver moonlight, for several seconds. And then the giant took a pace forward.

'Why did you kill Alberni?'

The question stopped Plenderleith in his tracks. He seemed to stand even taller in the dark. 'How did you know about that? I thought it was perfect.'

Skinner chuckled. 'You might be bright, Lennie, but nothing planned by the human mind is ever perfect. Remember Alberni's dog, in the garden?'

Lennie nodded. 'Yes, I was going to feed it, only I couldn't find anything to give it. Then I heard a car coming, so I got off my mark.'

'Christ,' said Skinner. 'Life's full of it. If you had fed that dog, I'd have bought the suicide. The investigation would have stopped right there and we wouldn't have linked Cocozza and Ainscow, at least not until far too late. You'd have been free and clear – if you'd just found a can of dog-food!'

He saw the big man smile and shrug his shoulders.

'But that's history. What happened? How did you wind up in L'Escala?'

'Tony came to see me in Shotts. We'd already set up the trip to Spain to look over that Rancho place. I was going out first – then Linda.' He paused. 'She was going to join me. But Tony said that there'd been a change of plan. He told me that he had found out, by accident, from a guy at the curling club, that the InterCosta thing was going to be rumbled. He said that he'd sent Cocozza to tell Ainscow to wind up the show and give him his dough back – plus profits, of course. He told me to pull my cash out of the bank as soon as I got to Spain, then go to L'Escala and tie off the loose end. Tony told Ainscow at the start that he should cut the guy in on the deal, but he wouldn't. He was greedy. So the wee Spaniard had to go. Shame, but there it was.'

'How did you do it?'

'It was easy. I'd already decided how I would do it. I just watched and waited. Then, when the guy's wife went to work, I nipped into the garage, set things up, and kicked over an oil-can to make a noise. When he came in to investigate, he was a goner. I didn't like killing him, but Tony was right. If he'd been left to talk to the police, the whole thing could have come back on Ainscow, and God knows where it would have gone from there. And, after Linda, it wasn't difficult at all.'

'Funny thing, though,' said Skinner. 'You needn't have bothered. The bloke at the other end of the chain, Vaudan – he was going to do it as well. You just beat him to it.

'Tell me about Linda. That's the bit that I don't understand. You go to jail and your boss shags your wife – not just that, he puts her on the game. When you come out you butcher her, then he's done in. You're the obvious choice for that one too, yet here you are telling me that Tony was like a father to you. Does that mean that you sold Linda to him, like a piece of meat?'

For the first time, the gentle voice hardened. 'No, Skinner. You've got that all wrong. Linda was a tart before I married her, and she stayed that way. She was a nympho: she couldn't get enough of it. She was always flashing her eyes around, and sometimes other bits as well. Of course, when I was about, no one would even look in her direction, but once I was sent up, she was off the leash. Tony gave her the flat, and he would have paid the housekeeping, but she told him that she wasn't being kept by him. She said she was going back to her old career. He offered to get her a job in Cocozza's office, but she'd have none of it. So he decided that if he couldn't persuade her, the next best thing was to control her. So he took her into the Powderhall place, and vetted the punters she saw. If anyone got too keen, he moved them on. He never laid a finger on her. When he took her out to the house, it was for a night off, nothing else. Tony couldn't stand her. If it hadn't been for me, she'd have been in the Water of Leith. Tony said that everyone has to have a weakness or they'd be too dangerous to let live. He said that she was mine.'

'All that time you were inside,' said Skinner quietly, 'did you plan to kill her?'

Big Lennie's shoulders slumped; he shook his head. 'No.' It was a whisper. 'I was tormented by the idea of leaving her again. I took the knife into the bedroom to cut her. I was going to mark her face. Not to get even, but to spoil her for the punters. Not for the sake of making her ugly, but as a sign to other guys: one that said "Be very careful of the man who did this". I took the knife in with me, tucked into the back of my jeans, and there she was, lying back wide open, saying "Come on, gimme." And so I did. And even as we were doing it, she was taunting me. She had her ways to torture you. I had forgotten how much they hurt. Then she talked about Ainscow, and how she loved it when he fucked her because he was so rough. She said that, beside him, I was just a big pussy. That was the last thing she ever said. I lost it. I snapped. Only one time in my life have I ever done violence in hot blood, and when I did – oh Christ, it had to be hers! Another reason for killing Ainscow.'

He began to move towards Skinner once more.

'Come on, Lennie, the whole story, then you can try your luck.

You're right. My boys aren't backing me up tonight. So tell me, then we'll go at it. When did you hear about Tony?'

'I read about it in Spain. I bought a copy of the *Daily Record*, and there it was. And I knew. I knew straight away.'

'You knew that when Tony sent Cocozza to tell Ainscow to shut the InterCosta operation down, Ainscow decided to do something completely different.'

Big Lennie nodded. 'That was *Tony*'s one great weakness, you see. He trusted people. Part of it was because he couldn't imagine anyone ever having the balls to cross him, but most of it was just plain gullibility. Tony was a savage guy at times, but he had standards. If Tony said you had a deal, you could take it to the bank, and if he said you were dead, you could book Warriston Crematorium. The last true man of his word.'

'Do you know how they did it?'

'Oh yes. That was one of the things Cocozza told me when we had our chat – when he didn't have that towel stuffed in his mouth to stop him screaming. Cocozza – Tony's good friend Cocozza – had keys to the house. He let Ainscow in. They fixed the alarm later to make it look like a break-in. They both waited in the bedroom for Tony to get in. The wee shit Cocozza hid in the wardrobe. Tony switched on the light and Ainscow was on him with the knife. He never had a chance.'

Lennie Plenderleith paused, with a smile of satisfaction. 'Neither did they. You should have seen Cocozza's face when he saw me. He looked like a spectator at his own funeral. As for Ainscow, he didn't even know who I was. I told him that Dick had sent me, and he followed me up here. He was a strong guy – but nowhere near strong enough to stay alive. Treacherous bastards,' added Lennie quietly. 'No way were they going to do that to him and live.

'I could have been off for good, Mr Skinner. I was free and clear, with a new identity and the income from that trust. The whole world was my bloody oyster, but it would always have tasted sour if I hadn't come back to pay my debt to my friend, and finish with these people.

'So after I did the business in Spain, I went to Liechtenstein with Tony's document, Tony's will, and took possession of his trust, my inheritance. Then, with my new passport and my new, genuine, Liechtenstein licence, I bought a car and made my way home. And now I've done the business here, almost. With you out of the way, I'll be free and clear again. So, Mr Skinner, it's time, as you said, to try our luck – and it's yours that's run out.'

Big Lennie moved forward with a speed and balance which were as unexpected as his voice. Skinner knew that the talking was over, and that he faced a fight for his life. The light was bad, and the path was

305

narrow, with the pool on his left, and foliage on his right. He backed off before the giant's advance, weighing him up as best as he could. Muscles bulged beneath his attacker's black top, and his jeans were tight around massive thighs.

Skinner broke his retreat, and feinted a karate kick, but Lennie reacted lightning-fast, swaying back and ready with a strike of his own. Skinner could tell that the man had no martial-arts training, yet realised that he was as deadly as any black belt, a natural fighter with enormous strength.

He backed off once more, then came in again with a second feint – a kick to the head. Once more Lennie leaned back instinctively, his hands up to catch the blow he thought was coming. But, instead, Skinner's foot changed direction and slammed into the side of his left knee. Lennie grunted, and sagged slightly, but he stayed upright and balanced. Skinner's momentum committed him to his next move: a sweeping chop to the throat with the cutting edge of his right hand. It would have been a finisher, even against such a formidable opponent, but his wrist was caught in mid-air, just short of the target. The big man jerked him up and towards him. Skinner knew what was coming, but he could only begin to pull back as Lennie's broad forehead crunched into the bridge of his nose. He heard a thunderous crack inside his head, and felt the hot blood flowing.

The fingers of a huge right hand clamped around his throat, and his wrist was suddenly released. Instinctively, skill and technique forgotten, he clawed at Lennie's face, digging for the eyes with his thumbs, luck more than judgement guiding him to his target. The big man snarled as pain made him release his death grip to push Skinner away. He shook his head, blinking. Skinner hit him: a straight right-hand punch square on the chin. It was a blow that might have stunned a horse, but it seemed only to renew the giant's strength and determination. He closed again.

'You're tough, all right,' Lennie said softly. 'But it won't be enough.'

Skinner tasted blood in his mouth. And then he tasted something else. An icy coldness flowed through him: a feeling that he had known before, one that he feared; a presence in him that very few had seen. He had wished him gone for ever, but now, when he needed him, his other self was back. He heard himself hiss in the darkness. 'I don't see a gun, Lennie. And without one, you'll be carried out of here, big and all as you are.'

For a second the giant looked at him, and something in his adversary's eyes made him pause. If there had been an escape route, that expression might have persuaded him to take it, but finally the

306

knowledge that there was nowhere else to go made him close in once more.

This time Skinner did not back off. This time he stepped, lightning-fast, inside the outreaching arms. His cupped right hand smashed against the side of the great head. Lennie screamed as his eardrum burst, but the sound was choked off as steel-hard fingers slammed into his diaphragm. He doubled over slightly, head leaning forward, chin stuck out.

Skinner pivoted on his right foot. The heel of his right hand sped upwards toward its target, aimed in the final blow. But in that very second, the sole of his moccasin found a pool of water on the pathway. He slipped off-balance.

Now it was the wounded giant who was fighting for his life. He grabbed the smaller man, and used his brute force and bulk to bear him backwards towards the pool. Skinner gasped as the small of his back hit the concrete, and as the breath was forced from him by Lennie's weight. Then the thick fingers were round his throat once more, and his head and shoulders were forced under the surface. He was helpless. There was a roaring in his ears. His eyes felt as if they were popping from their sockets. Somewhere in the depths of the pool he fancied he saw Ainscow, beckoning to him. And then another vision swam into his drowning mind. Jazz, his son, cradled by Sarah. She was dressed in black.

No! he roared in his mind. And he kicked upwards, with both knees and thighs, upwards with more strength than he had ever dreamed he possessed.

The great bulk of Lennie flew over him, and landed in the pool with a splash which sounded to Skinner, with his head still submerged, like an explosion. Again the fingers had left his throat. He swung himself up and out of the water, choking and gasping for breath. Seconds later, a huge hand slapped on to the concrete beside him, reaching for him. He scrambled to his feet, icy anger still coursing through him. He turned round to see both of Lennie's hands on the poolside, arms straightening as he hauled himself upright, like a great black creature emerging from an ocean.

Skinner stood facing him. He waited until both arms were straight, then kicked him with the outside edge of his right foot, with savage force, just above the right elbow. Then as the great trunk hung there helpless, he kicked him again without finesse, without technique, but as hard as he could, with his right instep, on the base of the jaw below the left ear. Big Lennie's desperate eyes glazed over and the huge arms lost all their strength. He slipped back into the water, unconscious, and disappeared beneath the surface.

Skinner slumped to his knees beside the pool, faint suddenly with exhaustion. A few feet away, Lennie Plenderleith's head and shoulders broke the surface once more. Skinner reached out weakly for him, but he had floated to the centre of the pool. He crouched there, wondering if he had strength left to dive in and pull the giant out, and if he had the will to subdue him once again, should he revive. He hauled himself painfully upright – and, as he did, the chamber was suddenly illuminated by the beam of a flashlight.

'Are you all right, sir?'

Skinner looked around. He stood in the spread of the light, his shirt soaked, his steel-grey hair plastered to his head, blood trickling from his broken nose, and from an angled cut over his left eye. His right foot was throbbing from the force of his last kick, and he stood awkwardly, trying to keep as much weight as possible on his left side.

Brian Mackie and Mario McGuire stood in the doorway, gazing at him in naked astonishment.

'Don't be fucking stupid, Brian. Of course I'm not all right! But I'm a fucking sight better than that guy in there – and better still than the one on the bottom. Now, fish Big Lennie out before he drowns, and handcuff him before he wakes up. I'd help but, quite frankly, I'm knackered!'

100

'They brought us here in the same ambulance, would you believe. Big Lennie's still badly concussed, but he's conscious and talking. His right arm's broken and they've just taken him off to set it. Otherwise he's not too bad. I kicked him hard enough to take a normal man's head right off, but they say all he'll have is a headache and a stiff neck for a couple of days, and that'll be it. I had another talk with him once he'd come round. He said that he'd make a statement to the Guardia Civil, admitting to killing Santi Alberni. So tomorrow morning you can call Gloria and tell her she can begin to look forward to sticking it up her insurance company.'

'That's great,' said Sarah, on the other end of the telephone. 'But what about you? You aren't kidding me, are you? You are fine?'

He glanced at his face in a mirror on the wall of the Royal Infirmary's Accident and Emergency Unit, from where he had been allowed to telephone his wife. He chuckled. 'I've been better looking, but, yes, love, I'm okay. Honest. They've straightened my nose and put a couple of stitches in my forehead. And they've taken pictures of my foot and satisfied themselves that it isn't broken. So I'll be limping home in a few hours.'

'A few hours! Why so long?'

'Because I'm going into the office to dictate a statement, while it's all still crystal clear in my head, for Ruth to type up in the morning.'

'Okay, I'll see you whenever. Just wear a paper bag over your head, if you think you might frighten the baby! He's with me just now and, as you can possibly hear, he's not best pleased at being wakened in the middle of the night!'

Bob laughed, a mixture of amusement and – though Sarah could not and, if he could avoid it, would *never* realise it – sudden relief at being alive to enjoy more moments with his wife and son.

'Oh,' said Sarah urgently. 'I almost forgot. How's Andy?'

'No problem. He's got a hard head, too. He was only out for a few minutes. It looked worse than it was. They've X-rayed him and stitched him up, and he's signed himself out. The doctor here offered him a bed for the night, but he said he'd rather sleep it off at home. I'd forgotten: he's signed off on two weeks' holiday. Now I'm off too. There's a driver waiting at the door for me. I had my car taken to Fettes in case I did wind up with my foot in plaster. Go back to sleep now, you and wee Jazz. I'll see you both in the morning.'

He hung up, wondering for that moment how Sarah had known of Andy Martin's accident. Then he shook his head and limped towards his driver at the door.

101

'So that's the story, Ruth,' said Skinner to his tape-recorder, as the early-shift staff began to wind their way up the drive below his office window in the early morning sunshine. 'That's Skinner's trail. It started in Edinburgh, wound through half a dozen countries, and ended back on our own doorstep. The story's full of greed and violence and death. But it's about honour, too. Big Lennie Plenderleith, or Dominic Jackson as he would have been for the rest of his life, is in a strange way one of the most honourable men I have ever met. He had his legacy, the sort of fortune the rest of us can only dream about, and he had a whole new life in front of him. As he said, he was free and clear. And yet he gambled it all, and he lost it all, to repay his debt of honour to Tony Manson. I tell you, Ruth, Big Lennie is certainly the toughest man I've ever come up against, but he sure as hell isn't the worst.'

The recorder whined a warning that its micro-cassette was about to run out.

'Right,' said Skinner as he switched it off and took out the tape, putting it beside two others in his typing tray. 'That's it. Home, Robert – but on the way let's call in to compare stitches with young Martin.'

He drove the BMW carefully through the morning rush hour, saving his still-aching foot as best he could, enduring the traffic queues which he normally hated, until he arrived outside the grey Victorian terrace just behind Haymarket where Andy Martin lived. He saw the familiar red sports hatch parked near the front door, with, fortuitously, a vacant space beside it. He parked, glancing in the driver's mirror as he climbed out of the car. He smiled, wincing, as he saw the swelling across the bridge of his nose, and the bruised bump around the cut.

'Let's see if you can beat that lot, boy,' he said to the sunny morning.

Martin's flat was on the second floor, and his injured foot made the climb awkward, but eventually he reached the blue-painted front door. He pressed the bell-push and waited. Thirty seconds passed without an answer. He pressed again, and waited for another minute. He smiled and shook his head.

'Dozy bastard,' he said. He pressed the bell for a third time and thumped the door with his fist. 'Polis!' he shouted, disguising his voice, 'Open up in there!'

There was a muffled response from within. At last the door swung open. There stood a young woman. She was wearing a man's satin robe, in blue, with the monogram 'AM' on the breast pocket. She was rubbing her hair vigorously with a huge peach-coloured towel. One of its corners had fallen across her face.

'I'm sorry,' said the hooded woman, her speech muffled by the towel. 'I was in the shower. Andy's just nipped down to the shops to buy a paper and some—'

As she spoke she looked up and, as she did so, her voice grew more distinct, and the towel fell from her face. The sentence tailed off unfinished as she stared at Skinner. Her eyes were wide, mirroring the blank astonishment in his. Her mouth, like his, hung open slightly.

Time stopped. Afterwards, neither would be able to say for how long they stood there in their frozen tableau. But in whatever time it was, in that time worlds moved and lives changed.

Eventually the woman recovered her voice, or at least a vestige of it. She smiled, tentatively.

'Hi, Pops.'